Might and Strength
of
Evil Bone

Fate of Vaeldor
BOOK 2
written by

Ronald G. Bellar

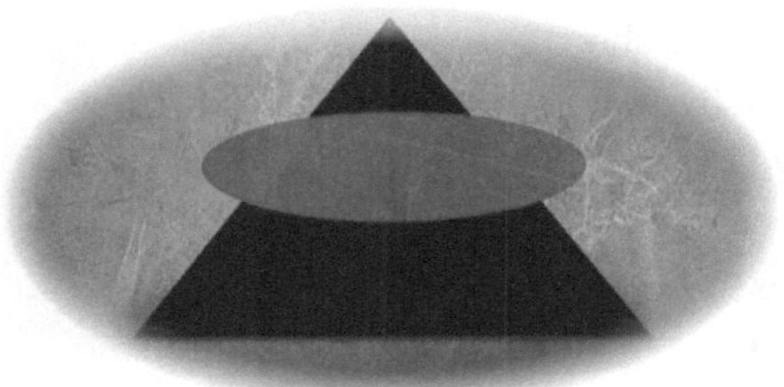

Vaeldor House LLC

Brighton, MI 48114

Might and Strength of Evil Bone

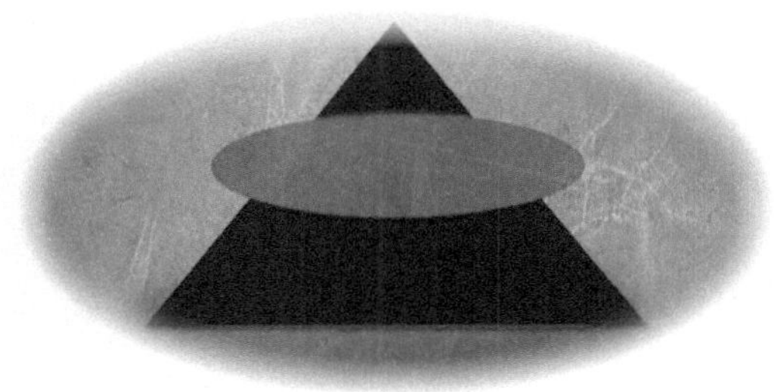

To my father, Ronald E Bellar.
He did everything he could for his kids.
May he rest in peace.

Dear Reader,

The Fate of Vaeldor is decided over several decades, and many characters are introduced throughout the series. For your convenience, a detailed glossary of names and pronunciations is provided at the back of Might and Strength of Evil Bone.

Some entries may act as small spoilers.

Fate of Vaeldor Series
(in reading order)

Alas! The One that Evil Brings
Might and Strength of Evil Bone
Eyes Open in Shadowy Hall (coming in 2023)

Visit Ronald G. Bellar's Facebook page at
https://www.facebook.com/vaeldorhouse

CONTENTS

Eraim's Journal Entry 34: Western Vaeldor

Andria
Ekland
Coranbiar M.
Bouldertown
Selt
Carbnum
Echo Valley Rapids
Vermallon F.
Lake Charal
Nira
Batorn Gulf
Steadshire
Berynye
House of Ulgarroth
Peltagar
Orlenfel F.
Tribenor
Benasti F.
Batorn R.
Sendorum
Orlenfel R.
Great East R.
Candermane Tunnel
Morimont R.
Palidur
Varlimor M.
Kalmaar
Morimont
Lake Garaard
Sardina
Darmhorog
Burmagaard
Starlight L.
Southwood
Barraday
Serpent's Range
Ironside Keep
Border Hills
Charndona
Denvale
Fire Hills
Belsal R.
Marcove
Ladal M.
Mud Lake
Moon Lake
Kembald
Menivrial F.
Krimbror R.
Endless Sea
Lambrek
W. Tusiv R.
Strie
Borleap M.
E. Tusiv R.
Stronghold
Trethel R.
sert of fire
Dright Sw.
Nomedd
Tarn Arum Jungle
Eraim's Journal Entry 35: Eastern Vaeldor

Prophecy of Trannum

As told by Seac the Seer

"Power of five, united by one,
Forth on journey, defy the sun.
Summer tastes winter, darkness draws near,
Sleeping do wake 'neath shadow of fear.

"From edge of old, bond does break,
At last revealed, One all did forsake.
Evil long subdued, the One long sought.
Centuries pass, power hard bought.

"Alas! the One that Evil brings,
Takes the lands, takes the kings.
Forces gather, dark secrets unknown.
Death march begins from One's throne.
Under sunless sky, o'er blanket of cold,
Fall of strength by treacheries unfold.
Dark power grows, living join through death.
By might of Lords, Hallowed Land is wrest.

"Many a hero, born to die.
Trial of time, the battles cry.
Companies four, to take the test,
Set forth on perilous quest.
Seek to end at dark throne,
Might and strength of Evil Bone.
Power shatters, dust does fall.
Eyes open in shadowy hall."

Chapter 1

Siege of Darmhorng

Just outside the city of Peltagarr and south of the Batorn Gulf stood Castle Berynyc. In days of peace, Baron Rasnar sat upon the throne there, keeping a loose watch over the border with Nira and overseeing the fleet of ships that made up the infamous Kalmiran armada. He governed the most prosperous land within the realm of Kalmaar, rolling with scenic hills, abundant in wild stallions, and supplying crops to the southern regions. Now, however, the baron's head was planted firmly onto the end of a tall pike atop the castle wall; a reminder to everyone it was not a time of peace. The years had not been kind to Rasnar, as his head had decomposed some time ago, and all that remained was a cracked and broken skull. But the people of the surrounding territory remembered the visage all too well.

This was how Gruzim preferred it.

Since the conquest of Kalmaar ended more than a decade ago, it was in Castle Berynyc that the Lord of Benasti had been placed. There, he ruled over the northernmost barony of the dominion, as well as southern Nira. Gruzim was responsible for holding siege over the cowardly elves of Orlenfel Forest and maintaining control of the Great East River bridges. Hobgoblins and krukari flocked to him from lands distant and near, as was their nature when one of their own grew in power, and they relished in their good fortunes while they roamed the territory and terrorized its citizens.

It was a peaceful life, and Gruzim hated every minute of it. He had grown up in Benasti Forest, where every day was a fight for survival, and he was lord over that chaos. Gruzim's new position would see him grow fat and weak. Refusing to allow this fate for his elite Soldiers of Blood, the Zurkan, he sent them back to Benasti until something more befitting of their skills came along.

Gruzim contemplated this while a servant cleaned the last traces of blood from the steps before his throne; the very spot where another servant had attempted to explain away her tardiness in bringing Gruzim his breakfast. This was proof that the years of idleness had worn upon him. Normally, he refused to stain his spearhead with the blood of peasants—they were not worthy of such a death. But a warrior needed combat, and a warlord needed to conquer. Sardina was defeated and Palidur toppled several years ago by the undead, but still there were no battles for Gruzim to fight. To the south, Tarm ruled over the rest of Kalmaar, as well as all of Marcove, and this troubled Gruzim further. Why the weak human was handed such power and a great lord such as himself made a mere gate warden of the growing empire, he could not begin to understand.

Something had to change, and soon.

Gruzim's thoughts were interrupted when Malgabi arrived—another bug that needed to be crushed. Gruzim remembered when he first met the strange crossbreed of human and undead in Garthglen Swamp several years ago. Malgabi claimed to be from Marcove, and he spoke with a silver tongue. Gruzim detested the creature as much now as he did then, but Malgabi was the voice of Trannum, so Gruzim tolerated him. His tolerance, however, went only so far.

The messenger *boy* brought news of a war council to be held in Darmhorng in two weeks, to discuss the next phase of the plan. Great. Another day of listening to Tarm's advisors squabble about casualties, routes, and backup plans. Did the fools forget whom they served? Did they not realize the immortality that awaited in the end? With the Death Lords on their side, they should mount an immediate and unending assault upon the enemy until all lay dead.

Death Lords... A power beyond mortal reach. If any doubted the strength of the master, they need only behold the mightiest warriors of darkness. Each was unique, but all shared the desire to quash life. Their mere presence dropped the bravest soldiers to their knees. Though Gruzim had not seen Trannum since that day in the Stone Eagle Mountains, when Gruzim traveled with the feeble paladin, Merssa, and overrated Vecnor, he knew the undead kings to be but a trifle of the necromancer's true power.

Fine. He would attend the war council. Because it was the master's wish.

Gruzim arrived at Darmhorng with a squadron of Zurkan in his wake. The Benasti banner flew high, a plain flag the color of blood, as well as the standard of unity with the master, a red flag with a blue oval set upon a triangle of black. Missing was the Kalmiran flag. Gruzim refused to display the waste of cloth, and although this topic was often brought up at these meetings, none of the weak humans were willing to do more than bicker about it.

Leaving his soldiers outside, Gruzim reported to the war room.

Malgabi was late, of course, and Tarm was hesitant to start without the worm's presence, so Gruzim left for the kitchen to grab something to eat. A table laden with food had been provided, but the meat was not as rare as Gruzim preferred.

After descending a flight of stairs, Gruzim was mildly surprised to see Queen Mayry. The queen rarely made an appearance when the leaders were gathered. She wore a revealing blue gown and gazed at Gruzim from an open doorway; and she slid into the library beyond with a seductive smile. Mayry was beautiful as humans go, but Gruzim did not play games, and he continued to the kitchen.

Upon his return with a bloody leg of lamb in hand, Mayry stood in the doorway again. This time, she stared intently.

"Master Gruzim." Her voice held the slightest tremor, obviously annoyed with his insolence. "I would be honored by your presence for a moment."

Gruzim allowed the food to roll about his mouth while the juices seeped from his lips and into his short, coarse beard. Her reference to him as *master* intrigued him, so he obliged.

Mayry closed the door and her smile returned. "We are quite alone. So feel free to speak your mind."

"I always speak my mind," Gruzim said without interest, and red spittle flew from his mouth. The queen did not flinch, not even when spots of it found their way onto her dress, and this aroused Gruzim's suspicions. "What game are you playing, wench?"

"You are much too great a warrior to be wasting away in the north." She was unfazed by his choice of words.

"On with it." Gruzim grew bored.

"You know, of course, of my son, Solinin?" Mayry moved along a bookshelf, scanning the titles.

"Of course." Gruzim furrowed his brow.

"Did you also know that I had a son before him?" Glancing over her shoulder when no response came, she continued. "His name was Durl. But he disappeared one day."

"I don't care," Gruzim said without emotion. "Do you think I ate him?"

"It was Tarm!" Ire flared in her eyes. "I know it was! He's been acting strangely ever since taking the throne. I could see the way he looked at my darling Durl... With *pity*!" The last word was drenched in disgust. "I know not how he did it, but my boy was not kidnapped, as that bastard claims. Who would *dare* take him?" Mayry threw her arms up, as if expecting an answer.

Gruzim said nothing.

Mayry calmed. "I let it pass once I was again with child. And after Solinin was born, I kept a close watch on him with the help of those loyal to me. But we could not be with him at all times. Often, he accompanied his father for training, so he would one day become a great warrior."

Gruzim snorted at her choice of words. He never saw Tarm as a great warrior, but one barely competent as humans go.

"But Tarm did not train him in combat alone. Oh no!" Mayry's shield of decorum cracked. "That *bastard* taught him *honor*. Then my son starts showing signs of *morality*! My husband has done his best to make him useless to our cause!"

The way she said *our cause* sounded pleasing, and Gruzim's lip twisted into a grin.

Mayry paced with her head bowed. "And now he's gone too," she said in defeat. "I have only the note he left. He does not believe in what we are doing. He wishes for a better life." She looked Gruzim in the eyes, her rage returning. "These were not *his* words! They were the poison of his weak father! That man has taken my future kings from me!"

"I...don't...care." Gruzim emphasized each word.

Mayry's dark eyes burned momentarily. The rage then passed, and she smiled. "He has deprived me of what is mine. He also deprives you of what *should* be yours. And only *you* have the power to change this."

Gruzim stared at the queen. She was indeed beautiful. Her jaw and cheekbones were perfectly chiseled, her nose, though a bit long, suited her, and the way her dark, flowing hair tumbled down her back... She was the perfect portrait of a queen. Gruzim could see men killing one another to be with her. Weak men. And her pathetic plea for him to kill her husband... She was proving herself to be weak as well. Nevertheless, she had a point.

"What do I get out of it? If I were to do this?"

"It is for you as well as myself," Mayry said. "The throne will be yours, as it should be." She smiled. "And I will bear a child for you; one that will grow more powerful than even *you* can imagine!"

Gruzim was at a loss for words. He never anticipated *this*. Did Mayry expect him to believe his presence did not disgust her? Did she not expect him to see right through her? He already had sons — more than he needed. But as he gazed into her eyes, a grin crossed his face. She did not see a krukari before her, but strength and power. Mayry desired the same thing as he: eternal reign over Vaeldor.

Gruzim left the library, and Mayry did not stop him. She was more like him than he had realized. She understood his answer.

Upon returning to the war room, Gruzim found the meeting well underway. Malgabi stood at the head of the table, wearing his usual pompous grin.

"You're late," Malgabi said, bringing a snarl to Gruzim's lips.

"Let's continue," Tarm suggested.

The council was long and drawn out, and Malgabi revealed the master's desire to conquer the rest of Nira. The Marc claimed another harsh winter should make the kingdom ripe for the taking. Great. More snow. Gruzim understood the advantages of eternal winter over southern Nira, but the weather never ended there. Snow blanketed Gruzim's castle for more than six months of the year—a condition he had grown quite tired of—while the rest of Kalmaar enjoyed normal seasons. Malgabi explained that there would be a thaw, however, and the host of Benasti would march.

Tarm and the counselors insisted they play a role as well, but their objections held more meaning than that. They had no trust for Gruzim and only wished to control the Zurkan—a feeble attempt to keep the denizens of Benasti from growing too powerful. This disgusted Gruzim. Nevertheless, more important thoughts were swimming around his head and he allowed the humans to have their say. After another pointless hour, they were satisfied, and the meeting was adjourned.

Gruzim sat upon his horse for an hour after exiting Castle Darmhorng. At last, Malgabi rode from the gate.

"Gruzim!" The insect smiled. "You and yours will finally get to march. That must excite you."

"Be silent, fool!" Gruzim growled. "The plan will change soon enough."

"What do you mean?"

Though Malgabi maintained an arrogant tone, Gruzim sensed a slight trembling from the man—or whatever the Marc was. It made him want to slaughter the dog right then.

"Tarm will not be here upon your return," Gruzim informed the puppet.

Malgabi frowned. "That has not been ordered by the master."

"Just inform him I shall be king by the time you have returned to him." Gruzim sneered. "I will rid the land of this weak, false king. And tell him I expect a reward befitting of such a deed."

"And what might that be?"

Gruzim grinned. "I wish to be one of his elite."

"That would be..." Malgabi pondered, and then realization struck him. "That would be impossible!"

Gruzim's smile faded, and he glared at the worm.

"You tread on dangerous ground, my friend," Malgabi said upon finding his voice. "I suggest you take no further action until my return. It may surprise you to learn that Tarm made a request not unlike your own. The master found it humorous, to say the least, and denied it."

"I have made *no* requests." Gruzim gave a level stare. "Just do as I say."

"So be it." Malgabi's arrogance was lost. "But do not be surprised if the master is not pleased. And he may very well deal with you himself." The Marc dug his heels into the sides of his horse, and the animal sped down the road.

"I would expect nothing less," Gruzim muttered, and he returned to the Zurkan.

"Is it good news, Lord Gruzim?" his lieutenant asked. "Do we kill again?" The warrior grew excited at Gruzim's half grin. "We return to Berynyc, then?"

"Not yet," Gruzim said. "I have business here first."

Gruzim knew exactly what he wished to do and how to do it, without hours of planning. Tarm had employed mercenaries many years ago to boost the size of his army, hired swords with loyalty only to gold and silver, and the fool gave them land and made them nobles among the people of Kalmaar. Gruzim would never have ended a contract in such a manner.

Tracking the soldiers down was easy—most served as castle guards, and they were obviously not of the Kalmiran lineage. It was even easier to dazzle them with promises of more wealth and power than Tarm had provided; a hired blade could never turn down gold, no matter how much he had already accumulated, nor the chance to use his weapon again.

The pawns were then set, and Gruzim returned to Berynyc. He did not remain there long, however, and after a month he arrived at Darmhorng with his entire Zurkan force, ten thousand strong. Tarm's mercenaries had risen against the throne, using their high-ranking positions to take out most of the Royal Guard, and the king issued a call to arms. Being the closest army, and having been prepared to march already, Gruzim was the first to answer the call; and he knew he would arrive days, if not weeks, before all others.

The Zurkan marched on Darmhorng and toward the rear of the mercenary army—five thousand soldiers surrounding the castle. Horn blowers signaled Gruzim's arrival, and Darmhorng answered; and what remained of Tarm's Royal Guard issued from the gates while the Zurkan advanced upon the besieging force.

Gruzim could not help but laugh at the looks of shock and horror as the Soldiers of Blood ruthlessly slaughtered the mercenaries. The fools actually believed he would permit them to live once they had served their purpose! They allowed Gruzim to mobilize his army to the castle without confrontation, and now he presented them with their just reward. As they dwindled to almost nothing, they threw down their arms in surrender, but the Zurkan had their orders and none were spared.

Gruzim met Tarm on the battlefield. There was no great contest, no feats of skill, and no heroic battle worthy of song. Gruzim simply thrust his spear, catching Tarm off guard, and the tip pierced armor and flesh and passed completely through the king's body. Upon

Gruzim's command, the Zurkan then overwhelmed the rest of Darmhorng's soldiers.

Tarm lay on the ground, gasping for air, and Gruzim basked in the fallen king's pain. The weakling had been allowed to rule over the mightiest empire in Vaeldor for more than ten years, but when Gruzim yanked his weapon free, what remained of Tarm's life slipped away.

The Zurkan stormed the castle, and Gruzim entered to claim his crown, his throne, and his queen.

Two weeks after the death of Tarm, Malgabi returned—impressive considering the distance the Marc had traveled. The messenger did not look his usual pompous self, and he gave a sidelong glance toward Mayry, who held an icy stare. Gruzim did not know what arrangement the two had had in place before most recent events, nor did he care.

"King Gruzim," Malgabi said with some difficulty as he bowed. "Master sends his regards for a feat well done. He presents you with this token of appreciation." The Marc climbed the first couple steps of the dais, holding aloft a golden vial.

Gruzim accepted the gift.

Removing the stopper, Gruzim found a dark liquid within, and from it he smelled his own grave. But also there was power. Was it the power he longed for? Or poison sent to end the insolence of a disobedient servant?

"Is this all?" he asked.

"Just drink it." Malgabi's irritation surfaced. Perhaps the worm did not look forward to serving a king he could not push around.

"Tell the master I thank him for his gift," Gruzim said. But as Malgabi bowed, Gruzim added, "Never mind."

He pulled his spear from beside the throne, and before Malgabi rose, the sharpened edge flashed in a downward arc. The Marc's head bounced across the stone floor as the body collapsed, and black blood made its way down the steps from the open neck.

"I'm sure he already knows," Gruzim said with a sneer.

CHAPTER 2

CIRCLE OF FRIENDS

It was Ballrik's turn to buy the drinks, and from the bar he could see his table through the crowded tavern, where his friends still laughed at Magneer's joke. Life was pleasant, but times like this reminded Ballrik of his father. Deep down, Ballrik remained troubled by the way they parted company eleven years ago.

After pulling his father's unconscious body from Ironside Keep, the only word the man offered in gratitude was "Go." So Ballrik left to live with his Uncle Arkor in West Palidur, in Duke Rholmar's castle. Arkor had moved to Philen when Ballrik was very young and rarely visited the keep, but Ballrik held fond memories of his uncle with the wooden arm, and the way the man used it as a crossbow. Arkor was happy to see Ballrik and asked few questions, and Duke Rholmar provided a room every bit as lavish as the one Ballrik enjoyed while living at Ironside.

It was an easy life, and staying with Arkor was a natural fit, for Ballrik shared more in common with his uncle than he ever had with his father. Even so, the first couple of years seemed hollow without the Lord of the Keep. Then Magneer arrived.

Magneer, son to Pallit and Arrikan, came to live in the duke's castle nine years ago. "I am here to receive battle training from Rholmar's finest teachers," Magneer said with more than a bit of sarcasm, but he believed his parents sent him there to keep him away from the hostile lands of the east.

Magneer resented living so far from his home within the Coranthiar Mountains, but he and Ballrik built a great friendship, which helped to ease the situation. The two were inseparable most times, frequenting taverns or walking about the walled city, and there were many that mistook them for brothers. This confused Ballrik, for Magneer's stocky physique stood nearly a head shorter and he had dirty blonde hair, while Ballrik possessed dark hair and inherited his father's wiry frame.

Being a talented mountain ranger as his parents before him, Magneer taught Ballrik to hunt; and because Philen was a realm that seldom experienced winter, hunting occupied most of their time. The journey to the High Riser Mountains was long, and after making the trip a few times, Magneer adapted his skills and they enjoyed bountiful treks into Dakreal Forest. Ballrik was grateful for this, for they were able to spend more time hunting and less time traveling.

It was on one of their excursions into the forest that they encountered a krukari. Ballrik had never met a half-hobgoblin before, but he learned about their race from his father long ago; of their reputation for being thieves and cutthroats, as well as their knack for betraying those close to them if the price was right. But this krukari seemed nothing like the picture Ballrik's father painted.

Gruelenor was not much to look at. His skin was like wrinkled leather, and the dark, coarse hair falling to his shoulders also sprouted from the oddest places about his cheekbones—it was the only facial hair he possessed. Adding to the foreboding appearance were his reddish eyes, which made him seem angry all the time. Gruelenor was similar in size to Magneer, although not as broad in the shoulders, and his thin lips looked to have rarely known a smile. But he was a proficient hunter, and he held Ballrik in awe with his skills in archery.

Gruelenor claimed to be hunting more for survival than the sport Ballrik and Magneer enjoyed, and after combining their efforts, the three were rewarded with the most exciting day Ballrik had known. He and Magneer were so impressed that they insisted Gruelenor return to West Palidur with them. When Gruelenor balked, they explained the city to be nothing like the original Palidur, where outsiders were unwelcome. It took much more prodding still, and in the end Gruelenor accepted the invitation, saying he was growing tired of camping beneath the watchful eyes of Dakreal elves.

From that point on, Gruelenor called the city home, even though many of its citizens disapproved—most folks in those parts had no love for hobgoblins. Gruelenor adamantly refused all offers to stay in the castle, so Ballrik and Magneer helped him to secure a room at a nearby inn. Gruelenor insisted on paying his own way, and he often ventured into the forest to procure meats to sell and furs to trade. He soon made a name for himself among merchants, and he took up permanent residence at the inn, where a well-rewarded innkeeper and several patrons became used to his presence.

The next to join the party was Nidor, a barbarian out of Holindale. Nidor was dark in complexion, being from the Desert of Fire, and he declared himself a paladin—a strange claim for a barbarian, and unheard of by Ballrik. "I am following the path the Almighty Silcor has set before me," Nidor said in his deep voice, boasting of his devotion to the fire god.

Though nine years younger than Ballrik, Nidor was the tallest of the group, and beneath his clean-shaven head were muscles that rippled over his entire body, which was sparsely covered by animal skins most days. He spoke less than Gruelenor at times, but laughed as much as anyone. When Nidor chose to speak, his words usually carried strong meaning.

The newest addition was Solinin. Only sixteen years in age when he arrived nearly a year ago, Solinin was the youngest of the group, as well as the most attractive. His piercing blue eyes, chiseled facial features, and wavy black hair left him never wanting for admirers. He was well educated and able to read and write in several languages, and he possessed advanced skills with the sword for one his age. Solinin was of noble blood, of that Ballrik was certain, but the young man proved evasive when asked about his past.

Solinin came with a full purse and his generosity went unchecked, granting him immediate acceptance; and with the passage of time, he grew more at ease and laughed often. But he cared little for the others always referring to him as *Kid*, pointing out that he was not much younger than Nidor.

Ballrik had found a warm home among his uncle and friends, and he planned to live out his days in the carefree lifestyle Philen offered. This decision seemed unyielding, even after his father passed through four years ago. Vikur arrived with Poluran, seeking Ballrik's forgiveness, and Ballrik accepted the apology. He was happy to see his father's return to health, no doubt having much to do with the dwarf's company, but Ballrik could not grant the man's request for him to leave. He was content to stay, unable to imagine a life elsewhere.

Vikur's time in Philen stirred unusual behavior in Arkor. Ballrik believed his uncle to harbor guilt, not having been there to aid in Ironside's defense against the undead invasion. But the former Lord of Keep showed no grudge and never brought the subject to light. Ballrik hoped his father had finally found peace with the ordeal.

Though he admitted it to no one, Ballrik eagerly awaited the end of his father's weeklong visit, for it brought back horrible memories of the evil he witnessed in Ironside Keep. His sleep became haunted once again with the nightmares that plagued him for more than a year following the event, and it took another month to shake them after his father's departure. Here in Philen, evil seemed so far off as to not exist, and that was how he preferred it.

Ballrik sighed and returned to the table, eager to replace his thoughts with the pleasant ramblings of Magneer. But once Ballrik set down the drinks, Nidor stole their attention.

"I am going to the Front," the Dale said with his slight accent.

The laughter came to an abrupt halt. The Front was the Great East River, stretching from King Arman Lake to the Batorn Gulf. It was the line between Good and Evil. For over a decade, the undead made no attempts to push north of the river and showed no interest in entering Tenvale. The latter did not surprise Ballrik, for no one wished to incur the wrath of the mages, but his understanding of the

Wizard Kingdom ended there. He could not fathom Tenvale's reasons for declaring a neutral stance in the matter, allowing no forces to pass through their domain, living or otherwise.

"Surely you jest," Magneer said with a chuckle.

Ballrik knew Nidor to be incapable of such a feat. "Why would you...?" He could not finish the thought.

Nidor searched the table for the words. "I never had the chance to see Palidur in its days of glory." He lifted his eyes. "I was only nine when it fell into darkness. Though I know I would not have been welcomed, I always dreamed of one day seeing its bright buildings all the same, even if from outside its walls. Now the survivors of the Holy City hold the line at the river, not knowing defeat. They watch, ever vigilant over the cold lands to the south, or so I am told. Surely they are planning a counterattack as we speak. I must be there for this most noble cause."

"Are you sure this is what you want?" asked Ballrik.

"It is what I *must* do." Nidor looked at Ballrik. "Silcor has shown me this in my sleep. Warriors who are able must do what they can, before dormant evil awakens. If they do not, how long will it be before it creeps within the boundaries of even Philen?"

Ballrik gave a wry smile, unwilling to put any truth to the paladin's words.

"My parents are there," Magneer said.

"As is my father, most likely," Ballrik added.

"I wish to thank you all for your friendship." Nidor rose from his chair. "I will treasure it always. Perhaps we will meet again one day. For now, I bid you goodnight. A long road awaits come the morn." He bowed and exited the tavern.

The jovial night was cut short, and the table remained silent for several minutes. Their mugs sat untouched while they pondered the paladin's words.

"I have half a mind to join him," Magneer said at last.

Ballrik shook his head. "Not I."

"Nor I," Gruelenor and Solinin said in unison.

"I never wished to come here in the first place," Magneer muttered. He then looked at Ballrik. "These have been the best years of my life. But there will come a day when I wish to wed and have a child. And what type of life will that child have if everyone sits and awaits the fate the undead brings?" Magneer shook his head. "Blast my parents! I could be one of the warriors Nidor speaks of."

"You'll find your grave," Ballrik said. "I have seen the enemy." He gazed at his beer, reliving the memory. "Not even my father could stand against them." He turned to Magneer. "And we could only wish to be as great a warrior as he."

"Perhaps." Magneer slid his chair from the table. "There's only one way to find out." He rose and lifted his mug. "Until tomorrow." He took a long drink.

Ballrik sighed while the others drank deeply. "Let's get some rest. These matters are better discussed during the day."

They exited the building.

The hour was late and the streets barren, and the sounds of the tavern carried far into the warm night. Ballrik and his friends headed for the inn where Gruelenor and Solinin resided, but as they neared its doors, Gruelenor brought them to a halt.

"Did you see that?" the krukari asked in his rough voice, his attention held by a dark alley across the road.

Ballrik saw nothing.

"It's the drink, my friend." Magneer placed his arm around Gruelenor's shoulders. "Don't you worry. The little beasts will be gone by morning!"

"No!" Gruelenor shrugged off the ranger's arm and pulled his sword. "A pair of feet just disappeared into the alley."

"Someone is just taking a shortcut home," Solinin said in his youthful voice.

"They were being dragged!" Gruelenor growled, and he strode across the street.

They followed Gruelenor to the alley, and the krukari peered into the darkness. One benefit of being part hobgoblin, Ballrik had learned, was their superior vision at night, rivaling that of elves and dwarves. This was one reason Gruelenor proved such an efficient hunter, of that Ballrik was certain.

"Who's there!" Gruelenor said.

An eerie hiss answered, followed by a hoarse voice. "Come find out!"

A chill ran down Ballrik's spine as four sets of pale blue eyes hovered in the darkness. "Dunarchins!"

Ballrik ushered his friends away from the alley as he drew his sword, and Magneer and Solinin pulled their weapons as well. The lights drew closer, and four dunarchins emerged, just as hideous as Ballrik remembered. They wore chain shirts over sickly, dried-up yellow skin stretched tightly about their bones, and within their hollow eye sockets burned the blue lights. Brandishing swords, they advanced, one heading toward Ballrik, one for Magneer, and two bearing down on Gruelenor.

Ballrik danced back, fending off a couple of feeble attacks. Either the creature was lacking in combative skills, which Ballrik did not believe for a second, or it did not desire to kill him. In either case, he was not about to let it achieve its goal, whatever it may be, and he unleashed a flurry of strikes. Combining the fighting prowess of his father and the finesse of Krelnamir, the Cafior paladin that lived at Ironside Keep before its fall, Ballrik severed his opponent's left arm and followed with a gash across its stomach. The dunarchin staggered back, but then it surprised Ballrik when it knocked his sword to the street.

Ballrik employed one of his father's tactics next, feigning an attempt to retrieve his weapon. When the undead warrior moved to oppose him, he thrust his left hand, which had withdrawn the dagger from his belt, and the blade pierced the creature's chest. The attack lacked the effect Ballrik had hoped for, and the dunarchin pushed him away as it swung its sword back across. The tip of the blade left a minor cut on Ballrik's arm.

With a touch of panic, Ballrik dove for his weapon. It was an obvious maneuver, and as he grabbed his sword and rolled to his feet, the undead warrior brought down its pommel. Ballrik dodged, and the attack glanced off his shoulder.

The dunarchin definitely had no intention of killing him, for it could have done so with little difficulty had it used its blade. Ballrik made it pay for its mistake, slicing its chest open with an upward slash. The creature reeled as black blood sprayed forth, and he decapitated it with his next swing. Ballrik watched in disbelief as the body twitched several times before becoming still. He then remembered his companions.

Gruelenor fought a dunarchin while another lay at his feet, and the final undead warrior was dragging Magneer's limp body into the alley. Solinin did his best to foil the creature's plans, but the dunarchin seemed bent on claiming its prize, fending off the kid and continuing on its way.

"No!" Ballrik charged.

The dunarchin released Magneer as its eerie eyes fell on Ballrik. It then surprised Solinin with a vicious attack, and the young warrior barely parried the weapon aside.

Ballrik arrived and knocked the dunarchin's blade from its hand. He then struck the creature in the face with his gauntlet, causing it to stagger, and brought his sword down, splitting its skull. The dunarchin collapsed and ceased to move.

"He's alive." Gruelenor hovered over Magneer, having dispatched his foe.

"The thing hit him on the head pretty hard," Solinin said.

Ballrik scanned the nearby buildings. Shutters closed and eyes disappeared from open windows. No one would have aided them had things gone differently.

Warriors who are able must do what they can, before dormant evil awakens. If they do not, how long will it be before it creeps within the boundaries of even Philen?

Nidor had posed the question, and Ballrik now realized the answer all too well. Was no place safe from the necromancer?

"Kid, check on the body in the alley," Ballrik said.

Solinin nodded and darted off.

After the young warrior was gone, Ballrik turned to Gruelenor. "This may sound odd, but I do not believe the one I fought was trying to kill me."

Gruelenor looked up from the unconscious ranger. "No. Nor me. I used it to my advantage."

"This one wanted Magneer alive," Ballrik said, "but it definitely tried to kill Solinin. It makes little sense."

"You claimed they were dunarchins, did you not?" posed Gruelenor.

Ballrik nodded.

"Tell me, are you a firstborn?"

Ballrik hesitated. The krukari's knowledge of the dunarchins' relationship to firstborns caught him by surprise. He first heard of dunarchins from his father, and learned much more from Selanna. He even had the misfortune of witnessing their assault on Ironside Keep. But never had Ballrik discussed any of this with his friends, wishing to forget the creatures altogether. His father's words of the nature of krukari returned, but Ballrik tried to shake them. Gruelenor's leather-like skin and coarse hair were more hobgoblin-like than human, and the reddish tint to the krukari's eyes never failed to place strangers on edge. But Gruelenor had never given Ballrik cause to doubt.

"I am firstborn," Ballrik said at last. "As is Magneer."

"What about the kid?"

"I am not a firstborn." Solinin stood at the edge of the alley, and Ballrik wondered how much the kid had heard. "I had an older brother, though I never met him."

"Perhaps their hesitation to kill has something to do with that fact." Gruelenor glanced at a nearby dunarchin. "Maybe they wanted us alive. To become one of them."

"Then you're firstborn as well?" Ballrik tried to hide the suspicion in his voice.

"Until now, I didn't know." Gruelenor shrugged. "I have siblings. But I never knew if there were any before me. Perhaps now I do."

Ballrik gazed at the bodies. The presence of the undead brought doubts to his mind, and again he wondered about Gruelenor. But it was foolishness. Gruelenor was his friend. Gruelenor fought against the creatures and defeated two single handedly.

"The man in the alley is alive," Solinin said. "He has taken quite a knock to the head, though."

Ballrik nodded. "Let's get him and Magneer to the castle. Duke Rholmar must hear of this immediately."

"What about the bodies?" Solinin observed the street.

"Leave them." Ballrik looked at the closed windows. "Let everyone see what's in store for them if they choose to hide and do nothing."

The sun's light was just peeking through the eastern window of Nidor's room when he awoke. After collecting his gear, he paid the innkeeper and exited the building to retrieve his horse from the stables. To his surprise, the animal waited outside the door, ready to ride. Magneer was there as well, seated on his own horse and looking as though he had been in a brawl and lost. The ranger's head was swollen on the left side and his bloodshot eyes revealed a rough night's rest.

"I'm going with you," Magneer said, and the effort to speak brought the ranger visible pain.

"Are you well enough to ride?" Nidor tied his chain shirt and pack to his saddle.

"Well enough," Magneer replied. "The others await us at the gates. We thought you would have been ready to go much sooner than this."

Nidor climbed onto his saddle and smiled. "You are not going just because—"

"We all have our reasons, I'm sure. But together," Magneer shrugged, "who knows what we can accomplish?"

Nidor laughed, loud enough to make the ranger cringe. "That is very true! Silcor smiles on me today. Let us join the others."

CHAPTER 3

THE FRONT

Ballrik and his friends traveled through Fendora and into Moclen, spending almost every waking hour atop their horses and making good time. They stopped in Tikken City, and although Nidor had never seen the free city ruled by the Council of Wizards, the Dale showed no interest in browsing markets or seeing the sights. Ballrik, Magneer, and Solinin made the most of their evening, enjoying a couple hours within one of the city's many taverns before turning in for the night.

The next day, they crossed the Squire River. Nidor revealed a mild interest in the white stones of Korban Bridge, but he was no more willing to explore the famous Rivercross Market than he had been to visit Tikken City. Having missed out on some Tikken City fun, all but Gruelenor teased the barbarian, trying to coax him into spending an extra day in Rivercross. Nidor welcomed them to do so, adding that he would see them when they arrived in Sendorum.

Come morning, they all headed east.

The weather remained pleasant, allowing for minimal stops. After entering Sendorum, however, the air grew chilly, and they donned the furs they knew they would eventually require. It was not much longer before the first signs of snow appeared, and after a few miles the ground was covered in white.

Later that day, Palidur Bridge came into view—a legendary masterpiece of stonework turned gateway to evil. Ballrik gazed upon the wide passage spanning the gap that separated Sendorum from Sardina; the living from the undead. Below the bridge, the Great East

River raced into the east, refusing to yield to the icy air, and beyond the channel, Palidur was a dark fortress veiled by a wintry haze.

Within a valley north of the bridge lay the encampment of the Palidurians. The immense compound appeared as a small city, occupying an area once unpopulated and bearing only a road and open fields. Ballrik had never seen the outpost before, but Magneer had described the collection of tents in great detail, the ranger having spent a month there over a decade ago. Now, even Magneer seemed surprised at what was before them. Permanent structures of wood existed where Ballrik expected to see tents, and several wooden towers kept watch over the south. A wall of logs surrounded the entire encampment, but a stone wall was under construction just inside of it and was more than half complete.

Only two gates were visible, one to the north and one to the south. Being in no hurry to get a closer look at the bridge, Ballrik led the way to the northern gate, where grim-faced soldiers blocked entry.

"This ain't no place for a good time," said one of the guards, eyeing Ballrik and his friends.

Before Ballrik could respond, an aging soldier hurried down a tower ladder, shouting all the while.

"Let them in! Let them in! 'Tis Master Ballrik at the gate!"

Ballrik did not recognize the old man, but he appreciated the access that followed.

Grooms took their horses once they were inside, and the old guard motioned for Ballrik to follow. The man then led them toward the middle of the encampment.

"So good to see you, Master Ballrik," the guard said. "I recall when you were just a lad learning to hold a sword."

"Ah, yes." Ballrik realized the soldier to be one of the Palidurians that served at Ironside Keep before its fall. But there had been so many, he could not remember them all. A thought then plagued his mind: his father might be within the compound. He considered asking the guard, but decided it was better not to know.

Nidor's expression became one of astonishment as he viewed over ten thousand people gathered for a single cause. Young men watched veterans demonstrate the elements of combat, soldiers sharpened blades or practiced swordplay, smithies pounded on weapons and armor, and horsemen attacked swinging dummies without mercy. Eyes glanced more than once at Gruelenor and Nidor as they walked by, but unlike Palidur in days long past, no one seemed overly concerned with their presence.

They arrived at the center of the compound, where the largest structure stood. It was the only building made of stone that Ballrik could see, and well-dressed soldiers milled about while messengers came and went with various scrolls.

"Here we are," their guide said. "The residence and headquarters of High Paladin Merssa Goldmace, commander of all you see."

"I have heard many tales of this mighty warrior." Nidor gazed at the building in awe. "I have also been told that she is the greatest barrier between Evil and Vaeldor."

"At least when she's not being bossy or cranky," Magneer said with a grin, bringing frowns to Nidor and the guard.

"She's not always like that." Ballrik looked from Magneer to Nidor. "You have not been misinformed."

"You two know her?" the Dale asked. "You have never mentioned this before."

"Well," Magneer said, "you shall meet her soon enough."

Ballrik laughed as he slapped Nidor on the back, but his eyes continued to search for evidence of his father's presence.

The old guard spoke to a soldier at the door, and the soldier escorted them into the building without a word. They entered a room with a large table and several chairs, and Merssa was there, speaking with men Ballrik assumed to be captains or generals. Though she had always stood about as high as a Salenti elf, Merssa seemed smaller to Ballrik now. Upon seeing him and his friends, Merssa excused the soldiers and smiled.

"Ballrik! Magneer! How are you boys?" She looked up at them as she clasped arms with each in turn. Had it not been for her graying hair, Merssa would have appeared no older than when Ballrik last saw her at Ironside Keep over a decade ago. She had done well to stay fit, and her grip was surprisingly strong.

Ballrik introduced the others of the group, and Merssa looked each one up and down. She seemed especially interested in Gruelenor, but then her gaze fell upon Solinin, as if recognizing him but unable to recall from where. After a sigh, she smiled and led them through a couple of doors and into her personal quarters.

They entered a room large enough to seat a dozen occupants comfortably. Borse was there, relaxing on an overstuffed chair before the hearth and enjoying a pipe. The priest's head was completely bald and his eyebrows thick and white, but he appeared vibrant when he rose, standing as tall as ever. He embraced Ballrik with surprising strength, and then Magneer, and he urged them all to sit.

"Where's Cavalor?" asked Magneer.

Merssa waved a hand. "He's off somewhere. He keeps busy, training new soldiers and such. They come in by the hundreds every month these days."

Ballrik thought it odd for Merssa's son to be training others in combat. Cavalor could not be more than twenty years in age. Surely the compound possessed warriors with more experience to handle such tasks.

"So what brings you here?" Borse asked.

They looked at one another, hesitant to give an answer. Nidor then stood.

"I have come to offer all that I have to the cause." The Dale's words were spoken in a disciplined manner. A perfect soldier.

Merssa studied Nidor. "Indeed." Her gaze turned to the others. "Is that why all of you have come?"

"It is," Magneer said. "And we bring news of dunarchins in Philen."

Merssa's expression became as stone, and she motioned for Nidor to sit. She retrieved a kettle from an iron hook over the hearth and served everyone tea, an action catching Ballrik by surprise. Merssa then sat and insisted they tell their story, omitting no details. She listened to every word, and she leaned forward when Ballrik spoke of the dunarchins' seeming desire to take them alive. Once their tale was complete, she was silent for several seconds.

"You realize, of course, the Front is no place for the timid," she said at last, receiving nods of confirmation. "It's hard work, day and night. Everyone must do their part, lest evil expose the weakness they create and spread as a plague. It is serious business we perform, protecting all of Vaeldor from the filth of Trannum, with little or no time for holidays or pleasures."

"We understand all of this." Respect shone in Nidor's eyes. "Whatever duty you assign, I will be most honored to perform."

Merssa gave a half smile and looked at her husband. Borse nodded, answering some unasked question.

"Very well." She rose to her feet, a sign the visit was ending. "Meet me here tomorrow after breakfast. I shall have orders ready for you then."

"Is breakfast still before dawn?" Magneer chuckled, and he received a sharp glance from Merssa.

Some things had not changed.

Merssa assigned a soldier to show them the grounds, and the man led them along the streets, pointing out various buildings and introducing them to several officers. Like Palidur of old, the outpost had few taverns to speak of, and it lacked theaters, music, dancing, and everything else considered entertainment. Instead, it possessed barracks, stables, and armories, as all was focused on the future battle with the undead.

While passing through a large temple, they had a brief encounter with Nilborg and Soren, the High Priest and High Paladin of Soleran. At least, those had been their titles in Palidur. Ballrik was not sure if that was still the case. Nilborg had changed little since

Ballrik encountered him years ago, although the priest always appeared an aged man as far back as Ballrik could recall. Soren looked worn, graying more so than Merssa, and was shorter than Ballrik remembered. Both men showed great pleasure with Ballrik and Magneer having enlisted in the Front.

Near the end of the tour, they ran into Pallit, Magneer's father. Ballrik had spied the aging ranger speaking to a soldier, and he heard only a part of the conversation before their approach was noticed. Apparently, Magneer's parents had been stationed in the northern region of the Varlimor Mountains.

Pallit looked happy to see his son, though confused as to Magneer's presence within the compound. Upon hearing of their enlistment, Pallit took Magneer aside for a private conversation. Magneer did not discuss what was said, not even with Ballrik, but he mentioned his father was proud of them for showing such bravery.

The evening ended at a busy tavern, where they were served a decent meal and adequate beer, although they received only two tankards each. Afterwards, they bunked with five hundred soldiers. Before Ballrik fell asleep, he lay for at least an hour, staring at the ceiling and remembering his lavish room in Duke Rholmar's castle.

The sky was still dark and a fresh layer of snow covered the ground when Ballrik and his friends were awakened for breakfast. After a flavorless serving of gruel, they reported to the central building.

Merssa was in the war room, poring over a map and speaking with Soren. The Soleran paladin wore silver armor and appeared much taller than the previous day—perhaps Soren was not so worn as Ballrik thought. The paladins ceased their meeting and smiled; and while Soren took a seat, Merssa rolled the map and set it aside. She then unrolled a map of Nira.

"I am sending you to Nira," she said. "They are in need of strong warriors such as yourselves."

Ballrik and Magneer exchanged looks of confusion—they assumed they would remain within the compound. Gruelenor and Solinin appeared nervous. Nidor sat tall and proud.

"Isn't that where the Benasti scum watches over the river?" Magneer frowned. "I'd rather fight the undead than the Zurkan!"

"The Soldiers of Blood are merciless." Merssa gave Magneer a level stare. "But do not be hasty to speak such requests unless you're prepared to answer them. The undead never rest and never tire. And, I trust, you have not forgotten there are worse things than dunarchins among their ranks." She directed her last question at Ballrik, and he nodded slowly.

"I shall perform whatever duty you see fit," Nidor said.

"That is good." Merssa studied the barbarian paladin, seemingly pleased with his response. She turned to Ballrik and Magneer. "Because the Benasti folk guard the river no longer. It has not been so for months now. The winters are harsh there, and thousands of skeletons and zombies watch the bridges. Beyond them, who knows? Paladins and priests report a strong evil, though they have yet to see its source." Merssa paused, looking at Ballrik. "But you will not be on the river.

"To the north, beyond the snowline in the village of Steadshire, new recruits receive training." Merssa pointed to the village on the map. "It is where crops are grown and food is raised to feed the army to the south. It is also where smithies make and repair weapons and armor. That is where you will be stationed."

"It hardly seems a place in need of our services." Magneer did not conceal his disapproval. "We are not smithies or farmers, and I need no training."

"It is *definitely* in need of your services," Merssa said. "They lack trainers, and bandits prey on food and weapon caravans and sneak into the village at night to pillage what they may."

Magneer's disgust had yet to leave his face. "But—"

"Do not question the wisdom of the High Paladin!" Nidor surprised everyone in the room. "Not every duty in the effort against evil is desired by all. But they must all be performed to achieve victory."

"Yes." Merssa eyed the Dale as she pulled a tube from her belt. "In here are your orders." She extended the tube to Ballrik. "You will report to Steadshire in ten days and give this to Gramborn, the commander there. If you fail to show in that time, the orders will be void and you will be relieved of your duties. The choice is yours."

They returned to the tavern where they had eaten dinner the previous evening, and mixed emotions surrounded their table. Nidor, ever the obedient soldier, looked pleased with the task before them; Gruelenor and Solinin appeared relieved; Magneer was visibly upset. Ballrik thought of the life he left in West Palidur, now exchanged for a village life in Nira, and how everything was going to change forever...again.

"I must apologize to you all." Magneer broke the silence. "It's my father's doing, I'm sure."

"Nonsense," said Nidor. "Do not be hasty to enter the field of battle. Consider our mission a chance to learn what we may of the enemy. There are no doubt folks there who have lived under the threat of the necromancer for many years now, and they will be our teachers. I believe Silcor is sending me there for a purpose. And when the time comes, we *will* be called upon, of that you can be certain."

They all stared at the Dale, and for a moment Ballrik saw their assignment through Nidor's eyes. The paladin's words made sense, as usual. And at the very least, they would be together.

Chapter 4

Radaam

Vikur drummed his fingers on the table, his drink untouched before him. Poluran, meanwhile, finished consuming a third mug and signaled for a fourth. The dwarf had, perhaps, noticed Vikur's lack of thirst, but he paid it no heed. Vikur often drifted into moments of deep thought as of late; and since learning of Ballrik's enlistment in the Front, Vikur was at a loss. He did not fear for his son's life, but envied Ballrik's courage to return to an evil that defeated them once already.

Vikur stared into his mug, remembering. He recalled how the fall of Ironside Keep had nearly destroyed him, and how he would likely have perished in Tenvale afterward had it not been for Poluran. The dwarf showed unyielding patience upon finding Vikur near the eastern border of the Wizard Kingdom, and after a few weeks of care made him travel worthy, much to the liking of local mages. They then searched for friendlier surroundings, slowly at first and without aim, and after a year ended up in Sendorum.

Within the compound, Vikur saw old friends, including Merssa, Borse, and Pallit. He related to them all he had seen of the enemy before the keep fell, and though it was obvious they already knew much of what he had to say, no doubt from Selanna, they listened all the same. It was good to see familiar faces again, but Vikur felt out of place and could tell the others only humored him. So after a couple months, he and Poluran departed.

They journeyed to Tikken City, where Vikur had enjoyed many good times in the past. The free city was hardly how Vikur remember it, though, for the Council of Wizards kept its citizens on constant alert of the enemy across the water. Most folks spent the late hours in their homes with the doors locked, and the prevalent nightlife the city once boasted was as quiet as a whisper. Poluran was not without means, however, and the dwarf produced enough gold to keep doors open and ale flowing.

They remained for a couple of years within Tikken City's walls and became well known among the tavern folk. But Vikur's regret for his falling out with Ballrik was ever on his mind. Though he would rather have died in defense of Ironside Keep, as those before him were prepared to do, it was time to seek and offer forgiveness. So they left for Philen.

Ballrik met Vikur with visible apprehension—a welcome he probably deserved. And though his son forgave his harsh words of the past, Vikur knew their relationship was forever tainted. Realizing his presence in West Palidur brought undue stress, Vikur and Poluran departed after only a week's stay.

They headed north to Rornibur, so Poluran might put to rest affairs neglected while at Vikur's side. It took some amount of convincing on Poluran's part, but Vikur was allowed into the dwarf city beneath the mountain, a privilege the stout folk were never hasty to grant; and within the halls of stone, he gazed upon many splendors. Veins of silver and gold lined the floors, crystals reflected beautiful patterns on the walls when light drew near, and carvings and statues were abundant. Vikur thought it a crime that such magnificence was hidden from the world.

It did not take the dwarves long to become comfortable with Vikur's presence, and he remained with them for a couple of years. He made many friends, but again grew restless, this time for reasons he could not comprehend, and he and Poluran left the mountains.

They returned to Sendorum, and it was there that Vikur learned of Ballrik's assignment to Nira only a few days prior. Less than a week had passed since that day, and Vikur and Poluran were still within the compound, sitting to an evening drink.

"It's time to go," Vikur said.

"Already?" Poluran raised his bushy brow. "I've only just wet my lips!"

"That's not what I mean." Vikur lowered his voice. "My son has set the example. Moving from place to place has brought me no true peace. Only your company has kept me alive... As alive as I can be."

"We are to find young Ballrik, then?" asked Poluran.

Vikur gave the dwarf a level stare. "I aim to take back what is mine."

"You don't mean—"

"Ironside Keep!" Vikur grinned. "I don't expect you to join me. Just promise you'll not tell Merssa. She's putting together some grand plan or something." His eyes sank. "I don't believe she intends to use me in any capacity. Can you blame her?"

"How do you plan to...?" Poluran said in a hushed voice.

"I'm not sure." Vikur shrugged. "But I have many days ahead to figure it out."

"Even if you...succeed," Poluran leaned in close, "how would you hold it? Its walls are strong, but one man could not possibly—"

"You ask many questions, *Polabin*." Vikur winked.

The dwarf grinned, stretching the wrinkled skin and thick hair about his mouth. "I'm going with you, of course. So long as you let me bring a friend."

Vikur was confused.

"Clanghorr, you dolt!"

Vikur smiled. "I can see the look on Merssa's face when she battles her way to the pass and finds us running the keep!" He chuckled and drained his mug.

After enjoying a couple more tankards, the two turned in for the night.

The next morning, they departed from the compound. They followed the road west across Virch and headed south through Moclen. The only plan they put together thus far was to pass through Tenvale, for the Wizard Kingdom was untouched by the eternal winter. Many powerful mages existed there to turn away the snow, but there was no need, for Trannum did not cast his wintry torment over their realm. Merssa speculated it had something to do with the mysterious Wizards' Code or some other such nonsense. In any case, Tenvale held a neutral stance and made this point very clear, stating that any encroachment upon their soil would be considered an attack and be dealt with swiftly and harshly. Such were the oddities of wizards. They did not seem to care that a necromancer, dead for more centuries than Vikur cared to count, was destroying all things living around them. Would Trannum not deal with them once he conquered the rest of Vaeldor? Where will their precious realm be then, without the aid of brave warriors? Obviously, they learned nothing from the orb's possession of Solett all those years ago, after the wizard discovered one of Trannum's orbs and kept it for himself.

Though the Wizard Kingdom allowed no *armies* to march through their land, surely they would pay no heed to a mere human and dwarf. Or so Vikur thought. When they arrived at the Arman Ferry along the Prince Arman River, the mage that manned the boat eyed them suspiciously and demanded to know their business within Tenvale. Poluran was quick to answer.

"I am Poluran of Morimont," he fibbed. "My homeland lies in the Varlimor Mountains, as you probably well know, and that is where I aim for."

"And what of the human?" inquired the man in a dry voice.

"These are strange and evil times," Poluran said, "and only a fool would travel alone."

The mage's gaze burrowed into Poluran. "Do you not realize that leagues of undead-infested snow bar your way?"

"Do you *dare* deny a dwarf passage to his homeland?" Poluran furrowed his brow. "How I get there is none of your concern."

The man glared for what seemed like a minute. Vikur grew nervous that his companion had gone too far.

"I'll have your fare." The ferryman shrugged. "Far be it from me to tell you how to end your lives."

Once across the river, they rode southeast, avoiding cities and villages — Vikur wished to stay clear of wizards as much as possible. They skirted Boddrom Swamp and turned due east, following the Windy River until reaching the Ladal Mountains. The terrain grew rough and forced them a bit north, but posed no problems for travelers as experienced as they, and they neared the border of Sardina after only two weeks.

No snow was visible, but Vikur smelled it riding on a cool breeze out of the east. To the north was the village of Belltown, where Ballrik had taken Vikur after the fall of the keep. Vikur and his son had been most unwelcome there, but thanks to the timely arrival of Selanna, they were granted permission to stay until Vikur was able to move on. That was several years ago, and gazing upon the settlement made Vikur's spirit grow weary.

"I know what you're thinking," said Poluran. "But it's just a village. My stocks are depleted, as are your own, and I don't think we've enough furs for the winter ahead. But if your mind is unwilling, I'll take a quick jaunt myself and secure all we need. Melballa's not as strong as she used to be, but she can still carry enough for the both of us."

Vikur glanced at the overladen mule and gave a weak smile. "As I said before, Ballrik has set the example." He looked at Belltown. "Besides, if I can't enter a simple village, how can I return to the keep?"

Poluran nodded, and they headed north.

The lights of Belltown were flickering with the approaching dusk, but the stores were open and Vikur and Poluran purchased the furs and food supplies they required. As they exited the last merchant's shop, a mage in a gray robe halted them. A strange white insignia upon the right breast marked the man as a city watchman.

"What have we here?" The man's unibrow rose high above his long nose. "Interesting wares you've collected."

Poluran stepped forward. "Our business is our —"

"Spare me your remarks," spat the mage. "I am of the Border Guard, and it is my business to watch for suspicious persons entering this village. From what I have observed, there is sufficient evidence to hold you *both* for questioning."

"They are with me," said an approaching mage. The man wore a red robe and stood tall and muscular with a clean-shaven head. "Did you finish my errands, Vikur?"

Vikur needed only a moment to recognize the newcomer. The man looked the same as he did several years ago, when he helped Vikur retrieve one of Trannum's orbs from the Serpent's Range. He had aged well.

"Yes, Master Melac." Vikur bowed. "I believe we have everything you requested."

The guard's suspicious glare never wavered, but Melac's presence apparently changed the situation. With a snort, the man departed.

Melac waited for the nosy mage to disappear around a corner before speaking again. "Vikur! What brings you here?"

Vikur released a chuckle of relief. "That's a long story."

"I don't live far." The wizard nodded toward a road to the east. "Perhaps you can tell it over a draft."

The sun had set, and the thought of a drink before continuing appealed to Vikur. He accepted Melac's invitation. Poluran let go a deep sigh.

Melac led them to a modest house on the northeastern outskirts of the village, and there he tapped a keg and served a platter of bread and cheese. They enjoyed small talk for a while, but the conversations were solely between Melac and Vikur—Poluran appeared to have lost his voice. As the halfmoon rose high, the mage invited them to stay until morning. Poluran seemed eager to return to the road, gazing nervously at the strange components about the place, but he made no objections when Vikur accepted the offer.

They talked well into the night, finally touching on subjects concerning Trannum. Melac revealed that the Council of Wizards had placed him in Tenvale to keep track of comings and goings through the region, and that he had been living there since the quest for the orb in the Serpent's Range reached its end.

"I was aware of your arrival with Ballrik," Melac said, "and would have offered my help..." He bowed his head, looking ashamed. "But it was not within my orders to do so. I am deeply sorry. And I'm glad Selanna arrived when she did."

"Speak no more of it." Vikur gave Melac a hearty slap on the back, causing the mage to lurch. "The past is the past. The future is all that matters now!"

"And what does the future hold for the two of you?" posed Melac.

Vikur's smile vanished. But he saw no harm in sharing, and he gave a full account of their quest. Poluran bore an incredulous look, as if expecting the wizard to point out how crazy the notion was and raise an alarm. The dwarf relaxed, however, when Melac offered to join them. Vikur accepted.

Come morning, the three set out on foot while the village was still asleep. Vikur understood Poluran's hesitation to part with Melballa, but after explaining the mule's low chances of survival, the dwarf reluctantly left her to the care of the stables. They divvied the gear and made their way east until reaching the northern tip of the Ladal Mountains. There, they veered southeast.

By noon on the second day, the temperature had dropped significantly. The air was still, unlike the swirling winds about Palidur Bridge, but Vikur knew things would change for the worse before long and they donned their furs.

After another mile the snowline came into view, and it was not much longer before the white powder surrounded them. A flurry floated lazily from the sky, a peaceful winter afternoon on a midsummer's day, and as dusk approached, the Fire hills replaced the mountains to the south.

The hills created a barrier between civilization and the wild jungles of Tarn Arum, spanning for miles between the Ladal and Varlimor Mountains. Legends held them to have once been mountains themselves, before the Dragon Wars, but powerful magic used to flush out the large reptiles had destroyed their majestic peaks. Left behind were strange, reflective stones that shone orange with the setting sun; and when coupled with the haze that settled over the region every evening, the hills appeared to be alight—a beautiful vision to behold! But there was no such pleasure for Vikur, for snow covered the hilltops and clouds denied the dying sun's rays.

The air grew colder still as they pressed on and snow fell heavily at times. On the following day, the winds picked up and the countryside vanished beyond a veil of white—Vikur was unsure if it was new snow, or if gusts had lifted loose powder to blind them. That evening, Vikur lost all feeling in his face and his fingers were failing fast. Poluran dug a shallow hole and filled it with firewood from their packs, and with Melac's arcane assistance a fire was started and they huddled close.

The night passed slowly and none of them found sleep. For Vikur, it was not entirely the cold that held his eyes open, nor the fear of wild animals. He remained on constant alert for signs of the undead. But they saw and heard nothing, and with the morning they continued on their way.

Near midday of the following day, Vikur became concerned. Either they had wandered off course, or they did not cover as much ground as he had thought, for they should have found the source of Starlight Lake. Later that day, he discovered he had been mistaken on both counts. Southwood came into view, and he realized they had already crossed the river. The water had been buried beneath the snow.

Vikur turned into the hills, and it was an idea his companions grew immediately fond of, for many small caves existed to shelter them from stinging winds. Vikur knew the burrows were scattered throughout the rising terrain, but he never considered them viable shelters, for they were known to house vicious animals. Presently, the caves appeared long abandoned, and he felt silly for not having used them sooner.

They picked their way from cave to cave while the light lasted, resting often to warm their bones, and with the growing darkness they stopped within a sizeable grotto and made camp. The wind continued to howl and tried desperately to extinguish their fire, but it was unsuccessful in its task and the night passed without mishap.

Come morning, yet another layer of snow blanketed the area and concealed all tracks from the previous day. For some travelers this would have served as a detriment, as one could easily lose all sense of direction. As for Vikur, he was too familiar with the surroundings, and nothing could hinder him now.

They trudged along for better than a day and a half, breaking often within the caves. The weather continued in its attempts to dampen their spirits, but they did not waver, and even took the time to enjoy a snowball fight.

At last, Vikur found what he sought, and he cleared snow and debris from a small opening located low to the ground. He crawled a short distance until the space expanded, and there he stood. His companions entered while he searched the wall to the right, and after finding the lantern he knew was there, Melac lit the long-forgotten wick with a spell of fire.

They were in a small cave possessing flasks, firewood, shovels, ropes, and other items of survival. Vikur ignored them and moved along the back wall, feeling the cold stone with his equally cold hand. He located a loose rock and gave it a firm shove, and a dark passageway opened to the right—the secret entrance to Ironside Keep.

They gathered what gear they needed and entered the rough-hewn passage. The walls and floor were uneven, and crude steps descended now and then, taking them deeper beneath the hills. The air remained cool, but it paled compared to the winds above, and they removed their heavy fur cloaks.

They followed the tunnel late into the night and stopped within a small chamber. It was set up as a resting place, with a few old cots of straw surrounding a cold firepit, and rats scurried from their path as they dropped their gear and settled in. Melac then started a fire with wood they had taken from the cave's supplies.

"Dwarves dug this tunnel long ago," Vikur said while they heated some meat by the fire.

Poluran gazed at the chiseled walls with a critical eye. "They did not do so well."

"It was done in haste and secret," Vikur explained. "They did the job they were paid to do."

"That's no excuse for poor craftsmanship!"

The dwarf's voice echoed into the darkness of the corridors, bringing the conversation to a halt. Vikur listened, but it seemed nothing existed to hear the outburst.

"Have you thought about what awaits us when we reach the keep?" Melac brought Vikur's attention back to the fire.

Vikur shrugged. "I know what's there. Or at least what was." He took a deep breath. "Dunarchins, wraiths, and probably zombies and skeletons. Things you'd expect. But also a Death Lord resides there, or so I'm told."

"Radaam," Poluran added with a mouthful of food. "At least, Selanna thinks so."

"Do you honestly believe there to be a chance of success?" the wizard posed.

Again Vikur shrugged. "If nothing else, we might at least rid Vaeldor of one of those abominations. They took my home by surprise. It's time someone handed them a surprise of their own." He looked at Melac and grinned. "And I've a score to settle with this Radaam!"

"What about you?" Melac turned to Poluran. "What business takes you there?"

"My brother needs my help." Poluran nodded to Vikur. "And I never turn my back on family." After gazing into the fire, he added, "Besides, I have failed too many times where Trannum is concerned. Even with the most powerful weapon in all the land..." He shook his head, patting Clanghorr. "Two people I cared about lost their lives before my eyes through this entire ordeal, and I lost an orb to the enemy as well. I do not think there are many who would trust me anymore. I am old, even as dwarves go. Before my time comes, I would like to do one thing the Almighty Meldar can smile upon, so I might be accepted into His Grand Hall deep below this world."

"What about you?" Vikur turned the question on Melac. "You are young yet, for a wizard. Why have you joined us on a mission so dangerous?"

It was Melac's turn to search the crackling flames for answers. "The Council uses me as a spy on Tenvale's border. I have been there for years now, and my studies have come to a standstill. I feel my power waning. The enemy lies dormant atop a sea of snow unchecked, and of all the wizards I know, only Selanna has shown the courage to slip by their guard to keep a closer eye on them. I should be so brave. Now is my chance to make a difference." Melac turned to Vikur. "I do not honestly believe there to be much hope in claiming the keep. But at least we might stir the enemy ranks; maybe learn a few secrets they harbor before we're through. And," Melac winked, "perhaps we might do what no one has done thus far: destroy a Death Lord."

Vikur woke from a most uncomfortable sleep to discover that rats had eaten most of their food—the packs were open and half their contents splayed across the room. No one complained, though, not even Poluran. Who knew if they would have further need for sustenance? Relighting the lantern and gathering their gear, they exited the chamber.

After a few hours, they came upon a small hole in the southern wall of the passage. It was two feet above the floor and roughly a foot in diameter.

"That happened years ago," said Vikur, "but it's larger now. Apparently the tunnel was placed too close to some cavern or something. I never looked into it, though I always meant to. I was going to speak with the dwarves to see if they could seal it up." He sighed. "I guess it doesn't matter now."

Poluran bent over to peer through the opening, taking the lantern from Vikur and shedding its light into the darkness beyond. "It doesn't look like a cavern to me." The dwarf issued a snort and stuck his head through the hole. "It's more like...mines." He pulled back, looking at Vikur with wide eyes. "It can't be."

"What is it?" asked Vikur.

"The lost mines." Poluran spoke just above a whisper. "The birthplace of my race. Lornibur."

"What is Lornibur?" asked Melac.

"Exactly what I said!" Poluran snapped. "The beginning of my folk. Hundreds of miles of mines, containing more wealth than even the High Riser Mountains."

"Interesting," said Vikur. "But I'm sorry, my friend. We have no time to explore it further."

"Of course." Poluran nodded and handed the lantern back. "Maybe once we've finished."

Vikur gave a small chuckle. "Yes. Once we've finished."

They walked out the remainder of the day, camping again when they reached another chamber. This one contained a well, and they refilled their skins and ate what little food the rats had left them.

"We arrive at Ironside tomorrow," Vikur said, all thoughts of things good in his life fading.

They continued the next day without a word. Several sets of crude steps led upward, sometimes bearing straight and other times spiraling around pillars of stone. After a few miles, the passage terminated at a blank wall.

Vikur inhaled deeply and released it slowly. His breath was thicker than it had been deeper underground. He was sure the others noticed the steady decrease in temperature while they climbed, but no one made mention of it. Vikur moved closer to the tunnel's end, and his heart raced as he experienced the strange fear that invaded his body the last time he was within the walls of his home. He saw that Poluran and Melac sensed it as well, but they stood resolute, and Poluran nodded to continue.

To his left, Vikur located the loose stone that opened the secret door. He pushed it inward and the wall before them slid aside without a sound, releasing a gust of frigid air that danced with the lantern's flame. Vikur thought for a moment of the furs they abandoned, but soon he would no longer feel the chill, for his blood would be running hot.

They stepped through the portal and into a circular chamber adorned with murals and many niches—the crypt of Ironside Keep. The paintings depicted the Lords of the Keep, and the most recent mural, its paint barely touched by time, was of Vikur. It revealed him in better days, sitting in a large chair and holding the same sword appearing in the hands of the other lords; the sword currently resting in his scabbard.

Vikur gazed upon the self-portrait in silence. His eyes then drifted around the room, remembering things better forgotten. The niches, once sealed and containing the remains of his family, were empty. But Vikur recalled the ghastly corpses that rose years ago with the Wind of the Dead, and how he and Arkor defeated the skeletons and cleared the chamber.

He turned to the far end, where the image of the first Lord of Ironside was painted. Grellmor was as a giant, with one foot atop a mountain and his sword held high enough to reach the sun. The visage covered the entrance; a door set with intricate locks on either side to hold even the most talented thief at bay. It was a ruse, however, for a single mechanism bolted the door shut.

Kneeling on the floor, Vikur withdrew a special key, one constructed by dwarves when the keep was young. He slipped it into a natural-looking crack on the bottom of the door and moved it along the groove until feeling it catch. After turning it twice, he slid the key out, and the door moved silently into the wall to the right to reveal a circular storage chamber. Vikur returned the key to the pouch dangling around his neck and dropped it beneath his chain shirt. With a deep breath, he led the way into the base of the central tower.

All was quiet, and years of dust covered smashed crates and barrels. The crypt door moved silently back into place, revealing an image identical to the one on the opposite side, save for the many scratches marring its surface. The exterior false locks were damaged or destroyed as well—apparently the current occupants had given up hope of entering the tomb some time ago.

Vikur ascended steps along the arcing wall, and as he and his companions rose above the storage room, the curving stairwell became enclosed on either side. They passed a few archways on the inner wall revealing the kitchen, dining room, and library, and each looked to have been sacked. The next archway contained a large door on the outer wall. It led to the Great Hall, but Vikur ignored it and continued upward.

Upon reaching Ballrik's bedchamber, Vikur threw open the door, surprising a couple of dunarchins. It appeared the abominations had been using the room as personal quarters, though Vikur could not fathom why the sleepless needed such accommodations. Before the creatures could draw their weapons, his sword cut down one and Clanghorr the other. Vikur scowled in disgust and exited the chamber.

They continued up to the next door. Vikur's room. Vikur expected to find Radaam within, but when he opened the door, he was faced with four men. Living men. They were huddled in thick cloaks, warming themselves by the fireplace, and looked up without fear or concern.

"New recruits?" asked one in a heavy accent.

Vikur immediately knew them to be denizens of Selt, a realm ruled by demon-worshipping priests. He had only met one man from the northern kingdom in his lifetime, and the coward proved every repulsive rumor of Seltans to be true. The thug bullied commoners for pleasure and killed without remorse, and he remained vile until the end, when he expired upon Vikur's sword. As Vikur viewed the men before him now, he did not know what disgusted him more: that they were from Selt, or that they were among the living and serving the undead. In the end, he did not care. Either was sufficient reason to exterminate them.

Vikur strode forward with sword in hand, the blackish blood of the dunarchin still dripping from its edge, and before the Seltans could defend themselves, two were dead at his feet. Another fell, as Clanghorr cut the man in half with a single swing, and Vikur bore down on the final Seltan. The man showed no fear while unleashing attacks with both weapon and tongue, but Vikur was superior in skill and knocked the sword from the man's hand. Even without a weapon, the curses continued until Vikur's blade silenced the swine forever. Or so Vikur thought.

The corpses stirred—Vikur had forgotten about the transformation! Fortunately, Melac was prepared for the event, and the mage gestured at the fireplace. Bolts of flame jumped from the hearth and onto the zombies, and as Melac raised his hands, their bodies were engulfed. The fires grew hot, forcing Vikur and Poluran to retreat a step, and the zombies collapsed at their feet. Melac then lowered his hands and the flames died out, leaving behind charred, smelly remains.

Looking around the chamber, Vikur spit in disgust. The Seltans had obviously been staying there for some time. There were a couple additional cots present, and hung upon the wall were symbols of worship to the Seltans' evil deity, Demoligius—a vile being with hordes of demons at his beck and call. Vikur thought it an odd alliance between the necromancer and Demoligius, for one enjoyed eternal winter while the other's world was wreathed in flame. Shaking his head, Vikur led the way back downstairs.

They entered the Great Hall, a long chamber connecting all towers of the keep. Their footfalls echoed softly toward the east and west towers of the barren room, and Vikur froze when he spied the open iron door on the northern wall. The screams of the keep's defenders filled his head, and he remembered all too well the wraiths that had slipped through the cracks to unbar the door for the awaiting Death Lord—he could still feel the drain of the dark spirits upon his body. He squeezed his eyes shut until the screaming faded, and when he opened them again, he saw only the steps descending to the lower levels.

"Be alert for wraiths," he said.

They passed through the iron door, and as they descended the long, narrow stairwell, an icy wind played with all loose clothing. Within the entry chamber, the portcullis was twisted and the doors smashed, just as it had been when Vikur led the keep's soldiers in battle many years ago. The corpses of undead still littered the floor, now half buried in snow. To the right was the door leading to storage chambers, meeting rooms, and the lounge; the portion of the keep that served as an inn and tavern when peace ruled the land.

Vikur opened the door and proceeded, passing the many side rooms and heading straight to the end of the corridor. The intensity of the chill increased, growing almost unbearable, and as he reached the final door, he could sense the enemy on the other side. Throwing it open, he was not mistaken.

The lounge was surprisingly in good order. The bar was intact, as were most of the tables and chairs, and Vikur's throne-like seat, the one he used when boasting of his many adventures with travelers, had survived. Now, however, the new Lord of the Keep occupied it. Though Vikur teetered on the edge of consciousness when he last viewed the dark warrior, he knew it to be the same one that led the attack against the keep. Black plates covered the entire body of the Death Lord, and the only distinguishable features were the blue eyes burning beneath the helmet.

Vikur and his companions froze as the glowing eyes turned to meet them and the Death Lord rose. From its belt it unsheathed a wicked sword, a dark blade bearing many teeth along one edge, and attached to the hilt were strange hooks. The undead king pulled a smaller sword, one lacking in stature, and from it dripped a greenish-black liquid.

Vikur pointed his sword. "Radaam?"

The dark figure nodded once.

"I have come to claim what is mine." Vikur stepped forward. "Prepare to die!"

The kitchen door flew open and half a score of dunarchins and wraiths rushed into the lounge. Radaam halted them with a stare.

"Leave me," came a hollow voice from beneath the helmet.

The undead obeyed, slinking back through the door as if in fear.

Vikur was not sure if it surprised him more that the Death Lord sent the reinforcements away, or that the creature spoke. He had little time to consider the matter when the dark warrior crossed its blades and stepped forward.

Vikur met Radaam in the center of the room, and their weapons clashed with a resounding *clang*. Poluran remained back, Vikur's longtime friend knowing he would accept no help in this battle, and Vikur put forth a series of attacks. All the glum years of the recent past melted away as he forced Radaam back, and Vikur could not contain his laughter when he pressed the undead king against the bar. But the dark knight wormed free before Vikur scored a hit.

Radaam went on the offensive, making it obvious he had been toying with Vikur all along. The evil weapons swung too swiftly for Vikur to defend, and the teeth of the larger blade sliced through the metal rings of his shoulder and tore into his flesh. Pain coursed through Vikur's body as he struggled to hold his ground, and the purpose of the hooks became clear when they locked onto his sword. The weapon of his family was wrenched free, and everything moved slowly while it flew end over end across the room.

Poluran roared, but Vikur knew his friend would not arrive soon enough. The smaller blade found its way into Vikur's abdomen and his knees buckled; and with a cold, metal boot, Radaam pushed him to the floor.

Vikur's vision blurred as he lay on the flagstones. He desperately wished to regain his feet, but his body was unresponsive while the poison coursed through his veins. His stomach soured, and he was suddenly aware of thousands of undead in and around the keep. He sensed hundreds of ghouls crawling about the halls and wraiths circling the towers, and a legion of zombies and skeletons stood perfectly still upon the mountain pass, as if awaiting orders.

Within the chamber, Poluran battled in vain before Vikur's body. There was no victory, no escape, and no hope. Vikur had led his friends to their doom.

"No..." Vikur managed, just above a whisper. But he saw no more.

Poluran stepped between Radaam and Vikur. Watching Vikur fall was more than Poluran could bear, and anger roiled inside unlike any he could recall.

"Time to taste the rage of Clanghorr!" Poluran swung the mighty axe.

The Death Lord danced out of reach, and the weapon whistled through the air. Radaam then unleashed a series of attacks, unbalancing Poluran and causing him to tumble over a chair. He heard Melac chanting, and small bolts of fire struck the enemy, but the missiles dissipated upon the black plates and not a mark was left behind. The blue eyes turned on Melac, growing brighter as a whispering chant issued from beneath the dark helmet. Melac's body contorted, and the mage screamed out.

Poluran scrambled to his feet, taking in a deep breath as he pressed again. He swung his axe several times, but found no openings in the Death Lord's defense. So he changed his tactics. If he could not attack the warrior, he would attack the weapons. Then Radaam would taste Clanghorr's edge!

Blow after blow, Poluran hacked at the Death Lord's blades, and sparks flew from the black steel every time they connected. He then knocked the smaller sword from Radaam's grasp, but he was filled with horror when Clanghorr became locked within the hooks of the larger blade. Poluran was powerless to stop the Death Lord, and the axe was pulled free.

Poluran froze as his mind raced, and a ball of flame washed over Radaam. The fire burned Poluran as well, and he saw Melac standing tall—the mage had overcome the Death Lord's spell. Radaam's attention turned again to Melac, and Poluran scrambled for Clanghorr. He dove across the flagstones and seized the bronze handle, but before he could raise the weapon, Radaam's blade struck the floor, emitting sparks as it severed Poluran's arm at the elbow. Rolling onto his back, Poluran gazed through watery eyes at the monster towering above.

The Death Lord tilted its head, and its eyes grew brighter as it seemed to absorb the pain coursing through Poluran's body. Poluran closed his eyes and awaited the final blow, wishing for an end to his suffering, but the undead king would not grant that request soon enough.

Radaam kicked Poluran several feet from the axe, and Poluran was helpless as the Death Lord lifted him with one hand and pressed him against the wall. Another hollow chant issued from beneath its helmet, and the strange words penetrated Poluran's head, causing it to pound. His skull felt as if it were going to explode, and the pain traveled throughout his body as his limbs were torn from their sockets. He cried out, but his voice would never be heard again outside the walls of the keep.

Melac's magic failed to hold the Death Lord's attention. Much of his power went into the spell of fire, but Radaam only glanced at him, as if he were a mere nuisance; a pesky insect buzzing about the room. Melac's mind raced, unable to think of anything to do. The Death Lord held Poluran against the wall, incanting some dark spell to bring the dwarf dire pain, and Melac was powerless to stop it. He could only watch and await his own demise.

All was hopeless.

Or was it?

Melac saw Vikur's sword lying on the floor. Then he spotted Clanghorr. Both were special, and neither could be lost to the enemy. While the Death Lord took pleasure in its victory, Melac forced himself to move and he scooped up the weapons.

"Sorry, Poluran," he whispered, and he fled from the chamber without looking back.

Chapter 5

Steadshire

Ballrik pulled his horse to a halt. Nestled in a lush valley three hundred yards to the northeast was Steadshire. The village stood a few miles east of Vermallon Forest and just within sight of the southernmost peaks of the Coranthiar Mountain—small, dark mounds in the distance.

"Always known as a peaceful farming village," Solinin said to Ballrik.

Nidor nodded in agreement.

Ballrik had noticed the Dale seeking information about Steadshire before exiting the compound. Solinin spoke matter-of-factly, as usual. Ballrik did not know how the kid stored so much useless knowledge in that head.

"It once boasted a population of five hundred," Nidor added.

"I do not think that is the case anymore," said Magneer.

The influence of the Front had forced some expansion, and dozens of newer buildings existed along the village's southern edge. As well, Ballrik estimated there to be a couple thousand people at the very least. What were the words Nidor said to make their task seem noble and worthy while they made the journey? They were lost on Ballrik while he viewed the many farms, and he wondered what type of soldiers they would be training. Farmers?

"Let's go," he said with a sigh.

They entered the village, and it was easy to tell locals from soldiers and trainees. Most villagers appeared none too pleased with the occupation and cast leering glances toward Ballrik's group.

"Well," Ballrik scratched his chin, "we've made good time. Two days ahead of Merssa's schedule."

"Must be her age." Magneer chuckled. "But at least we have time for a couple nights of drinking."

Nidor furrowed his brow, as if considering Magneer's idea. "I would prefer to report to Commander Gramborn. He may have immediate needs."

Magneer's shoulders slumped, and he looked desperately at Ballrik. But there was no arguing or bargaining with the Dale. With another sigh, Ballrik hailed a passing soldier.

An escort delivered Ballrik and his friends to a building on the eastern edge of town. They were then led to a dining room and stood before a man large about the waist and possessing a mountainous presence. Commander Gramborn had undoubtedly been a powerful warrior at one time, but it was obvious his battle days were behind him, for a thick cane rested at the side of his chair. Gramborn looked over the scroll Ballrik handed him without so much as a glance at Ballrik's company, and he bellowed out a name.

"Delarrin!"

"Yes, sir!" A spirited young man rushed into the room. He appeared younger than Solinin, and though he stood like a soldier, he wore farmer's attire.

Great. They *would* be training farmers.

"These are trainers from the compound." Gramborn waved in Ballrik's direction. "Show 'em around and find 'em a place to stay. They'll be training in the northern quadrant." Gramborn handed the scroll to one of his servants and returned to the task at hand: eating his lunch and ignoring the company before him.

"Follow me, sirs!" Delarrin's grin stretched from ear to ear.

"I'm Delarrin," the young man said after they exited the building. "I've been watchin' soldiers come and go most my life, but now it's my turn. I'll be in the next bunch of recruits for trainin'. Maybe one of *you* will train me."

"Do not be hasty," Nidor said as they led their horses along the street. "War is unkind."

Delarrin looked at the paladin, appearing nervous—the lad had obviously never seen a Dale before. Then his confident expression returned. "I know. But I was never meant for farmin'. I'm really quick and good with my hands. Pop says I'd make a good bow shooter. But I think I was born to swing a sword."

"Bow shooter, huh?" Magneer gave Ballrik a wink.

"Yeah." Delarrin was oblivious to any patronization. "And I've been practicin' when I can. Anyways, I'll be more than happy to run errands and such—when I'm not servin' Lord Gramborn."

"Very good," said Ballrik politely. "Now, if you could show us around, we'd be most appreciative."

Delarrin led them toward the northern side of the village. He paused often to point out shops and describe random locals, and after half an hour they stopped outside the training grounds where Ballrik and his friends were to perform their duties.

A dried field of dirt sat before them, sectioned off with fences, and all equipment appeared dirty and in ill repair. One section housed dozens of battle dummies looking more like scarecrows; another contained targets for bow practice, most of them possessing broken twine and falling apart; and the largest area was obviously meant for riding. Stables stood nearby, only half of its stalls currently occupied, and the horses seemed better suited for working fields than riding into combat. Ballrik and Magneer sighed.

The tour resumed, and Delarrin showed them the locations of three taverns, explaining that civilians frequented one, trainees another, and ranking officers the third. They then continued north until all that remained were scattered farmhouses and fields of various crops. Delarrin halted before a large farmhouse flanked by a barn.

"These are yer quarters." Delarrin smiled, but then he frowned at the looks on their faces. "See, there ain't enough room for newcomers anymore, with the inns full of trainees. So new arrivals have to be boarded with the common folk."

Ballrik contained his chuckle, while Magneer's smirk extended to one side of his face. Apparently, Delarrin did not consider himself a villager. Their attention was then drawn to the approach of a grumpy-looking farmer.

"That's Dezlo," Delarrin said in a hushed voice. "You guys'll like him. He's been here longer than anyone."

Ballrik had his doubts.

Dezlo stopped several feet away and eyed them with contempt. The man was older, his hair disheveled, and he looked to have put in a day's work already. Delarrin introduced the farmer to everyone, but Dezlo said nothing. When Ballrik offered a hand in greeting, the man made no acknowledgement of the action.

"Hope to see ya on the battlegrounds!" Delarrin skipped off down the road.

An awkward silence followed while Dezlo continued to stare. Ballrik wondered if he should say something, but then the farmer spoke.

"You boys can stay in the barn. Yer on yer own at mealtime, 'less you pay yer way clear to sit at my table. Nothin's free in these parts — I don't care what yer Gramborn says. And when yer not busy with whatever you've come to do, I fully expect you to help around the farm. Even pampered folk such as yerselves must know somethin' useful to contribute."

Magneer and Solinin fought back a chuckle. Ballrik considered putting the man in his place; they were there to protect him, after all. But then Nidor spoke.

"We are most appreciative of your hospitality, kind sir. We are your humble servants and will contribute in any way we can to earn our stay." The Dale bowed.

Dezlo's jaw dropped, and he almost choked on his saliva. He then cleared his throat and the stern expression returned. "And my daughters are off limits. They're not here for yer pleasure, so don't get any ideas." Dezlo gave a snort. "All right, then. Follow me."

The farmer showed them to the barn—a sty made for the king of swine. Within lived a few pigs, a cow, and a draft horse, and several chickens roamed the area outside, though Ballrik noticed no coop. The straw appeared old and soiled, and the smell was the worst odor ever to defile Ballrik's senses. Dezlo left without another word.

Magneer chuckled. "And dad worried that I'd never find my path in life."

They toiled for hours to get the space clean enough as to be bearable, and made their quarters upon the loft to avoid sleeping with the animals. Once finished, they sat in a circle on the hay of their new room.

"Nidor," said Magneer once they were as comfortable as possible. "You really shouldn't speak for all of us. I do *not* intend to work this farm. I'm a ranger. And I'm here to train soldiers."

"I agree," said Solinin.

"I apologize." Nidor gave a slight bow. "But do not worry. I will make up for any work you choose not to perform."

"Blast you, Dale!" Ballrik held half a grin. "You'll make peasants of us yet!"

The dark man grinned, and they all laughed.

"How about his daughters?" Solinin chuckled. "I think he worries a bit much. Did you see the warts on his face?"

There came a distinct giggling from below, and they leaned over to spy three young women standing in the barn. It was Dezlo's daughters, come to look at the boarders. Solinin could not have been more wrong in his assumption, and Ballrik was held in awe of the beauty the three possessed. Magneer was first to descend to say hello, followed closely by Solinin, and Ballrik went next. Gruelenor and Nidor were hesitant, and they slowly made their way down the ladder.

The women were in their twenties and appeared to the contrary of their father. Their clothes were clean, their hair combed, and their attitude warm. With enchanting smiles, they introduced themselves. Lorin was the eldest, Kalette the middle sister, and the youngest was Della.

"Yeah, Kid," Magneer said to Solinin under his breath. "They're quite hideous!"

A few months passed, and Ballrik and his companions spent most of their days on the training fields, making them more suitable and teaching soldiers. They also did their part on the farm when time permitted, although Nidor and Gruelenor performed most of the work.

It did not take long for feelings to grow between some of them and Dezlo's daughters. Lorin was taken with Ballrik, Kalette with Magneer, and Della gave her love to Solinin. Gruelenor did not win favor from any of them, for obvious reasons, and they found Nidor fascinating—it seemed few citizens of Steadshire had ever heard of the dark-skinned race. The paladin honored Dezlo's wishes and kept clear of the women as much as possible, cautioning the others to do the same. They paid the Dale no heed.

The couples sneaked around for weeks until Dezlo discovered their secret meetings, and the farmer was upset, to say the least. His daughters formed a united front, pleading for him to accept the warriors into his heart as they had, and he toiled over the situation. Then, one day, Dezlo confronted Ballrik and his friends in the barn.

"I have to say, you boys have worked hard since arrivin'. And I can't deny word around town that yer respectable. Rumors claim yer trainin' to be quite extraordinary, though I don't care much for such matters. And after all, you are, in fact, healthy young men, skilled in combat and carryin' a fair amount of wealth to yer names. Most fathers would be delighted with all this. But the fact is that you'll one day march off to the south and never return." Dezlo sighed and shook his head. "You've stolen my girls' hearts, and there's no choice but to give my blessin'. I pray yer worthy of them."

Life became pleasant on the farm afterward, and with the following spring a great wedding took place, where the couples were joined at the village temple. Ballrik, Magneer, and Solinin moved into the large house, and although Gruelenor and Nidor were offered rooms as well, the two chose to remain in the barn.

Ballrik was content. Married life was a blessing, and every day brought new joy. Their reputation as trainers continued to grow, and all of Steadshire soon knew their names; and Gramborn was so impressed with their efficiency that he began granting them personal time. At Magneer's insistence, they spent most of that time hunting, reminding Ballrik of the fun they had enjoyed in Philen.

At first their expeditions led them into Vermallon Forest, where game was aplenty. As usual, Solinin exhibited exceptional skills for one his age, already having a firm grasp on tracking and baiting prey. Nidor seemingly participated only for the camaraderie. On their second outing, Gruelenor attempted to train the paladin in the use of the bow.

"What need have I for a bow with all of you around?" the Dale asked with a grin.

"At least learn to tread more softly." Magneer frowned. "You're scaring away the game."

During the third hunting trip, they found the Vermallon elves to be displeased with their lurking about the forest, especially with the likes of Gruelenor in company. They then headed north in search of friendlier grounds, and the farther they trekked, the more interesting the hunts became.

Again, life seemed well and the threat of the necromancer far away. Ballrik never imagined he could find such happiness outside Philen, but indeed he discovered much more than that. Besides great friends, he found love, and he missed Lorin dearly at the moment. Ballrik and his companions were on the third day of a seven-day leave, and had pressed farther north than ever before as they followed a wide stream to Lake Charal. It was a large lake, fed by a waterfall on its northern side that marked the end of the Echo Valley Rapids — a well-deserved name, as the sound of charging water resonated off the tall cliffs. The rapids grew louder while Ballrik and his friends rounded the lake, and this made Ballrik question whether Nidor had been mistaken about the noise he claimed to have detected.

"Did you hear that?" the paladin asked above the rushing water while the horses refreshed themselves at the lakeside.

"Hear what?" Magneer furrowed his brow.

"It was a wailing, I think." The Dale cocked his head to one side, pointing his ear to the east.

Magneer opened his mouth to speak, but Nidor held up a hand. The paladin then closed his eyes.

"Over there." Nidor looked to the northeast. "Something evil is afoot. I can feel it."

Anxiety crept into Ballrik's chest. Though he heard nothing, Nidor was never wrong. Ballrik also wondered whether they were still within the realm of Nira.

Without another word, Nidor took to a swift pace, and the others trailed after.

"This is pointless," Magneer said to Ballrik. "And I don't like leaving the horses behind."

"We won't go far." Ballrik hoped his words rang true. He was uneasy himself, but not about the horses. What was it Nidor had *felt*?

They jogged northeast a few hundred yards before rounding a small pond of still water and heading north. Nidor pushed through weeds as high as seven feet, and after a mile the sound of the rapids faded and the wailing was clear.

"It's the cry of an animal." Magneer's impatience was obvious. "Probably wounded in a fight. What a waste of time."

"It is not normal." Nidor's gaze never wavered from the tall grass ahead. "If it is an animal, it suffers unnatural pain."

The paladin bolted, sprinting due north and drawing his blade. The company labored to keep up, and the Dale halted near the edge of a clearing.

A black bear lay on the ground, bleeding from open wounds. Its fur was scorched in many places and it appeared unable to move, save for its head every so often to give a cry of pain. Circling about and hopping up and down from its body were several small humanoids with pointed tails. They were naked, though there existed no detail to determine sex, and almond eyes of pure black were large upon their heads. Dark, forked tongues licked their pale lips, and they revealed sharp teeth when they laughed at the misery of the animal. They continued to poke the poor beast with small, two-tined spears, and one of the little monsters coughed up fiery spittle onto the bear's fur, adding to its torment.

"Demons!" Nidor hissed.

They were the first words the Dale had uttered in anger that Ballrik could recall.

The paladin sprang into the clearing, striking a fiend before they were aware of his presence. His weapon cleaved the creature in two, and it emitted a shrill cry as it disappeared within swirling red vapor. The company charged after, towering above the underworld fiends that outnumbered them nearly two to one, and the demons hissed as they lowered their spears.

Ballrik gave a battle cry, hoping to scare off a few, but the demons appeared unconcerned and two of them bounded toward him on small legs. He tested them, feigning an attack to read their reactions, and they split in an attempt to flank him. Ballrik danced back a couple paces, keeping both of them before him, and the creatures scowled and cursed in an unknown language, visibly annoyed with his refusal to play along. One then leaped overhead while the other charged.

Ballrik realized their plan, and he dropped onto the grounded one with his back. A cloud of red smoke nearly blinded him as the monster was crushed, and its small spear was like a nail in his side.

He gritted his teeth as he swung his sword at the second demon, and its eyes opened wide as it descended, unable to change direction. Ballrik's blade sliced through its body and it was destroyed.

Two demons hounded Solinin, and one leaped into the air, drawing the kid's attention. Ballrik scrambled to his feet to help, but not before the grounded creature thrust its spear into Solinin's foot. The kid growled in pain and slashed at the fiend, but it ran through his legs while the other demon landed on his shoulder and spit into his left eye. Ballrik arrived, slashing the grounded imp while Solinin planted his dagger into the other, and both dissolved into red mist. Solinin then held one hand over his eye and removed the small weapon from his boot.

Magneer kicked dirt at a demon, striking it in the face as it jumped. The distraction worked, and he struck it down with ease. Gruelenor fought a pair of demons, skewering one while the other leaped onto his back. The second creature stuck its spear between Gruelenor's shoulders and spit on the wound, bringing pain to the krukari's face. Gruelenor reached for the little beast, but it clung like a spider and thrust its weapon several more times, filling each wound with its spittle.

Ballrik ran toward Gruelenor, but slowed when an imp cut him off. Switching from his father's training to Krelnamir's, he dispatched it quickly, and with a bit more finesse.

Nidor was now at Gruelenor's side. Gruelenor moved rigidly, attempting to swing his dagger without success, and Nidor stole the creature's attention with a roar. The demon leaped at the paladin, and Nidor dodged and came across with his blade, killing it. Ballrik then spied another demon descending onto the Dale's back.

"Nidor! Above you!"

A flash of fire greeted the little monster as it landed, and it jumped away with a shriek. Ballrik was not sure where the flames had come from, and the demon's almond eyes grew round as it stared at the paladin. Nidor brought his sword down, ending its existence.

Only one demon remained, and it toyed with Solinin, who still held his hand over his eye. Ballrik and Magneer arrived at the kid's side, but the creature dodged their attacks with short, quick hops. It scored a couple wounds, catching Ballrik on the arm with its spear and spitting in Magneer's face, and it giggled like a child while they chased it about. After leaping onto a boulder near the edge of the clearing, the imp released a mocking cackle as it looked to escape into the tall grass, but an arrow pierced it when it leaped again, fired from the bow of Gruelenor. The demon disappeared into the weeds, but the red smoke assured Ballrik it had been destroyed.

All was quiet. Even the bear ceased to make a sound, its corpse motionless on the trampled grass.

"What were those things?" Gruelenor dropped his bow and fell stiffly to one knee.

"As I said, they were demons." Nidor looked at the bear with pity. "The evil aura about them was unmistakable."

"I saw no aura," said Solinin. "I'll be lucky if I see again. It burns!"

Ballrik inspected Solinin's eye while pulling his waterskin. He did his best to flush the black, sticky substance left behind, but it proved difficult to remove.

"Where did the blasted things come from?" Magneer wiped at the black spittle on his cheek.

"Where do all demons come from?" Nidor looked at the ranger. "But now it is most important I tend to your wounds."

Nidor went to Gruelenor. The krukari leaned against a boulder, wincing in pain. Upon checking the injuries, the Dale's face darkened.

"You do not look good, my friend."

"I don't need to see the wounds to know that," Gruelenor growled through clenched teeth.

"This may burn for a moment." Nidor removed one of his leather gauntlets.

"It burns now!" Gruelenor cried. "I've had enough burning!"

Gruelenor then looked at Nidor in fear and wonder, as did Ballrik. The Dale's hand flickered with a deep orange flame, and he lowered it onto Gruelenor's back. Gruelenor cringed, but the tension on his face quickly eased and Nidor removed his hand.

"That burned more than the demon's spit!" Gruelenor stood, moving more fluidly. "But I must say it worked. The pain is gone."

"The demon's poison was invading your body," Nidor said. "I did not wish for it to kill you."

"But how...?" Ballrik still could not believe his eyes. "Why is it you've never shown us this talent before?"

"I have powers bestowed upon me by Almighty Silcor." Nidor looked at Ballrik. "I do not abuse His Gifts, for I am grateful and unworthy. And I do not brag about them, for He did not bless me with them to gain the favor of others."

"What *other* powers do you possess?" Gruelenor picked up his weapons and secured them to his belt.

"Who else is infected?" Nidor turned to the others.

Solinin and Magneer stepped forward.

While the paladin tended to the two, Ballrik continued to gaze in wonder. Nidor had healing powers like a priest in high favor. To Ballrik's knowledge, not even Merssa could perform such a feat. Then there was the fire that rose against the demon attempting to jump onto Nidor's back. Ballrik decided it was not the time to bring it up, and he walked about the clearing in search of clues as to the demons' origin. He was not concerned about his own injuries—the spear wounds barely hurt, and none of the creatures had spit on him.

While Ballrik looked around, he realized just how far they had traveled. They were at the eastern edge of Echo Valley. The mountains loomed very near, and the boundaries of Nira were definitely behind them.

Gruelenor joined Ballrik, and they looked beyond the boulder where the last creature had attempted its escape. After a short walk through tall grass, they discovered another clearing twenty yards away. It dwarfed the one with the bear, covering an area larger than all of Steadshire. The remains of meals, discarded debris, and stakes tied to ropes littered the ground, as well as evidence of hundreds of bonfires and several charred corpses.

Gruelenor shook his head. "An army was here."

"Get the others," Ballrik said, and Gruelenor hastened back to the first clearing.

Ballrik scanned the surrounding landscape. Not far off, dark spots were evident on the cliffs to the east. Caves.

He sighed. "What have we gotten ourselves into?"

Chapter 6

The Gate

Ballrik waited until Gruelenor returned with the company, and they all stared in wonder.

"They're Seltan soldiers." Solinin nudged a corpse with his boot.

"And they were tortured before they met their fates," added Magneer.

"They often fight one another." Solinin looked up from the body. "Torture is just part of losing the fight. I'm sure it had no other significance than a bit of fun for them."

"A strong evil is near," Nidor said. "I feel it. Stronger than the small demons."

"Stronger?" Solinin paled. "More demons?"

"I am not sure." Nidor scanned the cliffs. "But it is much stronger."

"I have never fought demons before today," admitted Ballrik. "But from my father's stories, those creatures could not have been very powerful as demons go. Yet, something foul remains in the air. It hangs like an invisible fog."

"My father fought with Vikur against Ragab in the Stone Eagles," said Magneer. "He said the very air about it caused his stomach to sour. I feel I could vomit at any moment."

Now that Magneer mentioned it, Ballrik realized his stomach was unsettled as well.

"I do not wish to fight another demon." Solinin exhibited fear for the first time since Ballrik had known him. "Especially a stronger one!"

"Neither do I, Kid." Gruelenor turned to Ballrik and Magneer. "When your fathers battled Ragab, I believe they had the likes of Selanna with them. And as everyone here knows, she is a powerful mage and something we lack."

"Nevertheless, evil is near." Nidor pointed toward the cave openings. "There."

"I think we should return to Steadshire." Solinin looked at Ballrik. "If an army was encamped here, who knows where they're headed? I'm sure Selt would like nothing more than to take advantage of Nira's situation these dark days."

"They march on Nira," Nidor said, "of that I have no doubt. But they march with demons in their ranks, and large ones at that. Do you not see the charred tracks?"

Ballrik observed the areas of blackened grass. He believed them to be campfire remains at first glance, but they contained no bits of wood or piles of ash. Some were as long as five feet across, with strides of ten feet between them.

"Who's the tracker now?" Magneer released a nervous chuckle.

No one found any humor.

"Where have they come from?" Ballrik took another look, hoping the paladin was mistaken.

"Seltans have always been known to deal with demons," Solinin said.

"Yes." Ballrik shook his head. "But I've never heard of them possessing an army of the things."

"It takes a gate to allow them access to our world." Nidor's attention never veered from the caves. "And it must be a powerful one to allow this many through."

Ballrik furrowed his brow. "A gate?"

"A door connecting Vaeldor to their world." The paladin turned to Ballrik. "One that remains opened until it is closed."

"What...?" Magneer frowned. "How do you know this?"

"A story," Nidor replied. "Told to me by a traveler, a few nights before we left on this hunting trip. At the time, it held little meaning. But now..."

"Who was this traveler?" Ballrik grew suspicious.

"I do not know." Nidor shook his head slightly. "He was an elf, of the Salenti or Dakreal variety, I think, for he was not so tall as the Vermallon elves we have met. He came to the farm while the rest of you were busy. I was sitting outside the barn, having a late supper after weeding the tomato plants, and he happened upon me from the direction of the forest. He declared himself a traveler, though I saw neither horse nor gear to prove such a claim. From his garb, I am sure he was a wizard. He offered to tell me a story in return for some food and direction to Vermallon Road. I gave him what remained on my plate and set him on the correct path, assuring him I needed no payment for being hospitable. But he insisted on telling me his story, so I obliged him.

"He spoke of a warrior named Vennimor, who battled the Legions of Hell to rid Vaeldor of evil. I did not think much of the tale until recently, for he described the very demons we just faced." Nidor shook his head. "He also spoke of a gate. A door to the underworld. He said only beings of extraordinary power could open such a door, and that they could only accomplish it with the use of a valuable object. That object would become the key, and only *it* would have the power to close the portal. I thought it strange he shared this with me. It seemed a matter for wizards. But I thanked him and he departed."

"Was he giving you a warning?" Magneer raised a brow. "It seems odd that he described something we had yet to encounter. Only Seac the Seer can foretell the future."

"Perhaps he had not spoken of the future," Nidor said. "Perhaps he had seen them for himself. I do not pretend to understand why he told *me* these things, but I feel Silcor sent him, to make sure I did the right thing when the time came. That time is now. There is a gate within those caves." Nidor returned his attention to the cliffs. "And if what the traveler told me holds true, closing it is the only way to save Steadshire, as well as anything else in the demons' path. I do not ask any of you to join me, but it is something I must do."

"You know we're with you." Ballrik put his hand on Nidor's shoulder.

Magneer nodded, as did Gruelenor. After a sigh and a shake of his head, Solinin nodded as well.

"We have no time to spare," said Magneer. "From the looks of things, the army left at least six days ago. And judging by the size of the force, it'll take them maybe a week to reach Steadshire, if that is where they're aiming."

Nidor headed for the caves and everyone followed. The way was easy, for there existed a path of trampled growth bearing eastward.

"So we must find the key to shut the gate?" Ballrik asked while they walked.

Nidor nodded. "That is what the elf told me."

"And how does closing it help us now?" Ballrik posed. "I mean, since it appears so many demons have already entered our world?"

"The key must pass through the gate," Nidor said. "When it does, according to the elf, it will pull all that passed through the portal with it."

"What will the key look like?" asked Magneer.

"I am not sure." Nidor shook his head. "But I believe it will be obvious when we see it."

"What if there's a demon in these caves?" Solinin's face was ashen. "A bigger one? How will we combat it without a wizard?"

"I have no doubt that one is there," said Nidor. "And as we draw nearer, it becomes more evident. But I will keep it occupied while the four of you close the gate."

Ballrik and Magneer exchanged glances. Ballrik knew Nidor's dedication to the destruction of evil was strong, but he had not realized how strong it was until that moment.

After trekking more than a mile, they reached the eastern cliffs. Three caves were at various heights among the rising ground, and worn paths revealed years of traffic between them. Nidor closed his eyes and slowly rotated until facing the cave on the left. He opened his eyes.

"There. That is where the evil feels foulest."

It was the largest opening of the three, spanning over fifteen feet across at its widest point and well over twenty feet in height. They approached with weapons ready, and as they neared, a hot breeze brought them to a halt.

"It's dark," Solinin said.

Gruelenor pulled a torch from his pack and began working his flint and steel. Nidor touched the end with his finger and it ignited instantly.

Magneer raised a brow. "You have many talents you've concealed from us."

Nidor grabbed the torch and stepped into the tunnel.

Ballrik entered, followed by the others, and his eyes moved constantly about the crude passage. The tunnel stretched more than a hundred yards, twisting left and right and sloping downward, and as they pressed deeper, the air grew warmer and the odor of burning incense reached Ballrik's nose. A strange chanting then echoed softly down the corridor, bringing Nidor to a halt.

The paladin proceeded at a slower pace, and as they rounded another bend, a light became visible ahead and to the right. To the left, the shadow of a horrific beast moved about, placing Ballrik's nerves on edge. He gripped his weapon tighter.

Nidor inched forward, sliding along the wall, and Ballrik followed the paladin's lead. The Dale glanced around the bend before creeping farther, and Ballrik craned his neck to spy a large chamber. Unlike the tunnel, the walls of the room were smooth stone, and in the center stood a four-armed demonic statue, eight feet in height. Two hands stretched overhead with an enormous sword lain across them, and the lower arms reached down with palms up, the left one holding a decapitated head with its eyes missing and the other containing a pair of eyes. The warm breeze danced with many candles set within tall candelabrums, giving the statue's shadow its lifelike appearance, and chanting before the stone figure was a man dressed in red robes with black trim.

The company stepped quietly into the chamber, but after only a few feet, the robed figure turned and they stopped.

"Welcome, all of you," the man said with a thick accent. His voice was calm, as one speaking to expected guests, and around his neck hung a black talon clutching a small heart. "Here is where you meet your doom!"

The figure resumed chanting, and his eyes turned black.

Nidor rushed forward, pulling up short when three small demons, like the ones from the field, came bounding from an archway across the chamber. While the paladin attacked the lead creature, Ballrik and Magneer faced the other two.

Unlike the imps in the clearing, these did not operate in tandem, and Ballrik gave ground before lunging forward. The fiend jumped over the attack, but Ballrik only half extended, anticipating the maneuver. He slashed upward, splitting the demon in two before it reached its apex.

Magneer had just skewered his opponent, and the other demon clung to the ceiling and spat at Nidor. The paladin dodged the smoking saliva and threw the torch, but the fiend remained out of reach. Solinin, meanwhile, advanced on the robed figure.

The man released a brilliant flash from his palm and Solinin fell, screaming in agony with his hands over his face. The mage then conjured a flaming sphere between his hands, eying Ballrik and Magneer while the ball increased in size, but the sphere fizzled when an arrow pierced his chest and he collapsed. Looking back, Ballrik saw Gruelenor already nocking another arrow. The squeal of the small demon then stole Ballrik's attention, and Nidor stood before a momentary swirl of red smoke.

The room was quiet—even Solinin's cries ceased as the kid peeked through spread fingers. Ballrik was about to ask Nidor to check on the young warrior when a low growl came from the opposite archway. An inhuman screech followed, and it raced down the tunnel and likely across Echo Valley.

Nidor ran to Solinin and placed his flaming hand on the kid's reddened face. Solinin flinched at the paladin's touch, but then his body eased.

"The gate must be beyond the arch," Nidor said as the fire engulfing his hand winked out.

"Yes, but what comes from it now?" Magneer lifted his sword and faced the archway.

Nidor helped Solinin to his feet. Solinin's color had returned, thanks to the paladin's healing talent, but his eyes were wide and his lip quivered as he picked up his sword.

A clicking sound came from the archway, like claws on stone, and it was accompanied by a strange gurgling. A large, ram-like head then passed through the opening, and it gazed upon the company with red, cat-like eyes. Its limbs were long and lanky, and it ducked as it entered; and from its leathery skin protruded several bony spikes, the longest of which was a two-foot horn upon its forehead. It gurgled with delight as it spied the occupants of the room, revealing pointed teeth within its cruel smile.

"It's just as my father described!" Ballrik gasped. "Ragab!"

"Find the key!" Nidor strode forth to gain the demon's attention, and a growl rolled in the back of the monster's throat. "Come face the wrath of Silcor!" Nidor raised his sword.

Ballrik led Magneer and Gruelenor around the edge of the room while Nidor met Ragab near the statue, and the demon released a hissing roar that threw the paladin into the wall. Ragab then turned on Ballrik as he arrived at the arch, and it belched flames from the pit of its stomach. Magneer retreated while Ballrik froze; and he would have taken the blast fully had Gruelenor not shoved him through the archway. Ballrik tumbled into the next chamber, chased by Gruelenor's cry of pain.

Nidor felt as though a horse had kicked him into the wall when Ragab roared, but the pain hastily departed. He had trained his whole life, learning to repress such feelings, and now that training was hard at work. As he regained his feet, he saw the demon spit its Hell Fire onto his companions, and Gruelenor took most of the blast while shoving Ballrik to safety. Ragab then wore a cunning smile as Magneer charged it, and it crouched and spun, sticking out a barbed foot and catching the ranger by surprise. Magneer was knocked to the floor, and the demon pounced like a cat, piercing the ranger's shoulders with the spikes on its hands. Its black tongue lashed about in anticipation as it reared, and Magneer's eyes grew wide, staring at the long horn atop its head.

Nidor moved swiftly and slashed his sword across the creature's back, spilling its dark green blood. The spiny beast released Magneer with an angry hiss and lunged for Nidor, but he retreated a step, narrowly avoiding the attack. Nidor then jumped over its swinging leg and came down with his blade, scoring a gash on the demon's thigh.

Magneer had regained his feet, and he thrust his sword into the creature's lower back, causing the demon to leap. It caught hold of the ceiling, where it clung like a giant insect and spit its fire. Magneer rolled quickly away while Nidor allowed the flames to wash over him, and when the demon's mouth closed, he was unscathed.

"I am a paladin of Silcor!" Nidor said. "Your fire cannot harm me!"

Ragab crawled along the ceiling, staring at Nidor as if searching for a weakness. The demon dropped and roared, sending its shock wave and casting Nidor into the wall. Nidor gasped, unable to shut out the pain this time. The monster then leaped upon him, but Silcor kept his body pure from the touch of evil, and there was a flash of divine fire. Ragab jumped away with a shriek, a maneuver proving ill for Magneer. The ranger had been rushing to help, and the demon crashed into him, knocking him to the floor.

Magneer was pinned again, this time beneath Ragab's full weight. The enraged demon jumped to its feet, snatching the ranger by the throat with one of its six-fingered hands, and Nidor saw just how wounded his friend was. Blood seeped from puncture holes in more places than Nidor could count, and he realized Magneer had not completely escaped the last blast of fire. The demon squeezed slowly, grinning at Nidor as its spikes cut deeper into his companion's flesh. Magneer's head wavered, consciousness slipping away.

Ballrik rose to a knee and stared. He wished to make sure his friends were all right, but the scene before him stole his breath. Two braziers hung from the ceiling of the large room he had tumbled into, suspended by thick chains and emitting wisps of yellow smoke. Between the braziers stood a podium holding a black tome, and just as in the previous chamber, several candles illuminated the room. Red curtains covered the walls, save for an area occupied by an archway opposite Ballrik, and it was the arch that held his attention. It appeared to be drawn in blood upon the wall, and filling it was a swirling red mist. He was sure the arch was the source of the warm breeze.

Ballrik stood as the curtain to his left opened, and from behind it emerged a figure dressed in black robes with red trim. The man's head was clean-shaven and covered with strange sigils. The symbols traveled down his neck and disappeared beneath his robes, only to reemerge from his sleeves and proceed to his fingertips.

"You should have stayed in the other room." The figure's voice was harsh and bore the same accent as the first man. "The Ragab would have dealt you a death much less painful." With his final word, his eyes glowed red. He then uttered an incomprehensible command while extending his finger, and a glowing red ball shot forth.

Ballrik attempted to dodge, but the sphere knocked him to the floor. Every muscle in his body twitched as his nerves lit up, and though the spasms ceased after a few seconds, the pain lingered and he could not move.

The mage laughed an evil cackle, but then he released a gasp. Ballrik could not see what happened, but he knew his companions had arrived.

Blisters covered Gruelenor's body and he found it hard to breathe. He wanted to close his eyes and let unconsciousness claim him, but then he heard a strange voice speaking in the other room.

Gruelenor knew Ballrik was alone, and he forced himself to stand. Every movement brought excruciating pain, worse even than what the small demons inflicted in the field, and he staggered to the arch without looking back. Ballrik lay unmoving, and a figure with glowing red eyes laughed while pulling a long dagger from beneath his robes.

Gruelenor repressed all feeling and nocked an arrow. He let loose the bowstring, scoring a lethal hit, and the glow faded from the robed man's eyes as he stared at the feathered shaft protruding from his chest.

"Who dares...?" The man glared at Gruelenor, baring his teeth and emitting a hiss. But then he collapsed.

Gruelenor went to Ballrik as fast as his body allowed.

"Find the key!" Ballrik said through clenched teeth, apparently unable to move. "Don't worry about me. Just find it!"

Gruelenor scanned the room. Nothing looked out of the ordinary, with the exception of a glowing archway. The curtain to his left then moved, and he dropped his bow and rammed through the drape with his shoulder. He felt the resistance of a smaller figure as he burst into a corridor, and sprawled upon the floor was a woman robed and tattooed similarly to the bald man. She hissed as she scrambled on hands and feet to escape down the hallway, but Gruelenor pulled his sword and cleaved deeply into her neck.

She collapsed.

The passageway ran twenty paces before opening into a smaller chamber. Gruelenor continued to fight the burning pain as he hurried along its length, and he entered an evil room of worship. Another four-armed demonic statue stood to one side, and to the other was an altar covered by the bloody remains of a decapitated body. The ceiling was blackened in the center, a result of the fire below it, and a small hole carried smoke to destinations unknown.

Nothing looked valuable enough to be the key Nidor described. But then Gruelenor noticed a glint from the statue's lower left hand. Upon closer inspection, he found a golden scepter encrusted with jewels—an item worthy of the wealthiest king in all the realms. Even the newly etched runes along its handle did little to weaken its appearance. It was the key. It had to be.

Ragab grinned at Magneer's limp form, gurgling with delight as it tilted its head to admire its work. Nidor charged, but the demon had been awaiting this, and it cast its prisoner at him. He was knocked to the floor beneath Magneer as he caught the ranger, and in a single bound the monster landed inches from them. Ragab reared back to skewer them both, but then the demon whipped around with a growl.

Solinin stood with the monster's blood running the length of his sword. Nidor was not sure where the kid had gotten off to, but he was pleased with Solinin's return. Solinin swung again, and there was the ringing of steel on steel as Ragab caught the kid's blade in its large hand. The monster swept its leg around and knocked Solinin to the floor, wrenching the sword from his grasp and tossing it aside.

Nidor crawled from beneath Magneer as Solinin scrambled to his feet and sought refuge behind the statue. The demon leaped onto the sculpture and hissed, and Nidor was too late as the monster showered Solinin in a stream of fire.

"Nidor!" Solinin managed as he collapsed.

Swinging his blade with every bit of strength he could muster, Nidor sliced the demon's leg. Ragab hissed, jerking its wounded limb away and rocking the statue. The demon then leaped, and the monument toppled onto a table, splintering the wood and spilling candles across the floor—the wicks continued to burn as the candles rolled about. Nidor had expected the retreat, and when the creature landed, he was there, dealing another wicked blow with his sword.

Ragab rose to its full height and backed against the wall, and they eyed each other for a moment. Nidor was alone, and he wondered if he had understood Silcor correctly. He allowed his companions to take this quest with him, but never did he think the price would be so high. Magneer lay to his right and Solinin to his left, and it was obvious Ballrik and Gruelenor had been unable to close the gate—Nidor wondered if they still lived. His body was battered and blood ran down his face, and even as he fought to suppress the pain, it was taking hold. Ragab stood tall, but green blood covered the demon's once brownish skin and Nidor knew it to be close to defeat. Still, Ragab smiled.

Remorse for the fate of Nidor's friends plagued his mind, but he shut it out. He needed to close the gate before Nira fell and Trannum's army crossed the river. He had to make a move, and soon, for his head was beginning to swim and he was unsure how much longer his body could hold out.

With a roar, Nidor thrust his sword. Ragab danced aside and the weapon struck the wall, and before Nidor could recoil, the demon slammed its large fist onto the blade and snapped the sword in two. Turning back to Nidor, Ragab's toothy grin broadened as it gurgled with delight.

Gruelenor returned to the chamber of the gate. He wasted no time and hurled the scepter at the swirling red mist, but it did not reach its destination. A thick, spider-like web appeared and seized the key inches from the arch.

The robed man stood, his eyes rekindled and the arrow still protruding from his chest. He grinned, extending his finger, and a red sphere sped across the room. Even as Gruelenor dodged, the sphere altered its path and struck him. He collapsed, his muscles tightening and horrible pain adding to his already-broken body.

The robed figure lifted the dagger and approached, and Gruelenor was powerless to stop him. Then Gruelenor spotted Ballrik across the room, and to Gruelenor's surprise his companion was standing. Ballrik moved toward the gate, and though the first couple of steps were shaky, he picked up speed and was soon running.

"Take care of Lorin!" he shouted, alerting the robed man to his presence. But nothing could be done as he leaped through the web, snatching the scepter and disappearing through the mist.

"No!" gasped the man, the glow of his eyes fading.

The mist turned gray and reversed direction, moving faster and pulling a steady rush of air into it. The suction became stronger with each passing second, lifting papers and other light objects but failing to extinguish the candles; and though the items swirled about the room, none of them entered the arch. Soon the chamber roared with deafening screams as hundreds of vaporous shapes were swept into the gate. Gruelenor squeezed his eyes shut as the shrieks attempted to take what sanity remained… All went silent.

Gruelenor opened his eyes. The gray mist was gone, leaving only a wall of stone and the writings of blood that formed the arch. The robed figure stared with mouth agape. He then snarled at Gruelenor, lifting the dagger as he resumed his chant and his eyes burned red.

Nidor clutched his broken sword, knowing Ragab's next move would be his end. But when the demon opened its mouth, its body became transparent, taking on a mist-like appearance. A hot wind rushed through the chamber, sweeping Ragab away and through the arch where Ballrik and Gruelenor had disappeared. Shortly after, hundreds of smoky forms flew by, screaming and clawing haplessly at the air. It lasted for what seemed like a minute, and the room stilled and all was quiet. Someone had shut the gate.

Nidor hurried into the other chamber. A robed figure held a long dagger over Gruelenor, and Nidor knew the man to be a dark priest. An arrow protruded from the priest's chest where his heart should be, and still the man chanted some evil ceremony. Nidor did not know if Gruelenor lived, but he would not stand by and watch his companion sacrificed to an evil god.

He rushed in, unnoticed as the figure lifted the dagger, and hewed the priest with his broken blade. Dark blood oozed from where the shard cleaved deep into the skull, releasing a reddish steam into the air, and the body collapsed and ceased to move.

All traces of evil faded. Nidor stood alone.

CHAPTER 7

Snow and Lightning

old still," Nidor said. "This will hurt a bit."

Gruelenor's body lay crumpled on the floor, covered in burns, but he was alive. It amazed Nidor the krukari could move. He exhaled as he applied his healing flame, and Gruelenor winced. The blisters faded, but there was scarring from Ragab's fire Nidor could not cure. Gruelenor would suffer some pain for a time.

"Help me up." Gruelenor's voice was more hoarse than usual.

Nidor's eyes went to the arch of blood while he assisted his companion. He then looked around the room.

"He's gone," Gruelenor said. "I tried to..." He shook his head. "If I had just... It was the only way to get the key through the gate. I thought...or hoped he'd be sent back...but..."

"No." Nidor sensed deep guilt within the krukari. "But his deed was great. There must have been a thousand demons banished from our world. And who knows what evil they have wrought already? Even Ragab was about to get the better of me. But their terror has ended."

Gruelenor walked to where Ballrik's sword lay on the floor. Lifting the weapon, he stuck it into his belt.

The first chamber was a mess. The statue and table were in pieces and candles created eerie shadows from their random locations around the room. Solinin and Magneer remained motionless, but then Nidor saw Solinin's hand twitch.

"He's alive!" Nidor rushed to the young warrior. "Check on Magneer."

Ragab's fire had badly blistered Solinin's face. Taking in a slow, steady breath, Nidor released it with a prayer on his lips. He felt drained, and did not know if he possessed the energy to heal the kid, but when he held out his hand, the flames encompassed it at once.

"Thank Silcor," he said with relief.

Solinin screamed out at Nidor's touch, eyes wide and staring blankly at the ceiling. He then calmed as his eyes shut, and he moved back into a state of peaceful unconsciousness. Just as with Gruelenor, Solinin's face bore permanent scarring, and Nidor thought it a shame. Unlike Gruelenor, it was a dire change in appearance for the comely warrior.

"He's alive." Gruelenor hovered over Magneer. "But barely."

Nidor checked on Magneer. Puncture holes covered the ranger's body and much blood had been lost.

"Once more," Nidor whispered. "I beg of you."

Again Nidor concentrated, and again Silcor answered his prayer. Magneer was then healed, but he would need time to regain his strength.

"You're pale." Gruelenor stared at Nidor. "Did the Ragab do this to you?"

Nidor looked at his arms. They were lighter in color than he could ever recall. "I am drained. But there is no time to tarry. We must make for Steadshire... If it still exists." His last words he uttered to himself.

"What about *your* injuries?" Gruelenor asked.

"They will have to wait." Nidor gave a wry smile. He knew if he expended more energy, he would have nothing left to carry himself or his companions from the cave.

It did not take long to rouse Magneer and Solinin, and Gruelenor recounted Ballrik's fate. Both were stunned, unable to find any words.

After collecting themselves, Nidor assisted Magneer and they followed the tunnel back to Echo Valley. Though it seemed an eternity since they entered, not much time had passed and there was better than an hour of sunlight left.

They retraced their steps through the clearings and toward the river. Magneer struggled, but grew stronger with every step, and he was soon moving under his own power. This was a relief to Nidor, as his pain had surged beyond any he had ever endured. He continued to monitor Magneer, for the ranger remained pale and shivered often, even within the warm evening air.

The rapids greeted Nidor's ears at last, and dusk engulfed the land while they pursued the sound. With the arrival of night, they reached the river. They followed the water south under the light of the halfmoon, when the clouds allowed the moon to shine, and arrived at the hill where the rapids spilled into Lake Charal.

"Thanks be to Silcor," Nidor said upon seeing the horses obediently waiting by the lakeside. He then assisted Magneer, and they made their way down the slope.

They drank deeply from the waterskins on their saddles, and Gruelenor fished out a warm cloak for Magneer. They then mounted and rode south as swiftly as the horses could safely carry them, finally stopping late into the night when Magneer wavered in the saddle. The blood loss had taken its toll on the ranger, and he looked like he might pass out.

"I need an hour," Magneer said. "Just an hour. I'll be ready then."

They did not unpack blankets or make a fire. The evening was pleasant enough, and they wanted a quick departure once the hour was spent.

Nidor tended to the horses before taking a seat to keep watch. Solinin and Gruelenor were resting peacefully, but Magneer sat, not even attempting to sleep, and his eyes were distant. Nidor moved closer to the ranger, so as not to disturb the others.

"I miss him too."

Magneer shook his head. "The loss of Ballrik will take time. I have known him for so long... I cannot remember when we weren't together. Guilt will plague me for not following him into that room." He looked Nidor in the eyes. "But it's Kalette that is on my mind. If the demons made it to Steadshire..."

Nidor sighed. "I wish I could say that they did not. But I do not know. For now, I think we will make better time if you get some rest. I will wake you in an hour."

Magneer nodded, and after a deep breath he laid down. Sleep overcame him swiftly.

Finally feeling some energy had returned, Nidor summoned his healing flame and tended to his wounds. He discovered a couple of cuts he did not remember receiving, but mostly he was badly bruised from crashing into the walls. Once finished, he kept watch over the dark land, pondering Selt's involvement in the war against Trannum. Did the invasion of Nira have anything to do with the enemy to the south? Or was an evil realm taking advantage of a neighbor's dire situation? If Trannum was part of it, did Ballrik close the gate in time to thwart the necromancer's plans? All Nidor could do was hope.

The hour had nearly passed when his thoughts were interrupted. Solinin approached, and even beneath the intermittent moonlight, Nidor saw the disfiguring scars across the right side of the kid's face.

"I'm sorry," Solinin said in a hushed voice. "For leaving you back in the cave. I don't know what came over me. I had never been so scared."

Nidor had noticed the shameful look haunting Solinin since they exited the cave. "Free your mind. Though you carry yourself with the wisdom of one much older, few experienced warriors could have stood before Ragab. You showed great courage when you saved my life, as well as Magneer's. Think no more of it."

"Thanks." Solinin appeared unconvinced. "I'll wake the others."

They returned to their saddles and moved on. Magneer no longer shivered, but he remained pale, almost glowing in the night; and though his guidance was needed to keep a direct path, Nidor called upon him only when necessary. After several miles, they spotted dark shapes on the ground and came to a halt. It was the remains of a battle. The bodies consisted of Niran and Seltan soldiers, and the Nirans outnumbered the Seltans at least four to one. Many of the Nirans were mutilated and badly burned.

Concern plagued Solinin's scarred face. "How long ago was this battle fought?"

Magneer slid gingerly from his horse and examined the bodies beneath the moonlight. "They are cold. More than a day has passed since this battle. The remaining force split afterward; half headed southeast and half right for Steadshire. We best not linger."

They traveled at a quicker pace, powered by their fear for the fate of Steadshire. The sky grew brighter with the approaching dawn, and a couple miles later the village appeared in the distance. Dark smoke rose from several locations, and on the ground ahead lay hundreds of bodies—evidence of another battle. Some corpses showed savage wounds, some were scorched, and others were burned beyond recognition. Most of the recognizable dead were soldiers and trainees of Steadshire.

They hastened into the village, and were relieved to find Gramborn in control. The large man sat atop a horse, barking orders while soldiers put out lingering fires and collected the wounded. It appeared that most of the buildings on the northern edge had been razed by flame.

"Where were *you*?" a middle-aged man scowled at the company. "The great trainers! Bah!"

Nidor was speechless.

"I'm going to the farm." Magneer started his horse down a street to the right without awaiting a response.

Though Gramborn had yet to notice their arrival, Nidor felt compelled to report immediately. But how could he ignore the desperation in his friends' eyes? He nodded, and they hurried after Magneer.

Dezlo's farm appeared intact, though fire had devastated most of the fields, and the wide-open barn revealed wounded soldiers and civilians. Dezlo's daughters moved about with buckets of water and bandages, cleaning and dressing injuries with the help of other townswomen.

The front door of the farmhouse opened and Dezlo stepped out. The old farmer stared at Nidor, his look more dour than usual. Magneer and Solinin rushed to their wives without a word to their father-in-law and Gruelenor accompanied them. Nidor dismounted and joined the farmer on the porch.

"Seems you boys left just in time." Dezlo watched Nidor's companions dismount upon reaching the barn.

Nidor bowed his head. "We had no idea what Steadshire had in store for it."

"If not for the elves," the farmer shrugged, "we'd all be burned up."

"The elves?"

"From Vermallon." Dezlo nodded toward the great forest, not far to the west. "They held the invaders off as best they could."

"I am truly sorry," Nidor said, "but we —"

"No." Dezlo shook his head and sat on a bench. "I don't mean to blame you. You'll receive enough of that from others 'round here. In fact, I have no doubt it was you boys what got rid of the demons." The farmer eyed Nidor. "Even the elves were bein' bested by the Seltan forces, what with all those strange creatures settin' fires and such. But then, all of a sudden, the things shrieked the most ear-piercin' screams I've ever heard and disappeared. All of 'em. That was the turnin' point of the whole battle, 'cause the Seltans were no match for the elves without their *pets*."

Nidor watched Kalette and Della comfort Lorin. They had obviously learned of Ballrik's fate.

Dezlo followed the direction of Nidor's gaze. "I noticed not all of you returned. And now my greatest fears begin."

A figure startled them, suddenly standing on the porch. It was a Vermallon elf. He was almost as tall as Nidor, and he wore green leather riddled with scratches and puncture marks, some of which showed traces of blood. A fine sword was sheathed at his waist and a bow hung over his shoulder, and perspiration saturated his dirty blonde hair.

"The southern line holds no longer," the elf said in a stern voice.

"What?" Nidor and the farmer voiced in unison.

"The bridges have been crossed." The elf gazed into the distant south. "Nothing now stands between the undead and this place, save for a few thousand elves."

Nidor released a long exhale and shook his head. If the Seltans had been working with Trannum, they were a successful distraction. With Nira's focus shifted northward, the enemy advanced from the south.

"We cannot fight them alone," the elf said. "Our agents travel to every village to gather what help we can."

Lorin's heart shattered with Gruelenor's words, and he was powerless to comfort her. Her sisters came to her aid, as did Solinin and Magneer, and Gruelenor suddenly felt out of place and walked away. He recalled when life was easier; when he had no friends. In some ways, he longed for those days.

Back at the farmhouse, an elf conversed with Nidor and Dezlo on the porch. The elf then disappeared around the back of the house, and Nidor looked Gruelenor's way with a grim expression. The elf's news surely did not improve matters. Nidor sprung from the porch and ran toward Gruelenor.

"Magneer! Solinin!" Nidor called as he neared.

"What awaits us now?" Gruelenor asked.

The Dale shook his head and said nothing. Once the others had joined them, he spoke.

"The enemy is on the move. They have crossed the Great East River and head this way. Vermallon elves oppose them as we speak, but they fight a losing battle without help."

"I don't know how useful *we* can be." Though much improved, Magneer was still pale.

"I'm ready," said Solinin, the scars on his face giving the words a dangerous feel to them.

"I'll do what must be done." Though Gruelenor feared what lay ahead, he meant it. Ballrik, the man he held in the highest regard, was gone. All because Gruelenor failed to throw the scepter through the gate. And now he had broken Lorin's heart. It was more than he could bear.

At that moment, the daughters arrived. Tears streaked Lorin's cheeks and Della's eyes never left Solinin's face. Kalette's expression was one of anger and suspicion.

"What is happening?" Kalette said, looking at Magneer. She then glared at Gruelenor and Nidor.

Magneer and Solinin looked at each other but said nothing. Gruelenor remained silent, having already caused enough pain. Nidor spoke.

"The undead march against Steadshire and all of Nira. We must oppose them."

"No!" Tears welled in Kalette's eyes. "We must flee. Pack our things and move far away."

"I wish to do nothing but that very thing, my love." Magneer gained everyone's attention. "But if able warriors fail to do what they can, how long before evil finds us, no matter where we hide?"

Nidor nodded, as if the words had not been his own.

"The boys is right," said Dezlo. Gruelenor had not noticed the old man's approach. "This is what they came for. And there's no one else I want defending my home."

Lorin and Della cried harder while Kalette's eyes fired daggers at Nidor. The three then returned to the barn.

"Now you boys do quickly what you have to do." Dezlo turned to Nidor. "And the sooner the better. No sense draggin' this thing out till the zombies destroy what's left of my farm." The farmer headed back to the house.

Magneer's gaze followed Kalette, who resumed caring for the wounded while Della sat with Lorin. Every now and again, Kalette shot a glare Magneer's way.

"Let's go," Magneer said.

Nidor and his companions rode south along the street, searching for soldiers and all abled villagers, but they found none. It seemed women and children were all that Steadshire offered. Nidor hailed a woman holding the hand of a little girl.

"Please. Can you tell me where the soldiers have gone?"

"What do you care?" the woman spat. "Where were you? That's a better question. I've heard a lot of talk about you trainers. Great swordsman! But no one seems to have seen you after the demons arrived."

"The soldiers went south," the little girl said.

"Trenny!" The woman glared at the child.

"What?" The girl looked confused. "That elf told Commander Gramborn—"

"That's enough!" The woman walked away at a brisk pace, dragging the girl along.

Nidor watched the two until they disappeared around a corner. Though he knew the demons would have destroyed Steadshire had the gate remained open, regardless of whether he and his companions were present for the attack, he could not help feeling responsible for the devastation the village suffered.

"Let's find Commander Gramborn," he said, and they rode at a quicker pace.

Upon reaching the southern edge of town, they found a gathering of nearly three hundred soldiers, a third of the force that once existed. Many civilians were present as well, holding a variety of makeshift weapons. Gramborn was mounted and dressed in armor, and strapped to his horse was a large hammer. The commander moved slowly about while barking orders, but fell silent when he spotted Nidor. He then revealed a grateful smile.

"There you are," Gramborn bellowed as they neared. "I see you have horses. Good. There aren't many left."

Nidor's eyes dropped. "I am sorry Commander—"

"I am no stranger to battle." Gramborn's expression was stern. "I know what I saw. And I suspect I know why the village still stands. We will speak no more of it. All that matters is the battle ahead."

Nidor nodded.

"It won't be an easy road." Gramborn looked at Nidor's companions. "I shall need all five of you to lead this contingent." The commander frowned. "Or…as many of you as I can get." Pity filled his eyes.

Nidor bowed his head. "We are yours to command."

Gramborn gave a nod. He then resumed shouting orders at the small force.

A young warrior ran up beside Nidor's horse, his face grim. It was Delarrin, wearing a chain shirt and helmet, and Nidor noticed a bloodstained bandage on the lad's upper left arm. Delarrin appeared much older than he did a few days ago, when Nidor had worked with him in the training pens. Perhaps the assault on Steadshire had aged him.

"I shall not let you down, Master Nidor!" Delarrin called up. "And I brought you this." The young soldier extended the hilt of a sword. "I noticed your scabbard was empty."

The blade was plain to look at, obviously made by a less-than-masterful weaponsmith, but Nidor accepted the gift. He smiled wryly at Delarrin, wishing to send the boy home. But the road ahead could spare no soldiers.

"Thank you, Delarrin." It was all Nidor could think of to say.

Nidor made a quick assessment of his friends. Gruelenor appeared to have made a full recovery from his wounds, though the warrior's mind seemed haunted. Solinin's face was grim. Magneer's color was rapidly returning, but Nidor continued to worry about the ranger. He hoped Magneer would continue to improve before they reached the battle.

All was ready, and Gramborn blew his horn to begin the march. Nidor and Magneer rode to the commander's left and Gruelenor and Solinin to his right. Behind them were the only other mounted warriors, five in all. The soldiers and villagers were mingled, and they walked a steady pace with swords, pitchforks, shovels, and the like. More than half wore armor, and nearly all carried furs in anticipation of the cold. The trained warriors bore grim looks, while the slightest noise or movement outside their ranks startled the commoners.

The day was warm and the sun bright. But after a mile, clouds riding a cool breeze out of the south swallowed the orb and the sky became gray. Evening arrived, and they continued through most of the night; and with the morning, the wind grew colder and the clouds darker, and the soldiers donned their furs. The early hours saw occasional snowflakes dancing about, and by lunchtime, the flurries gave way to larger flakes. Before long, the land was covered in white, four miles sooner than Nidor had expected.

An hour later, the first signs of war became known. Shouts and the clash of steel greeted Nidor's ears, but he saw nothing beyond a veil of snow. Behind him, the fatigue on the soldiers' cold faces and anxiety in their eyes were plain, but they pressed on, and the battle came into view at last. Elves were locked in combat with zombies, skeletons, ghouls, and dunarchins, and some of the zombies were Nirans that once guarded the Great East Bridges. Soldiers from other villages fought beside the elves, but the horde of undead appeared endless and the defenders were surrounded.

Gramborn sounded the horn, and the Steadshire force charged. Nidor gave a battle cry, smiting all enemies coming within reach, and his companions were close behind, fighting to either side. Gramborn showed surprising skills, dealing massive blows with the enormous hammer, and though the men of Steadshire were but trainees and farmers, they fought valiantly behind their leaders.

The small army drove a wedge into the undead, but failed to reach those already seasoned by the battlefield. Nidor and Magneer pressed deeper than most, becoming separated from all allies, and they were forced from horseback when the enemy dragged their mounts to the ground. They stood back to back, fighting zombies and ghouls, and dispatched the creatures without taking an injury. Battling demons and traveling with little or no sleep took its toll, however, and as a group of dunarchins approached, Nidor's weapon hung lower.

Then Gruelenor arrived.

Still mounted, Gruelenor struck down a dunarchin while his horse trampled another. He then slew two ghouls and trampled three skeletons, clearing the immediate area.

"Where's Solinin?" shouted Nidor.

"I haven't seen him," Gruelenor called back.

Nidor caught a glimpse of Gramborn. The commander was unhorsed and battling dunarchins.

"I'm going after Gramborn!"

Nidor did not get far when he spotted three zombies dragging Delarrin to the ground. Nidor slew the creatures and two others as he hastened to the young soldier's side, but he was too late. The lad lay wide-eyed upon the snow, with too many wounds to count.

"No!" gasped Magneer as he and Gruelenor caught up, and Gruelenor's brows drew together.

Nidor's strength was renewed as his blood boiled, and he cleaved his way through the enemy to where he last saw the commander. But he found only the large man's horse mutilated upon the snow. A path of bodies stretched beyond sight, as well as a trail of blood, and Nidor realized Gramborn to be wounded, if not dead.

There came a roar to the west. Nidor turned to spy an army of elves charging—reinforcements from the forest. The elves carried great energy and new hope as they drove into the undead, and even the dunarchins were hard pressed to match their skill. The tide shifted, and Nidor sensed those around him growing eager. But then things changed.

The snow stopped falling, and thunder shook the ground as lightning flashed across the sky. Next came an eerie, hollow roar that ended in a hiss, and the fighting nearly ceased as all attention turned skyward. The winds picked up, carrying a new chill that unsettled soldiers and caused most farmers to cower, and a skeletal beast descended from the clouds upon bony wings. It was greater than fifty feet in length, with a toothy maw and long tail, and from its eye sockets shone points of blue light. Mounted atop the monster's back was a dark rider possessing the same glowing eyes. The warrior wore black armor and held high a long spear; and lightning struck the weapon, surrounding it with a crackling energy that brought the wielder no harm.

"Death Lord!" shouted Magneer.

The skeletal mount swept across the battlefield, twenty feet above the din. It released another roar, the cry of a dragon's cursed spirit, and the farmers and several Nirans fled. The monster then landed among a squadron of dunarchins, allowing its rider to dismount, and it breathed a brownish-yellow cloud onto a group of men and elves. The victims' screams lasted only seconds before falling silent.

Nidor's attention turned to the bodies surrounding him. It was as if the Wind of the Dead had blown across the battlefield, and the corpses of humans and elves began to stir. He then battled zombies of those that once fought by his side, and with every passing moment the chill of the Death Lord deepened.

"We must find Solinin!" Magneer said.

"There!" Gruelenor pointed his sword from atop his horse. "He's surrounded! This way!" He charged his mount.

Nidor and Magneer followed the trail left by Gruelenor, fighting all the while. The air was like ice when Solinin came into view, and only a few paces from the kid stood the Death Lord.

Solinin had not seen his companions for some time. He would have liked nothing better than to track them down, but fifty soldiers followed him and the enemy was all around. Ghouls had torn into Solinin's horse with claws and fangs when he first entered the melee, forcing him from the saddle as the poor beast was slaughtered. He and his men slew the fiends, only to see them replaced by a hundred zombies.

Things looked grim until Gramborn appeared, and the morale of the soldiers soared as they witnessed their commander strike down the enemy two at a time. Moments later, Gramborn was unhorsed within a group of dunarchins. Solinin led the charge to give aid, but a squadron of ghouls impeded them and his men fell to half their number. The elfish reinforcements then arrived with a roar and the ghouls were slain.

Solinin scanned the battlefield. He saw neither Gramborn nor his friends. His heart sank as he imagined the worst, but he continued to battle. The enemy's numbers thinned with the arrival of the elves, and Solinin sensed the excitement of those around him rise. But then a Death Lord descended from the clouds and landed less than thirty yards away.

Fear struck Solinin—a feeling he experienced not too long ago within the caves of Selt. Some of his soldiers dropped their weapons and abandoned the cause, but he refused to retreat, remembering how he left his companions to face Ragab. It would never happen again.

"Watch yourselves!" Solinin warned those around him as fallen allies stirred. The transformation into zombies was an event he knew to be forthcoming with the undead king's arrival.

To the right, Solinin spied greater than a score of men and elves charging the undead dragon. The skeletal monster towered above the battlefield and released its evil breath; and screams of torment lasted only seconds within the sickly yellow vapor. The cloud dissipated, leaving behind twisted, withered forms.

Solinin remained strong, as did those with him, and they destroyed the newly formed zombies surrounding them. But as the next wave of undead arrived, a deepening chill invaded Solinin's body. The Death Lord approached.

"I will not run!" Solinin struck down a ghoul and then a dunarchin. "I will not run!"

Less than twenty yards away stood the Death Lord, and the dunarchins parted before it. Solinin held his ground, lifting his weapon in challenge, and his eyes locked onto the long spear. He had seen it before.

"Gruzim!"

Solinin had encountered the Benasti king on many occasions in the distant past. But Gruzim had not been a Death Lord then. Solinin's father warned him never to trust the vile krukari, and to stay as clear as was possible, and Solinin never forgot those words. Even after meeting Gruelenor in Philen, it had taken Solinin a couple months before he truly considered the krukari a friend.

Gruzim's glowing eyes pierced Solinin's soul, and from the spear came crackles of lightning. "Solinin," a hollow voice uttered from beneath the helmet. "So we meet again."

"That is your cruel fate!"

Solinin charged and slashed with his sword, but Gruzim turned the blade aside. The shaft of the spear then struck Solinin below the jaw and knocked him onto his back. He gazed up and saw the Death Lord standing above him.

"How fitting for you to share the fate of your father." Gruzim raised the evil weapon. "Death at the tip of my spear."

Solinin coughed blood as the weapon plunged into his chest, and he grasped the shaft while the point passed completely through him and into the snow. The energy surrounding the spear then coursed through his body and he convulsed.

"I'll tell your *dear* mother you said hello." Gruzim twisted the weapon.

Gruelenor went numb as he watched Solinin fall.

"No!" Nidor hacked at the undead separating them from the kid.

Gruelenor rode past the paladin, trampling ghouls and dunarchins and closing the gap, and the Death Lord jerked free the spear and pointed it Gruelenor's way. Lightning issued from the weapon and struck his horse, and he was thrown from the saddle. Gruelenor scrambled to his feet as the dark warrior neared, but then the evil king halted.

"What a waste," the Death Lord said.

The hollow voice was different, but Gruelenor recognized it. He knew the weapon as well, but the lightning was a new feature. "Father?" he asked, dreading the reply.

"You disappoint me." Gruzim's voice held no emotion. "You never returned to Benasti."

"I don't believe in your ways!" Gruelenor spat. He was ready to die for his convictions and knew he soon would. But he refused to turn his back on his friends.

"So be it." Gruzim lowered the spear. "At least you'll make a fine dunarchin."

A large hammer crashed into the Death Lord's helmet. Gramborn struck Gruzim from behind, leaving a sizable dent, but he did not land another blow. The long edge of the spear came around, slicing open Gramborn's stomach, and crackling energy engulfed his body when the point pierced his thigh.

Gruelenor rushed to Gramborn's aid, stopping short when his undead father kicked the large man to the ground. Lightning continued to issue from the spear, and Gruelenor could only watch as the energy danced about the commander's body. Gruzim stared at Gruelenor through it all, and Gruelenor could feel the grin beneath the dark helmet.

Nidor reached Gruelenor's side, and Gruelenor's mind raced. He thought of Ballrik; of Lorin; of Solinin. His desire to fight his father was strong, and although he knew it would be his end, he welcomed it. But he could not die just yet. Ballrik had charged Gruelenor with one last favor, and he would not let his friend down. Not again. Gruelenor grabbed hold of Nidor's arm.

"We must retreat!"

"What?" Nidor's look was one of shock.

"The battle is lost," Gruelenor said. "And I have a promise to keep."

Nidor scanned the battlefield. Gramborn's body was unmoving and the Death Lord headed toward them. To the left, the corpse of Solinin had joined the ever-growing undead army. Escape would soon be impossible.

"Retreat!" Nidor called out as Magneer joined them, and the ranger looked relieved to hear the order.

"Retreat!" all three shouted again and again as they battled their way north.

Humans and elves responded, withdrawing from the battlefield without hesitation. It almost seemed that the enemy allowed them to escape, and there was no pursuit.

Gruelenor gazed back after they were clear of the undead. Thunder continued to pound the land as lightning flashed, and the last thing he saw before turning away was the haunting eyes of his father, shining eerily through the haze.

Chapter 8

Zhomians

Even after the call for retreat spread, many failed to emerge from the snowy battlefield alive. What remained of the forces of humans and elves walked together without speaking, and once the snow faded, the elves parted company and headed west. Likewise, Nirans split from the host to return to their villages until all that was left were the citizens of Steadshire. Everyone then looked to Nidor.

Nidor kept a steady pace, making sure the wounded received assistance, and they left no one behind. They arrived in Steadshire the following evening with a quarter of what had marched. Most of the villagers began packing to head north and hide among the mountains and fields, regardless of Nidor's warnings that it would only be a matter of time before the undead sniffed them out. It seemed no one had ears for him now that they were home.

A few villagers refused to abandon Steadshire, including Dezlo. The old farmer did, however, wish for his daughters to be spared his fate.

"*I* will remain," Nidor said to Dezlo. "Take your daughters to safety."

"Nonsense!" Dezlo sighed. "I've seen a lot in my days, what with soldiers comin' and goin', and yer the most noble man I've ever met. And if yer sword's as good as yer soul, I reckon you'll be needed for a much greater cause." The farmer gazed at Vermallon Forest. "Besides, I'm too old to be travelin' anymore. Now get off my property!"

Dezlo's daughters were less than willing to part with their father, and Nidor feared they might have to be forced to do so. In the end, Dezlo made them see reason.

Barely a word had been uttered since that day, nearly a week ago. Presently, Nidor led the way along Vermallon Road while Gruelenor brought up the rear, both of them on foot. Between them, Magneer and Kalette shared a horse and the widows, Lorin and Della, shared another. The road was long and quiet and they saw no patrols—Magneer speculated the elves had gathered on the eastern border to establish a new front. As well, bandits and forest creatures did not hamper them, and if any were present, they did not show themselves.

Nidor walked with a heavy heart, knowing he had failed in his efforts against Trannum. And now Nira would be the next dominion to fall to the necromancer. Two of Nidor's friends were dead, friends who had had no plans to join the Front until he revealed his wishes to do so, and he encountered a Death Lord and knew himself to be no match for such a monster.

Then there was the exchange between Gruelenor and the Death Lord. Shouting was common during battle, but why did they hold a conversation? In what Nidor assumed to be the hobgoblin language? Did Gruelenor know the Death Lord? From what Nidor witnessed, Gruelenor was angry, and it did not appear to be a friendly discussion. But they definitely seemed familiar with one another. Gruelenor did not realize Nidor overheard the interaction, Nidor was sure, and he decided not to reveal it. At every opportunity, Gruelenor proved faithful beyond a doubt. Gruelenor would be judged on his actions.

Nidor sighed when the end of the forest arrived. The past several days had been dreary beneath the canopy of branches, and he hoped the sunlight would help to warm their hearts. Unfortunately, fate had other plans, and when he exited the woodland he was stopped in his tracks.

A woman and two young men nearly barreled into Nidor as they ran across the road from the north. When he looked after them, he saw the woman glancing over her shoulder in fear. Realizing he was not the object of her concern, he turned to see a warrior in chain armor giving chase and waving a sword like a madman. Nidor had little time to think, and he wrestled the man to the ground.

"Whoa there, soldier," Nidor said. "Do you not have better things to do than pursue women and children?"

The man rolled over with a sneer, but as their eyes met, they froze. Besides evil, a paladin always knew when faced with another paladin, and Nidor hastily moved from atop the man and helped him to his feet.

"Forgive me." Nidor bowed his head. "I am Nidor. Paladin of Silcor."

"And I am Sullis," the man said. "Paladin of Brondor."

Nidor did not know what to think. Paladins of the battle deity were almost as uncommon as paladins from Holindale. Sullis was older, perhaps twice Nidor's age, and obviously very experienced. But why would he pursue a woman and two boys barely old enough to be called men?

Sullis scanned the landscape and released a sigh. The figures were gone.

"Please," said Nidor, "forgive my hasty actions. I only acted on what I saw."

The man's face softened and he nodded once. "I hold no ill will toward you, Dale."

The Brondor paladin's recognition of Nidor's heritage caught him by surprise.

Sullis sheathed his sword. "I likely would have done the same." His hand returned to his weapon when Nidor's companions exited the forest.

"They are with me." Nidor said.

"You sure?" The man glared at Gruelenor.

"I swear upon my soul."

"You can't be too careful." The Brondor paladin relaxed again. "The enemy has many faces." He eyed Nidor. "Even friendly ones."

"What do you mean?"

"You asked me about those I pursue." Sullis glanced to the south and then back at Nidor. "Come with me and you shall learn of something most disturbing. The newest attempt, perhaps, of the necromancer to infiltrate the living."

Nidor looked at his companions. Gruelenor and Magneer held doubtful expressions while the women seemed disinterested. None of them appeared ready for an excursion of any sort. But this could be important. Turning to Sullis, Nidor said, "Wait here a moment."

He went to his company. Kalette glared at him, as if warning him not to take her husband.

"The next city is a few miles away," Nidor said. "Take the ladies and wait for me at the easternmost inn. I shall join you there tonight. Tomorrow evening at the latest."

Magneer glanced at Kalette before nodding. Gruelenor gave a wanting look, as if he would rather go with Nidor. He pursed his lips and nodded.

Nidor followed the Brondor paladin along the forest's edge to the south. He could tell Sullis was a skilled tracker, and they moved at a brisk pace, stopping several times for Sullis to scan the ground. After a couple miles were behind them, the Brondor paladin smiled.

"They're near," Sullis said. "I know not where exactly, but I'm sure of it. Though the boys can run for days, the woman needs rest."

"Why do you chase them?" Nidor asked. Thus far, the Brondor paladin offered no clues as to his interest in the three.

Sullis held Nidor with a stern gaze. "A strange breed of man was spawned in the realm of Andria. They possess hearts as black as a demon's. They beat not, but the abominations live all the same."

"Zombies?" Nidor asked.

"*Zombies?*" Sullis frowned. "Did they look like zombies to you?"

Nidor had seen enough zombies, ghouls, and dunarchins to last a lifetime, and the three that crossed his path earlier looked nothing like any of those fell creatures. The Brondor paladin was surely mistaken.

Sullis sighed. "The Andrians call them zhomians. It means *black hearts* in their tongue."

Nidor furrowed his brow. "How could those three be of the undead?"

"I don't know if I'd call them undead, exactly." Sullis stared forward in thought. "I'm unsure of *what* to call them. Their hearts only beat when necessary. Put one down and you'll see what I mean. That is when the heart begins to work. The creatures come back to life."

"How can this be?"

Sullis shook his head. "All I know is what an Andrian shaman told me."

Nidor frowned. And he was sure Sullis sensed his growing confusion.

"Perhaps I should start from the beginning."

Nidor nodded. "Please."

"For many centuries, a temple of Brondor has existed off the Shield River in Harbnum. It was built to teach others of the Faith, and I have long been one of those teachers. Several months ago I journeyed to Wornduir, a village near the southern border of Andria, and that is where I met the shaman. He spoke of a small hunting settlement along the Coranthiar Mountains that had been devastated. He knew not how, and the score of women and handful of children that survived were tight-lipped and refused to speak of it. Wornduir accepted the refugees without hesitation.

"All was normal at first, according to the shaman. But over the next several years, many of the women gave birth, and the shaman claimed the children to be unnatural. They made no sounds as they entered the world, and he detected no heartbeats. But they lived. As infants, they did not weep, laugh, or show joy of any kind. He also claimed that if you look at them just right, you can see small points of blue light deep within their eyes. But the villagers ignored the shaman's warnings, for the mothers seemed normal and loved their children as mothers do. Then one of the children suffered a horrible accident; one that brought about the child's death — or rather, should have.

"The lad was trampled by a horse in the street and lay unmoving. But moments later, he rose to his feet. His wounds were gone, leaving behind only bloodstained clothing. The shaman's words then returned to the people of Wornduir, and they banished all that had come seeking refuge."

"Perhaps there is another reason." Nidor doubted his own suggestion as he uttered it. The blue points of light could not be overlooked.

Sullis shook his head. "After learning of this, I searched for these women and their offspring. They had moved on to live in the wild, but I stumbled upon a small gathering of them." He furrowed his brow. "The children, most in their teens, were using an Andrian hunter to perform a bizarre ceremony. They tied the man to a tree, and he bled from several long cuts. The zhomians chanted while the mothers kneeled and bowed… My blood burned hot that day!" His eyes lit up. "I broke up their little ritual, dealing swift death to many! But they did not remain dead. The mothers became mere zombies, but the children appeared just as they had before. Their wounds had vanished.

"They scattered in all directions, but I hunted one down and pinned him to the ground. I looked into his eyes and saw what the shaman spoke of: the blue lights. They were hard to detect at first; the angle and lighting need to be right. But they were revealed to me, and it was then that I decided to see the rest for myself."

Sullis's face hardened. "I placed my ear to his chest… There was no heartbeat. So I cut into him with my knife. The creature didn't even scream, as any mortal would have, and I continued until I discovered the black heart. It was motionless at first, but started to beat quickly, pumping out a dark liquid. The wound began to close and I ripped the evil organ free, and still it beat in my hand. I cast it away and it slowed, but it would not stop… Not until I put my knife into it." He paled. "The smell almost caused me to vomit. But it ceased to move at last."

Nidor cringed, sickened by the detailed account. "What of the body?"

"When I pulled out the heart, the body died," Sullis replied. "I left it there, as a warning that I'm aware of their little secret. And I've been hunting them ever since. I have destroyed a dozen offspring, and half as many mothers. Most of them over the past couple of months." Sullis scanned the landscape. "I've followed *this* group south for several days now."

Nidor said nothing, nor had he time to, for the Brondor paladin snapped to attention.

"There they are!" Sullis pointed to three figures running up a hill not far away.

They picked up the pursuit, and the older paladin's pace surprised Nidor. They soon overtook their quarry, and Sullis brought one of the boys down with his pommel to the back of the young man's skull.

Nidor nearly grabbed the other boy, but the woman threw herself before him and caused him to stumble. He dragged her to the ground, pinning her by her wrists while she screamed and attempted to claw her way free. Behind Nidor, Sullis had removed the black heart and cast it aside. It pumped dark ichor onto the grass, and Nidor watched in horror, wishing it was a dream.

Sullis wiped his blade clean and smashed the organ beneath his boot, splattering its fluid onto his leggings. The Brondor paladin then approached, shaking his head.

"The boys are the larger threat." He scanned the landscape. The other zhomian had disappeared. "She's one of the mothers. She doesn't possess the black heart."

The woman pled with Nidor, though he did not understand her words, and Sullis yelled at her in her own language. The two held a brief conversation, the woman in a state of panic and Sullis using an overbearing tone.

"She wants to know why we hunt her and her children," Sullis said.

Nidor turned to Sullis. "Perhaps she does not know."

Sullis shook his head. "You cannot put her to the blade, can you?"

Nidor looked into her eyes. There was nothing but fear. He sensed no evil. He sighed.

"I do not know the ways of Silcor," Sullis furrowed his brow, "but Brondor demands her death. I know she does not emanate evil, and neither do some zhomians. But if we allow her to go free, she will produce more of those *things*. If you cannot do what must be done, then I will."

Nidor thought hard. He could not shake the feeling the woman was innocent of intentional evil doing. But neither could he refute the words of Sullis. Releasing his hold, Nidor rose and walked away; and her scream echoed off the trees of the nearby forest until Sullis silenced her. Nidor felt ill and he did not look back. Not even when the Brondor paladin slew her a second time, after her corpse began to rise.

"I'm sorry." Sullis put a hand on Nidor's shoulder. "Perhaps you should return to your friends. I, on the other hand, have some hunting to do."

Nidor said nothing as Sullis ran off in the direction the final zhomian had disappeared.

The sky was orange, red, and pink with the setting sun. But it held no beauty for Nidor. At that moment, he did not know if beauty existed. Turning north, it was time to return to his companions.

Chapter 9

Call to Arms!

Merssa sat in the war room, gazing at the empty chairs surrounding the table. It was an hour before dawn, and soon the vacant seats would be filled. Sleep had been nearly impossible, so she decided to spend a few hours alone with her thoughts before the day's council began.

Many years had passed since Palidur fell to Trannum's Death Lords. Since that fateful day, Merssa lived north of the Great East River within a compound of her creation. There, she schemed, plotted, and prepared for a war that would one day throw down the necromancer and restore glory to her beloved Holy City. Every month, warriors and soldiers offered their services, and even young men, untrained in combat, joined the cause by the hundreds. Training and organization of the latter took time, but for years it seemed time was all Merssa had.

Merssa's family was ever on her mind as well. Borse was older, and time had not been kind. Over twenty years Merssa's senior, Borse's face was lined with deep wrinkles, his eyebrows thick and white, and several brown spots decorated his hands, arms, and bald head. But he was ever the loving husband, and wise beyond all priests Merssa had ever known. Cavalor, her son, was a fine warrior, sharp of mind and strong in character. Merssa had always hoped he would become a Paladin of Cafior, but alas, it was not meant to be. Cavalor's dedication was unwavering and his convictions strong, but becoming a Holy Knight was not the decision of the warrior alone, rather a spiritual unity between warrior and deity. And it seemed there existed something within Cavalor's soul that prevented it. Merssa and Borse raised Cavalor the best way they knew how, but he was not of their blood, and one only needed to look at him to know this to be true. The flowing blonde hair of his youth, now black, ended just above his shoulders, and his piercing, dark eyes and sharp facial features never left him wanting for female admirers—an unlikely product from such ordinary folk as Merssa and Borse. Often Merssa wondered if his true heritage played a role in Cafior's denial, but that would have to remain a mystery. She chose long ago to love him as her own, and never to question Selanna as to where he had come from. Cavalor was Merssa's son, and he had grown into a leader among men.

Over the past few years, Selanna and Eraim captured Merssa's deepest respect. Selanna kept a constant watch on the enemy while Eraim gave great detail to otherwise mundane maps. Though lacking the magical benefits of Selanna, Eraim's talents in stealth, one time creating a barrier between the elf and Merssa, brought them closer together. How the elves accomplished such feats among the undead without detection baffled Merssa, but she knew better than to ask questions.

Elgarroth Sandanari was often within the compound as well, a wizard Merssa used to distrust. The mysterious elf proved wise in matters concerning Trannum, always presenting points Merssa had not considered. Merssa welcomed this, for she had no experience in battling ancient necromancers that should have perished a thousand years ago. Over the past several months, Merssa spent no less than one day a week with the wizard. Though she once considered him unapproachable, Elgarroth was mortal in her eyes, capable of normal conversation and laughter—the latter shocking Merssa and making her uneasy at times.

Most recently, Merssa was grieved to hear news of the deaths of Vikur and Poluran at the hands of Radaam. Melac had accompanied the two in an attempt to free Ironside Keep, and he barely escaped with his life. Before departing, Melac collected Vikur's sword, an heirloom handed down many generations, and Clanghorr, the mighty dwarfish battleaxe that brought an end to the evil of Trannum's orb in the Silent Marsh many years ago. Though Merssa was upset with the loss of life, not to mention the execution of such a hopeless venture, there was nothing to be done and she spared Melac too much ridicule. She did, however, demand to know how the mage had escaped.

"I figured Radaam to look for me to flee to the west," Melac said, "so I made my way into Marcove. The path was not easy. The enemy was everywhere, and it took a year just to reach Kalmaar. I scavenged for food wherever I could find it... I will not speak further on that matter." Melac swallowed the lump in his throat. "Upon reaching Kalmaar, the country opened up, and I hastened into the snowy regions of Nira. But then I was stumped by the river. Legions of undead surrounded the bridges, so I remained a safe distance from the westernmost bridge and kept watch. It seemed the abominations would never present an opportunity to cross, but then a snowstorm arrived and they stirred at last. They marched across the river and headed north, and I was able to proceed at last. Nothing then opposed me until Vermallon Road. Elves surrounded me, and it was a most welcome sight. Upon hearing my news, they ushered me quickly through their realm."

After hearing Melac's tale, Merssa dismissed the mage so he could find much needed nourishment and rest.

The fall of Nira troubled Merssa, and her thoughts went to Ballrik and Magneer, who she had sent to Steadshire more than a year ago. She placed a request with Vermallon elves, asking to receive any news of the young warriors' whereabouts—if news *could* be found. This became unnecessary when Magneer arrived a few days later.

It moved Merssa to hear of Ballrik's fate, and as she gazed at the Sword of Ironside, she realized the line of Vikur had ended. But Borse informed her that Ballrik's widow, Lorin, was with child, as were both of Lorin's sisters, and Merssa's heart eased a little. When learning of Ballrik's final words to Gruelenor, Merssa passed the Ironside sword to the krukari for safe keeping. This caught all who knew Merssa by surprise, for she had never shown such trust in a half-hobgoblin—especially not after the treachery of Gruzim.

The news did not stop there, and Nidor described the newest Death Lord; one unseen by Selanna or Eraim. Merssa immediately realized it to be Gruzim, and she cursed the day she met him. The Dale also informed Merssa of the zhomians, and she went numb, remembering the village in Andria where she had journeyed years ago in search of Trannum's orb. Merssa recalled the women bathing in the pond where the orb was kept, but she did not heed Wezlok's opinion. The elf wizard thought they should exterminate the barbarians, but in Merssa's mercy she allowed the women to live. And her decision had turned to evil. What part these new creatures would play in the war to come, she was not sure, and it left an uneasiness in the pit of her stomach. From that day on, she gazed longer at those within the encampment, searching for blue lights within the backs of their eyes.

Gruelenor and Magneer departed the day after their arrival to return to Philen, where they hoped Magneer's wife and her sisters would be safe. But the warriors swore to return as soon as possible. It pleased Merssa that Nidor remained behind, for within the Dale she saw her younger self. He was a bit humbler, perhaps, but the similarity between their auras was undeniable, and Merssa sensed he would prove important in the upcoming war. The young paladin grew restless and needed something to occupy his time, so Merssa set Nidor up as Captain of the River Watch.

Things were moving fast, and Merssa feared they were veering in the wrong direction. So without awaiting further counsel from Selanna or Elgarroth, she put forth the call, informing all kingdoms that the time to march was at hand.

Virch was the first to answer, allocating ten thousand soldiers, and Harbnum responded with five thousand more. A week later, Moclen sent word that eight thousand would soon arrive. Responses were slow from Urell Coast, Philen, and Neja, the latter a realm Merssa would never have thought to ask for help in earlier days, and at Nidor's request she sent word to Holindale. Merssa had not done so previously, for organizing barbarians could prove difficult and hinder her plans. But the Silcor paladin assured her the Dales were capable of great deeds.

From Salenti Forest came three thousand elves, and among them were Selanna and Eraim. The two elves enjoyed the youthful beauty Merssa had known for over forty years, and she was glad to see their return. She expected Selanna to question her decision to move forward, but the mage did nothing beyond giving Merssa a smile and a hug.

Sullis then arrived; a warrior Nidor had spoken of. The Brondor paladin was ten years Merssa's younger and full of energy, and with him was another paladin of his order by the name of Landerik. The young paladin looked about Cavalor's age, and he was just as handsome, though in a different way. Landerik's build was slender, and he possessed long brown hair and bright blue eyes. He carried more than a bit of arrogance, and Merssa hoped he would overcome that trait before it led to an ill fate.

Only a couple days after arriving, Sullis discovered three zhomians within the encampment. They were guards, stationed to keep watch over the Great East River for the past couple of years. The zhomians appeared as ordinary men, but when questioned, they fell into trances of emotionless unfeeling and said nothing. Sullis insisted they be put to death, but Merssa declined—a decision Sullis vehemently disagreed with. She chose instead to imprison them, hoping something might yet be learned. After the discovery of the three, at least a dozen guards deserted their posts, disappearing over Palidur Bridge one night, and Merssa's heart sank. She did not know what the infiltrators knew of her plans, and there was little she could do about it.

Pallit and Arrikan arrived next. The rangers had been working as spies since the compound was built, and they spent most of their time patrolling the northern reaches of the Varlimor Mountains. They were not as young as the days when the orbs were sought, and the past couple of years saw them grow thinner. Borse reminded Merssa that she, herself, was not a young warrior anymore when she thought of leaving the two out of future plans, and she assured her husband she would take that into consideration.

To Merssa's surprise, Wezlok offered his services. She thought her last meeting with the Lorian wizard in Andria would have deterred him from further assistance, but Wezlok arrived from Maple Lore, a woodland offering no other help. The Lorian appeared the same as when Merssa saw him last, except that his white hair was longer, hanging halfway down his back, and the top had some spiking to it. Merssa thought Wezlok's arrival to be timely, for her plans required four mages; and other than Selanna and Melac, there was Rybeal, the wizard that had accompanied Poluran into Garthglen Swamp. Merssa accepted Wezlok's enlistment.

Gruelenor and Magneer then returned from Philen, and with them was Rholmar. The Arronaus paladin and Duke of West Palidur was a most inspirational sight for Merssa and Soren, and with Rholmar were ten thousand Philen soldiers. Arkor, too, was in company. After learning of the deaths of his brother and nephew, the one-armed warrior could stay put no longer. Arkor was a bit more robust than when Merssa last saw him, but his eyes were determined.

Next came four thousand warriors out of Neja, and with them was Brem. The priest of Frayorna appeared almost as a Salenti elf, an observation Selanna and Eraim would whole heartedly disagree with, but his deep, non-melodic voice gave him away as a marteese. The half-elf had assisted Poluran in Garthglen Swamp with Rybeal, and though the mission failed, Brem was a most welcome addition.

Soon after the arrival of the Nejans came three thousand soldiers from Urell Coast.

Xorlunder of Orlenfel Forest arrived with his daughter Lorylla, both armed with exquisite bows and swords. The gray elves were taller than any elves Merssa had ever encountered, and she quickly grew fond of their disciplined attitude. Unfortunately, there were no others of their kindred willing to leave their forest.

"We still hold Orlenfel against the Benasti scum," Xorlunder said, his voice deeper than Merssa was accustomed to in elves. "And there are a couple thousand of my folk ready to aid if ever allied forces arrive."

A pair of dwarves presented themselves as well. Millord of Rornibur was the largest dwarf Merssa had ever seen. Greyor of Morimont, though smaller in stature, appeared confident and contained a certain cunning in his eyes. Greyor also possessed a much longer beard, the whiskers falling to the dwarf's knees.

"We heard of my cousin's death back home." Millord spoke of Poluran with a grim face. "And I have brought two thousand soldiers of Rornibur to do what must be done."

"Though I have not seen my kindred for many years," added Greyor, who had been unable to journey home since the occupations of Sardina and Kalmaar, "I am sure they await your decision to advance before they will march. Until then, I am at your disposal."

Later that night, Merssa requested an audience with Millord, where she presented him with Clanghorr. The dwarf gazed in silence upon the weapon; and though Merssa detected sorrow for the loss of his cousin, there was also joy that the mighty axe was not lost.

Merssa now possessed a sizeable army, and all was almost ready. She sat at the table, awaiting the other members of her council so the finishing touches could be added to the plan. It was midwinter, and with the coming of spring, the war would begin. There was still no word from Holindale, and there would be nothing coming from Tenvale. But this did not surprise Merssa, and she no longer cared. She felt young again, and though Palidur would not appear in the splendor of its glory days, she was eager to once again set foot in her fair city.

Chapter 10

Off into the Night

Nidor felt alone within the compound. Gruelenor and Magneer escorted Dezlo's daughters to Philen over a month ago, and Merssa was constantly busy; and with most soldiers uncomfortable in the company of a barbarian out of Holindale, there was no one for Nidor to speak with. Sullis joined the Front, and he spent his time working with recruits, but after Nidor's encounter with the Brondor paladin outside Vermallon Forest, he kept his distance.

To keep himself busy, Nidor enlisted in the River Guard and patrolled through the nights. He practically had to beg Merssa for the position, for she insisted he rest after his ordeal in Nira, but he needed to remain active. So Merssa made him captain.

Of the soldiers under his command, Nidor became quick friends with Grimmen, a man from Harbnum. They enjoyed several conversations, usually about current events, but also they shared many of life's experiences. The soldier reminded Nidor of Ballrik, for Grimmen often told boastful jokes, always with a touch of seriousness.

A week after Sullis flushed the zhomians from the compound, Nidor made a strange discovery. His patrol was resting at one of the many bonfires placed to warm soldiers on duty, and he noticed Grimmen wandering into the darkness. Nidor called the man's name, but the soldier darted off into the night. A bit confused, Nidor gave chase.

"Stop!" Nidor grabbed hold of Grimmen's shoulder, twenty yards from Palidur Bridge.

Grimmen spun, causing Nidor to take a step back. The soldier's features were barely visible beneath the waning light of the moon, but the points of blue light within Grimmen's eyes were unmistakable. Nidor unsheathed his sword.

"Wait!" Grimmen raised his hands. "Please, no."

Nidor balked. He had shared meals and drinks with the man for a month. "You are one of them!"

"I am," Grimmen said. "But I'm not."

Nidor kept his sword ready, but he did not strike. "What do you speak of?"

"You're a paladin," Grimmen said. "Can you not sense evil?"

Nidor stared at the soldier. There was nothing. But he remembered the words of Sullis. The Brondor paladin warned Nidor that not all zhomians emanated evil.

"I am not like the others you have seen," Grimmen said. "I was born with the black heart, yes. But not all of us are evil. Not all of us are under *his* control."

"What do you mean?" Nidor was still unsure.

Grimmen sighed. "Trannum did not plan our creation. It just sort of...happened. We were born. We were not normal, and we knew this without being told such. We were innocent at first, as any child, but as we aged, thoughts of evil entered our hearts and dark deeds were done. But not all of us gave in to these temptations. Some of us loathed those that did."

"Why did you not stop them?" Nidor asked. "Or fight them?"

"We...feared them," Grimmen stammered. "There were so many of them and so few of us. So we hid among them as best we could. Then there was the calling."

"Calling?"

Grimmen looked at the starless sky. "We all receive it eventually, though not at the same time. There are some that have yet to receive it still. It wasn't a message, but a feeling upon the wind; a yearning to journey south. One by one we answered, unable to deny it." He gazed off to the south, as if his vision could pierce the snow beyond the river. "I remember when it came to me. It wasn't hard to avoid the watch here, for we see well enough in the dark and have no need for warmth. I passed through the mountains and into Nomedd. To him. With several of others like me.

"Trannum desired servants that could walk among the living. His success finally came to him by accident." Grimmen's Andrian accent, previously well concealed, now became heavy. "Dimarr, the leader of the village where my poor mother lived, placed one of the necromancer's orbs into a pond. The women bathed in this pond and were forever tainted, cursed to give birth to others like myself. But as I said, not all of us have turned to evil. We were drawn to Trannum, yes. But we did not all like what we found when we arrived. A gathering of us exists that despises him and what he has done to us... To our mothers! We call ourselves zhokards, black warriors in my native tongue. We are cursed. We have no souls. We are doomed to be hunted by the likes of Sullis. And when he destroys us, we do not have the comfort of knowing we will be accepted into the halls of any god. More likely we'll become servants to Trannum in some other form, since *he* is our creator. We would love nothing more than to see him destroyed. We believe it is the only way for us to be free."

Nidor's body shook as the intense chill penetrated his bones.

"Here." Grimmen removed his fur cloak and handed it to Nidor. "Remember, we do not feel cold. Nor do we feel heat, lest it be fire against our skin."

Nidor draped the cloak over his own and gazed at Grimmen a moment longer. The soldier either told the truth, or he was well rehearsed in his tale. Nidor chose to believe the former. "How many zhomians are there?"

Grimmen shrugged. "I can't say for sure. Fifty, maybe."

From the way Sullis had spoken, Nidor figured there to be much less. "Why are you here? And why did you not leave when the other zhomians fled?"

"I was sent to keep an eye on the zhomians," Grimmen said. "To see what they're up to. As for fleeing, I dared not do so when they had. They report to Palidur, where Lord Cadorn awaits news. But now that his spies have returned, I can slip by unnoticed and report to my superiors."

Nidor pursed his lips. Then a thought occurred to him. "Come back with me. I believe your tale, and I think Merssa will listen. She is wise, and we could use your knowledge against our common enemy."

Grimmen shook his head. "I cannot. Though I know you speak sincerely, there are too many that would not trust me. Sullis is greatly feared by zhomians and zhokards alike. In any event, I must report what has transpired here."

Nidor gazed at the ground. The snow was only ankle deep north of the river, but the chill crept into his boots and up his legs, strengthening his desire to return to the fire. He searched for a convincing argument.

Grimmen sighed. "I cannot go back with you. But I will do my best to persuade my folk to help if we can. We are very secretive, though, and convincing them will be difficult, to say the least. If Trannum were to discover us, we would not live another day."

"How will we be able to tell you and zhomians apart?" Nidor asked. "Now that I am aware of your kind, I do not wish to harm any of you."

Grimmen stared in silence, as if struggling with inner turmoil. "It is in our greeting," the soldier said at last. "In any greeting, really. From a clasping of arms to a simple hello in any language. Watch." Grimmen bowed. "Good day, sir." As he spoke, he traced a symbol on his stomach with the middle finger of his left hand. The motion was subtle, and Nidor did not notice it at first, but Grimmen repeated it several times, pointing it out and having Nidor try it as well.

"There you are." Grimmen nodded with satisfaction after the tenth try. "Show this only to those you are certain you can trust, and I'll do my best to convince others to offer help if possible. But as I said, we are fearful of Trannum, and will likely side with the enemy before allowing anyone to expose us."

"There is much I would like to ask," Nidor said.

"I know. But I really must go. Before it's too late."

Nidor nodded, and they clasped arms; and Grimmen smirked when Nidor performed the zhokard greeting.

"Until we meet again." Grimmen ran off, disappearing onto the bridge.

"Until next time," Nidor said quietly, hoping he had not committed a grave error.

Later that night, an hour before dawn, Nidor went to the central building of the compound. He knew there had been a council meeting earlier, and Merssa was still in the war room, poring over papers. She looked as though she had not slept in weeks, and Cavalor was with her, appearing just as exhausted.

Merssa looked up, and she beckoned Nidor to enter and have a seat.

"Aren't you on duty?" Her eyes returned to the parchments before her.

Nidor took in a deep breath. He then revealed the entire conversation with Grimmen, and Merssa abandoned the papers while she listened without expression or interruption. Once Nidor finished, Merssa continued to stare. Cavalor did not move or make a sound.

"Why don't you get some rest?" Merssa said at last, and she began shuffling through the papers again.

Nidor could not tell if she was upset or agreed with his decision. He thought of asking, but then she spoke again.

"Go. Get some rest."

Chapter 11

Council of the Allies

It was early spring, and Merssa stood at the head of the large table in the war room. To her right sat Borse and Cavalor, and next to them were Rholmar and Arkor. Melac, Rybeal, and Wezlok occupied the next three chairs, followed by Xorlunder and his daughter Lorylla, Brem, and then Millord and Greyor. To her left were other displaced citizens of Palidur, Nilborg and Soren, and then came Selanna, Eraim, Pallit, and Arrikan. Magneer, Gruelenor, and Nidor followed, and Sullis and Landerik finished the side. All faces were grim while they awaited Merssa to speak, and a potent energy surrounded them.

It was beyond time for the council to begin, and Merssa wished to do just that. Instead, she continued to look at those seated before her, stalling until Elgarroth arrived. Just as her patience was spent, the wizard entered. He took a seat behind Merssa and to her left, and there he remained quiet.

Some things never changed. Merssa wondered if the elf held his ear to the door, waiting for the right moment to make his presence known. She released a calming breath before speaking.

"The day has come. It is time to take back what Trannum stole from us. All peoples have lost something to him, or will in the days to come if Vaeldor is unwilling to put a stop to the undead. Great peril awaits everyone in this room, and not all will survive. Any who are not committed to see it through may take their leave immediately."

The council was silent. With a nod, Merssa continued.

"We have learned much of our enemy over the years. We know of his weapons, his minions, and where most of them are located. And through years of debate and counsel, we are ready to move forward at last. But I caution you: we must follow the plan *exactly*, for failure of any one part could prove disastrous for all."

Merssa nodded to Cavalor, and he unrolled a large map onto the table. It depicted eastern Vaeldor, from Selt to Nomedd and all lands east of King Arman, and many notes were marked upon it.

"Trannum resides here." Merssa pointed to a black square in Nomedd labeled STRONGHOLD. "We will form four separate units, and though not all four are tasked with combating Trannum directly, I do not place any one mission as more important or more dangerous. The necromancer has spread out his greatest weapons, the Death Lords, and this plays into our hands. We will strike from multiple fronts, keeping the undead kings from joining forces or lending aid to their master; an event most undesirable."

"*Companies four...*" Eraim recited from the prophecy, as the elf often did.

"The war will begin with two direct assaults." Merssa pointed out a pair of thick lines on the map. "The South Army will take Palidur Bridge into Sardina, and the North Army will march through Vermallon and into Nira. Some in this room will accompany these forces, while others will make their way in secret to Trannum's stronghold." Merssa glanced over her shoulder. Elgarroth nodded, reaffirming what they had discussed at great length: Merssa's own part in the war. She was not entirely pleased, wanting to be there personally to ensure Trannum's demise, but she had given in to the wisdom of Elgarroth and accepted her role—at least, she was trying to accept it. "I know everyone here has reason to see the necromancer destroyed, but I assure you we are all part of the same plan. And I stress again that *all* parts are of equal importance."

Merssa released a slow breath. She then revealed the primary objectives for the North Army. This large force was to mobilize through Vermallon, Nira, and into Kalmaar, where it would march on Darmhorng. Merssa admitted there would be heavy resistance and many casualties, but also that reinforcements would be attained along the way. She informed them the army should encounter at least two Death Lords, Gruzim and Anduiff, but she concealed the fact that their success was not a necessity. They only needed to survive long enough to keep the Death Lords from aiding Trannum. Elgarroth, Selanna, Soren, and Merssa's family knew this, and it weighed upon Merssa's soul, as did other parts of the plan. But sharing too much information would only crush the hopes of many.

Merssa spoke of the South Army next. Their objectives were to take back Palidur and Ironside Keep, and from there march into Marcove to make a direct assault on Kembald. Throughout the route they would likely face three Death Lords: Cadorn in Palidur, Radaam at Ironside Keep, and Gulthar in Kembald. Just as the North Army, the South Army's survival was not a requirement to win the war.

"And now, as Eraim put it, the *companies four*." Merssa eyed the council. "Here, the objectives are more involved. Let me begin with the Darmhorng Mission."

Merssa explained the goals of the companies marching with the North and South Armies. Upon completion, she revealed the register for each. The Darmhorng Mission, to march with the North Army, included Sullis, Xorlunder, Nidor, Melac, Gruelenor, and Magneer. The company leading the South Army consisted of Cavalor, Landerik, Wezlok, Arkor, and Merssa.

As for the third and fourth companies, the ones to assault Trannum directly, Merssa referred to them as the Mission of the Mines and the Mission of the Swamp.

"From information provided by Melac," Merssa said, "we have learned of a secret tunnel, within which exists access to the mines of Lornibur, according to Poluran."

Millord and Greyor sat up, as if they had nodded off and suddenly awoken.

"As luck would have it," Merssa continued, "Elgarroth possesses an ancient map, showing the maze of tunnels to stretch all the way to Nomedd."

"If that is so," Greyor stood upon his chair, "then I *must* travel in that company."

Millord nodded in agreement, patting Clanghorr. The weapon had been resting on his lap throughout the meeting.

Merssa gave a wry smile. She was displeased with the interruption, but she understood their interest in the matter. Of course, the plan included the dwarves in the Mission of the Mines, to best utilize their skills. Also going were Eraim, Selanna, Arrikan, and Brem.

The final roster, consisting of Soren, Nilborg, Rybeal, Pallit, Rholmar, and Lorylla, was to take on the Mission of the Swamp. They were to journey across the Fire Hills and into the wild lands south of the Varlimor Mountains. The company would then traverse Dright Swamp and head east to Trannum's stronghold. Besides zombies, opposition along the way was unknown, but the hope was that the company remained unseen and unlooked for.

"If all goes to plan," Merssa said with forced optimism, "Trannum will send his forces to deal with the armies, and there should be minimal resistance left in Nomedd to protect him."

"What of the remaining Death Lords?" inquired Rholmar. "I have heard you mention five, yet I have learned that eight exist."

"Unfortunately, we do not know where every Death Lord is, or will be," Merssa replied. "Jurak, Dunuthar, and Velgaad do not remain in one place too long. They have been seen in Trannum's stronghold, flying over Kalmaar or Sardina, and sometimes they are nowhere to be found. I know this presents a problem, but the hope is that we lure them to the major battles and away from their master."

"What of the rising dead?" Magneer asked. "When we fought against the Death Lord in Nira, all allies that fell in battle rose against us. How are we to combat an army that grows even as we fight?"

"From what we have learned," Borse replied, "it is only within the vicinity of a Death Lord that the dead rise. The aura surrounding them bears the same effect the Wind of the Dead once possessed, but we believe we have a way to counter this evil. Over the next few days, everyone will receive a blessing from one of our priests; the same blessing the dead of Palidur used to receive. You see, in the days when the Wind of the Dead plagued the lands, Palidur's dead remained at peace."

"A blessing for the dead?" Magneer frowned.

"Yes, it *was* performed on the dead," Borse said. "But I believe it will be just as effective on the living."

"You *believe*?" Sullis stood with a furrowed brow. "You don't know for sure?"

"Please sit," Merssa said firmly. Though she had become more tolerant over the years, she did not take kindly to anyone speaking to her husband in such a manner. "Borse is wise, with a close connection to the Almighty Cafior. I believe in him, and I believe it will work. The only way to be absolutely sure would be to send someone to their death across Palidur Bridge and see if they rise. I can think of no one willing to volunteer for such a mission. Would you?" Merssa raised an eyebrow.

"If my temple were in charge," Sullis took his seat, "that is exactly what we would do. We would not risk the lives of the true warriors. But I know that is not the way of you Palidurians, and so we will have to hope for the best."

Merssa had heard rumors that Brondor paladins were ruthless and warlike, and now she realized those rumors to be understated. She continued to stare while Sullis shared a murmur with Landerik, and the young paladin nodded with a sarcastic smile. Next to them, Nidor appeared disturbed by what was said.

"What of the snow?" asked Brem, the marteese's deep, non-melodic voice lacking the volume of most others within the room.

"The snowline ends in northern Kalmaar for the North Army," Selanna answered, "and in Kembald for the South Army. The mines, of course, will be free of it. But the Fire Hills are covered. When last I saw, the land beyond the hills was clear."

Additional questions were voiced, and though they seemed irrelevant in Merssa's opinion, they helped to ease the minds of those that asked them. So she permitted the queries, allowing Cavalor, Selanna, and Soren to provide the answers. The topic then changed to that of the individual missions, and they spent the next few hours filling in the details.

The evening grew late, and once all questions were exhausted, Merssa brought the meeting to an end.

"Let's get some rest," she said. She then looked at Elgarroth, who gave a single nod.

Over the next several days, the compound was alive with activity. Blades were sharpened and armor checked, and soldiers were split into the two armies and briefed by their generals. Nilborg and Borse worked day and night with other priests, holding large ceremonies to administer the Blessings of the Dead. They traced symbols upon every soldier's head with holy water and oils, and chanted in prayer while placing wooden pendants around the warriors' necks. Merssa had seen the ceremony performed many times in the distant past, but seeing it bestowed upon the living made her skin crawl.

Pallit, Arrikan, and Magneer spent the final days together. Each had a separate path to travel in the war, for their skills as rangers were needed in multiple locations. Though Magneer had shown contempt for his parents in the recent past, they were a happy family and laughed often. Merssa was glad to see this. She knew the chance of them all surviving to be small.

Selanna and Eraim joined the Salenti elves, and their assembly was the most raucous of all gatherings. Xorlunder and Lorylla joined the army of elves, their grayish skin, silver hair, and height making them appear out of place, but they had no other kindred present. The two remained close, seemingly uneasy with the merriment—such were the ways of Salenti folk, even on the verge of war.

Gruelenor was alone most of the time. He was the sole krukari within the compound, and it seemed Nidor and Magneer were the only ones willing to converse with him. But Magneer was with his parents and Nidor was often busy. Merssa held sympathy for Gruelenor, but there was nothing to be done.

Merssa decided it wise to have Nidor shadow her while preparations were made, so the Dale might learn how Palidurians put plans into action. She also thought it best to distract Nidor, knowing the disappointment he held for his kindred failing to offer aid in the war. One night, Merssa spoke to the Silcor paladin about his decision to allow Grimmen to leave, telling him she would likely have done the same. She further explained that there would be no attempts to recruit the zhokards.

"To rely on a force that may or may not help us in time of need would present terrible risks," Merssa said. "Perhaps more terrible than those we already face. But do not worry. All of this shall remain between us."

With all preparations in place, Merssa spent the final two days with her family and they laughed often. On the last night, before the war was to begin, she sat alone in her study, staring at the darkening shadows. She did not notice her husband enter.

"How are you, my dear?" Borse handed Merssa a warm mug of tea.

"As well as I need to be," she said softly, absently accepting the drink.

Merssa was pulled from her trance when Borse sat next to her on the divan. She smiled, but there was no joy in it. The missions plagued her mind, as did the fact that she would not be the one to destroy Trannum. So many things could go wrong, and she would not be there to ensure his defeat. Elgarroth counseled against it. The wizard reminded Merssa of Trannum's plot to lure the survivors of Palidur across the bridge—her in particular. He insisted that if she was not among the attacking armies, the necromancer would look for her elsewhere, and perhaps discover one or both of the smaller companies approaching in secret. It was the plight that haunted Merssa the most. Then Borse added to her concerns.

"I'm going with you."

"What?" Merssa sat up, her mind scrambling for words.

"You cannot change my mind." Borse smiled. He looked every bit his age, more than seven decades behind him now, and the late nights had formed permanent crescents beneath his eyes. But his smile was genuine.

"I do not think it wise," Merssa said.

"You, of all people, know I do not make decisions based on emotion alone." Borse took her hand. "I know of the dangers ahead. But I sense there will be a need for my assistance before it is over."

It was useless to argue. In all the years Merssa had known Borse, even before she loved him, he had always followed the path that Cafior set before him. If that path now led into the war against the undead, she could not deny him.

They sat quietly for the rest of the night, drifting into restful slumber within each other's arms.

CHAPTER 12

PALIDUR BRIDGE

The South Army was poised and awaiting orders. Merssa sat atop her horse at the lead, with Cavalor to her right and Borse to her left. The spring sun labored, but with the power of the collective prayers of the compound, a significant amount of snow north of the river had been melted. Now, only a couple hundred yards of cold, wet ground lay between the army and Palidur Bridge. Beyond, a land of eternal winter awaited.

At Merssa's instruction, Wezlok reported to the front, and his eyes narrowed as he gazed across the bridge.

"What do you see?" Merssa detected nothing, save for the northern half of the bridge. After that, a snowy haze hung like a curtain.

"It is difficult." The elf pursed his lips while the wind danced with the spikes of his hair. "The snow is thick, but I can make out the city. As far as I can tell, the walls are unmanned."

Merssa was no fool. The zhomians knew the war was coming. They may not have known the details, since Sullis flushed them out before actual orders were given, but the thousands of soldiers arriving from various kingdoms certainly told them that much. No. The city was ready. Of that, Merssa was sure.

She bit her lip. Never had she imagined being on the outside of defenses that once kept her safe. Palidur was fortified with catapults, strategically placed to defend against enemies attempting to cross the river, and upon the bridge there existed little cover. Any forces lucky enough to survive the catapults then faced over a thousand crossbows from atop the city walls. Merssa had briefed her men on these facts, and looking back now, she dreaded to issue the next command.

The lead squadron held shields nearly as tall as the soldiers themselves. The tops were bright blue to represent Arronaus, the right sides brown for Cafior, and the left sides dark blue for Soleran—a perfect representation of the three sectors of the Holy City. Behind the shields, the faces of the platoon were grim. They would be the first to set foot on the bridge, and they knew no hope awaited them after that.

With a heavy heart, Merssa nodded, and Cavalor lifted his hand and gave the order. The squadron raised their shields and rapped their swords upon them twice to signal their readiness. Merssa nodded again, and Cavalor twirled his hand in a circle overhead.

Three hundred soldiers from various kingdoms marched twenty abreast, stepping onto the first flagstones of the mighty Palidur Bridge. It was a wide street, straight and flat for half a mile before falling snow concealed it. The air was stale while they made their way, and a cool breeze greeted them as they neared the snowstorm, but no attacks were forthcoming. A pair of massive pillars marked the center of the construction, stretching from the riverbed to a point fifty feet overhead. The pillar to the right was carved in the likeness of Vennimor, paladin and founder of Palidur, and the opposite portrayed Bormungdaher, dwarf king of old that commissioned the bridge as a gift to the paladin hero. Though the pillars stood as bastions to ward off evil and inspire brotherhood, no one found the will to look up.

With snow in their faces, the soldiers picked up the pace to a jog. Their mail jingled, and the breeze grew colder as sleet whipped from left to right. The bridge was soon covered in white, and farther on the shadow that was Palidur came into view. Cold stung all exposed skin, but they remained strong, and with less than a quarter mile to the bridge's end, the city attacked.

Over the walls came boulders, like dark birds taking flight and disappearing into the snowy sky. They reappeared overhead with little warning and crashed upon the first five ranks. Stones over four feet in diameter crushed soldiers or shattered on impact, but the deadliest ones bounced and rolled, trampling warriors or knocking them into the icy water fifty yards below. The sound of shattering rock barely died off when a second barrage arrived, and this time the stones reached the twelfth rank. Another volley crashed down, and another, until only two score of soldiers remained.

The strength of Palidur Bridge was beyond measure, and the flagstones withstood the bombardment. The surviving soldiers proved just as stout in heart, advancing as fast as they could, but the pace became difficult when they reached the deeper snow. Short-range catapults then attacked, launching fiery kegs and coating everything in burning oil. The mighty bridge remained unharmed, but none of the first squadron survived.

More boulders descended, this time heading for the second company. The soldiers witnessed the onslaught of the first platoon from fifty yards away, but little did this benefit them, and they did not make it much farther before suffering the same grim fate.

Another fifty yards back, the third squadron received minimal casualties from flying rocks, as only three of the missiles opposed them. Upon reaching the flaming oil, the snow was completely melted, but the sight of burning bodies was disheartening all the same. More kegs arrived, setting fire to half the unit, but the other half continued toward the southern edge of the bridge. The weather calmed and Palidur became clear — a tall, proud city upon pure white. Dark forms then lined the walls, and before any soldier set foot off the far end, arrows filled the sky. No one survived.

And so it went. Five squadrons fell before any reached the southern bank. Still, the soldiers advanced. Among the rubble and soot, more than a thousand bodies covered the bridge, and below, the Great East River swept away hundreds more. Over two thousand soldiers littered the snow outside the walls of Palidur, and the number continued to grow.

Merssa knew taking Palidur would be costly, but it was a necessary goal. She gave the command for the host to advance, as a dozen squadrons had done before them, and she led the way on foot—the bridge was too cluttered for riding and the horses were left behind.

The pillars of Vennimor and Bormungdaher had suffered minor chipping from the catapults, but Merssa barely noticed while she moved from boulder to boulder. In the distance, the eighth squadron was failing at the base of Palidur's walls, and barrels of some liquid that did not ignite pelted the twelfth squadron a hundred yards ahead.

A shower of boulders arrived, and one crashed near to Merssa. She fell behind a large rock in time to escape harm, but Cavalor and Landerik took minor injuries from spraying debris. Merssa resumed the pace, and they made it twenty more yards when she spied another grouping of stones overhead.

"Take cover!"

She bolted forward, stepping over rubble and bodies as quickly as she could. The rocks crashed down as Merssa pulled a discarded shield over herself, and the shell was struck several times while she remained unharmed. Casting the shield aside, she looked behind her. The first few ranks had been devastated. Landerik survived, having used the corpse of a soldier to protect himself—Merssa hoped it had been a corpse. Wezlok also appeared unharmed. Cavalor was gone.

"Cavalor!"

Dread filled Merssa as her mind raced. Surely he had not studied as much as any scholar, trained harder than any soldier, and risen to be a leader among men just to die upon Palidur Bridge at the beginning of the war. She spied gauntlets gripping the edge of the road and she rushed to them.

Blood streaked the right side of Cavalor's face as he held on over the rushing water. Extending her arm, Merssa pulled him onto the bridge with strength surprising even herself.

"Watch yourself!" she barked as she climbed to her feet.

Cavalor nodded.

Only snow descended at the moment. Merssa knew some time existed while the catapults were reloaded, and she issued the next order.

"Full charge!"

Merssa sprinted as fast as her legs could carry her. Barrels crashed all around, but the aim was poor and the attacks served only to drench her in beer—either the city ran out of oil, or the mindless undead had procured the wrong stock. She soon set foot upon the trampled snow outside her precious city, and fifty yards farther the twelfth squadron assaulted the gate of the Cafior Sector.

A volley of arrows stole Merssa's attention, and she kneeled behind the shield of an unfortunate soldier. A couple of missiles caromed off the shell and one pierced through, but the steel snagged the arrow inches from her face.

The South Army rushed from the bridge as the catapults fell silent and the undead on the walls doubled. Arrows again filled the sky, felling soldiers by the hundreds, but the host was too great and they returned fire. The attack had little effect on the zombies and even less on the skeletons, but many dunarchins and ghouls fell from the battlements. Merssa then saw what she eagerly awaited: three battering rams and several ladders had made it across the bridge intact.

She dropped the shield and waved her arm; and Cavalor and Landerik led the rams to the gates, where soldiers surrounded them with shields overhead. The rams were employed immediately, where the first one struck, then the second, then the third. The process repeated over and over, sounding like a drum. Several soldiers fell, pierced by arrows from dunarchins above, but others took their places and the drumming continued.

Merssa knew the gates to be sturdy, and beyond them existed the mighty portcullis. Once the soldiers breached the doors, they would be denied entry by the iron gate and cruelly attacked from above. But she planned to enter by other means.

The ladders were constructed to the perfect height for Palidur's walls, and a dozen had survived the bridge. Four men bore each, and on Merssa's command they raced across the field beneath a shower of arrows. Seven ladders reached their destinations and were immediately raised, but ghouls and dunarchins sent them crashing before they could be scaled.

Merssa surveyed the battlements. Fifty yards to the left of the gate was a group of skeletons with crossbows. "Grab that ladder and follow me!" she ordered five soldiers stepping from the bridge.

The men pulled the ladder from the hands of dead soldiers and followed Merssa. Two were felled by arrows, and Merssa took their place, pausing only when an arrow pierced her thigh. She clenched her teeth and continued, and upon reaching the wall, the ladder was raised into the skeletons' midst.

Just as Merssa hoped, the brainless undead failed to knock the ladder over while she ascended. The skeletons attempted to shoot her, but when they aimed the weapons downward, the arrows fell before the triggers were pulled. Merssa heard the *twang* of the cables repeat as the archers reloaded and tried again, and again the arrows dropped to the ground.

She reached the top and grabbed her mace, and from the weapon shone the golden glow of her faith. It had been too many years since Merssa last basked in the aura's warmth, and it fueled her strength as she reduced the skeletons to piles of bones. Soldiers filed onto the wall as she continued along the battlements, and soon greater than fifty undead were destroyed or knocked to the ground below, making room for the remaining ladders to be placed. A loud *crack* then issued from the gates—the doors were beginning to give.

"Clear the battlements!" Merssa shouted as soldiers stormed the wall.

Merssa gazed upon her city. Though covered in snow, she could see that most of the Cafior Sector lay in ruin. At the portcullis, more than a hundred skeletons and zombies awaited the invading army, and crawling along the streets were packs of ghouls, ducking into piles of rubble.

"Follow me!" she ordered a group of men arriving to the top of the wall, and she descended a flight of stone steps into the city.

Over forty men ran in Merssa's wake as she charged into the rear of the zombies and skeletons guarding the portcullis. The undead were no match for her well-trained soldiers, and she experienced few casualties while the creatures were defeated. Beyond the gate, she saw the massive bar across the wooden doors snap, and she ordered a dozen men to enter the tower and raise the portcullis. She then gathered the remaining soldiers and proceeded deeper into the Cafior Sector.

Evil permeated the streets and the stench of ghouls was thick. A pack of the creatures hissed after Merssa flushed them from a ruined building, and she destroyed five while her soldiers defeated the rest. The monsters claimed four victims of their own. Eight dunarchins then approached, and seven held swords while one chanted. Bolts of lightning issued from the undead mage's fingertips, and three soldiers screamed as they fell.

Merssa met the dunarchins, and she destroyed the lead figure with a single blow. Two others stopped to do battle, but they were no match for her, as training, love for her city, and dedication to her deity burned hot. Merssa knocked aside their swings and dodged left and right, and within seconds, she slew them both. She then turned on the spell caster, and it focused on her as well.

A small, fiery ball sizzled past Merssa, striking the dunarchin mage. Flames engulfed the creature, and it hissed as it collapsed onto the snow. Wezlok had arrived, and not a moment too soon, as the dunarchins had taken out half of Merssa's men. She was also relieved to see Cavalor approaching, and Landerik, Borse, and Arkor were close behind. Her spirits rose, and she advanced on the next dunarchin.

The South Army spilled into the Cafior Sector, destroying the undead without mercy, and Merssa ordered her general to search every building and take the rest of the city. As for her, she made for the Grand Cathedral at the heart of Palidur, and with her went the others of her company.

The air became frigid as they battled to the center of the city, and a tingling sensation worked its way down Merssa's back, causing her skin to crawl. She ignored the fear and passed through the open gates to the cathedral, but what she found was a faded silver street, crumbled statues of warrior angels, and a building long toppled. Standing beside the rubble was a Death Lord.

Merssa stepped forward, sizing up her enemy while Cavalor and Landerik took positions at the Soleran and Arronaus gates. The Death Lord stood over six feet tall and was clad entirely in black plate armor, and a full helm rested upon his head, revealing only two points of blue light. In his right hand was a wicked black sword, while his left clutched a dark mace. His glowing eyes bore into Merssa, and she was suddenly aware of her heart pounding in her chest. From the notes in Eraim's journal, Merssa had no doubt of whom she faced.

"I've come for you, Cadorn!"

The evil warrior raised the mace, and from it issued a dark flash. Pain wracked Merssa's body, as if her bones were trying to escape, and from the sounds behind her, she knew her companions suffered as well. Selanna warned Merssa that Trannum's generals possessed many abilities, but the elf had not been able to discern those powers, and Merssa was caught off guard.

From beneath Cadorn's helmet issued a mocking chuckle as the Death Lord approached, and Merssa clenched her teeth and rose to her full height, paling to that of her enemy's. Cadorn swung the sword and then the mace, and Merssa fended off the attacks and countered. The pain coursing through her body unbalanced her, and she missed her mark. An arrow then shattered upon the black armor, as Arkor's wooden-arm crossbow proved useless, and the Death Lord paid the attack no heed.

Merssa's pain suddenly eased and the glow of her mace grew brighter. Though she could not see Borse, her husband having remained outside the inner sanctum with Wezlok, she knew it to be his doing, for she felt Cafior's touch upon her soul. Cadorn balked, and his glowing eyes shifted, as if seeking the source of the intervention.

Having abandoned his post, Landerik attacked the Death Lord's right flank. The evil warrior sidestepped the young paladin's thrust and brought down the pommel of his sword, knocking Landerik to the street. Before Cadorn followed with the mace, Merssa moved in with a flurry that left golden streams in the air. Cadorn fell back, turning aside all but one attack, and her weapon struck the dark breastplate. A spark resulted, and Cadorn staggered to the side.

The Death Lord took a sideways stance, regarding Merssa for a moment while Arkor dragged Landerik to safety. Cadorn then advanced with both weapons, forcing Merssa to parry many blows, and the assault was fast and unending. The dark sword knocked her mace to the street and the golden aura faded; and the evil mace followed, crashing into her chest.

Merssa staggered, and upon her breastplate was a black mark where the weapon had struck. Every wound received while crossing the bridge and storming the city lit up, as evil invaded her body, and she fought to remain standing. Unable to lift her arms, she gazed up at her enemy, awaiting Cadorn's next strike, but the Death Lord's attention turned skyward when a terrible roar came from the clouds.

Borse and Wezlok entered the inner sanctum in haste as an undead dragon descended and released its horrible breath. Borse stood tall, shouting a prayer while the beast flew only a few feet above their heads; and even as the yellow cloud issued, it dissipated, consumed by divine power.

Merssa forced herself into a defensive stance with much effort and faced Cadorn. But the dragon made another pass, this time snatching the Death Lord in its bony talon and lifting him into the clouds. The dire cold faded and the fear lifted from Merssa's heart.

Cadorn was gone.

Palidur was freed as the remaining undead fell; and though the city cheered, Merssa did not share in the celebration. Borse later cleansed her body of the darkness inflicted by the Death Lord's mace, but he could not take away the sorrow and confusion that plagued Merssa's soul. The South Army started out over twenty thousand strong, but now their numbers were only half that amount. It could have been worse, Merssa knew and fully expected—the undead failed to utilize the city's defenses as well as they could have. And why did Cadorn flee without much of a fight? What was Trannum up to?

Standing once again within the walls of Palidur did not have the effect Merssa thought it would. The city seemed more a desolate graveyard than a holy place. She did find comfort in that her family had survived, and as Borse later pointed out, none of the fallen soldiers had risen against them. The blessings had worked. But for how long, Merssa would have to wait and see.

CHAPTER 13

VERMALLON ROAD

Even as the South Army crossed Palidur Bridge, the North Army had been on the move for two weeks. With over forty thousand men, it was a breathtaking sight to behold. Rank upon rank of soldiers marched with grim looks of determination: dwarves of Rornibur, elves of Salenti, and humans from various kingdoms. They skirted several villages along their route, and the commoners never failed to gather and cheer.

A few days after rounding Tribenor, Vermallon Forest came into view in all its vastness. The road then bent northeasterly, and the army followed it another week before turning onto Vermallon Road. The wide path accommodated four carts abreast, providing ample room to march sixteen across, and the pace was easier than when passing over the uneven fields of Sendorum.

Lush branches became entangled high above, casting shadows over much of the road, and it was not long before the canopy grew thick. Though this offered relief from the burning sun that had shone for days in the open country, most soldiers were filled with regret, for winter and gloom awaited on the opposite end of the woodland, and they knew not whether they would feel the sun's rays again.

Camping on Vermallon Road proved challenging, as space was cramped with tents, horses, wagons, and soldiers. Travelers would have been hard pressed to pass by, but in such dark days, not even merchants were seen journeying between Harbnum and Nira.

On the sixth day since entering Vermallon Forest, not quite halfway through the woodland, a captain arrived to the rear ranks to report to Sullis. Merssa had put the Brondor paladin in charge—a decision Nidor questioned.

"Do not forget that he is very experienced," Merssa told Nidor before they left the compound. "Just as you, I don't agree with all his beliefs. But in the end, he is a commander of warriors and will do whatever it takes to destroy evil."

The explanation did little to comfort Nidor, and Sullis making him second in command only compounded the situation. Now, Nidor spent almost every waking hour with the Brondor paladin.

"Why have we stopped?" asked Sullis.

"Vermallon elves are on the road," the captain replied. "They bring ill news. It would seem Trannum's forces are on the move. They have invaded the forest and the defense of Vermallon is breached."

"This is ill news indeed," said Xorlunder.

The gray elf scanned the woodland, as if his unusual eyes could pierce the trees. Nidor had never seen black eyes with white pupils before, but he knew what it was like to be viewed as different, and he tried not to stare. Xorlunder stood nearly as tall as Nidor, possessing smooth grayish skin and long silver hair, and everything he possessed was of the utmost quality. Though his frame was slim, appearing almost fragile, Nidor bore no illusions as to the elf's abilities in battle. Xorlunder held a fancy bow made of dark wood, as if eager to put it to good use.

"Is it Benasti scum or the undead?" the elf posed.

"It is the undead," the captain replied. "But the Vermallon elves believe hobgoblins and Kalmirans follow in their wake."

"We do not part company with the host for another three days." Xorlunder turned to Sullis. "Perhaps we should advance the plan a bit."

Nidor was going to agree with the tall elf, but Sullis spoke first.

"We honor the plan. Merssa said there are to be no deviations."

"Surely she believed the elves still held the forest," Nidor said. "I am sure she intended for us to use our heads."

"And so we shall." Sullis shot Nidor a stern gaze. "When the time calls for it. Let us not forget that an army marches with us. Besides, the elves must maintain *some* control. No sense endangering the entire war with hasty actions." The Brondor paladin turned to the captain. "We press on. Deploy additional scouts and keep your eyes open."

"As you command." The captain bowed and departed.

"I do not like this." Xorlunder continued scanning the woodland. "For our part, the way is supposed to be secret. We can ill afford to be seen separating from the host when the time comes."

"Today or three days from now," Sullis shook his head, "they could spot us either way. And we cannot complete our objective if we are outnumbered and slain among the trees. Our best hope is to stay with the army as long as possible."

Xorlunder relented, but his frown remained.

Nidor did not argue. Surely this was the experience Merssa had mentioned. He needed to trust in her, even if he did not trust the Brondor paladin.

Later that evening, while camping on the road, Sullis approached Nidor.

"I do not know the ways of Silcor," the Brondor paladin said, as he often did, "but you need to think with your blade. True warriors of Brondor do not run and hide. Why, if this plan were of *my* creation, we would march all the way to Darmhorng. And we wouldn't be stopping to recruit elves or dwarves."

"But this is a war for all the realms," Nidor said. "Do elves and dwarves not have a right to fight for their homes?"

"That is the only reason I am willing to follow this *stealth* mission at all." Sullis frowned. "In my order, stealth is for the weak. Of *course* Xorlunder looks to run into the trees at the first sign of danger—I expect nothing less. He is an elf, after all, and an odd one at that. But it surprised me to see you agree with him."

"My only concern is for winning the war." Nidor was more than a bit annoyed. Was the paladin calling him a coward?

"Good." Sullis nodded. "Then we are in agreement."

Sullis left Nidor alone—and slightly confused. Gruelenor then joined him.

"What was that about?"

"Nothing." Nidor shook his head. "Now, if you'll forgive me, I must say some prayers." He walked to the edge of the road.

The next day was trying. Snipers attacked from either side of the road on several occasions, and the hidden archers always launched a couple of volleys before disappearing into the wilderness. The attacks continued, and though less than fifty men were lost, soldiers were becoming anxious.

"Where are the blasted elves?" grumbled Magneer after the fourth such attack. "Shouldn't they be clearing the trees about the road before us?"

"The Vermallon elves are not part of the plan," Xorlunder said in his deep voice. "And more than likely, they are protecting their own. We know not what the enemy has wrought upon their homes."

"It is just a few soldiers." Sullis shrugged. "That's what they're there for."

Nidor was appalled. He wondered if Sullis saw *him* that way, or the others of the company for that matter.

The night watch was tripled and fires kept small, so as not to shed too much illumination. Still, the darkness brought more frequent attacks. The enemy used no lights, making it hard to detect their presence, so dwarves and elves were deployed throughout the ranks. Finally, a villain was felled by an elf's arrow. It was a hobgoblin.

"Just as I suspected." Sullis gazed at the corpse that was brought to him. "That explains why they have no need for lamps."

"We should have parted ways yesterday." Xorlunder was visibly upset, and his white eyes seemed to glow. "There is no way to keep our passing secret now."

Sullis was silent, his brow furrowed. "I still don't like deviating from the plan," he said at last. "But, I suppose, to best utilize *all* of our skills, we should depart as soon as possible." He looked at the darkening trees. "Of course, proceeding at night would favor the hobgoblins." He turned to the company. "We leave at first light." To Magneer, he added, "Inform the general."

Magneer glanced Nidor's way before carrying out the command, likely annoyed at being used as a lackey.

"Let's get some rest," Sullis said. "Who knows what the morning will bring?"

With the brightening of the forest, horns sounded to begin the day's march for the North Army. Nidor heard it from a mile away while he and the company picked their way through the trees on foot. Xorlunder was at the lead, followed by Sullis, Nidor, Magneer, Melac, and then Gruelenor. The tall elf stopped often to reference the map Eraim had provided, but always he shook his head.

"Any of it making sense yet?" asked Sullis.

"No." Xorlunder rolled the map. "But eventually we will see one of these landmarks."

They headed southeast. Xorlunder paid close attention to the surroundings, inspecting every broken branch and trampled piece of vegetation, and everyone kept their eyes and ears alert. After several miles were between them and Vermallon Road, they paused for a late lunch and Xorlunder climbed a tree. The gray elf leaped nimbly from branch to branch, disappearing from sight.

"Why did Merssa put *him* in charge?" Magneer posed quietly to Nidor, nodding toward Sullis. "I never thought I'd rather be under my father's command before now." He smirked at Nidor. "I think if we had a privy, he'd make *me* clean it."

Nidor could always count on Magneer to make him smile.

Xorlunder dropped lightly to the ground. "We seem to be on course. Soon, I think, we shall find the path Eraim has lain for us."

"Let's hope so." Sullis spit a piece of bone onto the forest floor. "Otherwise it will take twice as long to locate the ford she mentioned." The Brondor paladin stood. "Time to move."

They walked all day and deep into the night, encountering no hobgoblins or undead. But neither were there any signs they had made it onto Eraim's route. Nidor became concerned, and within Sullis, Magneer, and Xorlunder he sensed growing frustrations. Melac appeared at ease, and Gruelenor was hard to read, as usual. After resting a few hours, they returned to their task with the first hint of light.

"Are you in need of assistance?" Magneer asked Xorlunder during a break for lunch, evidently unable to contain himself any longer. "I am skilled in both tracking and map reading."

"If you wish to take the lead, then perhaps you should!" The elf rose from his squatted position to look down at the ranger. "But I doubt you would fare better in this forest than I, *mountain* man."

"Anything is better than wandering aimlessly and waiting for the enemy to find us," said Magneer.

"Enough!" Sullis glared at them both. "We will get nowhere squabbling among—"

"Quiet!" Xorlunder cocked his head to one side. "Something approaches from the northwest."

Sullis surveyed the forest. "Get from sight."

"Could they be elves?" asked Magneer.

"Their steps fall too heavily for elves." Xorlunder furrowed his brow. "Lest they be seriously wounded."

"Get from sight!" Sullis said again. "Now!"

They concealed themselves behind trees, and soon Nidor detected the approaching footsteps, and lots of them. Seconds later, he heard voices he was sure belonged to hobgoblins. He did not understand the words, but he got a general feeling from the tones used. The first one spoke harshly. Another posed a question. Then there was sniffing, followed by rustling, as if someone was crawling upon the ground. Next came an exclamation.

"Attack!" Sullis shouted.

Nidor sprang from his position to see a band of hobgoblins, and before the enemy could react, Sullis hacked down two. Nidor was then by the Brondor paladin's side, and together they defeated four more.

A couple of hobgoblins lay at Gruelenor's feet, and three others were strewn, each with an arrow through the heart. To the right, Magneer leaped over his fallen opponent and charged the final two hobgoblins as the fiends attempted to flee. One tumbled across the forest floor, pierced by Xorlunder's arrow, and the last hobgoblin disappeared. Magneer abandoned his chase, kicking the ground in frustration.

"Benasti scum!" Xorlunder spat onto a hobgoblin corpse. "Why were they tracking us? How did they know to look for us?"

Nidor thought he saw Xorlunder shoot a glare Gruelenor's way.

"Who knows?" Sullis looked troubled. "Perhaps they are aware of our mission."

"They couldn't possibly know," said Melac, perfectly calm. "Nobody knew the plan before the night it was revealed to us, save for Merssa and a few of her trusted friends."

"Perhaps not all zhomians were flushed out," said Sullis. "There were too many soldiers at that encampment. I could not check every single one. Damn! I told Merssa to *kill* those prisoners."

Nidor's mind went to Grimmen, but he discarded the thought. Grimmen departed days before the final council.

"There is another possibility." Xorlunder stared pointedly at Gruelenor this time.

"Not a chance!" Magneer turned to the elf. "I have known Gruelenor for years. Until we joined the Front, he'd never even *been* to this side of King Arman."

"No." Sullis addressed Xorlunder. "You let the tale of Gruzim distract you. He was a prince of Benasti, let's not forget. There's another reason. It *must* be the work of zhomians. There are probably some marching with the North Army as we speak."

Nidor kept silent, an uneasiness in the pit of his stomach. Gruelenor had been acting differently since Ballrik's death, but Nidor did not believe for a moment his friend would betray them. He was sure Xorlunder's dislike of Gruelenor had to do with the Benasti siege upon Orlenfel Forest.

"In any case," Magneer said, "we must get moving. If they *are* tracking us, they'll return with greater numbers."

"Not only greater numbers," Xorlunder looked at Sullis, "but with Zurkan as well. These were mere grunts."

They left the battle scene at a quickened pace and placed a few miles behind them. Xorlunder paused now and again to view Eraim's map, always following the action with a sigh or a shake of his head. On occasion, the elf ascended to the treetops for a better look, but he returned each time with a sour expression. As darkness encroached, the company halted.

"I don't think we should stop," said Magneer. "It will not be safe."

"If we travel at night," Sullis turned to Xorlunder, "can you find your way?"

"This forest is unfamiliar and growing denser." Xorlunder shook his head. "The river draws nearer with every step, and if we do not arrive according to Eraim's instruction, we could search for hours before finding the ford."

"But who knows if we'll *ever* find our way onto that map?" argued Magneer. "Why should the night be any different from the day?"

Xorlunder appeared none too pleased with the comment.

"We shall stop." Sullis sighed. "There's no choice. We cannot afford to lose more time searching for that raft."

"Let us pray we have bought ourselves a night at least." Xorlunder's tone held little hope.

"We'll guard in shifts," said Sullis. "Nidor and I will take the first watch, Xorlunder and Gruelenor the second, and then Melac and Magneer."

Xorlunder glared at Gruelenor. "Perhaps I would be better placed on the first or last shift."

"Perhaps." Gruelenor eyed the elf.

"You'll do as I say!" Sullis said. "We are not here to become friends. Of all of us, you two possess the strongest sight in the darkness. We shall be in need of it when the truest dark of the forest is upon us."

The two fell silent, but they maintained eye contact for several more seconds.

The night passed with no sign of the hobgoblins. Come morning, the company continued. They did not make it far when Xorlunder voiced the elfish phrase for alarm.

"*Mees! Mees!*" The elf slung his bow over his shoulder and drew his sword, facing the forest ahead.

They pulled their weapons and advanced, and Nidor saw at least a score of zombies standing among the trees. As if awakened by the company's presence, the undead opened their eyes and hissed, baring yellow teeth and moving as quickly as ghouls. The similarity to ghouls ended there, however, for they wielded swords and walked erect.

Xorlunder began the battle, swinging his sword in a vicious arc, and as he did so, Nidor saw the blade become red hot. The elf cleaved the heads of the first two zombies, dropping the corpses with smoke rising from their necks, and he fended off a third one's sword with ease.

Having no time to marvel over Xorlunder's heated weapon, Nidor darted around a couple of trees and attacked the undead with savage swings. Though the creatures were faster than normal zombies and held swords, their skills paled, and he destroyed five without taking an injury.

The battle ended and all was quiet. Melac stood against a tree, lowering his hands.

"These zombies were strange." Xorlunder looked at the headless corpses at his feet. "I have never seen them move so quickly, or wield weapons."

"Nor have I." Sullis scanned the trees. "And I destroyed many of them years ago, after the Wind of the Dead blew over Harbnum."

"The enemy takes pleasure in creating new breeds," Melac said. "Be glad these were only zombies. The time will come soon enough when our true skills will be put to the test."

"Well," Magneer looked over the battle scene, "this will leave an easy trail to follow."

"It cannot be helped." Xorlunder sheathed his sword.

Nidor noticed Magneer had taken a wound on the arm. Although it did not look serious, Nidor pulled some bandages to wrap it.

"No time," Sullis said. "We need to keep moving."

Nidor put the bandages away, receiving a wry smile from Magneer.

Xorlunder returned to the lead, turning more east than south. After half the day was spent, his shoulders slumped.

"Eraim gave us very few landmarks." The elf turned to Sullis. "Perhaps it *would* have been wise for us to remain with the host, as was your desire."

The Brondor paladin sighed. "That means nothing now."

"They've returned!" Gruelenor called from the rear of the group.

Hobgoblins approached from the west, and a pair of large animals led the way. The beasts stood over five feet high and were covered by filthy yellow fur, and fangs jutted from their long, narrow muzzles. But it was their red eyes that captured Nidor's attention. Though he had never seen the creatures before, he was sure they were Benasti wolves. Nidor read about the animals while at the compound, wanting to learn all he could of Benasti Forest after his encounter with Gruzim. The wolves were said to be especially cruel, preferring to torture their prey, and their skill at keeping their victims alive for several minutes while they feasted was well documented. There looked to be better than a score of Benasti warriors in the mongrels' wake, but the denseness of the woodland made it difficult to know for sure. The animals lifted their noses from the ground and roared as they spied their targets, sounding more in likeness to lions.

The hobgoblins released thick chains around the wolves' necks, and the beasts charged.

"To arms!" Sullis sprang forth with sword in hand.

Xorlunder launched arrows. Each found its mark through leaves and branches, and three hobgoblins fell. Sullis then met one of the terrible wolves, and the beast stood nearly as tall as the paladin. Sullis dodged to the side when the hound lunged, and he swung his blade, catching the animal on the hind leg. It growled as it scrambled from his reach, dragging the wounded limb behind it.

"You'll pounce no more today!" the Brondor paladin shouted as Nidor and Gruelenor charged past him to face the second wolf.

The hairs on the back of Nidor's neck rose when the animal bared its teeth, but then Gruelenor glowered at the monster, and its snarl faded as its eyes grew wide. Nidor was not sure what had come over the wolf, but he took advantage and dropped it with a fatal blow to the throat. He and Gruelenor then met the advance of five hobgoblins, dropping all of them with little difficulty.

Nidor spied a Benasti warrior skirting the trees toward Magneer's flank. The ranger stood over two enemy corpses and had just cleaved a third.

"Magneer!" Nidor called. "To your right!"

The warning became unnecessary when a shimmering light struck the hobgoblin, launching it into an unyielding tree. The evil warrior fell to the ground and ceased to move. Nidor looked past Magneer and received a nod from Melac.

Nidor rejoined Gruelenor, and they felled four more hobgoblins. Greater than a score now littered the forest floor, but the number of attackers continued to grow. It was as if a small army was upon them.

"There are too many!" Nidor shouted. "We must flee before we are overwhelmed!" While he spoke, more dark shapes moved among the trees to the left and right. "They are flanking us!"

Sullis added another hobgoblin to the tally of bodies, and then Nidor saw a black shaft suddenly protruding from the paladin's side.

"Archers!" Sullis grimaced while searching the forest.

Nidor spotted the line of Benasti bowmen, just as an arrow whistled past his head and a second one pierced his right shoulder. The missile bit deep and the pain was great, but he shut it out and cleaved an advancing hobgoblin.

"We must go!" shouted Xorlunder. "Now!"

"Melac!" Sullis called. "The archers!"

While Melac chanted, Nidor saw a hobgoblin approaching the mage from the side. He lowered his left shoulder and rushed, crashing into the fiend as Melac's spell was released; and a loud cracking of wood sounded not far away while Nidor skewered the Benasti warrior. Turning, he saw several large branches had fallen onto the bowmen.

"Fly! Now!" Sullis commanded.

Xorlunder continued shooting as Nidor climbed to his feet and ran past with Gruelenor. Ahead, Magneer led the way with Melac close behind—the two combined sword and magic to clear a path. Xorlunder then overtook them all, and Nidor slowed when he noticed Sullis struggling to keep the pace.

"Go!" Sullis said. "Do not wait for me. The mission must not fail because of me!"

"Keep moving, old man!" Nidor's tone held no kindness. "I cannot allow them to capture you!"

Sullis continued to labor, but he wore a satisfied grin. "Now you're thinking like a *true* warrior!"

Nidor stooped to give Sullis a shoulder to lean on, slowing his own pace, and Xorlunder released an arrow or two any time pursuit grew too close. Nidor then saw the elf's bow aimed straight at him. The arrow whistled just over his head, striking a wolf as it rounded a tree, and the shaft buried deep into the animal's throat. The creature failed to release even the smallest cry before tumbling to the ground.

Sullis stumbled and nearly fell, and Nidor threw the paladin over his shoulder, ignoring the protests that ensued. He was hampered then, but he pressed on, refusing to leave Sullis behind.

Suddenly, the trees gave way, replaced by a small clearing. A wooden house occupied the center, surrounded by a tidy yard of well-kept flowerbeds, and before the cabin, an elf sat on a log next to a fire.

Nidor's head spun. The company came to a halt, and he fell, spilling Sullis onto the ground. No hobgoblins pursued, but their shouts split to either side of the clearing and faded into the south.

"Elgarroth?" Xorlunder's eyes narrowed.

Everyone gaped in confusion as the small elf stood from the log and smiled. His white hair hung to his shoulders and his green eyes appeared to shine.

"Do not worry," Elgarroth said. "You are safe. Very few can find this place. Lucky for *you*, I suppose."

"This is indeed most fortunate." Xorlunder frowned. "Lest we have been overrun and slain."

"I promise you that has not happened." Elgarroth smiled. "Now come to the fireside and tend to your wounds."

Chapter 14

The Ford

Nidor was dumbfounded. Elgarroth. The traveler that came to him in Nira speaking of demons and gates; the same elf he saw with Merssa many times in the compound afterward. For months, Nidor had thought of asking the wizard about that day in Steadshire, but there was never an opportunity. It seemed Elgarroth appeared when a council was to be held and vanished once it was over. Never did Nidor see the wizard arrive or depart. He chose not to mention any of this to Merssa, because he feared Elgarroth might overhear him, and he learned long ago from the elders of his clan that a wizard's business was a wizard's business and no one else's.

"Come, we have wounds to treat."

Sullis shook Nidor from his thoughts. He looked at his companions, reminded of the arrow in Sullis's side and the cut on Magneer's arm. The pain then returned to his shoulder and he grimaced.

"I'll look after you first," he said to Sullis, and he received no argument while he eased the Brondor paladin onto a log near the fire.

Sullis nearly passed out while Nidor extracted the barbed arrowhead. The Brondor paladin then gaped in disbelief when Nidor called upon Silcor's Healing Fire and the flame engulfed his hand. He placed it on the wound and Sullis tensed, but then the paladin released a long breath.

"I was expecting an *herbal* treatment!" Sullis continued to stare in amazement. "You possess the skills of a great priest." He inspected his side. Not even a scar remained.

"Silcor has blessed me with gifts beyond my deserving," Nidor said.

"You're humble." It was difficult to know if Sullis was issuing an insult or a compliment. "But I would not be too hasty to make that judgment."

Nidor gave a wry smile and turned his attention to Magneer's arm.

"Take care of yourself first." Magneer spoke with more than a little force.

Normally, Nidor would have refused. His wounds always came last. He did not wish to offend Silcor with acts of self-worth—the powers were granted to serve. But with the look on Magneer's face, Nidor removed the arrow from his own shoulder and applied the flame, enjoying its fiery relief. Magneer nodded in satisfaction, and Nidor took care of the ranger's arm next.

Xorlunder and Melac possessed no visible wounds, and they watched Nidor with curious eyes as they seated themselves on a log by the fire. Several paces away, Gruelenor kept watch on the trees. Nidor noticed a couple of minor injuries on his krukari companion, but when he approached, it did not surprise him to see Gruelenor wave him off. He returned to the fire.

An elf stepped from the house bearing a large iron kettle. He was the most muscular elf Nidor had ever seen, taller than Salenti elves, but shorter than that of the Vermallon clans—a denizen of Dakreal Forest? Without a word or introduction forthcoming from Elgarroth, the servant placed the kettle on a hook above the fire and returned to the house.

"You can relax for the moment." Elgarroth turned to Gruelenor. "They will not find you here."

Gruelenor glanced back, but remained where he stood. Elgarroth smiled and spoke to Sullis.

"I see you have recovered quite nicely. Nidor possesses exceptional talents, does he not?"

Nidor avoided the wizard's gaze. Did no one understand it was not *he* that healed others? All praises belonged to Silcor.

Sullis nodded and looked at Nidor. "With this kind of healing, we should be able to depart at once."

"It seems that things have gone a bit awry." Elgarroth lifted his brow.

Sullis sighed, glancing at Xorlunder and Melac. "They might have been worse had we not come upon your home. But we cannot stay. Not even for tea."

"You will not get far before you are discovered," the wizard said. "Hobgoblins and more infest the area, searching for you."

"But why?" asked Xorlunder. "How did they know where to look for us? Or even that they should?"

"Trannum is cunning," Elgarroth nodded, "as well as farsighted. He has spies in many forms, be it undead, zhomian, or even among the living. And there has been plenty of time to seek the paths by which some have entered into his lands over the years. He knew the members of the Front would not sit idle forever."

"Can you see us through?" asked Magneer. "Surely your powers can hide us from their eyes."

"You have the aid of a wizard already, son of Pallit," replied Elgarroth.

Melac shifted on the log.

"And alas," the elf mage added, "I have many duties in need of my attention."

Elgarroth paused when the servant stepped from the cabin bearing clay mugs. The muscular elf removed the kettle and filled the cups with steaming water. After adding herbs, each of the company was served, including Gruelenor. The servant returned to the house.

"But," Elgarroth said once the door was shut, "you may stay until such a time that it is safe to continue. I will then set you on the path to the ford."

Sullis shook his head. "But the plan—"

"Do not worry." Elgarroth turned to the Brondor paladin, maintaining his calm demeanor. "Your delay will not bring ruin to the war. We made the plan with room for the unexpected, I assure you."

"But if you can hide your home from all eyes," Sullis spilled his tea in frustration, "then why can you not hide us from the hunters and let us be on our way?"

"It is enough that he has sheltered us from the enemy," Melac said with more emotion than Nidor was accustomed to. "Do not forget that we would have failed already, had he not allowed us to enter his home."

Everyone fell silent. Elgarroth puffed on his pipe, gazing at the fire as if he were alone.

"Master Elgarroth." Xorlunder gained the wizard's attention. "Can you tell us if the North Army is faring well?"

The wizard gazed to the northeast, as if the trees did not exist. "They have reached the first signs of snow within the forest. The snipers continue to hound them, but they are too large a force to deter. It is a shame the elves of Vermallon cannot help. Trannum has wisely kept them busy."

Sullis looked at the company and frowned. "We will stay then." The paladin turned to Elgarroth. "At least until a time you deem it safe to leave… So long as it's not too long. Merssa has put much trust in you. I suppose I should do the same."

Five days passed, and during that time they stayed in a large tent erected by the elf servant, whom everyone believed to be mute. They did their best to pass the time; Sullis sharpened blades, Xorlunder inspected arrows, Melac read from a book provided by Elgarroth, and Magneer and Gruelenor shared quiet conversations. Nidor had hoped to catch Gruelenor alone, feeling guilty for not defending his friend from Xorlunder's earlier accusations, but it seemed Gruelenor was avoiding him, so he let it be.

Everyone grew restless, except for Elgarroth. The wizard went about his daily affairs, often disappearing into the house for hours, but every day he provided bits of information to ease their minds, even if only a little. The North Army was doing battle in Nira and working their way south toward the first bridge. Resistance thus far was small, for the assault upon Vermallon Forest had spread the enemy thin. Of news to the south, Elgarroth said only that the South Army was slowly moving through Sardina.

That evening, while the others were occupied with their own affairs, Nidor found the wizard enjoying a pipe near the fire that never ran out of fuel. With the amount of firewood the elf servant had chopped since Nidor's arrival, it surprised him enough trees still existed to hide the house from the world.

"Paladin of Silcor." Elgarroth acknowledged Nidor's approach without looking. "Please, have a seat."

Nidor accepted the invitation, but he did not speak. Though he had been awaiting this opportunity, he began to doubt that it was truly Elgarroth that had come to him in Steadshire.

"Put your mind at ease," the elf said. "You did well in the caves of Selt. Much better than most would have."

That confirmed it.

"I have been wanting to ask..." Nidor paused, trying to decide which question to pose, in case the wizard allowed him only one. Why had the talk of gates been brought to *him*? Why impersonate a traveler in doing such? He shook his head. "No. That does not matter. But if I may, what of Ballrik? Where is he?"

"Of where he is and where he had gone," the elf replied, "you need not concern yourself. His act was one of great valor, but unfortunately, it will be known only to a few. Of his fate, he was spared the gruesome end that surely awaited him. Though his actions brought certain death unto him, he was not lost to the world of demons. Worry not of him or his whereabouts. Realize only that he has played an important role in making success in this war possible."

Nidor was not sure he understood Elgarroth's answer, but a great weight lifted. He smiled and asked no other questions.

Nearing evening of the eighth day since their arrival, Elgarroth informed the company the time had come. The North Army was assaulting the westernmost bridge over the Great East River, and the enemy's attention was drawn toward it.

"The party that hunted you has moved off to the east," Elgarroth added, "but the forest is not clear of danger."

"At last!" Sullis grinned. The paladin had threatened several times over the past couple days to go insane if he had to stay a moment longer. "Not that I don't appreciate what you've done for us," he said to Elgarroth. "It's just—"

Elgarroth smiled, holding up a hand. "I understand. Already *I* have tarried too long." He uttered the last comment softly. "If you exit around the back of the house, you will find yourselves upon Eraim's map. I wish you luck."

They thanked Elgarroth as the elf walked toward the house. After one last wave, the wizard entered the dwelling and left them alone.

"I just hope it's not too late," Sullis muttered.

"He wouldn't have kept us this long if it would have proven ill," Melac said.

Sullis gave the mage a wry smile.

At the rear of the house, they found a small path entering the trees. They followed it with Xorlunder at the lead, and after twenty paces it disappeared. Nidor looked back and noticed it had vanished completely. There was no sign of the path, the clearing, or the wizard's house.

"He has been true to his word!" Xorlunder pointed to a gnarled tree with a root protruding from the ground, appearing as a hand reaching from the grave. "It is morbid, but unmistakably one of Eraim's landmarks."

They headed south with renewed strength. Darkness arrived with no signs of hobgoblins, wolves, or undead, and while they camped everything remained quiet. The next day, just after noon, Xorlunder grew excited.

"I hear the river. It is not far now."

"Stay alert," said Nidor. "Elgarroth warned the woods are not safe."

"Yes." Sullis nodded. "Keep your eyes open and weapons at the ready."

Xorlunder continued, checking Eraim's map often and scanning the surrounding forest. The elf stopped before an old cedar bent in a strange position, and Nidor now detected the unmistakable sound of rushing water.

"This must be it." Xorlunder gazed at the large tree. Shaking his head and speaking in a level tone, he added, "Eraim described it as a squatting dog."

"I see it!" Magneer pointed. "The big tree is the body, that small tree the tail, and that other tree looks like a—"

"I did not say I failed to see what she—" Xorlunder sighed, looking again at the map. Then he nodded with satisfaction to Sullis. "We are on course."

"Those rocks are definitely a pile of—"

"I said I see it!" Xorlunder walked away.

From the tree, Xorlunder marched deliberate steps south, west, southwest, and then due south until the river was before them. To the left, a mountain river joined forces with the Great East River, creating an impassable torrent of raging water. Across the river, above the trees and less than a mile away, the Candermane Falls roared.

Xorlunder walked a careful line, stopping well before the junction of rivers. Near the bank, the elf stooped among the undergrowth between a couple of large maples and uncovered a hidden raft. It amazed Nidor at how well the construction of small logs had blended with the surrounding foliage, and he realized Xorlunder's apprehension at approaching from the wrong position—large maples were everywhere, and it could have taken hours to find the raft otherwise. From one of the two trees, Magneer located a rope concealed by natural growth around the tree's trunk, and Xorlunder pulled some of its slack from the river and locked it into a harness upon the raft.

"What was that?" Melac said above the rushing water, peering into the trees to the northeast while Xorlunder steadied the raft onto the river.

Everyone froze and scanned the woodland. Nothing stirred.

"I thought I saw something moving." The mage sighed. "Perhaps it was just a rodent."

"Let us go." Sullis glared at the forest with contempt. "And leave this place behind."

They loaded onto the raft, and Xorlunder began pulling them across the river. Magneer seemed to grow anxious and assisted the elf, and the construction groaned as the current pulled them and the rope stretched thin. But the ford held.

They neared halfway across when Nidor's heart sank. From beyond the trees along the northern bank stepped hobgoblins and Kalmiran soldiers, as well as a group of dunarchins, and all were armed with bows. It made Nidor sick to see the living working with the undead.

"Archers!" he shouted.

A volley was released, and two of the missiles struck Nidor as he moved to protect Magneer and Xorlunder, one in the thigh and the other in his arm. Another pierced Gruelenor's right side while one found its way into Magneer's forearm. The remaining arrows landed in the water or stuck into the raft.

"Xorlunder! Gruelenor! Your bows!"

Before Sullis finished the order, Xorlunder had already swung his bow from his shoulder and fired an arrow, taking out a hobgoblin. Gruelenor was not so swift, and the elf felled two more by the time he fired a shot.

A second volley was released from the shore, and as a dunarchin cast a spell, the incoming missiles were suddenly alight. Nidor knocked aside a flaming arrow with his sword as a second one grazed his neck, and one pierced Xorlunder's shoulder while another struck Gruelenor in the chest. Several missiles stuck into the raft, setting fire to the wet timbers at once.

Nidor spread his fingers, and his vision was tinted deep orange as he called upon Silcor's aid. He wrapped his will around the flames, pulling them into himself until the fires dissipated into harmless smoke, and little did he feel their heat, for his soul burned hotter. He exhaled and his vision returned to normal.

Gruelenor's face was twisted from pain, but he stood tall, nocking arrows and dropping two more Kalmiran soldiers. Xorlunder felled three more hobgoblins, and Melac released a globe of fire that struck the ground near the dunarchins. The ensuing explosion cast three of the undead into the forest, never to be seen again.

Sullis joined Magneer, and the two pulled the rope. The raft picked up speed, but also it rocked violently as it fought against the current. This did nothing for Gruelenor's marksmanship and his next shot landed on the shore, but Xorlunder was ever on the mark, dropping a Kalmiran soldier that had just struck the rope with a sword.

Lightning streaked from the dunarchin mage, enveloping Nidor in convulsing pain. He fell to the deck, very near to the water, and Magneer dragged him from the edge. Gruelenor sat in the middle of the raft, shaking his head—the krukari experienced the lightning as well.

Another volley arrived, and an arrow struck Melac in the chest, nearly driving the mage overboard as he collapsed. Magneer received an arrow in the leg and Sullis one in the upper back; and though the Brondor paladin slowed, he continued pulling the rope.

The southern shore was still twenty yards off, and Nidor wondered how many of them would make it across the river alive, if any. Then the arrows ceased as a new arrival emerged from the trees—a large warrior covered in black armor. The figure wielded a great sword in each hand, and Nidor's heart sank further.

"No!" Xorlunder gasped.

In their current state, they were no match for a Death Lord. But to Nidor's surprise, the dark warrior cleaved the head of the dunarchin mage as the creature prepared to release another spell. The hobgoblins and Kalmirans backed away, retraining their bows on the warrior, and the undead firstborns pulled their swords.

Three more dunarchins fell at the Death Lord's feet as the archers fired, and four of the missiles found their marks but failed to penetrate the black plates. The figure continued swinging both swords with deadly precision, striking down the remaining dunarchins and several archers. Two other bowmen collapsed, pierced by Xorlunder's arrows, and the final three hobgoblins fled into the forest.

The raft reached the opposite bank at last, and Sullis secured it to the shore.

"What of the dark stranger?" asked Xorlunder above the distant roar of the falls.

The armored figure stood motionless across the water, gazing at them.

"Strange behavior for a Death Lord." Magneer limped onto the shore with some effort.

"He does not feel like one," Nidor said, remembering the unbearable chill that surrounded Gruzim. He helped Gruelenor from the raft, looking over his shoulder to keep an eye on the warrior. "And his eyes do not glow."

Sullis glanced across the river and shook his head. "I don't know. If times were different, I would send the raft back and learn his name; maybe even challenge him to a duel. But I do not know this to be anything other than a ruse, and we are in no shape to confront him. Let us be off before he grows wings!"

Sullis swung his sword onto the rope, severing it, and he shoved the raft into the water to be claimed by the rapids. The Brondor paladin then winced as he lifted the unmoving mage onto his shoulder and headed south.

Nidor, Gruelenor, and Xorlunder hesitated for one last glance across the river. Both swords were sheathed upon the figure's back and the warrior remained still. Xorlunder held up a hand and nodded in thanks, but the figure did not respond. They then moved to catch up with Sullis.

Wounded and weary, they left the river behind and made their way through scattered trees. To the left, the icy water cut a deep channel as it raced to join the waterway, and ahead the falls rose above the treetops, issuing from a cliff among the northern reaches of the Varlimor Mountains.

Every uphill step brought Nidor increasing pain, and he knew Gruelenor to be worse off than himself. He wondered how the krukari endured such agony.

"We must stop!" Nidor called out. "We cannot go on as we are."

Sullis dropped to one knee and placed the mage on the ground. "Do what you can," he said to Nidor. "But you must hurry. We do not know what is behind us. Nor how long the river will delay him."

CHAPTER 15

CANDERMANE TUNNEL

Nidor saw Gruelenor wince when he wrapped his fiery hand around the shaft protruding from the krukari's chest. He withdrew the arrow, healing his companion as he did so, and upon extracting the barbed point Gruelenor passed out. The wound was gone, leaving only a small scar. Gruelenor would recover. The second arrow was not so dire, and Nidor removed it as well.

"Melac is beyond my skill." Sullis was kneeling over the mage.

Nidor hurried to the wizard. Melac was in worse shape than Gruelenor had been, and the arrow was close to his heart. Nidor repeated the procedure, expending even more spiritual energy and driving himself almost to exhaustion. The wound closed, but Melac remained pale and he labored to breathe.

"He will need to rest," Nidor said. "He was far, very near to Death's Door, and will not recover too quickly."

"We'll give him what time we can." Sullis gazed down the slope. Only the rushing water and trees were visible. "We cannot stay long. Even if the dark warrior finds no way across the river, he may head east to the bridges. If he *is* our enemy, he'll alert them to our whereabouts."

Nidor tended to Sullis next, and together they cared for the others. The Brondor paladin applied herbs and wrapped wounds while Nidor cured all major injuries, taking care of himself last. He then sat heavily against a tree, lightheaded and fighting to keep his eyes open.

The sun was high, and scattered trees provided a wide view of the area, but the falls masked all sound. Gruelenor and Melac rested peacefully, and Magneer took a couple of long drinks from the river before rolling onto his back to do the same. Sullis and Xorlunder stood to either side, keeping watch on the forest and sky.

Nidor closed his eyes and allowed his senses to take over. He detected no evil. The air was cool, more so than was typical for early summer, and they were not yet high enough for the chillier regions of the mountains. This concerned Nidor, but it did not prevent sleep from taking hold.

Nidor awoke to Sullis shaking him. It was as if he had just fallen asleep seconds ago.

"It has been an hour," the Brondor paladin said, scanning the trees. "We cannot tarry any longer, but Melac will not wake. I'll have to carry him." Sullis walked toward the sleeping mage. "I have an ill feeling I cannot shake."

Gruelenor squatted over Nidor, looking much better than Nidor had expected.

"Are you all right?" Gruelenor extended a hand.

"I am fine." Nidor accepted his companion's help and was pulled to his feet. In truth, he could use a few more hours of sleep.

"Perhaps we should rest a bit longer once we are in the tunnel," Xorlunder said, eyeing Nidor with concern.

Nidor wondered how dire he appeared to draw such attention.

"Perhaps." Sullis lifted Melac over his shoulder. "But first we must get some distance behind us."

They resumed the climb, and not long afterward, patches of snow forced them to use tree limbs to steady themselves. Sullis had the hardest job with the extra weight he bore, but Magneer assisted the paladin through the rougher spots. The falls grew deafening as Candermane drew nearer, and trees became scarce, consisting solely of pines. Cold water sprayed often, creating ice along the channel's edge, and after another thirty yards, high cliffs allowed no farther progression to the south. To the left, the falls poured from a ledge fifty feet above.

Sullis placed Melac on the ground, and Magneer and Gruelenor kept watch on the descending slope. Xorlunder pulled Eraim's map and surveyed the area. His eyes then narrowed on four small pines.

"There." Xorlunder gave a nod.

The elf headed toward the trees and Nidor followed. The pines were close together, and Xorlunder pushed his way through the branches in the middle.

"There is a recess in the cliff wall," the elf said. "It may be a tight squeeze for some of you, but this must be it. I feel a breeze coming from within."

"We have located the tunnel!" Nidor called to the others.

Sullis sighed and lifted Melac back onto his shoulder. After reporting to the trees, he turned to Magneer.

"This is where you take the lead."

Magneer disappeared through the branches, returning moments later. "We'll need a torch."

No one possessed a dry torch, as the constant spray had drenched their gear. Magneer attempted to bring one to light, but it was hopeless.

Nidor placed his hand on the ranger's shoulder. "Hold out the torch."

Magneer complied, and Nidor touched the end, igniting it. Magneer gave a nod of thanks.

They pushed through the branches and into the opening. Magneer led the way, followed by Xorlunder, Sullis bearing Melac, Nidor, and Gruelenor. The ceiling and walls were saturated and the passage narrow, causing problems for Sullis, but after twenty feet the tunnel widened and things progressed more easily.

They trudged through brown puddles upon an uneven floor, and though muffled, the sound of the falls grew in strength. After another fifteen yards, the passageway widened further and the ceiling towered overhead. Water dripped from stalactites, creating a layer of slime beneath their feet, and all but Xorlunder placed a hand on the wall for added balance.

Ahead, light shone through a small window, accompanied by a constant spray of water. Nidor could see the window had been chiseled into a perfect square, and he wondered what purpose it served. Outside, the falls plunged into the raging river a hundred feet below, and the roar was louder than it had been elsewhere. The spray intensified when the company hurried by, as if objecting to their presence, and Magneer shielded the torch while icy water drenched them again. They left the window behind, and Candermane faded with it.

The tunnel twisted before them, always veering in what had to be an easterly direction, and soon the floor was dry, save for the wet prints left by their boots. The rough-hewn ceiling then shrank to eight feet, and after another mile they entered a small room.

A stone table sat to one side of the chamber, flanked by a couple of stone benches, and in the back corner was an iron-bound chest next to a basin of water. A firepit near the table held ashes, and next to the table was a neatly stacked pile of wood.

Xorlunder moved to the far side of the room to inspect the continuing tunnel. He turned back with a satisfied nod. Gruelenor, meanwhile, put an ear to the passage they had been following, and after a moment the tension in his shoulders eased.

All seemed secure, and Nidor sat on a bench and leaned against the wall while Sullis placed Melac on the table. Gruelenor moved to the far exit and held his sword ready, and Xorlunder joined Magneer as the ranger inspected the chest.

"It doesn't appear to have been here long," Magneer said. "It's not locked." He lifted the lid.

"We owe Eraim many thanks." Xorlunder set his bow aside. He then helped Magneer pull blankets, small packs, and dried leaves from the chest.

Sullis's brow furrowed upon seeing the leaves. "Healing herbs." He moved in for a closer inspection. "And rare ones at that, found deep within Vermallon. I've not seen these since my youth."

"They should come in useful." Magneer nodded toward Nidor.

Watching through the slits of his eyelids, Nidor gave a smile of approval.

"I do not know what use he'll be if we continue draining his energy this way," Magneer said to Sullis. "We'll need his sword once we reach the end of this tunnel."

"I shall be ready." Nidor smiled.

"I think it best we rest here a while," Xorlunder said. "Even if the black warrior has managed to cross the river, he may never find this passage."

"Night is near enough, I think." Sullis sighed. "We'll get some sleep. But I don't trust this place. No telling what creatures have wandered into it over the years. We'll keep watch on both tunnels."

They huddled in blankets and ate dried meats from the packages Eraim left for them, save for Melac, who was covered by two blankets and had not moved. Magneer arranged the wood into the pit and Xorlunder set it alight with the torch, but the chill emanating from the walls did not allow the heat to travel far, and they crept close. After the meal, Nidor shut his eyes and found sleep.

Nidor awoke to Xorlunder's touch. It did not feel like morning yet, but he was refreshed, and he breathed a sigh of relief to see Melac awake. The mage's coloring was restored, and the man listened while Magneer explained all that had transpired since the ford.

After a small breakfast, they added the remaining supplies of the chest to their packs. Magneer and Sullis then lit fresh torches before smothering the fire, and Magneer led the way into the eastern passage.

The tunnel stretched for miles, winding ever eastward and veering south at times. They followed it another day, sleeping in a second chamber Eraim had stocked with thick furs, and several hours into the following day they detected a fresh breeze. It was cool, bearing the scent of snow, and revealed to Nidor just how stale the air had become.

Another fifty yards, and the tunnel ended much like it began. The walls closed to a two-foot gap, veering sharply to the right, and the company exited into a copse of firs and maples.

A frigid wind cut into them while they stepped onto a snowy land. Nidor shivered as the breeze stung all exposed skin, and though the sun lay behind gray clouds, the day was bright and he shielded his eyes. They stood just east of the northern peaks of Varlimor, pinned between Vermallon Forest and stray mountains reaching out to the east, and all around them was undisturbed snow.

"No one has been this way in some time," said Xorlunder while they donned the fur cloaks. "Our tracks will be easy to spot. That is, if anyone is around to see them."

"A Death Lord will notice them easily enough if one flies over." Melac eyed the sky.

"Perhaps we should remain within the mountains and head south," said Magneer. "That would offer cover, as well as make our passing harder to detect."

"I agree." Sullis nodded to Magneer. "Lead on."

They headed southeast upon the rough, snow-covered terrain dotted by trees and boulders. The way was tricky, as occasional snowdrifts or sheer walls forced them east and west, but under Magneer's guidance they progressed. To Nidor's surprise, the chilling winds calmed as the day waned, and though no one made mention of it, he was sure the others noticed as well. Before the creeping shadows of evening engulfed them, Magneer located an outcropping of rock to serve as shelter for the night.

"There'll be no fire," said Sullis, pity obvious in his eyes. "Prepare for a cold stay."

While the company pulled blankets from their packs and laid them out, Xorlunder stood motionless upon a tall boulder, gazing through a window in the mountains to the east. Nidor followed the elf's gaze, but he saw only white land beneath a gray sky.

"What is it?" asked Melac.

"Smoke," Xorlunder replied. "It is thick and widespread. I wonder if it is the North Army. They should be in Peltagarr by now, if everything has gone to plan."

"Let us hope it is so," Nidor said with as much optimism as he could muster.

Xorlunder gave a small nod and dropped from the rock.

The winds returned through the night, and the urge to start a fire became difficult to resist. But Sullis remained resolute, and they huddled close, shivering violently and finding little sleep.

They resumed their trek at first light. The terrain grew rugged and they had to use ropes at times, but the air warmed while the day progressed, providing some relief. With the arrival of evening they turned due east, and though the land below showed patches of green, around the company it was not so—snow and boulders were all the mountains offered.

Magneer discovered a small cave appearing unused for some time, and they set up camp. Feeling fortunate that nothing had spotted them thus far, Sullis again decided against having a fire, even when the night chill invaded. But they were sheltered from the wind, and everyone found sleep.

As usual, Gruelenor and Xorlunder guarded the darkest part of the night. They stood to either side of the cave entrance, much closer than Gruelenor was comfortable with, gazing onto the still land. Their shift was nearly over, with nothing to report but a howling wind, and Xorlunder spoke.

"I cannot help but wonder about the warrior in black."

Gruelenor gave the elf a sidelong glance. For several nights they stood guard, and neither had uttered a word. Xorlunder had no love for Gruelenor, and Gruelenor bore no trust for the strange elf of

Orlenfel. He learned at a young age the ways of gray elves. They were reclusive, owning an ancient magic that came to all members of their race from sources unknown, and they kept that secret safe. About the only time a gray elf ever strayed from Orlenfel was in pursuit of killing hobgoblins or krukari. Though Gruelenor gained all his knowledge of gray elves from biased teachers he would never wish upon his own children—if he ever had any—he could not shake the distrust he felt. He offered no response.

"I almost feel we should have sent the raft back for him," Xorlunder added.

"It's hard to say," Gruelenor said at last, shooting the elf another glance. Were it not for his strong vision, Xorlunder would have blended perfectly with the cave wall. "But one thing's for sure: it was no Death Lord."

"What then?" Xorlunder turned to face Gruelenor. "Who would travel through Vermallon alone these days? It was a dangerous place before the war began, and it is even more so now."

Gruelenor shrugged. "I suppose. But if you can best a score of archers without a scratch, I guess you can go any place you wish."

Moments of silence followed. Xorlunder then spoke again.

"Where do you come from?"

Gruelenor did not know how to answer, or that he should. His mouth opened as he considered his response. "I have no home," he said at last. "Lest you call an inn room in Philen home." Gruelenor continued to gaze down the dark mountainside, and he could sense the elf's white eyes upon him.

"I have slain many hobgoblins and half-hobgoblins." Xorlunder furrowed his brow. "But never have I encountered a krukari with your skill and courage."

Gruelenor narrowed his eyes at the elf. Was Xorlunder trying to trick him into saying something? He remained silent.

"And I have never met one that did not wish good folks ill tidings," the elf added. "I hope you will continue to surprise me before it is over."

After another couple minutes of silence, Xorlunder headed deeper into the cave.

"We best wake Magneer and Nidor," the elf said. "I do not know about you, but I am very much in need of rest this night."

Gruelenor followed.

Four days passed while they continued east, veering south whenever the terrain allowed. Much to Nidor's relief, the air grew warmer with each day and the snow thinned. Having grown up in the desert, winter was a season he had only experienced since enlisting in the Front, and he was beyond weary of it. Patches of hard soil and plant life became more numerous and small groups of trees provided additional cover, and still the company saw and encountered nothing.

As darkness swallowed the mountainside that evening, Magneer located a shallow cave to shelter them. Once they were settled, Sullis made an announcement.

"We shall exit the mountains come morning."

"And what then?" asked Magneer. "We'll have no more cover."

"I've been pondering that," said Sullis. "According to the plan, the army is supposed to be stealing the enemy's attention while we pass between Benasti Forest and Lake Garaard, a journey needing two weeks. I do not believe we can count on that distraction anymore, not since the enemy seems to know of our presence, and our progress so far has been too slow." Sullis sighed. "Even so, two weeks beneath the open sky is too risky. There's only one choice." He looked at Xorlunder. "We'll need to conceal ourselves within the forest."

"Enter Benasti?" The elf's brows drew together, his eyes seeming to glow within the dim moonlight that seeped into the dank chamber.

"Only barely," Sullis said. "Enough to escape detection from above."

"That is just as dangerous as passing through the heart." Xorlunder shook his head. "Hobgoblins and wolves patrol the borders night and day."

"We could remain within the mountains a few days more." Magneer turned to Sullis. "Perhaps we'll find a way that does not slow us down so much. If we're lucky, we might even pass straight through the foothills and bypass Benasti all together."

"According to Eraim," said Sullis, "the foothills are where the Benasti wolves breed."

Nidor remembered reading that fact. He was surprised he had forgotten it.

"And besides," the Brondor paladin added, "I'll not waste countless more days searching for a path that may or may not exist."

"Is that more perilous than traveling beneath the open sky where a Death Lord may see us?" Magneer asked. "Or braving Benasti? As Xorlunder says, if we enter the forest even a little, we might as well pass straight through it."

"We could do exactly that." Gruelenor turned all eyes on him. Though Magneer's words had been drenched in sarcasm, Gruelenor's stone expression left no room for jest.

"And get lost?" posed Sullis. "I doubt even Xorlunder could guide us through those trees of ill repute."

"I can," Gruelenor said.

"*You?*" Xorlunder raised his brow.

"Years ago, my path led me through." Gruelenor shrugged. "It is not such a dangerous road for one of my race. It's been a while, but I remember it well enough."

Sullis looked long and hard at Gruelenor. "We have lost many days. First at the House of Elgarroth, and now picking our way through the mountains. I mention passing through the forest because it would be unexpected and save us valuable time. Now I wonder at what cost?" His eyes narrowed, never straying from Gruelenor. "I have no trust for you, nor any other krukari for that matter. And I made this point known to Merssa before the march began. But she would not hear it. She insisted you remain with Nidor and Magneer. And now, when I suggest skirting Benasti, *you* offer to lead us through it."

Gruelenor did not flinch. He continued to meet the gaze of the Brondor paladin, unwavering and unreadable. But Nidor sensed anger building within his friend.

"Very well," Sullis said at last. "We will pass through Benasti. Perhaps the forest is depleted of most of its denizens by now."

Xorlunder stared at Gruelenor with his strange eyes. Melac displayed his usual calmness. Magneer looked unsure.

Nidor awoke to violent shakings at the hands of Sullis. The Brondor paladin had been the sole guard for the last leg of the watch, and it was still dark and the night had grown deathly cold. Nidor could just make out the others while Sullis shook each of them in turn, and everyone's breath was thick.

"Did any of you hear that?" Sullis sounded desperate.

"It feels like..." Magneer's voice trembled.

"A Death Lord approaches!" Melac said with alarm.

The cave grew colder still, and traces of ice formed on the walls. Next came a distant, hollow roar and hiss that echoed into the night—the call of an undead dragon.

"There it is again," Sullis said. "Never have I heard such a sound." The paladin held his sword as he moved to the entrance.

"When did you first hear it?" Xorlunder joined Sullis, holding an arrow to his bowstring.

"Only moments ago," the Brondor paladin replied.

"To the back of the cave!" Nidor pushed Sullis and Xorlunder from the opening. "Get from sight!"

The company fell as far from the entrance as the cave allowed, and there they shivered beneath the growing chill of the evil aura. Nidor knew not why the Death Lord had come. Did it spy their tracks? Had it been waiting for them? His heart pounded.

The roar came again, causing everyone to jump as it passed from east to north. Seconds later, it sounded to the west, this time higher in pitch and more like a wailing, but it was cut short. Several hisses followed, as if the monster encountered something in the night, and all went silent. A breeze then swept across the mountains from west to east as the chill faded and the fear subsided.

"What happened?" Magneer whispered.

"I don't know." Sullis ventured a couple of steps toward the cave mouth. "And I'm not sure I wish to find out."

"The warrior in black?" asked Xorlunder. "Perhaps he has done battle with the Death Lord."

"Gather your gear." Sullis's silhouette turned to face the company. "We exit the mountains now."

"If it *was* him," said Xorlunder, "should we not wait? It seems he is not on the enemy's side."

"I doubt it was he." Sullis stared at the elf as the darkness lightened. "And we can ill afford to wait and find out. All we know for sure is that a Death Lord flew overhead. And if it did meet with something to cause it to turn tail, I do not wish to find out what it was. Not now. Too much is at stake."

"For all we know," added Magneer, "it simply spied our tracks and returned to Darmhorng to give a report."

"Perhaps there were two of them," said Melac. "The noises might have been some form of communication."

"I wish to learn more." Xorlunder turned to Sullis. "But you are right. Whatever it was will have to remain a mystery."

They left the cave and made their way down the mountainside in the dark. The sky continued to brighten with the coming day, though clouds remained overhead, and by the time they exited the foothills it was morning.

Xorlunder returned to the lead, and they skirted the mountains at a running pace. No one showed signs of tiring for some time, and Nidor failed to notice the disappearance of the snow until a warm breeze brought them to a halt.

With heavy breaths, they scanned their surroundings. To the right the Varlimor Mountains loomed, showing snow in high places, but all around the company grass and wildflowers danced upon soft gusts of warm air. Summer had arrived.

"The snowline has receded farther north since I was last here," said Melac. "Northern Kalmaar was covered, from Batorn Gulf to the Serpent's Tail."

Sullis nodded to Xorlunder. "Let's continue."

They abandoned the furs among a collection of boulders and moved on, walking and running as strength allowed. They made no stops for several miles, not even for food, until Xorlunder froze.

"What is it?" asked Sullis between breaths. "What do you see?"

"Benasti," Xorlunder replied somberly.

The mountains were ending, and just beyond the easternmost peaks was a dark line extending to the horizon. Benasti Forest.

"Never in all my life did I think I would enter that place." Xorlunder's focus never strayed from the trees. "The most loathsome woodland in all of Vaeldor, and we harbor it as a haven."

Without another word, they continued.

The ground sloped downward as the failing peaks to the right became heavily wooded, and soon they were outside Benasti Forest. The trees appeared normal enough, and birds and animals went about their daily routines. Still, Xorlunder balked.

"This is wrong." Magneer sighed. "Though I've never been in these lands before, even I have heard tales of this forest. Perhaps Xorlunder's hesitation is warranted."

"Must we discuss this again?" Melac asked. "What would you suggest?"

"I still believe the mountains are the better choice." Magneer turned to Sullis. "The peaks are not so high in these parts. There are surely paths I can find. I'll see us safely through, wolves or no."

Sullis took in a deep breath, scanning the woodland before them. He then gazed east and north. Turning to Gruelenor, he said, "Now is your part."

Gruelenor glanced at Magneer and Nidor before stepping beneath the trees.

CHAPTER 16

SNOWY TRAIL

The South Army remained within the walls of Palidur for four days, searching every building and mound of rubble for hidden undead. The bodies of fallen allies were then gathered in a massive pile outside the city and set alight. Merssa ordered the burning with a heavy heart, for Cafior's way was to bury the dead. But she did not know how long the blessings would last, and she could not afford an undead infantry rising behind her. Borse said many prayers while the fire was lit, deeply saddened by the act, but he did not disagree with Merssa's decision.

On the fifth day, the army prepared to march. Supplies arrived from the outpost across the bridge, as well as horses, and additional soldiers fortified the Holy City—Merssa could not bear the thought of it falling back into enemy hands. Bundled in furs, the South Army set out for Charndova.

Merssa and a cavalry of two thousand trampled a path before the soldiers, and they headed southeast as directly as possible. Years of winter had concealed the roads, however, and small woodlands often pushed them southward, more so than Merssa preferred.

On the fourth day after leaving Palidur, they happened upon a village half buried in snow. They searched for survivors, but found none. Neither did they encounter any dead—or undead for that matter.

"Where are the people?" Cavalor furrowed his brow. "Dare I imagine what the necromancer has done with them?"

"I doubt he would kill them merely to increase his ranks," Merssa said. "Fallen soldiers would better serve his army than farmers. The people of this village were likely herded off as cattle." A morbid thought, but one she believed to be true.

"I don't know which fate I would choose for myself," Cavalor said.

"Choose neither!" Merssa snapped. "Your fate lies elsewhere."

Cavalor fell silent.

Six more days passed, and still they encountered nothing but snow—a perfect blanket of white, untouched by foot or hoof. The increasing chill bit through Merssa's furs, and there existed no soldier that did not long for camp and a warm fire. But the fires were not always enough, and they lost several men through the nights. Their bodies were frozen with the brightening of the sky; and just as in Palidur, the corpses were destroyed.

The next morning, the clouds darkened and snow began to fall. As it continued throughout the day, the flakes became larger and more numerous, obscuring sight beyond forty yards.

"He knows we approach," said Landerik.

"Of course he knows!" Merssa was feeling cranky from the cold.

"How far do you think we've made it?" asked Cavalor.

"We're a few days north of Starlight Lake." Arkor had been silent most of the trip, seemingly lost in thought. "At least, we would be if we had decent roads and weren't leading an army."

With the night came stronger winds that danced with the fires, and keeping warm seemed impossible. The snowfall continued, and by morning a fresh layer had partially buried the tents. Supplies were dug up, and the day was off to a late start.

"Trannum!" Merssa called out in frustration. "You are a coward hiding behind your snow!"

The flakes ceased, and Merssa wished she had said nothing.

The army moved on, and though the snowfall had stopped, a haze now hid all things distant. Shortly after lunch, a shadowy presence appeared ahead and to the left—the Varlimor Mountains were less than five miles away. The view lifted Merssa's heart, feeling progress had been made. But also she was uneasy, for they had ventured farther east than she intended.

They placed another mile behind them when Merssa heard screams and shouts. Cavalor, Landerik, and Arkor hastened to keep up as she rode to the commotion among the middle ranks, and she found over two hundred zombies attacking the foot soldiers. The creatures were blue from countless days of lying beneath the snow, and fresh blood stained the white ground from victims already claimed. The motions of the undead were fluent, more in likeness to ghouls, and Merssa was reminded of a zombie years ago near King Arman Lake, after the Wind of the Dead had blown a second time.

Although her soldiers were slow to respond, they found the courage to fight back once Merssa arrived. She crushed the skulls of no less than a score of the creatures, and beside her, Cavalor struck down another dozen. Arkor had dismounted, as fighting from the saddle proved difficult with only one hand, and Landerik covered the one-armed warrior's flank from atop his horse. A horn sounded as the cavalry joined the fray, and the undead were overwhelmed.

Merssa surveyed the bodies. She estimated a hundred soldiers had been lost.

"Gather the dead," she said to Landerik.

She returned to the lead with Cavalor at her side. The defiant look on Landerik's face did not escape Merssa's notice, but she had more important matters on her mind.

"What is it?" Cavalor asked, reading her expression.

Merssa shook her head. "Did you see how the men reacted? That will not do."

"They were caught off guard," her son said. "They will be ready next time."

"I pray you are correct." Merssa's heart hardened. "They will need to be. Or all hope is lost."

After burning the dead, the army continued.

The wind was in their faces, rising and falling and numbing Merssa's cheeks, and the day toiled as the snow became deep. With the arrival of dusk, they halted and prepared for another chilly night.

Merssa stood in her tent, poring over maps, when a deeper chill descended. With it came a familiar feeling of fear.

"Death Lord!"

She bolted outside. By the light of the fires, she saw soldiers scrambling about. Some ducked into tents, some hid among the gear, and others held weapons while searching the shadows.

"A Death Lord is near!" she called out, gazing into the sky. The night revealed nothing.

"To the south!"

Wezlok drew Merssa's attention to a patch of blackness just below the clouds, reminiscent of the haze surrounding the Silent Marsh. She clutched her mace as the darkness neared, and the hideous roar of an undead dragon caused several soldiers to cower. Merssa squinted, and she spied the shining eyes of the large creature, as well as the rider upon its back. Fine points of light shone like blue diamonds, and the warrior held high a scepter.

"Gulthar!" Merssa detested the taste of the name on her tongue.

The ancient king of Marcove flew twenty yards overhead, but he did not attack. The skeletal dragon glided past and circled back, but then it gave another roar as it turned to continue north.

"Light arrows!" Merssa shouted. "Shoot him down!"

The archers hesitated, their eyes unsure—Merssa doubted they wished to gain the undead king's attention. And so it was that a single arrow struck the Death Lord in the back. Arkor stood next to a bonfire, and upon his wooden arm was assembled the pieces of his crossbow. Already he was lighting a second arrow, and many archers joined him. Over a thousand missiles then lit up the night, some finding their marks but most disappearing into the distant snow, and the soldiers' fears were realized when the dragon turned. "It comes again!" yelled a soldier, and they scurried from its path.

"Keep firing!" Merssa ordered. Though the archers acted out of fear for their lives, she feared the Death Lord discovering things she wished to keep hidden.

Half the archers released another volley, adorning Gulthar's armor with several arrows, but the undead king remained seated. He pointed his scepter, and from it came a dart of black energy. It struck an archer, and the man screamed as he collapsed, all the life drained from his body. Gulthar did this three more times as he passed, dropping three more soldiers, and the dragon breathed its cloud, killing another score. The Death Lord and its mount then disappeared to the southeast and the chill faded.

"Why has he gone?" asked Cavalor.

Merssa shook her head. "It would seem Trannum is testing us."

The next few days dragged by. No Death Lord was seen, but the army wandered through three more nests of buried undead, and the ensuing battles claimed five hundred soldiers.

On the eighteenth day since leaving Palidur, Charndova was in sight at last. Its walls stood fifteen feet high, with snowdrifts climbing to the top along the western side, and one of the thick wooden doors of the north gate sat ajar.

All was quiet.

The commanders began shouting orders and leading troops to their proper locations around the city. One squadron made their way to the west gate while another pushed through the snow to the east gate. The cavalry remained with Merssa on a direct path for the north gate.

No attack prevented their approach, and Merssa signaled the horsemen to ride forward. They swung the doors open, revealing a half-buried city, and nothing stirred, save for loose snow on the wind.

"Be on your guard," Merssa said, and she entered.

The city remained silent. Merssa expected ghouls to jump from dark doorways or zombies to crawl from beneath the snow, but there was nothing. An evil presence existed, but it was distant. Perhaps miles away.

"Maybe it's like the village we saw two weeks ago." Cavalor scanned the city. "The people may have been taken."

Merssa stared at the vacant buildings. "This makes no tactical sense. This would have served as a mighty defense to our entering the mountain pass." She turned and addressed a horseman. "Go and fetch Borse."

Borse rode to the rear, for Merssa did not want her husband involved in direct combat. It was not long before he arrived.

"Tell me what you feel," Merssa said.

Borse closed his eyes and concentrated. "There was great evil here. But it was removed, not long ago." He opened his eyes and turned to Merssa. "A week perhaps. I also sense a presence. A distant evil."

"Perhaps it comes from the keep," said Arkor.

Borse shook his head. "The keep is too far away. It is closer, but I cannot say where."

Merssa addressed the cavalry captain. "Bring all forces into the city. I want every building and snow drift searched before nightfall." Turning to Cavalor, she added, "Secure buildings capable of sheltering the men and set a watch upon the walls. It might serve us well to camp indoors tonight."

CHAPTER 17

SECRET PATHS

Eraim studied the niches in the snow, where she was sure undead had been hiding for some time. It was enough to make her skin crawl.

"This doesn't look good." Soren gazed at the stack of burned bodies. Wisps of smoke still drifted high into the air.

"This is the fourth such pile we have seen," Selanna said. "Did the undead come from beneath the snow again?"

"Most certainly." Eraim returned to her saddle.

"How many soldiers march in the South Army?" Concern plagued Nilborg's rosy face.

Eraim considered the corpses. "A third of their original number, perhaps." Were the bodies not melted together, she might have given a better estimate.

"That isn't much." Rholmar shook his head and sighed. "Let us hope they can still complete their objective."

The members of the companies bound for the mines and swamp moved on in single file, as they had over the past ten days while riding in the wake of the South Army. They wore white furs from the great wolves of the north—Eraim had purchased them from Andrian hunters many months prior—and sat atop pure white horses, making them nearly invisible to prying eyes from above. This theory had gone untested, however, as they had seen nothing within the skies.

To the east, Eraim could just make out the Varlimor Mountains through the haze, a place with which she would soon become more acquainted. She shuddered at the thought, wondering if it would be better to remain *on* the frozen land than go under it.

The next day brought them within sight of Charndova. There were no signs of any battles having been fought outside its walls, and Eraim spied a dozen sentries—small, dark figures ambling along the ramparts.

"Are they undead?" Rholmar asked.

"No," Eraim replied. "They are of the South Army."

"Were they not supposed to have marched into the pass this morning?" Rholmar looked at Soren.

The Arronaus paladin nodded.

"I would dearly like to know how things have gone for them," murmured Nilborg. "What if they need our help?"

"Alas, we must trust Merssa," Soren said somberly. "And we have remained too long already."

The Soleran paladin led the way south, finally stepping from the trampled path of the army and riding onto untouched snow. A visible trail would now be left behind, but there was no choice in the matter. Their hopes lay in Merssa keeping the enemy's attention on her.

The towering mountains guided the company south, and after two days, the Southwood appeared on the right. Ahead, the Fire Hills came into view, and though Eraim knew the sun to be setting at that moment, the illusion of fire dancing upon the hill's reflective stones remained hidden. Even if the sun *were* to show itself, it would only amplify the sheen of white covering the rugged terrain. It was an odd sight, for winter rarely touched the Fire Hills; and on the occasions when it did, its visits were short. Eraim's heart ached with the realization that she had taken for granted the dazzling display of the past, and she wondered if she would ever witness it again.

"This will be our final evening together," said Soren while they readied to camp. "Our paths part come morning."

The night was cold and quiet, and as it had been throughout their journey, no fire was lit. Everyone paired up and burrowed into thick bundles of furs to keep warm, and they spoke no words, as all thoughts were surely bent on the days to follow.

With the morning, they shook off the chill as best they could. It was the day Eraim had been dreading most, at least for the time being. Not only did she realize she might never again see those headed for the swamp, but also she understood that once she entered the dwarfish mines, there was no guarantee she would ever find her way out.

Rybeal and Selanna used their powers to heat water, as they had done often over the course of the trek, and tea was made to warm everyone's insides. While they enjoyed the drink, Soren and Greyor split the gear for the two companies, the Soleran paladin keeping most of it within his possession. It was then time to say their goodbyes.

"Take care, my love." Arrikan gave Pallit a kiss.

"I will see you at the castle." Pallit offered a smile.

"May Arronaus watch over you," Rholmar said to Selanna and Eraim.

"He won't be able to." Millord shrugged. "His realm is the sky. 'Tis Cafior's blessings we need in the mines. Or if you really wish for the best, you'd better add a prayer to Meldar. 'Tis dwarf country we aim for!"

Rholmar smiled and bowed. "So be it, Master Millord. May Cafior's Will guide you, and Meldar's Might see you safely through."

The dwarf nodded with a grin of satisfaction.

"We'll see you at the castle," Soren said to Selanna.

"To confront the *Might and Strength of Evil Bone*," Eraim added without thinking.

CHAPTER 18

MOUNTAIN PASS

Merssa sat in a tavern near the center of Charndova, contemplating the situation. The battle for Palidur had been hard fought, and though the men exhibited great courage, their true fears surfaced after leaving the once-Holy City. They panicked and were unorganized when faced with the enemy's lowest minions, when the zombies had risen from the snow. This brought Merssa little confidence for the road ahead, for Ironside Keep possessed horrors yet to be experienced. No soldier was present when she fought Cadorn, and the meeting with Gulthar had been brief.

Even with the casualties sustained thus far, things should have been worse, and Merssa wondered why they had not been. Charndova was deserted. Why? The necromancer could have thwarted their advance or introduced heavy losses. The thought occurred that Trannum *wanted* her to enter the pass, and if he devastated her forces before she arrived, she might turn back and never spring the trap.

At present, Merssa sat in council with Borse, Cavalor, Arkor, Wezlok, and Landerik, as she had the past couple of nights, attempting to determine what Trannum was up to and how to counter it. But ideas were slim. They should have departed from Charndova two days ago, but Merssa's concerns caused her to balk; and as the sun set on the third day, she knew a decision must be made. The eyes of the enemy needed to remain affixed upon the North and South

Armies, and sitting idle too long could jeopardize those marching in secret.

"As I have said before," Landerik stirred Merssa from her thoughts, "we advance on Ironside and take it with as much force as we can muster." The young paladin stood and pounded his fist on the table with his next statement. "Brondor rewards those brave enough to march, and punishes those lacking the courage to act. Surely we'll lose lives, but is that not why we brought an army?"

"You have said this every night." Cavalor rose to glare across the table at the Brondor paladin. "And *our* opinions have not swayed. We need at least half our current number to take Kembald."

Landerik held a level gaze, not backing an inch. "The road to Kembald is through the pass, is it not?"

"The keep's defenses are strong," Arkor said. "If properly utilized, our entire force could be destroyed."

"*If* they are properly utilized!" Landerik pointed a finger in the air. "Which I do not believe will be the case. Did you see them atop the walls of Palidur?"

"Those were zombies and skeletons." Cavalor waved his hand. "There are surely dunarchins ahead, and they will prove much deadlier a foe. And let's not forget Radaam."

"Though I do not wholly agree with the young paladin," Wezlok issued a sidelong glance toward Landerik, "he is correct to a point. We have no choice but to proceed to the keep, for we can hardly achieve our objective in this city. It has been three days, and we have seen no sign of the enemy. Apparently, they are content with our presence here."

"And meanwhile," Landerik added, "they continue to prepare for our approach."

"Perhaps you would ride at the lead," Cavalor said, "since you are the *bravest* among us."

Landerik gave an arrogant grin. "I did not fear Cadorn, and I do not fear Radaam."

"And that's why you failed to keep your position in the heart of Palidur," said Cavalor. "Don't think I didn't notice you abandoning your post to attack the Death Lord. You are irresponsible, and cannot be trusted to—"

"Silence!" Merssa glared at the two until they took their seats. The arguments were the same as the night before, and the night before that. They were all correct. In the end, there was no option other than to proceed, and Merssa had put it off long enough. "We march in the morning." Her words brought a smirk to Landerik's face and concern to that of her son's. "Others are counting on us." She shook her head and sighed. "Inform the men."

Landerik, Cavalor, and Arkor stood.

"Pack only what we must," Merssa added. "The pass will surely be buried in snow, and we don't need unnecessary burdens weighing us down."

As the warriors left the tavern, an icy breeze swept through the room, reminding Merssa of the winter that awaited come morning. She looked at Borse, and he gave a half-hearted smile and patted her hand.

Cavalor walked with Arkor and Landerik toward the general's quarters. His mother made the only decision available, Cavalor knew, but he hated that Landerik was so pleased. The Brondor paladin had been speaking ill of the entire plan that took years to map out, even since before leaving Sendorum, and Cavalor had had enough.

"It's the right thing to do," Landerik said. "I just don't know why it takes you Palidurians so long to make decisions. No wonder your city fell."

"Guard your tongue!" Cavalor gave the paladin a shove. "I'll hear no more of your pompous words! Were it not for my mother and it were up to you, we all would have died on Palidur Bridge!"

"She's not even your mother," Landerik said under his breath with a sarcastic chuckle.

Fire rose from Cavalor's stomach and into his scalp. He moved toward the paladin, but Arkor stepped between them.

"We've a common enemy." The one-armed warrior put his hand on Cavalor's chest. "Or have you both forgotten? It's time we bend our minds on the necromancer, don't you think?"

Cavalor glared at Landerik. The paladin smiled. But Arkor was right and Cavalor yielded.

Arkor turned to Landerik. "*You* inform the general."

Landerik scowled as he walked away.

"Cavalor," Arkor said once they were alone. "I learned long ago not to let others bring me to anger by mere words. Had I not, I would never have found peace, or the great friendship I share with Duke Rholmar. My life, perhaps, might already be spent."

Cavalor gazed down the street where Landerik had gone. "My whole family is here." His ire turned to anxiety. "I fear after tomorrow there will be nothing left of it. My mother is strong and my father wise, but they are both aging. I fear for them, and for Vaeldor, for the land will be at a loss with their passing." He shook his head, gaining his composure. "As for me, I was raised to fight this war and have never planned a life beyond it. But my parents..."

"I know how you feel." Arkor placed his hand on Cavalor's shoulder. "I have lost much while stowing away in a far-off place. Had I been there for my brother in his hour of need, he might be alive today." He gazed at the night sky. It was overcast, as it had been since leaving the compound. "I do not plan on seeing any of my friends once this is over. Nor have I thought beyond retaking Ironside Keep for that matter. Long I took for granted that Vikur would remain Lord of the Keep until he had grown old and weary. Even when I learned of its fall and his misfortunes, I remained far away, thinking of it as only a story." Arkor's face was grim. "For that, I will never forgive myself. It's too late to save my brother. It's not too late to avenge him." After a moment, Arkor smiled. "Go now!" He swatted Cavalor on the back. "Go to your parents. The time of counsel is over. Enjoy this night with your family while it lasts."

Horns echoed off the mountains as Merssa sat on her horse before the east gate. The morning sun was yet an hour away, but the soldiers were prepped and ready. The wooden doors swung open and the march began.

A wind greeted them, as if a Death Lord was near, but Merssa knew there to be none—the aura of evil was still far off. The gusts continued, strong and constant, and as the sky attempted to brighten with the coming day, dark clouds rolled in and all remained gloomy.

Less than a mile was placed between the army and Charndova when the ground rose. The Varlimor Mountains loomed to the north and south, glaring down as the pass drew near, and undisturbed snow filled the gap between the mighty giants, creating an arc from one cliff to the other. Merssa pushed through snow six feet deep, but after a short distance it fell to a mere foot in depth. The cavalry then withdrew to the rear ranks while Merssa, Arkor, Cavalor, Landerik, and Wezlok remained mounted at the lead with several of the officers.

The road narrowed as the mountains closed in, forming high walls to either side, and the men marched eight across while the cavalry rode four abreast. A light snow fell, quickly becoming thick and steady, and with the swirling winds, Merssa's vision dropped to thirty yards. The sky then grew as dark as the night, and thirty yards shrank to thirty feet. Torches were lit, but the lights provided little help.

"And so he greets us," Wezlok said above the whistling wind.

Merssa did not respond.

A few more miles passed, and Merssa was weary from the chill. They had had the pleasure of resting indoors for three days with hearths blazing and windows shuttered, and though most of the daylight hours were spent outside, nothing could have prepared her for the winds that assaulted the pass.

It was well past noon, as far as Merssa could tell, when the mountains to the left were replaced by a steep drop into an unseen valley. The ravine was over a thousand feet below and served as one of the natural defenses for Ironside Keep. Unfortunately, the sudden disappearance of the wall caught a lieutenant by surprise, and he and his horse tumbled into darkness. Their faint screams were swallowed by the wind howling twice as loud with the opening of the pass.

Merssa slowed the pace, allowing the left side to tread more carefully. But after another half mile, the snow turned to ice and more lives were claimed by the gorge. She then issued orders to reduce the ranks, and the horses rode two by two while soldiers walked four abreast, hugging the wall rising hundreds of feet to the right.

The wind gusted stronger still, unhorsing a rider and casting him to his death, and soldiers fought to remain standing while some slid toward the ledge. They scrambled to grab hold of anything within reach, including one another, to stay on the road.

"We must pick up the pace!" Landerik shouted, his horse laboring to keep up with Merssa's and Arkor's. "We'll lose too many men at this rate!"

"Be still!" Merssa knew Landerik to have little concern for the actual loss of lives. She turned to Cavalor, her son riding beside the Brondor paladin. "Have them lock arms and form chains!"

Cavalor issued the order, and Merssa's words spread. How far the army stretched behind her, she could only imagine—three ranks of soldiers were all the storm revealed beyond her officers, and the torches failed to penetrate the veil of snow.

The road turned sharply northward, and after another quarter mile, it bent back to the east in a wide arc. The mountains then grew darker with the approaching night, and a stairwell appeared, carved into the rock on the right and winding its way upward. Farther on, the path continued until veering southward, and above them, the snow-covered keep rose into the storm, its windows dark and barely visible.

They had arrived.

A thunderous crash sounded back down the road, and muffled shouts accompanied the commotion.

"What's that?" Merssa looked over her shoulder in vain.

"Avalanche!" said Arkor.

The rockslide washed over the mountain pass like a dark wave, and stifled screams lasted only moments as soldiers were crushed or swept away. Thoughts of Borse came to Merssa, and she paled. But the horror did not end there, for the night grew deathly cold, and Merssa's heart pounded hard within her chest. A Death Lord approached.

Ahead, the snow swirled violently off the road and over the chasm, and the hollow roar of a skeletal dragon penetrated the wind as the beast rose from the depths. The monster was at least thirty feet long, and upon its back was the Death Lord. Arrows rained from the keep's towers as the dragon landed before Merssa, and another avalanche sounded back down the pass.

The trap was sprung. There was no hope for survival, let alone taking the keep.

"Go!" Merssa said to Arkor. "Full retreat! Get the men out of here!"

Merssa pulled her mace and turned to face the Death Lord. She held the weapon high, and it shed its golden light, penetrating the darkness better than any torch and revealing the enemy before her. It was not Radaam, but Jurak, judging by the enormous axe he wielded.

"I will not leave you!" Arkor pulled his sword.

The resolve on the one-armed warrior's face was unmistakable, but Merssa needed the troops to escape. She could hold off the Death Lord long enough for that... She hoped.

"You must! It's me he wants!" Merssa looked into Arkor's eyes. "I give command to you. You must return and finish this!" She glanced back at Cavalor. "Sound the retreat!"

Cavalor stared in shock, realizing the doom his mother accepted. He shook the thought and his wits returned, but when he raised the horn,

Landerik slapped it from his hand. It shattered on the ice and disappeared over the cliff.

"There will be no retreat!" The paladin pulled his sword. "Brondor smiles tonight!"

The battle rage in Landerik's eyes was almost maniacal, and Cavalor was powerless as the paladin sounded the horn to advance. Several horns echoed the call as the order traveled along the ranks.

"What have you done?" Cavalor demanded.

"What must be done!" Landerik laughed, clicking his heels and driving his horse toward the winding steps that led to the keep.

Merssa rode forward, hugging the wall to avoid the archers in the towers. Her eyes then grew wide when the horn sounded, for it was not the tone for retreat, but the signal to charge. She saw Landerik with the horn to his lips, and answering calls echoed in response. Next came the roar of the advancing army.

She had no time to ponder the situation further, for Jurak urged the dragon forward. The monster's skinless wings stirred the snow into a blinding torrent, but when Merssa twirled her mace overhead, the golden aura grew, causing the undead mount to rear and hiss. She charged, snapping several bones from the dragon's ribcage with a single swing and driving the creature back. Arkor joined her, having abandoned his saddle, but his sword had little effect.

The dragon continued backing from Merssa against its rider's wishes, and she heard the Death Lord cursing in a strange tongue. She pushed her enemy to within inches of the ledge... But then her horse lost its footing.

Merssa's mount, a faithful animal she had ridden for years, fought to remain standing as it slid from the road and disappeared over the cliff. Merssa jumped in time, grabbing hold of a rock protrusion to keep from sharing the animal's fate, but her mace slipped from her grasp and the golden light vanished.

The dragon's fear turned to malice and it snapped at Arkor. Its teeth sank into the flesh of the one-armed warrior's horse as he danced behind the animal, and he shrank against the cliff wall while the poor mount was thrown into the chasm. Merssa then gasped in horror when the bone dragon inhaled deeply. Yellow vapors swirled within its chest cavity, and she could do nothing as the creature thrust its long neck down the pass and released its poison onto the advancing army. Many screams ensued, short-lived and muffled by the wind.

Merssa did not look to see the results of the breath. She needed to reclaim her mace. She scrambled across the road, slipping as she lunged and grabbed hold of the weapon, and before she recovered, the dragon raked her left side with its claw. The bone talon sliced Merssa's silver armor as if it were leather, and she bore the pain while she rolled onto her back, holding the mace aloft. The golden glow returned and the monster reared.

Merssa regained her feet and shattered one of the dragon's bony wings. The beast retreated a step, but there was no room. It clawed frantically at the ice as its hindquarters slipped from the road, and its remaining wing flapped wildly, but its ability to fly was impaired. With a hissing shriek, the undead mount disappeared over the edge, but not before Jurak sprung from the dragon's back and rolled to his feet.

The Death Lord's eyes penetrated the storm, causing Merssa's heart to race, and with great effort she swallowed the pain of the dragon's claw and readied for the evil warrior's approach. The dark axe gleamed within Merssa's golden glow while Jurak swung it in circles from side to side—a weapon most men would have struggled to lift, the undead king played with it like a toy.

Jurak brought the axe down with amazing speed, and Merssa barely dodged the blow. The weapon bit into the road, cutting a foot deep and splattering black liquid onto the ice. Merssa countered, but Jurak evaded the strike while pulling his axe free. In the same motion, the Death Lord swung the weapon low, and Merssa jumped over the attack. But when she landed, she lost her footing and fell onto her back.

Jurak twirled the axe and brought it down, but the blow did not land. Arkor crashed into the Death Lord, screaming the war cry Vikur used when performing the same tactic. The simple maneuver unbalanced the dark king, and though he appeared undaunted by the slick road while fighting Merssa, Jurak slid from the pass. Unfortunately, Arkor followed.

"No!" Merssa scrambled, feebly reaching out her hand.

Arkor was gone.

Merssa released a gasp of exasperation and struck the road with her metal fist.

"Merssa!"

The muffled call came from below, and Merssa spotted a black hook planted into the road's edge. She crawled over to find Arkor dangling above the chasm, probably grateful at last for losing his arm all those years ago.

Merssa pounded her mace on the ice, creating jagged areas where she could brace her feet, and then she sat and removed her gauntlets. Leaning forward, she grabbed hold of the cold hook; and digging her boots into the niches, she used every bit of strength she possessed to pull Arkor onto the pass.

Merssa and Arkor panted as they climbed to their feet. Behind them, thousands of soldiers and horses littered the road, but the army must have gained access into the stronghold, for the clash of steel rang into the night.

Merssa pulled on her gauntlets while Arkor grabbed a sword to replace the one he lost to the chasm. They then raced up the steps and into the keep, passing a twisted gate and entering a gruesome chamber. More than a score of soldiers bled upon the floor, their eyes blank and unaware, and sharing the space were a dozen motionless ghouls. Screams and shouts echoed faintly from an open iron door, where a stairwell climbed to the upper levels, and to the left, another open door revealed additional sounds of battle.

"Borse! Cavalor!" Merssa called out. Though her side was hurting, she needed to find her family.

"I'll go up!" Arkor passed through the iron door and ascended the stairs.

Merssa entered the corridor leading to the keep's tavern. Bodies of soldiers and foes were strewn about the hallway's length, and most of the doors were open. From the third doorway on the right, a voice rose above the clash of steel. It was General Vargen.

Racing to the door, Merssa found Vargen with half a dozen soldiers. The general fought valiantly in the face of five dunarchins, but his men were outmatched and provided little help. Four soldiers were motionless on the floor alongside a pair of dunarchins, and Vargen added another undead firstborn to the tally.

Merssa's golden aura washed over the chamber as she advanced, and the dunarchins cowered while she smote two. Courage then lit up the soldiers' faces, and they destroyed the remaining two, losing one more of their companions in the effort.

"Have you seen Cavalor or Borse?" Merssa asked.

"I've not seen them." Vargen shook his head. "It has been chaos since we entered." His eyes were then downcast. "I am sorry we did not help against the Death Lord."

"There's nothing you could have done," Merssa said without patience, and she turned from the room to seek her family elsewhere.

Once in the hallway, Merssa stopped to listen. From beyond the tavern door at the far end came muffled sounds of battle. She ran and threw open the door to find Borse with a score of soldiers, battling a mixture of dunarchins and ghouls. Borse wielded his hammer, a weapon too large for one of his age, yet he swung it with ease, damning the creatures as he crushed them. A few bleeding wounds were visible on his body, but he stood taller than Merssa had seen him in years, reminiscent of the priest she met in Cafdella. Before she could offer help, the room was cleared of evil, and only the stench of the undead remained.

"Where's Cavalor?" Merssa asked.

"He went up to the towers." Borse's voice was deep and clear, as if he were twenty years younger. To the remaining soldiers, he said, "To the towers!"

Merssa had never seen Borse behave so. The men exhibited bravery beyond their means as the aura of his soul gave them strength, and she was sure they would follow him if he dove off the mountain pass.

She and Borse led the soldiers back to the stairs, and Vargen and several others joined them. Merssa was first to ascend the narrow steps, and she had to jump over a pair of hideous ghoul corpses — one was impaled upon a blade while the other looked to have had its head torn open. She continued into the Great Hall, where Arkor was locked in combat with a single dunarchin. To the left, Landerik and three soldiers were hard pressed by an endless stock of ghouls issuing from a tower, and to the right, Cavalor and Wezlok battled more than a dozen dunarchins.

Merssa ordered Vargen and most of the men to join Landerik, and with Borse, she led the remaining soldiers to aid her son.

"I'll go up!" Arkor said to Merssa, and he bolted for the stairs.

The turmoil in Merssa's eyes did not escape Arkor's notice, and concern for her family was plain upon her face. He wished he could remain to help, but the keep was the only family Arkor had left. He needed to take it back.

Corpses of fallen soldiers and undead littered the stairwell, but Arkor ignored them, racing two steps at a time until a pair of ghouls impeded him. Fresh blood stained their lips and claws, and Arkor thrust his sword into the lead ghoul and drove it into the other. Dark, nauseating ichor spilled onto the steps while the fiend bit and scratched Arkor, but he did nothing to fend off the attacks. He buried the blade to the hilt, killing the abomination, and then impaled the head of the other ghoul with his hook. The creature clawed frantically at his arm, but its efforts were wasted on the wooden shaft; and Arkor bore down, ripping open its skull in a manner to make the most seasoned warrior ill. Black blood and gray brain matter sprayed Arkor as the ghoul went limp.

Arkor trampled the corpses, failing to notice the burning scratches on his body and leaving the sword planted into its victim. He passed through the second iron door, striding over more bodies, and as he neared the last door he heard an explosion.

Within the Great Hall, Arkor found Wezlok standing before three dunarchins. The undead firstborns lay motionless, burning before a charred wall. To the left, Landerik and ten men fought a pack of ghouls, and at least forty corpses of both friend and foe littered the chamber.

Arkor rushed to the central tower door. He knew not why, but he felt drawn. It burst open, and Cavalor stumbled from it, pursued by four dunarchins. Arkor lifted another sword from one of the fallen and charged, destroying the first dunarchin with a single blow. Side by side with Cavalor, they dispatched the other three, taking a couple of minor wounds themselves.

"Dunarchins!" Wezlok yelled. "To the west!"

Arkor turned to see a dozen more undead firstborns issuing from the west tower. He and Cavalor moved to welcome the newcomers, but the door to the central tower swung open and Arkor froze. Standing there was a single dunarchin, taller than any other he had seen. Its yellow skin clung to its bones and its glowing eyes burned into Arkor as it hissed with hatred. But also Arkor noticed several scars upon its face, as well as other familiar characteristics.

"Brother?" he gasped in disbelief.

Vikur had become a dunarchin!

Arkor had never fought against his brother before, save for the sibling spats of their youth. He had always believed Vikur to be an excellent swordsman, and now Arkor realized it to be true as he fended off a flurry of strikes. Or did facing the man for whose predicament he felt responsible unbalance him? The only thing he knew for sure was that this creature was skilled and carried a mighty blade, and Arkor was on his heels in the defense of his life.

The dunarchin hissed with malice as it swung again and again, and Arkor gave ground with every blow. He managed only a few attacks of his own, but the Vikur-dunarchin turned them aside. With its next attack, the undead Lord of the Keep shattered the blade Arkor held and knocked him to the floor. The creature then snarled as it raised its sword for the final strike.

"Vikur!" Arkor cried.

Vikur hesitated, his scowl fading. His eyes dimmed, as if something deep inside recalled another life. "Brother?" The voice was hoarse, but it was Vikur's. Bowing his head, Vikur turned his blade and offered the hilt.

Arkor stared in disbelief, hesitant to take hold.

"You must!" Vikur's voice became sharper. "I don't know how long I can fight the urge that burns within." Even as Vikur spoke, his eyes pulsed with the blue light.

Arkor rose, seizing the weapon, and hatred returned to the cold eyes. The Vikur-dunarchin reached for Arkor, the icy hands locking around his throat, and Arkor thrust the sword, piercing his brother's chest. Vikur's fingers tightened, and Arkor wished they would complete their task, but he forced the blade downward, slicing open his brother's torso. The hands then relaxed, and the Vikur-dunarchin fell to its knees.

Vikur looked at Arkor, and the glow of his eyes dimmed again. "Thank you," he hissed. "My brother."

The eyes went dark, and the body collapsed.

CHAPTER 19

FIRE HILLS

R holmar rode behind Pallit as the ranger led the way into the Fire Hills. Soren went next, and then Nilborg, Rybeal, and Lorylla. The hills were known to be difficult terrain, and never-ending winter did nothing to remedy that while they traversed tricky, ice-coated slopes and deep snow. Rholmar was sure Pallit called upon all of his experience to proceed.

As the day grew late, a concealed pit claimed Pallit's horse, and the beast thrashed as it vanished. Rholmar pulled Pallit from the saddle in time, and everyone stared in disbelief as the hole filled in with snow to await its next victim. Pallit then traveled on foot, sometimes half submerged, and the pace slowed.

Just as Selanna promised, the hills possessed many caves, and shelter was easy enough to find the first night. But as the second day ended, the dark openings were hidden by snow. That evening the winds picked up, as if noticing the company's presence, and had it not been for Rybeal's magic, a fire would have been impossible.

The next morning was marginally brighter than the night, for storm clouds settled overhead. Soren's horse lay frozen, having passed while the company slept, and the Soleran paladin doubled up with Nilborg.

The scenery was unchanged for several hours, and had it not been for the Varlimor Mountains, barely visible through the haze to the left, Rholmar would have thought they traveled in circles. The winds grew stronger as noon came and went, and heavy snow descended; and as Rholmar's limbs became numb, a feeling that seemed to be shared by all, they had no choice but to stop. Lorylla unpacked one of the five remaining bundles of firewood from her horse, and Rybeal used his magic to warm the tinder and bring it to flame.

"This will prove ill," Pallit said to Rholmar and Soren. "At this rate, we will run out of wood long before our need diminishes."

"How far have we to go?" asked Soren.

Pallit shrugged and sighed. "This land is unfamiliar to me. As best I can figure from what Selanna told me, it'll be at least three days. Maybe more if the weather doesn't change for the better."

A bone-chilling wind drew all attention skyward. No Death Lord flew overhead, and the company relaxed as the gust diminished.

A half hour passed when they picked up again—the fire provided little relief, and the snow had accumulated three more inches. They progressed slower than the previous day, and with the mountains lost behind the thick snowfall, Rholmar hoped they maintained a southerly route.

They stopped for the night when the sky darkened, but sleep was impossible in the whipping snow, and not even Rybeal's magic kept the fire burning. After a few hours, they abandoned the notion of camp and continued. Rholmar worried about losing their way in the dark, but he did not argue—it was better than dying beneath the snow creeping up their legs.

Everyone traveled on foot, as riding had become hazardous. Furs covered every inch of their bodies and were drawn tightly about their faces, but the attire was no match for the storm. They stumbled through the night, and though Rholmar's feet were numb and his legs frozen, he pushed on, leading his horse as best he could.

With the morning came no comfort, as the blizzard continued to build and pelted them with sleet. The day was half over when Pallit pointed to a group of evergreens, barely visible through the curtain of white, and they made for the trees. Reaching them took almost an hour, for the snow proved deep, and upon arriving Pallit's shoulders slumped. The trees were spread apart, providing little protection from the wind.

"We have to go under!" the ranger said above the rushing air. "It's our only hope!"

They dug into the snow with small shovels, but it was slow going and loose powder collapsed any tunnel they managed. Pallit then took sole charge of the task, looking quite at home in his efforts. Rholmar recalled Coranthiar Mountain winters to last half the year, surely having prepared the ranger for such a feat, and after another hour the shelter was complete.

Pallit looked at the horses. "We have to turn them loose." He turned to Soren. "They'll have a better chance on their own."

"We'll miss them later," said Soren.

Rholmar nodded. There was yet a distance to cover, and the lack of horses would make the way more difficult, as well as increase the amount of gear they would each need to carry.

"It seems a crime." Pity filled Lorylla's white eyes.

They removed the saddles and put their packs in the shelter. Lorylla then spoke to the animals in her native tongue before slapping her steed on the hindquarters, and the horses bolted into the storm, vanishing in seconds. With one last wave of the gray elf's slender, fur-covered arm, she crawled into the shelter to join with the others. Rholmar followed.

Pallit continued to labor within the hollow, collecting snow and packing it onto the walls with the aid of his water flask. Half of the blankets were placed on the floor while the rest were pulled over their shoulders, and though it remained chilly, the absence of the wind made it bearable.

Soren wrapped his arm around Nilborg, concern on the paladin's face. "How are you holding?"

"I'll be fine," Nilborg said through blue lips. "I only wish we could have a fire."

Rholmar noticed the pity still present in Lorylla's eyes. Looking at the others, he realized how the cold emphasized every wrinkle on their faces, and he wondered if the elf's earlier concern had been for the horses. Lorylla's expression moved from pity to doubt, and she released a small sigh before climbing beneath the furs.

Rholmar closed his eyes. "Almighty Arronaus," he prayed to the deity of the sky, "let this storm abate, that we might see our way through."

He took his place with the others.

Rholmar awoke. The shelter had held, though the entrance was blocked by snow, and the only sound was a chorus of gentle snoring. To his surprise, he felt well rested, and he knew it must be morning. He attempted to rise, but Rybeal was lying across his legs and Pallit was nestled against his back.

"Let us wake," Rholmar said aloud, stirring the others.

They looked around. Silence. If the wind still whipped through the trees, the company was too deep for Rholmar to hear it.

"Has the storm passed?" Nilborg asked.

Pallit grabbed his shovel. "There's one way to find out."

The ranger maneuvered to where the entrance had been the previous night. He tunneled three feet before light spilled into the shelter.

"It has passed," he called back.

Everyone collected their gear and made for the surface.

It was like a new land. Peaceful, undisturbed hills of white rolled as far as Rholmar could see. The clouds were brighter, the snowfall had ceased, and the wind was but a mere breeze blowing now and again.

"Thank Arronaus," Rholmar said to himself, and Lorylla gave him a nod.

The mountains had returned, dark and tall beyond a light haze, but they were smaller since Rholmar last viewed them.

Soren sighed. "How far off course have we wandered?"

"This will cost us at least another day." Pallit shook his head. "I wonder if we've moved south at all."

"All is not lost." Rholmar placed his hand on the ranger's shoulder. "But all the same, we've no time to waste."

Pallit gave a wry smile and nodded.

They marched again, slower than before without horses to carry their supplies, and Pallit walked in a southeasterly direction as much as the terrain allowed. In some areas they were forced to climb, and the absence of horses proved a small blessing, for an alternate route would have been necessary otherwise. Regardless, Rholmar missed the beasts.

The day passed, and still the Fire Hills stretched beyond sight. The mountains, however, loomed closer once again, and Pallit turned due south the next morning. As they neared noon of the following day, the snow became thinner and the air warmer. Rholmar felt like a kid, having had his fill with a long winter and eagerly awaiting the approaching spring. Their pace quickened, and an hour later the snow was patchy, creating large pools of slush. In the distance, the hills ended and green land reached the southern horizon.

"We made better time than I could've hoped," Pallit said, "given the circumstances."

"It is summer there." Lorylla peered at the country below, enjoying a sharper view than Rholmar. She closed her eyes and inhaled deeply, as if smelling something fragrant on the warm breeze. A few strands of silver hair danced about her face while she released the breath slowly, coming as close to a smile as Rholmar could ever recall. Her eyes opened, and she gazed to the southeast. "They are distant, but I can see the Twin Rivers and Mud Lake."

Rholmar sighed. Not much farther now.

No one thought for a moment of stopping for lunch, and they trudged down the slopes. The ground became firmer while they progressed, and soon they were jogging on dry, rocky soil. They shed their furs as the air grew hot, and with the setting of the sun, they stepped upon a long field of tall grass and wildflowers.

Glancing at the snow-covered hills to the north, the night in the blizzard seemed a bad dream to Rholmar. He put his hand on Pallit's shoulder.

"Well done, my friend!"

Pallit gazed at the Varlimor peaks. "I pray Arrikan found an easier path."

CHAPTER 20

LORNIBUR

Eraim led her company west, following the Fire Hills toward Southwood with Selanna at her side. Millord and Greyor rode close behind, almost pushing Eraim with a sense of urgency to reach the mines. Next came Brem and Arrikan. Eraim knew exactly where she aimed for, even though a few more feet of snow had covered the land since she last viewed it, and they traveled a direct route. Night was upon them when they reached the junction of the forest and hills, and when Eraim looked back, she wished it would snow—a trampled path clearly marked their passing.

"We best not stop," she said to Selanna. "Our tracks could be spotted by morning and we may never reach—"

"Not all of us speak elf!" Millord's brow furrowed enough to conceal the upper half of his eyes. "I'd appreciate you using a tongue agreeable to all. Especially if it involves the mission."

Eraim knew the dwarves to be more than eager for a chance to see the ancient home of their ancestors, and the distrustful looks they gave when she spoke in the elfish language never escaped her notice. So naturally she used her native tongue as much as possible.

"We will not be stopping anytime soon," Selanna said in the common speech. "We must continue in the dark."

"We dwarves need no sleep yet." Millord waved a hand. "Nor do we require light. We can travel twice as far as any of you this night."

"Indeed," Eraim muttered.

The concealed moon dully illuminated the white land while Eraim skirted Southwood. Once the forest was behind them, she rode another quarter mile before entering the hills. Though covered in snow, she knew of a route posing no hazards, and a half hour later she dismounted.

Kneeling next to a long stick protruding from the ground, a marker Eraim had placed months ago, she dug into the packed snow with her shovel. Soon, an opening was uncovered, about three feet high and three feet wide.

Eraim stood. "This is it."

The company unsaddled the horses. Eraim then whispered in elfish to her mare, who whinnied in understanding, and she flashed an innocent smile in response to the dwarves' suspicious glares. With a couple of snorts, her horse led the other animals west toward Tenvale. Just before passing beyond sight, Lilli and Dandi changed from white to brown and black, as Selanna's spell was released and the Salenti horses resumed their natural colors.

Eraim crawled through the opening, and by the time the company joined her, she had already lit her lantern. They stood in a small, natural-looking grotto with a low ceiling. The room was empty, save for the flagons of water and leather sacks containing dried meats and breads Eraim had stashed several months earlier. All stocks were frozen.

"It is late." Selanna sounded weary. "Perhaps we should rest awhile."

"I think we should move on." Greyor drummed his fingers on the head of the hammer strapped to his waist.

"We *should* move a bit farther," Eraim said. "There is a place where we can have a fire."

To this suggestion, no one argued, and they piled the saddles in a corner and gathered the frozen stocks. Eraim then opened a secret door to the rear of the hollow and stepped into the tunnel beyond. It was the very passage Vikur, Poluran, and Melac had used to sneak into Ironside Keep, and Eraim pondered this with sorrow. If only Vikur had waited a little longer...

They walked a few miles along the dank tunnel until reaching the resting chamber. A firepit rested in the middle of the floor, and above it a blackened shaft a few inches in diameter bore into the ceiling. Dry wood filled the pit and six cots encircled it—the room was exactly as Eraim had left it.

They could not rest for long, but a few hours would do them good, and they claimed their cots while Millord lit a fire. At Eraim's insistence, they guarded in shifts. She was untrusting of the tunnel and knew not whether the occupants of the keep had discovered its existence. Sleep then came easily enough.

Selanna opened her eyes and gazed about. Noises had stirred her from sleep. Millord and Greyor were sharing the final watch, and their constant movements and low grumblings had awakened the others, too. It was obvious the dwarves were eager to continue.

"Good." Millord nodded. "You're all awake. Might as well get an early start."

Selanna looked at Eraim, who rolled her eyes.

They rose and gathered their gear.

The passageway continued, veering left and right and often sloping downward. After several hours they halted before a burned-out torch lying on the floor, and Eraim inspected the wall to the right. All appeared normal at first glance, but then it became obvious that part of the tunnel was discolored. It was the breach Melac had spoken of. Eraim had cleverly disguised it to prevent further discovery of its existence.

While Eraim dug into the patch, Selanna gazed farther down the passage. Her thoughts wandered to Merssa, and the desire to continue entered her mind. She could not shake the feeling that the paladin of Cafior needed her help.

"Even if we were to continue," Brem said softly, "Vikur possessed the only key to grant us access. And from what Arkor said, I doubt even Eraim could open the crypt door."

"Do not underestimate Eraim." Selanna issued a smile she did not feel. "But we must trust that all is well, else doom awaits us. Regardless of whether or not we pass through the mines."

Eraim broke through the mud, revealing a hole a couple feet above the tunnel floor, and without a word she slipped through. Selanna followed, and by the small light Eraim carried, the differences between the new corridor and the one bound for Ironside were clear. The walls and floors of Lornibur were finely chiseled, as was the ceiling fifteen feet overhead, and beautiful arches decorated with hammers and anvils in bas-relief were spaced every twenty yards. A larger arch was nearby, covered by unfamiliar runes.

Brem crawled through the breach next. Being about the size of Selanna, it was a task easily performed. Arrikan's shoulders and hips were slightly broader than those before her, and after some wriggling she squeezed through.

The dwarves hesitated on the other side, eying the hole with doubt. Millord, the larger of the two, shrugged and approached. With a deep breath, he poked through his arms and head. He then placed his large hands on the wall and gave a heave... He was stuck. Lodged at the chest.

"I knew this elf hole wouldn't work!" Millord glared at Eraim. "It might be well and good for elves, ladies, and marteese, but for us dwarves — Hey! Stop that!" Millord's last words were shouted back at the hole. "You'll pull my leg off!"

"Shh!" Eraim hissed. "There may be things living in the mines. Let us not alert them to our presence!"

"If I could just reach Clanghorr," Millord grumbled, "I'd carve a proper arch!"

"Selanna!" Eraim said. "Please do something before he brings the mines down upon us."

Selanna had been enjoying the show, but her smile dropped and she cleared her throat. "Yes, of course."

She tried to appear more serious as she chanted a few words, and the wall below the dwarf turned to mud. Millord slid down the pile of thick, wet dirt, looking none too pleased.

"Brakkeet!" Millord cursed in the dwarfish tongue. "I was about to pull myself through! And now look at me!" Filth covered him from his knees to his chest, including much of his brown beard. "I'll be introducing myself to Lornibur looking like this!"

"Quiet!" Eraim snapped. "We are not here for the mines. Or do you need reminding?"

Millord sighed and nodded, wiping his armor in vain with a muddy gauntlet. His jaw then dropped as he looked upon the tunnel; and his lips started moving, as if trying to comprehend the runes engraved along the edges of the archway.

"Lornibur!" Greyor gasped, his head poking through the breach. He attempted to step over the mess, but his right boot sank into the sludge, and it would leave a soiled print with every stride for at least the next hundred yards.

"This way." Eraim went left without so much as a glance at the map.

They traversed dusty corridors ranging from ten to twenty feet wide, and a rusty rail traveled along the center of most of them. The perfect shaping of the walls was constant throughout, and Selanna found the detail impressive when considering the time and organization necessary to perform such consistency. Bas-relief images of dwarves performing several tasks continued from corridor to corridor, as if telling a story, but Selanna would need weeks, possibly months, to interpret what they meant. As interesting as the scenery was, Selanna detested being underground; of traveling beneath miles of dirt and stone that might collapse at any moment. She took in a slow breath and thought about the trees of Salenti.

Soon they passed through many vaulted chambers with ceilings cloaked in darkness. In these vast halls, veins of ore glittered gold and silver within the walls while every sound echoed to reaches unknown. In some rooms Eraim's lamp sparkled off crystal deposits, creating myriads of shifting colors that danced around the chambers. Millord and Greyor needed prodding in these rooms, as the two wished to remain and bask awhile. It surprised Selanna how quiet the dwarves had been thus far, as if sharing even a single word might cause them to miss something.

After a mile was placed behind the company, several intersections containing four to eight directions lined the way, as well as occasional stairwells. Just like the rest of the mines, the stone steps were expertly crafted, and they spiraled around pillars of granite striated with quartz of yellow, blue, and red jasper. Eraim made brief stops at these junctions to determine the proper direction, and during these pauses Millord and Greyor found their voices, speaking in hushed tones in their own language. Though she understood the speech, Selanna thought it to be very hypocritical of the two.

The company moved on this way for a week with no encounters, stopping to rest within rooms of Eraim's choosing. Each of the resting chambers bore a single point of entry and possessed large furnishings or rusted mine carts, which Eraim insisted they use as cover against unwanted discovery. Although the mines appeared to be abandoned, Eraim seemed fidgety, and Selanna wondered if there were any details her friend had not shared. The dwarves gladly volunteered to guard most nights, still awestruck and unable to sleep, but nothing was detected outside the occasional dripping of water.

On the eighth day, the scenery changed. The rail was broken in several places, or pieces of it were missing, and most mine carts were smashed. Sections of the perfect walls were plagued by long cracks, and in most rooms boulders and blocks of stone were scattered, having fallen from the ceilings.

In one passage, Selanna stopped to inspect brown smudges splayed on the wall. The lines were smooth and deliberate, as if forming symbols or words in some language, but she held no comprehension of their meaning.

"The mines appear to be falling apart." Brem gazed at the ceiling, barely visible within Eraim's light.

"Nonsense!" snapped Millord. "The construction is superior to any! Built to last throughout the ages. Something must be tearing them apart."

Greyor nodded in agreement.

They moved on. A short distance later, they encountered large scratches traveling horizontally along a chamber wall. It was as if an enormous creature had gouged the stone with a powerful, three-fingered claw.

"What made these?" Brem held his hand up to one of the jagged lines, able to fit it within the groove.

"I am not sure," said Eraim. "I have never seen anything to make such a mark."

"We best be ready." Arrikan pulled her blade.

The corridors became cluttered with debris as they pressed on, and Eraim slowed the pace, taking care to move as silently as possible—a pointless task, for the dwarves' mail jingled with each heavy step. After another mile, Eraim stopped to peer in all directions of a six-way intersection.

"I hear something," she whispered.

Selanna heard it as well, and from the look on Brem's face, so did he. It was like a group of naked feet shuffling along the corridor to the left.

"Are they coming or going?" asked Brem.

"They are going," Eraim replied. "But what they are, I wonder." Looking at Selanna, she said, "Perhaps I should have a peek. Alone." She eyed the dwarves with the last word.

Selanna nodded, and Eraim placed her lamp on the floor and vanished down the hallway without a sound. She returned minutes later, her expression one of concern.

"What is it?" asked Arrikan.

"Well," Eraim glanced over her shoulder, "at first there was a large reptile clinging to the ceiling. I did not see it in the dark, and the blasted thing nearly caught me with its tongue!"

"Cavern lizards." Millord snorted. "Mere pests."

"This was no cavern lizard." Eraim frowned. "It could have swallowed me whole."

"A reptile could not have made the noises we heard," Selanna said.

"No." Eraim shook her head. "Further on, I saw what I thought to be goblins."

At these words, the dwarves' brows drew together.

"But they were a bit tall for goblins," Eraim added.

"Hobgoblins?" Arrikan frowned. "I've never known them to dwell in caverns or mines."

"They were much too short for hobgoblins," Eraim replied.

"What were they doing?" asked Brem.

"They moved in rank. Like a guard patrol."

"Probably afraid of cavern lizards." Millord chuckled as he nudged Greyor.

"It was not a cavern lizard." Eraim frowned. "And I doubt they were guarding against the reptiles, for they were wearing the creatures' skins. They most likely hunt the things for food."

"Then what would they be guarding against?" posed Arrikan. "Is there something else down here to fear?"

Millord raised Clanghorr. "It'll be an army of dwarves if they remain after this Trannum is destroyed!"

The dwarf spoke more boisterous than Selanna was comfortable with, and she sent him a sharp glare. "This *Trannum* is very powerful and demands your full attention."

Millord gave a wry smile.

"Perhaps they fear whatever made the scratches on the walls," said Brem. "Similar markings are on the ceiling." He looked upward. "So either it climbs walls like the cavern lizards, or it is very tall."

"Not cavern lizards," Eraim muttered, following the marteese's gaze.

Selanna looked at the ceiling, where another set of claw marks ran for at least ten feet. Her attention was then drawn back down the corridor, for the sound of shuffling returned, faster and louder.

"They are headed this way," Eraim said.

Millord shook his head. "They must have seen you spying on them."

Selanna ignored the dwarf's accusation. She knew better than that. More likely, it was Millord's voice bouncing along the corridors that gave them away.

"There is a chamber not far back." Eraim looked over her shoulder. "Let us make for it. We do not need a confrontation if we can avoid it." She aimed her last comment at the dwarves, who seemed eager to begin the extermination of the mines.

"And if a confrontation *is* unavoidable," Selanna added, "I prefer not to be caught in this passage."

They backtracked more than a hundred yards to the chamber Eraim had mentioned. It appeared to be a junction room for mine carts. A score of tunnels entered the enormous round hall through grand archways, and rails from each were joined in its center. There, evidence of many levers existed for shifting tracks, but only a few remained intact. A couple dozen carts were scattered, most toppled or damaged and all showing severe signs of rust.

"Conceal yourselves," Selanna said.

"Clanghorr is insulted," grumbled Millord. "Dwarves of Rornibur do not *conceal* themselves!"

"Nor do dwarves of Morimont," added Greyor.

"Be still!" Selanna snapped. "There are more important matters at hand."

The dwarves obeyed, and Millord squatted behind an overturned cart while Greyor dropped to a knee among chunks of the ceiling that had fallen.

Eraim extinguished the lantern and everything went dark. Selanna knew this did not present too much of an issue for her, Eraim, and Brem, and even less for the dwarves, but Arrikan would be blind. Selanna squatted next to Arrikan behind two carts, placing her hand on the ranger's shoulder.

They waited several minutes without a sound beyond the occasional rattle of the dwarves' armor, the warriors no doubt hoping for a fight. Then soft shuffling echoed throughout the chamber. The movement stopped, replaced by sniffing, a couple of chirps, and a grunt. It then resumed, more slowly and getting closer.

Selanna watched Millord shift his feet in anticipation of battle, and she shook her head when he lifted himself onto his toes to peek over the cart. She decided she might as well have a look herself, and she peered around the carts concealing her and Arrikan.

Many dark shapes moved about the chamber, each of them standing at least a few inches taller than four feet. They were thin, with arms reaching almost to their knees, and they made their way without lights as they sniffed the floor and debris. Though Selanna could not make out the details of their features, she noticed spears in their hands, ready to strike. One pointed its weapon in Millord's direction, emitting a grunt, and the figures began moving toward the dwarf.

"Rats in the mines," Millord whispered to Greyor in their own tongue.

One of the creatures emitted a screech, as if detecting the dwarf's voice, and the mine dwellers charged.

Selanna stepped into the open and cast forth her magical light. Though it only dimly illuminated a portion of the room, it revealed the humanoids and ceased their advance as they shaded their red eyes. Eraim claimed they appeared goblin-like, but it was obvious they were not goblins. They stood half a foot taller and their skin was pale, not at all like the leathery hide of the sworn enemy of the dwarves. Patches of crude armor made from thick reptile hides covered their torsos, and in their hands were spears crafted from thin shards of the railing system. With poor aim, they launched several of the weapons before bolting through various archways.

Eraim and Arrikan stood with bows ready while the dwarves jumped from their hiding places. Raising Clanghorr, Millord gave chase.

"Let them go!" Selanna shouted. "We do not fight unless we have no choice."

Millord scowled and came to a stop, glaring at the dark archways where the creatures had departed. "One day, I'll rid Lornibur of these pests!"

Selanna allowed her light to fade after Eraim relit the lantern, and they returned to the corridor. They were more alert now, as the mines no longer seemed abandoned, but after another mile there were no signs of the mine dwellers.

Just as Selanna relaxed, Eraim came to a halt. Latched to the wall ahead was a large reptile. It was ten feet long and remained motionless, appearing as a decorative statue. Millord stepped forward with Clanghorr in hand, but Eraim grabbed his shoulder and pointed to the ceiling. A second lizard clung there, matching the stone perfectly. Millord had almost walked beneath it.

"Is there another way around?" Selanna whispered.

Eraim shrugged. "Not according to the map. But it is old and does not show every passage."

Eraim nodded to Arrikan, and they both fitted arrows to their bowstrings before taking aim at the lizard on the ceiling. Eraim nodded again and they fired. Arrikan's arrow pierced the creature between the shoulders and Eraim's sank into its skull between the eyes. Its body fell lifelessly to the floor, and the second lizard advanced.

Millord stood poised, his axe ready to strike, but he was surprised when the reptile closed the gap in but a second. Before he could swing, the lizard was upon him, gnashing with a toothy maw as large as his head. Its jaws snapped inches from Millord's nose as he jumped back, and Greyor's hammer crashed onto its skull, crushing it.

"Fast devils." Millord stared at the corpse as blood issued from its mouth. "These aren't cavern lizards!"

Eraim sighed.

"Now that I've seen them," Greyor nudged the lizard's head with his boot, "I wonder if the mine folk hunt them, or if it's the other way around."

"Or both," said Arrikan. "In Andria, the barbarians hunt the griffons of the mountains, a beast most would prefer to avoid if given the choice. And the griffons hunt the barbarians as well."

"My mind is still on the scratches," said Brem. "The claws on these creatures are far too small."

"We should move." Eraim's eyes darted about the walls and ceiling. "We have remained here too long."

A few more miles passed, and it was beyond time for rest, but they continued, searching for a chamber from where they could defend themselves. Before one could be located, a pile of rubble strewn across the passage brought them to a halt. To either side was a gaping hole greater than ten feet in diameter.

"What is this?" Selanna had never seen anything like it before. Not at this size. The edges were jagged, as if carved with powerful claws, and the one to the left bent downward while the right turned upward.

Eraim shook her head.

"I don't like the looks of it," Millord said.

Eraim gazed down the hole to the left. "Let us move on before whatever did this returns."

They passed over the debris and followed a curving hallway to the right. After fifty yards, another pile of rubble reached almost to the ceiling. Eraim ascended to peer through a three-foot gap at the top, and when she turned back, her face was paler than usual.

"Two more holes," she said. "One emits steam and smells of charred flesh." Eraim then answered Selanna's next question before it could be asked. "There is no other way around."

Selanna scaled the mound, and Eraim held Mithkahr as they slid down the opposite side. Selanna noticed the left hole curved away and to the right, while the other delved steeply into the mountain. Hot air issued from the latter, and upon it was the pungent odor

Eraim had mentioned. No sound emitted from either hole, and Mithkahr remained dull, assuring Selanna that no evil was too near.

The shuffling returned, back the way the company had come, and Selanna heard stones being kicked as the feet passed over the first debris pile. Brem joined Selanna and Eraim, and from his expression, he detected the noise as well.

"They've returned," Arrikan called from atop the rubble, just before Selanna could voice a warning.

"And in larger numbers," added Greyor from the other side of the pile.

"Hurry!" Selanna was no longer concerned with speaking too loudly. "Over the rocks."

Arrikan pulled her bow as she looked back. "Let's go," the ranger said in the dwarfish language.

It seemed everyone in the company understood the speech.

Greyor appeared next, followed by Millord. They slid skillfully down the other side, landing on their feet with weapons in hand. Millord bore a sour look.

"The time will come to show them I am no prey!" the dwarf growled.

Arrikan joined the company, her eyes wide. "The tunnel is full of the things. We need to move."

Eraim led the way down the corridor. The passage was long, with several branches on either side, but also there were more excavations throughout its length. Some were larger than others, and all appeared to have been dug by enormous claws.

"Are we marching into the creature's lair?" asked Arrikan.

"Our path lies to the left," Eraim said. "At the next intersection."

They moved at a hurried pace, and Selanna heard the pale creatures clambering over the second mound. Eraim turned left at the junction and they ran; and after fifty yards, they entered a large chamber unlike the others they had seen thus far. The ceiling rose only twenty feet overhead and was supported by many pillars, but at least half the supports were damaged or broken, possibly caused by the crude tunnels plunging into the walls, floor, and ceiling. Several archways existed to either side of the room, and from a couple to the left side issued the humanoids, shielding their eyes with one hand and holding rail-spears with the other. Shouting and squawking in their strange language, they charged.

"Now we fight!" Millord advanced, and Greyor was close behind.

The mine dwellers' combative skills were lacking, and their bodies were so thin that Millord cleaved through two with each of his first few swings. Greyor's hammer sent three others flying, and Selanna heard the crushing of bones with each blow. The humanoids balked at the sight of the raging dwarves, but as their numbers continued to grow, their faces became determined.

Arrikan assisted with her bow, keeping a couple of mine dwellers from flanking Millord and Greyor. Selanna added flashes of light that proved even more effective than the arrows, and the humanoids' approach was slowed.

"To the right!" Eraim pointed to an archway across the room. "We must hurry!"

The mine dwellers now poured through four different openings, including the one the company had used. Over three score were present, and still more arrived.

"Greyor!" Selanna shouted. "We cannot win!" She flashed her lights toward the humanoids to the rear, halting their charge.

Greyor slowed to notice the growing mass of mine dwellers. But then he resumed his assault. Selanna thought the dwarf to have gone mad, and she searched for a spell to assist in the matter, but then Greyor called to his friend in the dwarfish tongue.

"We must go! Before we are swallowed up!"

After one last swing, Millord joined Greyor, and they rushed toward the others, who were now halfway across the chamber. The humanoids were faster than the dwarves and closed, so Eraim assisted Arrikan, piercing the nearest pursuers with arrows until the dwarves caught up. Eraim then slung her bow over her shoulder and led the way through the arch she had indicated.

The sound of pursuit continued into the corridor, and a few spears clattered on the floor behind the company. One spear nearly tripped Millord, but Greyor steadied his companion and the dwarves kept the pace. Any time the mine dwellers drew too near, Arrikan fired an arrow and Selanna cast a flash to increase the gap.

Upon reaching a five-way intersection, Eraim paused with a rare look of confusion. With a nod, she headed forward and to the right. The corridor opened into another large room, one free of debris, and the humanoids were not far behind.

Selanna trailed Eraim as they ran across the chamber, heading for a single archway at the opposite end. But when they reached the center, the floor cracked like thin ice. It might have held for Selanna and Eraim, maybe even Brem, had the marteese's human heritage not added a bit too much fat, but when Arrikan and the dwarves stepped onto it, not to mention the many pursuers, it collapsed. Selanna became disoriented as she fell into a maze of descending tunnels, and she lost track of her companions.

CHAPTER 21

BENASTI FOREST

Nidor followed Gruelenor into the infamous woodland, and next walked Sullis, Magneer, Melac, and Xorlunder. Nidor saw no path to speak of, but Gruelenor walked a confident pace, each step as sure as the last. Outside of Gruelenor, everyone's nerves seemed on edge, and every noise drew immediate attention. It was not long before the rodents and birds disappeared, and Nidor wondered if living in the evil forest taught the animals to dwell on the outskirts, or if they kept quiet and out of sight.

A few miles passed without mishap and the air grew humid. They removed the rest of their warm gear, and Xorlunder buried the furs among undergrowth as best he could to conceal their passing. As the day drew to a close, the company paused to look to the west. The rays of the dying sun filtered through the leaves, a sight they had not known since setting foot on Vermallon Road. The view lasted only a moment and was gone. It was as if the clouds had corrected their mistake and slammed the door shut.

"We should stop," Sullis said. "All things considered, it was a good day. Let's not press our luck in the night."

"No fire." Gruelenor dropped his pack to the ground.

"Wouldn't a fire keep the wolves away?" asked Magneer.

Gruelenor shook his head. "It'll invite them."

They settled in, posting the usual guards. While eating bread from the packs provided by Eraim, Nidor pondered Sullis's words from before they entered the forest. The Brondor paladin speculated that the denizens of Benasti might be away to fight the war. Nidor hoped the theory proved true. Perhaps they might pass through the forest unnoticed and make up for lost time. He then noticed Sullis's troubled expression. The paladin had worn the look since their last night in the cave. Nidor moved to sit next to him.

"Was that the first time you experienced the aura of a Death Lord?" he asked.

Sullis almost looked ashamed. "Yes. I hold a great deal of respect for those of you who have faced something so evil and foul. My courage waned with every second, and I had not even *seen* the creature. I only hope I have not insulted Brondor with the cowardice that ran through my veins."

"None of us have ever *faced* one," Nidor said. "After Gruzim arrived, we were forced to retreat. So do not question your —"

"Now that I have experienced one," Sullis shook his head, "they shall never affect me so again. Ever!"

Nidor fell silent and left the paladin to his thoughts.

Sleep was difficult, and the night seemed like it would never end. But morning came. Nidor was grateful for this, and he whispered his thanks to Silcor.

Gruelenor picked up the unseen path and they continued south. The forest grew brighter than the previous day, despite the dark clouds hiding the sun, but the trees crowded together to block most of the light shortly after noon. Gruelenor said nothing, and his ever-vigilant face showed no signs of concern or fear, but his pace quickened.

As dusk neared, the woodland became overgrown with thickets and large thorns clutched at everyone's boots and leggings. A direct path was impossible, and they veered left and right while always bearing southward. Nidor felt anxious, but Gruelenor's expression was unchanged.

The forest grew dark with the coming of night, and a musty smell arose from the moist soil. If not for the trees, Nidor would have sworn they were underground. They settled in for some rest, and a distant howl caused all but Gruelenor's eyes to dart about the woodland. The krukari cocked his head for a moment, and then leaned against a tree and closed his eyes.

It was the darkest part of the night. Gruelenor stood to one side of his sleeping companions, while Xorlunder guarded the other. Nearing the end of their shift, Gruelenor detected a movement to his right, and within the darkness he saw a krukari gazing at him from behind a tree. He had not seen the face for years.

"What have we here, brother?" The krukari spoke just above a whisper in the hobgoblin tongue.

Gruelenor glanced at his companions. Xorlunder sat motionless while the others remained asleep. "Korgun," he whispered with disgust. "I thought I smelled you."

"So you've come back," Korgun said. "The *strongest* of us all, yet the last to return alive. Most of us figured *Brazan* claimed you."

Gruelenor scowled at the mention of the journey taken by the sons of the ruling power of Benasti; a quest all princes endured before they could challenge the throne. Gruelenor had not seen Benasti since he began that expedition at age thirteen. Korgun likely never strayed far when his turn arrived. Though a skilled tracker, Korgun was never much with a blade, and he could not hope to rival any of his brothers in combat. Gruelenor had no doubt Korgun focused instead on being the best at what he knew—a sneak.

"I'm quite alive," Gruelenor hissed. "Now keep your voice down."

"I see you have brought sacrifices." Korgun bent his neck around the tree to spy the campsite. "They should make for a grand feast!" He raised a brow. "But why are you taking such a strange route home, I wonder?"

"They're not for you." Gruelenor's blood began to boil.

"Then it *is* true!" Korgun said, almost too loudly. "You have not returned to join us. You damaged your mind somewhere over the last fifteen years, you have."

"Keep your voice down," Gruelenor growled, "or I'll have your tongue!"

"Father told us of your meeting in Nira." Korgun smiled. "What do you think of him now? Quite an accomplishment, if you ask me."

"He's an abomination," Gruelenor spat, "bent to another's will. He has abandoned you and all who dwell here. You are nothing but pawns to him now."

"What do you mean, *now*?" Korgun chuckled. "When has anyone been anything but a pawn to Father? And you're wrong. He's still in control, have no doubt. He's unlike the others. And he has plans, yes. Big plans. Plans for some of us, I suppose. Or perhaps for *all* of us." Korgun grinned. "One way or another."

Gruelenor turned back toward the camp. Still, no one stirred.

"It's not too late," Korgun said. "You can show your loyalty to Father and Benasti. Turn these spies over to me. Now."

In one swift motion, Gruelenor held Korgun by the throat. "Know this, brother," Gruelenor said through clenched teeth. "The next time I see you, you best have a sword in your hand. There's a better life for me and I plan on having it. So make no mistake. I will not hesitate to gut you like the pig you are!" He released Korgun with a shove.

Korgun rubbed his throat, ire reflecting in his eyes. "I'll return." He took a few steps back. "Mark my words." He sped off into the trees.

Gruelenor heard Xorlunder's approach.

"It is time to wake Nidor and Magneer," the elf said.

Gruelenor nodded, glancing at the leaves still swaying with the hasty departure of his sibling. As he and Xorlunder walked back toward the others, the elf spoke again.

"Perhaps you forget I am an elf." Xorlunder stopped. "I hear much over great distances, especially when all else is silent."

Gruelenor panicked, his lips moving as he searched for something to say. But nothing came out.

"And I understand the hobgoblin speech as well," Xorlunder added.

"I have nothing to do with this place anymore," Gruelenor grumbled.

"Perhaps." Xorlunder furrowed his brow. "Had I overheard that conversation a week ago, I would have shot you full of arrows before you knew I listened. But now... Things are different. I believe you, though I do not agree with letting him go. Had I a clear shot, he would not have made it far. But I guess blood runs deep. I do not know if ever I could slay one of my own, and I hope I never face that test. But tell me, if he is to return, how long do we have?"

"I did not spare him out of family obligation." Gruelenor looked up at the elf. "He was not alone. He's never alone. We could have taken him and his party, but at what cost to us, I don't know. If he goes to the main village, we'll have at least a day before he returns with greater numbers."

Xorlunder nodded. "I think the others should know of your ties to this place. You have friends here, and I do not think it right that you hide this from them."

"Please!" Gruelenor could feel his shield cracking; the barrier that kept his true self secret. "Say nothing. Not now. It will not help us win this war."

Xorlunder continued to study Gruelenor, as if searching for something. "Very well. It is between us for now. But I will keep an eye on you until we are safe from these borders. Though I trust you to be honest in your words, if they swarm us tomorrow and it meant your life, will you remain loyal to us? Perhaps someday I will hold that trust. And I hope to. But when this is over—"

"When it's over," Gruelenor said.

They awoke Nidor and Magneer and settled in for some sleep. Gruelenor found none.

Come morning, Gruelenor took to a swift pace again. Xorlunder walked to the rear with bow ready, but Gruelenor saw no sign of Korgun's return. He did, however, discover wolf tracks later that afternoon. Trusting Magneer's skills above his own, he called the ranger forward to inspect them.

"These were made early this morning," Magneer said. "They came from the south and passed on to the north."

Gruelenor scanned the contorted trunks and briars inhabiting the area and sighed. They were more than halfway through the forest, but the wolves were circling, testing the range of the company's speed, and the darkest part of Benasti was yet ahead. If only the humans had better vision in the night, they might have a chance.

"There will be no rest tonight." Gruelenor took in a deep breath and pressed on.

As dusk neared, they crossed the Batorn River. It was a shallow waterway, calm throughout most of its length, and easily traversed. The wolves would not be fooled for long, though, and Gruelenor knew it might buy them a few hours at best. Perhaps that would be enough.

They walked through the night, and the forest became exceptionally dark. Gruelenor expected this, but the pace grew slower than he had hoped while he and Xorlunder kept the company in line. As the woodland brightened with the morning, Sullis decided to chance an hour's rest. Gruelenor was uncomfortable with the decision and did not sleep, but the time passed without interruption, and they picked up and moved on.

The new day was much like the last. But when dusk arrived, Gruelenor recognized the signs before them: a tuft of fur on a briar; the smell of a hound's urine on a tree; an intentional scratch on the soil. The attack was coming.

"We should camp." He shot a concerned look Xorlunder's way. They stood a better chance if they did not wander into an ambush in the dark of night.

"We best be on high alert." Xorlunder followed Gruelenor's lead. "I have seen signs of hobgoblins. Recent ones. And with the wolf tracks we saw yesterday, we can only thank the gods we have gone this long undiscovered. Now, I feel our luck to be running thin."

"Why did you wait to share this?" Sullis glared at the elf.

"I spotted the tracks a short time ago," Xorlunder replied. "They were old enough to ignore while we were moving. But now that we are to stay in one place..."

Sullis sighed, frustration obvious on the Brondor paladin's face. He placed Melac on duty with Xorlunder and Gruelenor to watch the first half of the night, and the others sat against trees to try and find sleep.

Gruelenor took his place to the south while Melac sat near the sleeping bodies. Xorlunder climbed a tree to the north side, disappearing from sight. The night was especially dark and quiet, and sweat beaded on Gruelenor's brow while his eyes and ears searched the surrounding trees. He could not live with himself if one of his companions fell at the hands of his kin. Biting his lip, he fought the urge to wake the others.

Melac looked his way, the mage's eyes emitting a slight glow in the darkness. Without another thought, Gruelenor waved his arm, motioning that he heard something. Melac squinted until seeming to realize the signal, and this was confirmed when the wizard roused the others.

Sullis and Magneer pulled their swords and turned their heads left and right. Gruelenor was sure they saw nothing beyond a few feet, but he hoped Melac would remedy that when the time came. Nidor moved to join Gruelenor, navigating through the trees surprisingly well in the dark. Gruelenor wondered if the paladin had concealed yet another talent.

"It would seem our luck has run dry." Nidor spoke just above a whisper. "It is just as Xorlunder feared."

A pang of guilt struck Gruelenor for not having divulged his past to his friends, now more than ever. Xorlunder opened a window in Gruelenor's mind that could never close, and his lips parted as he felt the words upon his tongue. But the sound of approaching feet caught his attention, rushing through the forest from the northeast with no attempts at stealth.

Melac's magic illuminated the area, and from beyond the trees came better than a score of screaming hobgoblins and krukari. The enemy advanced without rank or order, meaning no Zurkan were among them, and two fell with arrows in their chests while Sullis charged.

Gruelenor and Nidor rushed to join their companions, but stopped when a couple of wolves appeared to the left. The monstrous hounds ran in a line, with one trailing the other by ten feet.

"Take the leader!" said Gruelenor. He knew the second wolf would use the first as a distraction, and he moved to the Dale's flank and readied his sword.

The lead wolf crouched as it came to a stop, drawing Nidor's lunge, and the other wolf pounced. Gruelenor thrust his blade, piercing the second wolf's chest and steering it away from the paladin, and Nidor skewered the first wolf's throat. Both animals were slain, but two wolves replaced them while four others rushed past, and their lion-like roars filled the woodland.

Gruelenor closed on the next wolf. Having traveled for years with Ballrik, he picked up a few things, and he slid feet first into the animal, slicing his sword through its front leg. The wolf was caught by surprise and lost the limb. Gruelenor rose and dealt a lethal blow to its chest, and he turned to see Nidor had defeated the other wolf.

They pursued the mongrels that had run past. Beyond the animals, Gruelenor saw his companions battling. Half a dozen hobgoblins and krukari were motionless, pierced by arrows, as well as a pair of wolves. Three Benasti warriors were dead at Sullis's feet and four were charred upon the ground before Melac. Magneer stood to the mage's flank, and a couple hobgoblins lay slain before him.

But the scene changed in an instant. Sullis was surrounded, and Magneer was driven away from Melac by a large krukari dressed in heavy chain armor. The tall Benasti warrior wore a dark red cape, and two stripes of blood stretched across each of his cheeks, as well as from forehead to nostrils. A Zurkan had come after all.

Nidor must have shared Gruelenor's view, for the paladin's eyes and sword were alight with the orange, fire-like glow. Nidor sliced into a wolf's shoulder, burning away fur and scorching its flesh, and the animal bolted into the forest with its tail between its legs, sounding hideous cries.

Gruelenor squared off with another wolf. He glared into its eyes, and in the hobgoblin tongue, he shouted, *"Braak!"*

The hound growled as it turned and slinked into the woods, obeying his command.

Gruelenor saw Melac thrust his hands forward, and a krukari flew twenty feet and into the trunk of a tree, splitting the bark. The mage then jumped, grabbing a branch fifteen feet overhead as a wolf leaped. The animal missed his boots by an inch at most.

"Magneer!" Melac called. "I need help!"

Magneer's attention was bent on the Zurkan. The ranger looked to have scored a few wounds, but the Benasti warrior remained unhindered. Magneer was steered around trees, fending off the Zurkan's large hammer as best he could.

Sullis was also in trouble, as a krukari had flanked the paladin and gashed his side. Worse still, Gruelenor spied Korgun near the tree where Xorlunder was perched. Korgun fired a crossbow, pinning the elf's leg to the branch it was wrapped around.

Gruelenor attempted to reach Melac, but several hobgoblins blocked his path. The Benasti soldiers pulled up short, gaping in disbelief. Perhaps they could not fathom a prince of Benasti fighting against them; one they knew to have been trained by Gruzim; the former favorite to become the next Lord of Benasti. Gruelenor saw that fear in their eyes, and as he smote one, the others fled into the forest.

Gruelenor gained the attention of the wolf beneath Melac after another of its failed attempts to reach the mage. The beast was young and did not know Gruelenor, and it growled with its hackles raised. Gruelenor smiled, waving his blade back and forth, and the animal feigned a few lunges, snapping its teeth while it circled. The beast then charged when Gruelenor stumbled over a hobgoblin corpse. He lifted his sword, and the weapon bit deep into the animal's chest as the mongrel's fangs grabbed hold of his chain shirt. It drove Gruelenor to the ground as its jaws squeezed, piercing armor and flesh, and he pushed the blade deeper in a contest to see who would fail first. The wolf relaxed at last and Gruelenor claimed victory; and he heaved the animal to the side and rose to check on his companions.

The Zurkan's hammer struck Magneer's shoulder, knocking the ranger to the ground. The krukari twirled the heavy weapon with ease and drove down another blow, but a ball of flame knocked the warrior sideways and the attack missed. Gruelenor looked to see Melac sitting on the branch he had clung to moments before, and the mage's focus turned to Sullis. Behind Gruelenor, Nidor battled two wolves, and the animals exhibited several patches of burned fur. Gruelenor ran to Magneer.

Magneer had regained his feet, and he fought desperately until the Zurkan sent his blade flying into a bush. The ranger pulled a knife and did his best to stay out of reach, but he was backed against a tree and he froze.

Gruelenor arrived, and the Zurkan turned. There was a brief pause when their eyes met, and though the enemy stood taller and was twice as large, Gruelenor held no fear. Magneer remained still, as if afraid to move.

"The *prince*," the Zurkan mocked in the hobgoblin tongue, sizing up Gruelenor while twirling the hammer.

"You're outmatched," Gruelenor said in the same language, and he almost believed his words. Just as the princes of Benasti, the Zurkan trained in combat constantly. They were always the largest of their kind, and this one was large even for a Zurkan. Gruelenor did not look forward to fighting him. "You can walk away."

The Zurkan snarled and swung the hammer. Gruelenor steered the attack aside, and when he countered, his opponent was equal to the task. They exchanged several blows in the same manner, and twice Gruelenor felt the breeze of the large weapon brush by his head. But he proved superior, scoring a deep gash into the Zurkan's right side and staggering the Soldier of Blood. Gruelenor followed with an upward swing, splitting open the warrior's chest. The Zurkan collapsed, and its blood flooded the pits the hammerhead left upon the ground.

Gruelenor shot a glance Magneer's way. The ranger appeared confused, but gave a slight nod. Gruelenor then turned to Sullis.

The Brondor paladin favored his left side, but he had strength enough to kick a hobgoblin in the chest and square off with a krukari. Sullis roared, holding his sword with both hands, and bore down upon his foe. The krukari parried the blows aside and was pressed against a tree, where Sullis knocked the blade from the Benasti soldier's hand. The final blow came when the paladin's weapon sliced deep into his enemy's neck, becoming lodged within the gnarled tree as well.

A wolf moved in on Sullis's flank, and Gruelenor charged to give aid, but the gray elf arrived before him. Xorlunder must have pulled his leg from the crossbow bolt, for the bloody shaft still protruded from the branch, and he dropped onto the animal's back. The wolf reared and howled with rage as it attempted to dislodge the elf, but he maintained his hold, piercing a knife between the mongrel's shoulders and grabbing fur with his free hand. The animal bolted, bucking and gnashing in vain until it crashed into the trunk of an unforgiving tree. Xorlunder leaped as the wolf collapsed, traveling more gracefully than Gruelenor would have thought possible with the wounded leg. But the elf's landing was not so smooth, and he tumbled across the ground and disappeared into a patch of tall bushes.

All was quiet. Nidor returned from chasing off the last couple of wolves, his eyes no longer burning and his blade scorched from hilt to tip. Xorlunder crawled from the underbrush. Sullis pulled his blade free of the tree, allowing the krukari's corpse to fall, and Melac floated down from the branch.

"Are you all right?" Magneer eyed the wound on Gruelenor's abdomen.

"Get your shoulder looked at!" Gruelenor turned to the trees where the final attackers had fled.

A pang of guilt gnawed at Gruelenor for speaking to his friend in such a manner. He was not sure how much of his exchange with the Zurkan had been overheard, or if the ranger understood the hobgoblin language. He glanced back at Magneer with a sigh of frustration.

Magneer frowned. He nodded and headed toward Nidor, who was inspecting Xorlunder's leg.

"Do not trouble yourself." Sullis halted Nidor. "You shouldn't drain yourself as you did at Candermane. Had you lacked any strength this night, I dare not think of the outcome. We have strong healing herbs, thanks to Eraim. I suggest we use them."

Nidor nodded, and relief was obvious in the Dale's sigh.

The paladins busied themselves, applying herbs and dressing wounds. For Magneer's shoulder, Nidor called upon his healing fire to mend the crushed bones. Nidor healed Xorlunder's leg as well, for the elf's pace would have been hampered otherwise.

Gruelenor scanned the trees. Korgun was not through with them, of that he was sure.

Chapter 22

Ogres!

Once everyone's wounds were treated, the company moved on beneath Melac's light. The pace was slower than usual to allow the healing herbs time to work, but Nidor was grateful to have conserved his energy. Not all of Silcor's Gifts were too taxing—seeing in the dark was easy enough and setting his blade alight was bearable. But had he healed every wound sustained by his companions, he would probably lack the strength to walk.

They placed several miles between them and the battle site, and the forest brightened, revealing in better detail the gnarled trees, briars, and fruitless brambles plaguing the woodland. There, Gruelenor came to a halt.

"We should be safe for a while."

"Melac," said Sullis. "Let's chance a bit more light."

The mage increased the illumination, allowing Nidor and Sullis to check on bandages and make sure all injuries were progressing. Nidor had never used the herbs provided by Eraim, and he immediately understood Sullis's praise for them—most wounds had already closed. Nidor then spotted blood and twisted chain links on Gruelenor's stomach. The wound had escaped notice after the battle ended, but it was obvious within the light.

"You're bleeding," Nidor said.

Gruelenor shrugged, but Nidor was sure the injury caused pain. He gave a level stare until his friend lifted the chain shirt and allowed him to have a look.

"We were fortunate," Nidor said while he prepared herbs. "Things could have been worse."

"We are fortunate only one of them was Zurkan," murmured Gruelenor.

"Zurkan?"

Gruelenor hesitated, seemingly unsure if he wished to say more. "The strongest of the Benasti warriors. They are the Soldiers of Blood. The Zurkan. Fearless and skilled above all others."

"I see." Nidor wrapped a bandage around Gruelenor's abdomen. "You must be speaking of the one with the hammer."

Gruelenor nodded.

"Your wound is not as bad as it appeared," Nidor said. "It should be better by morning." As he spoke, the forest brightened further. Morning had arrived. "Well," he smirked, "maybe not by *morning*."

Gruelenor lowered his shirt without emotion. He appreciated the Dale's care. But he was undeserving, and it would have been better to allow the wound to fester.

With a heavy heart, he walked about, inspecting the trees and bushes. Broken branches were overhead and most of the underbrush was flattened. They had drifted farther east than Gruelenor intended, and it was not good. Xorlunder was then beside him.

"What is it?" The elf spoke just above a whisper.

Gruelenor shook his head. "Ogres. They live along the southern border of the forest. They hold no allegiance to the tribes of Benasti, but often work with them."

Xorlunder cocked his head to the side. "I hear nothing that is near. Perhaps we should get some rest while it remains so. We shall be in need of strength if we are to encounter an ogre."

Gruelenor gave a slight nod of approval, but he held little hope. Even well rested, encountering an ogre could prove disastrous.

Xorlunder looked at Sullis and raised his voice, gaining everyone's attention. "Ogres. The tracks are days old. We should rest while we can."

Sullis nodded.

Hours passed with no signs of ogres, hobgoblins, or any other denizens of Benasti. It was just after midday, and Gruelenor's wounds felt almost as if they had never existed. And now it was time to move.

The company marched with weapons ready. Gruelenor veered west, crossing back across Batorn River and leaving the water behind in hopes of avoiding the ogres. There were a dozen of the giants calling Benasti home—at least it had been so when Gruelenor lived in the forest—and being a lazy group, they did not travel far from the river to hunt. But they were a cunning bunch, and not to be underestimated.

The woodland grew brighter as the trees opened up, and small animals returned, scampering from the company's path. A weight lifted from Gruelenor's shoulders—the end of the forest drew near.

"I hear something," Xorlunder said.

The company halted, and the hairs on the back of Gruelenor's neck rose as he listened. There was the snapping of a tree limb, followed by a leaf-laden branch falling. Next came a thud. Then another. And another. Something large approached.

"Ogre…" Gruelenor shook his head.

Sullis motioned for Magneer and Nidor to take positions toward the approaching monster. The Brondor paladin then waved Gruelenor, Xorlunder, and Melac to back off and get from sight. Sullis remained in plain view with his weapon drawn.

Thud! Thud! The sound drew closer. Then it halted. Next came sniffing. The thudding resumed.

Gruelenor stood behind a maple, craning his neck to have a look. Beyond a thick birch was a tall figure, visible on either side of the trunk. Its legs looked capable of squashing a full-grown man and the arms were immense, and in one hand was a small tree, stripped of all limbs. The monster's skin was the color of spoiling fowl, with many dark patches, and covering its massive torso were several bearskins, sewn together to make a tunic. The ogre peered around the tree, ducking beneath branches that dangled ten feet above the ground. Its bushy brows lowered as it scanned the forest with reddish eyes and sniffed with its bulbous nose, and upon spotting Sullis, it revealed its misshapen yellow-and-black teeth with a wide grin.

"Meat for my shtew!" The ogre sprayed saliva while it spoke in a deep, rumbling voice.

"Be on your way, ogre!" Sullis said. "I am a paladin of Brondor, and I am only passing through. There is easier prey to catch."

The ogre belched a hearty laugh and stepped around the tree, placing a large hand on its trunk. The tree yielded as the brute pushed by, and it seemed to sigh in relief when the hand was removed.

"I shmell more meat!" The ogre sniffed again, turning left and right to spy Nidor and Magneer.

Xorlunder stepped forward with an arrow fitted to his bowstring, and Gruelenor joined the elf. Melac remained hidden.

The ogre laughed. "Your puny toysh not hurt me! But I tell you what. Give me one shlab of meat, and I let other shlabs go."

Gruelenor could almost hear Sullis's thoughts. The Brondor paladin, though usually more than eager to battle, wished to avoid this confrontation. Apparently, Sullis also realized the ogre would not leave empty-handed.

"We can give you the food from our packs," he said.

The brute scratched its chin, as if considering the offer. But then came heavy footfalls from the north. The ogre laughed even louder than before as it slapped its large hand on its thigh. It had been stalling.

Melac stepped from the brush to join Gruelenor. "I believe another—"

Gruelenor lifted a brow.

"Yes, of course." Melac nodded.

Sullis glared at the ogre, and the monster stopped laughing as its lips curled into an evil grin.

"Korgun shaid that meat wush on the way. Meat with sharp toysh. Sho I invite friend for dinner!"

Battle was imminent. Gruelenor knew this. Sullis knew it as well, and the paladin charged.

The ogre received a gash across its obese stomach as Sullis scored the first wound, but the behemoth seemed oblivious and swung its club. The paladin ducked beneath the massive weapon, and the wind of the attack nearly knocked him to the ground.

Xorlunder launched three arrows, piercing the ogre's neck, shoulder, and chest. Still, the hulking monster took no notice, turning its attention to Nidor and Magneer, who had inflicted wounds to its sides. The ogre flailed its giant maul at the two, taking out a couple of trees, and Sullis lunged, thrusting his blade upward and impaling the creature to the hilt. The ogre could not ignore this wound, and it roared as it kicked the Brondor paladin with one of its massive legs. Sullis flew several yards until halted by a tree, and he crashed to the ground. He struggled to rise and collapsed again.

Gruelenor wished to help, but the second ogre had arrived. He put his back to a tree as the monster stopped next to him, its eyes locked on Melac. Though smaller than the first ogre, it was three times the girth of Gruelenor, and as it took a step toward the mage, Gruelenor came around with a savage attack. His sword cut into the monster's stomach, and it roared as it thrust a long spear. Gruelenor jumped aside, and the weapon pierced the forest floor.

Melac stole the ogre's attention as he chanted, and from his hands issued a brilliant flash. The ogre staggered back a step, releasing its spear to shield its eyes. Gruelenor pressed, scoring several more wounds, but he soon found himself in peril when the ogre's sight returned and it swung a fist larger than his head. The attack landed on his chest and sent him tumbling into the underbrush.

Nidor continued his assault on the larger ogre while Magneer attacked from the other side. The monster swung its maul, grazing Nidor as he dodged to his left; and so deadly was the force that Nidor was knocked to the ground and the forest began to spin.

Nidor shook his head to clear it, but the trees still rotated and all sound seemed far away. He saw Magneer, alone before the ogre, and the ranger raced around a tree while the monster pressed. Xorlunder arrived with sword in hand, and Nidor's vision continued to play with him as the elf leaped onto the ogre's shoulders—an impossible feat. Xorlunder inflicted smoking wounds to the ogre's head and neck, and Magneer thrust his sword into its leg. The monster swung its club, landing a solid blow that sent the ranger into a tree.

Nidor forced himself to stand, and his blade lit up with fire. His vision cleared as Xorlunder dropped from the ogre's shoulders to add a smoldering gash to its thigh, and the massive brute turned on the elf. It brought down its club, and Xorlunder evaded the attack as it crashed onto the ground and shook the forest.

Renewing his assault, Nidor added scorching wounds to the massive body. The ogre grimaced and fell against a tree, and the trunk bent beneath the monster's weight. Nidor and Xorlunder inflicted several more gashes until the ogre dropped to its knees, and the elf dashed away, leaving Nidor alone with the ailing foe.

From within the vegetation, Gruelenor saw Melac release a globe of fire that struck the smaller ogre on the chest. The flames washed over the creature, resulting only in charred skin. The ogre pulled the spear from the ground as it turned its angry eyes on Melac, and the mage released several more spells in defense. He snapped the spear in half; the ogre kept coming. He brought down branches; the ogre kept coming. He launched spheres that exploded on impact; the ogre kept coming. Melac's magic only served to slow the monster and bring it to greater rage.

Gruelenor pulled himself from the briars and gave a Ballrik-like roar, stealing the ogre's attention and allowing Melac to dart behind a tree. Standing alone before the unarmed foe, Gruelenor readied his blade. He danced about, drawing several swinging fists, and used small trees for cover—many were marred and a few crashed to the ground. The ogre's attacks were so wild that Gruelenor could not find an opportunity to counter.

Xorlunder was then next to Gruelenor, and they split before the brute to attack from either side while Melac launched more exploding globes. The ogre continued flailing its fists, and a glancing blow knocked Gruelenor to his knees, but he recovered and rolled to his feet.

Another ogre's approach thundered through the trees, and the monster before Gruelenor gave a bloody smile. Gruelenor's heart sank when he spotted the new arrival.

The third ogre arrived out of the east, and it was larger than the first two. The behemoth looked at the fallen ogre, where Nidor struck the final blow, and to its right was the smallest of its group, scorched and bloody and without a weapon. Its eyes narrowed, and it roared, causing even the smaller ogre to cringe.

The colossal foe charged Nidor with its maul held high, and its footfalls shook the forest while its club tore through branches twenty feet overhead. Nidor ducked the tree-club, but he bounced off the ogre's knee and tumbled several yards away. The fire on his sword disappeared as the blade flew free, and Nidor struggled, trying to regain his feet.

Gruelenor's mind raced as the enormous ogre looked his way. The smaller ogre was hurting and near defeat, but Sullis, Nidor, and Magneer were down, and Melac proved ineffective.

Then another figure appeared.

A large warrior entered from the north, obviously not an ogre at only seven feet in height, and it was clad in black armor with a large black sword in its hand. It was the same warrior that defeated the archers at the ford in Vermallon Forest. Gruelenor was not sure if Xorlunder noticed the new arrival, for the gray elf resumed his assault upon the smaller ogre.

Trusting Xorlunder to finish the wounded foe, Gruelenor charged the giant ogre. He pulled up, however, when the monster took notice of the dark warrior, and it appeared as though fear had entered the ogre's eyes.

The ogre swung its maul, but the black figure exhibited great strength and knocked the club aside. With deadly accuracy, the warrior put forth an exhibition, scoring four deep gashes while drawing a second, equally large sword from his back to add three more. The ogre stumbled and looked to retreat, but the warrior was relentless; and after a few more vicious strikes, the monster collapsed, taking out two trees.

The entire exchange had taken less than ten seconds, and the stranger turned to face the smaller ogre. Defying the wounds that plagued the monster's body, the ogre fled into the woods with surprising speed.

Gruelenor stood with sword ready, watching the stranger in black, and Xorlunder arrived at Gruelenor's side. Sullis struggled to prop himself against a tree, staring at the large warrior, and Melac stepped forward with hands raised, as if ready to cast a spell.

Nidor climbed to his feet with some effort and stepped before the figure. "Thank you, stranger."

The tallest person Gruelenor had ever known, Nidor stood half a head shorter than the warrior.

The Dale extended his arm in greeting. "We are indebted to you twice now."

The warrior sheathed the swords on his back and removed his helmet. He was a handsome man, and he shook his dark hair and turned his blue eyes on the company. His gaze was penetrating and his face grim. "There is no debt." The man's voice was deep. He clasped arms with Nidor before turning to the trees behind him. "Umbarc! Come!"

Chapter 23

The Dark Warrior

The man before Nidor appeared young, perhaps Magneer's age, but wisdom shone in his eyes.

"Vecnor?" Xorlunder's expression was caught between joy and disbelief. "Can this be?"

"Impossible." Nidor glanced at the elf.

Vecnor was but a legend. Nidor heard tales of the Black Rogue in Holindale, as the name served to inspire even the lowest of fighters in times of need. *Fight like Vecnor!* was a statement used often during Nidor's training, and *Vecnor give me strength* was another when warriors faced impossible odds. It was said that Vecnor single handedly defeated an army of undead within Tikken City two decades ago. But it was just a story. Even if it were true, the man standing before Nidor was too young to have accomplished it.

"That is my name," said the warrior in black.

"Nidor!" Gruelenor called, kneeling over Magneer.

Nidor felt ashamed for having forgotten about his friend's condition, and he rushed to Magneer, who was sitting with Gruelenor's help. The ranger's leg was bent in an awkward position, blood issued from his mouth, nose, and ear, and scratches covered all exposed flesh. Magneer appeared grateful to see Nidor's flaming hand, but as it came into contact, the ranger cringed. The reaction was short-lived and his breathing eased.

Nidor turned to Sullis next. Though in obvious pain, the Brondor paladin made his way to stand before Vecnor.

"Your name is Vecnor, you say?" Sullis furrowed his brow. "I am a paladin of the Temple of Brondor, and that name is held high among my order in Harbnum, for he is the champion of my religion. But the warrior who used that name lived many years ago, so I would reconsider boasting such claims in my presence, whether in jest or otherwise."

"Regardless," Vecnor offered a slight bow, "Vecnor is my birth name. I do not claim to be the same Vecnor you speak of, but if you wish to address me, that is the name I answer to."

Sullis considered the warrior. "Very well. And by whose authority do you act? Why have you trailed us?"

"I act on my own authority, as far as it concerns you." Vecnor's response caused Sullis's frown to deepen. "As to why I have trailed you, I think you should be grateful that it is so. But if you must know, it was requested that I provide what help I can. I am aware of your mission, and I offer my sword."

There was a pause while Sullis studied Vecnor, dealing with some inner turmoil. It was clear Sullis did not care for the tone in which the warrior addressed him, and he probably did not believe the man's story. But how could anyone deny Vecnor's timely arrival? With the skill and strength the man exhibited, such an ally would be of great assistance on the road ahead.

"This man is who he claims to be." Xorlunder broke the silence. "It is he who came to Orlenfel, battling through hundreds of hobgoblins to convince me to part with my clan and give aid to this war. This is great news indeed, and it fills me with hope renewed!"

Vecnor nodded to the elf. "Good to see you, Xorlunder."

Sullis never took his eyes from Vecnor. Nor did he flinch when touched by Nidor's healing hand. Nidor thought it odd, but Vecnor lacked the usual look of surprise for his healing talent.

"You say you are aware of our mission," Sullis said once Nidor finished, drumming his fingers on the pommel of his sword. "What else do you know?"

"I know that the North Army has suffered heavy casualties. But they reached Orlenfel at last and defeated the besiegers."

Xorlunder stood taller with these words.

"The gray elves now accompany the army," Vecnor added, "but they will be greatly outnumbered upon reaching Darmhorng, for a legion of undead marches out of the south to meet them."

"That should not pose too dire a threat." Xorlunder lifted his chin. "Even if dunarchins march with the enemy, my clan will show them to be no match."

"That is not all," said Vecnor. "After the North Army crossed the Great East River, the Death Lord, Gruzim, flew to the north to lead another host of undead from Selt, and they now march in the army's wake."

At the mention of Gruzim, Nidor thought he saw Vecnor glance in Gruelenor's direction. Gruelenor eyed the forest floor.

"Your words make it appear the war is lost already." Sullis continued to exhibit distrust. "Have you any *good* tidings for us?"

"Though Burmagaard is filled with Zurkan, mercenaries, and bandits that once hid in the wilderness," Vecnor replied, "there are many who would rise and fight against the evil. They are loyal to Priestess Elloria, and they await her return."

"Elloria?" Xorlunder furrowed his brow. "The one that accompanied me into the Serpent's Range many years ago?"

"The same."

"She is the High Priestess of Brondor in Kalmaar," Xorlunder said to Sullis, sparking the paladin's interest. "Though it has been years since last I saw her, I recall her to have been an excellent warrior."

"Where might we find her?" Sullis asked Vecnor.

"I'm afraid that is another problem." Vecnor's face became grim. "She is within the dungeons of Darmhorng."

"I am confused as to whether your coming is a blessing or one of ill omen." Sullis shook his head. "With every bit of hope you offer, you take away twice as much."

"There is a way to free her," Vecnor said. "And with her freedom, not only will her following surface from hiding, but so will many Kalmirans who have lost all hope. It is a dangerous path, but one that must be traveled."

"There are to be no deviations from the plan." Sullis grew more heated with each word. "We have strict orders. If one company fails, the entire war could collapse. I won't have that on my head."

"There is more at stake here than your orders and your pride." Vecnor raised a brow. "There are the lives of all that call Vaeldor home. And the war has already suffered. No part of the plan has gone as hoped."

"What do you mean?" Sullis's suspicion returned.

"There is nothing specific I can share with you," Vecnor replied. "I only know, on good authority, that things have gone awry elsewhere. The plan needs to evolve if the war is to be won."

"Surely he brings tidings from Elgarroth." Xorlunder looked at Vecnor for confirmation, but the warrior said nothing. "Elgarroth is one of the creators of the plan," the elf turned to Sullis. "And if the great wizard sees fit for us to alter our path, we must consider it."

"What of the dwarves, then?" Sullis glanced from Xorlunder to Vecnor. "You say they outnumber us. Why would we not proceed to the mountains to seek their aid, as the plan dictates?"

"Our need for their help has not diminished," Vecnor replied. "The dwarves are more important than ever."

Sullis lit up with realization. "You aim to split our company."

Vecnor nodded.

"Does it not make more sense to journey to Morimont together?" posed Magneer, having recovered enough to join the conversation. "From there, we can return to free the priestess with an army."

Vecnor shook his head. "It would be too late. Trannum's minions keep watch on Morimont, for the necromancer realizes the inevitable recruitment of the dwarves. Once they set out, the enemy will send a force to meet them, and while this may seem to deplete Darmhorng's defenses and serve the North Army, it does not come close to evening the odds. But with the emergence of Elloria, we can create another force; one unlooked for and within their midst."

Sullis's brow furrowed as he pondered Vecnor's words. "It seems logical. But the enemy is tricky."

Nidor was unsure if Sullis was talking to himself or Vecnor.

"The day is not yet spent." The Brondor paladin looked at Vecnor. "And we cannot tarry any longer. Let us leave this accursed forest, so I might have a moment to think."

Before heading out, Sullis used herbs to treat all injuries Nidor had not, including those Nidor sustained. Nidor was drained from treating Magneer, Sullis, and Xorlunder, not to mention the energy he expended while battling the ogres, and he took this time to sit against a tree and rest.

Magneer's wounds were gone, but the ranger was a bit shaky, so Vecnor lifted him onto Umbarc. Magneer marveled at the large Andrian steed, and though Nidor could tell the animal was advanced in years, he was impressed with its unmistakable strength. Once Sullis finished with his task, Gruelenor helped Nidor to his feet.

Lunchtime came and went while they marched to the south, but the blood of the ogres decorating the company's cloaks and armor suppressed their appetites. They happened upon a brook and halted long enough to cleanse themselves as best they could, and Nidor also took time to clean the silt the Fires of Silcor had left on his sword.

Very few words were spoken while they continued their trek, save for Gruelenor and Xorlunder pointing out signs of passage on the terrain before them. Before long, they reached the forest's edge, and the sun found a small window to greet them, shining just above the distant mountains to the west and sparkling off Lake Garaard. The vision ended quickly, however, as clouds moved in to correct the oversight.

Sullis stood motionless, gazing across the vast lake at Darmhorng Castle. A mighty fortress, it appeared as nothing more than a simple shelter of stone in the distance, and beyond were the walls of Burmagaard. Above the castle, storm clouds hovered, and occasional strokes of lightning pierced the ground, followed by rumbles of thunder several seconds later. Other than the lightning, nothing moved.

At last, Sullis spoke.

"I do not doubt your sincerity." The Brondor paladin turned to Vecnor. "You know much that we do, that is obvious, as well as things we do not. But our orders are strict, and I should send you on your way."

Xorlunder's shoulders slumped. "You must—"

"However," Sullis shot the elf a glance, "I would be a fool not to heed your words. So my decision is this: I will continue to Morimont to complete our mission and speak with the dwarves." He turned to the company. "As to where the rest of your paths lie, I leave that up to you."

Nidor was dumbstruck. It was unlike Sullis to allow others to make decisions.

"I alone know the way to Morimont," Magneer said. "I will go with you, Sullis."

Sullis nodded.

Nidor thought Magneer would have jumped at the chance to get out from under the Brondor paladin's control.

Xorlunder looked back and forth between Sullis and Vecnor. "I must follow Vecnor in this matter. My part was to lead you through Vermallon and around Benasti, objectives now achieved. The dwarf city is no place for my kind."

"I will join Vecnor as well," said Gruelenor. "Morimont is no better suited for one of my race than it is for an elf. I can offer little assistance outside my sword from this point, and I believe it to be better placed in freeing the priestess."

"I must divert to Darmhorng as well," Melac said. "They will surely be in need of my talents if they are to break into the dungeon."

Sullis looked at Nidor, and before Nidor offered a response, the Brondor paladin spoke.

"You will join them."

Nidor was not sure how to respond, and it took a few seconds to find his voice. "What if you are discovered? Two cannot combat a Death Lord, nor an army of undead."

"Our paths remain the same for better than a day yet," said Vecnor to Sullis. "After that, Umbarc will carry you swiftly to Morimont." Vecnor then addressed Nidor. "You can ease your mind, for it is unlikely they'll encounter the enemy until the dwarves set foot from the mountains."

"It's settled then," said Sullis.

They traveled west, remaining just inside the trees until Benasti offered no more cover. By then, dusk had arrived, and they continued under darkness. The water's edge was a perfect guide, and the towering pillars of shadow, the Varlimor Mountains, grew taller with every passing mile. They walked through the rest of the night among tall reeds and scattered trees, and insects were almost deafening while the pests enjoyed sampling their blood. The moon peeked from behind the clouds now and again to reflect off the water, but its visits never lasted long.

As the sky brightened with the morning, they found a small thicket to shelter them and halted for some sleep. Nidor felt much stronger, and he took the first watch with Sullis. All was quiet for some time, but then the Brondor paladin spoke.

"I'm sending you to Darmhorng for a reason." He looked Nidor in the eyes. "Though there is no evil about the man, I do not wholly trust him." Sullis checked to make sure no one was listening. "I've watched you closely. You have a soft heart, but a clear head. I'm trusting you'll use your best judgment, so that no evil comes of this. Remember, the fate of Vaeldor is in the balance."

Nidor said nothing. He was shocked to hear Sullis speak so. In the beginning, Nidor had not wished to be grouped with the Brondor paladin. But since leaving Sendorum, Sullis had made sound decisions for the most part, based on the circumstances. Perhaps Merssa had been right in choosing Sullis, and Nidor felt he would miss the man's leadership.

The day passed, and they headed out at dusk. After a few hours, the lake narrowed until meeting the swift Morimont River that fed it.

"Another mile and the water is shallow enough to cross," said Vecnor. "That's where we'll part ways."

The river moved rapidly against them, and just as Vecnor claimed, an area existed where it widened and the water was only a couple feet deep at most. At that point, they halted.

Magneer looked at Nidor and Gruelenor with troubled eyes, and Nidor realized they might never see the ranger again. They exchanged arm clasps and then hugs.

"We'll see you in Darmhorng," Nidor said.

Magneer nodded, and he and Sullis mounted Umbarc. Sullis grabbed hold of the reins and turned to the company.

"May Brondor guide your swords!"

CHAPTER 24

DENVALE

The battle for Ironside Keep lasted deep into the night. The stronghold was a mess. Broken furnishings and dead soldiers were strewn about, as well as hundreds of dunarchins and ghouls, and thousands of soldiers littered the mountain pass while thousands more lay at the bottom of the gorge. Cavalor took charge of clearing the lounge of bodies so Merssa might have a place to ponder the situation, and there she sat, everyone leaving her to her thoughts.

The next leg of the mission was to march on Denvale and then Kembald, destroying all that opposed them. They were then to lay siege to Castle Lambrak, the stronghold where the kings of Marcove ruled before the arrival of the Death Lords. The siege was only a ruse, however, to draw the attention of Nomedd and lure the enemy from their master's side. The plan had taken years to develop, but with only fifty soldiers under Merssa's command, it could not work. Landerik's foolish actions had cost them dearly.

A couple of hours passed before Borse entered the room, and behind her husband walked Cavalor, Wezlok, and Landerik. Their faces were grim, except for Landerik's. The young paladin wore a look of scorn, his usual sign of disrespect for all that treated him as anything other than a superior. But this time, his animosity was aimed at himself. He offered no arguments or excuses when Merssa scolded him earlier; he said nothing at all, standing with his head bowed in shame. Landerik's love for battle had gotten the better of him, as well as his need to prove himself to his battle god, and he realized his mistake too late. Merssa had not chastised Landerik as severely as she had wished, for they would require his sword in the days to come, and she dared not crush his spirit entirely.

"The men have fortified the keep's defenses under Arkor's direction," Cavalor said.

Merssa nodded, feeling pity for the one-armed warrior. After destroying the Vikur-dunarchin, Arkor discovered Vikur's key, and he placed his brother's body in the family tomb. Vikur's will must have truly been strong, for he managed to keep secret the only key capable of opening the tower crypt, hiding it in a place where only Arkor could find it. Merssa ordered that Arkor be left alone to mourn over the twisted corpse of the former Lord of the Keep. Arkor resurfaced an hour later, showing no more sorrow, but his face was grim. Merssa put him in charge of the keep, and she had not seen him since.

"Have you come to any decisions yet?" Borse asked.

Merssa stared at Landerik. The paladin bowed his head and did not meet her gaze. She then looked at Borse, and his smile calmed her, relieving some of the anger that burned within. "We must press forward...somehow." Her last word was just above a whisper.

"I don't see how." Cavalor shot Landerik a sidelong glance.

"We *will* press on." Merssa's voice grew stronger. "We'll just have to find another way to achieve our goal."

"What do you have in mind?" Wezlok sat on the other side of the table, keeping his distance. Through it all, the elf continued to display his loathing for everyone, but Merssa paid his attitude no heed. He would never hinder the mission.

"We have no army," Merssa said. "That is obvious. So we cannot simply march into Marcove as originally intended." She slid her seat back and stood. "But we must continue, all the same. We must reach Kembald and draw attention to ourselves at Castle Lambrak, well enough to complete our goal."

"I do not see how that is possible." Wezlok eyed Landerik. Had the wizard had his way, the young paladin would be resting at the bottom of the chasm.

Merssa glared at the elf for the interruption. Her eyes then dropped to the table. She felt much more her age as of late. The last time she passed a mirror, she noticed her hair was consumed by gray. She dug deep, searching for the warrior within herself. "We may not be able to lay siege to the castle, but we might still gain access beyond its walls."

"And what would that accomplish?" Wezlok's demeanor remained calm.

"Once inside," Merssa replied, "we take out the Death Lord that resides there. Then Trannum's attention will surely turn our way."

"Take the castle?" Cavalor's incredulous tone showed his lack of faith in the new plan. "Even if we were able to do so, then what? How are five people going to defend a castle against Trannum's minions?"

"We are not meant to." Wezlok's focus remained on Merssa.

She stared at the occupants of the room, a deathly calm settling over her. "Our mission was never one of survival. We are but a necessary tool for the cause of Good. Surviving is not required in the end." Merssa kept her eyes from meeting Cavalor's. This was not the fate she would have chosen for her son. "We might not be able to hold the castle against the forces of Trannum, but we might be able to distract them long enough to achieve our objective. That is all that matters."

"What about Arkor?" Wezlok asked.

"I do not believe he'll abandon this place," Merssa said. "I doubt he possesses the heart to continue. But under his direction, I'm confident the keep will not fall again into enemy control."

There was a moment of silence. Then Landerik spoke.

"I know my deeds have proven ill. But I swear by my sword I will put it to right. If you'll give me the chance."

"For your actions, I owe you nothing," Merssa said evenly. "If days were different, I would do more than just leave you behind. But

I cannot deny your skills. Perhaps you'll receive the chance you seek before it's over."

"It is late, and we should get some rest." Borse gazed at Merssa, as if he wished to speak to her in private. "We are all weary from battle, so harbor no concerns this night. Arkor will protect our sleep. In the morning, we prepare for the days ahead."

Wezlok departed without hesitation. Landerik lingered, as if wanting to say more, but then he exited. Borse and Cavalor remained seated, staring at Merssa.

Borse leaned forward in his chair. "I sense there to be more on your mind."

Merssa opened her mouth, but nothing came out. She always knew her family could perish in this mission, but she never believed it would happen until now. "I think one of us should remain." She looked at Cavalor.

"You cannot leave me behind!" Her son stood. "This is what I have trained for my whole life. True, your new plan caught me by surprise. But I'm ready. If I turn back now, my life would have no meaning."

Merssa continued to stare and her shoulders slumped. Cavalor was right. She had deprived him of a normal youth, raising him to fight the necromancer. Though she always considered the war to be her responsibility, she feared she might not live long enough to see it through. So she raised her son to lead in the event that she could not. Merssa was the worst mother in all of Vaeldor. She looked at Borse.

"You know I must continue as well." Her husband spoke in his typical, fatherly tone. Not long ago, he stood tall and menacing above the enemy. Now, he appeared the aged priest again, wrinkled and worn. "I know what you feel in your heart, but I have a duty before Cafior, just as you. Just as Cavalor."

Merssa released a deep sigh.

The following morning, they returned to the lounge. Arkor was there as well, and they took their seats at the tavern's largest table.

"I hear that I have fallen from the company." Arkor's grim expression was unchanged from the previous night.

"I thought you might wish to remain." Merssa looked at the one-armed warrior. "The pass must not fall again. Evil must not have freedom to roam into the west."

"Once Trannum is destroyed," Arkor said, "there will be no worry of evil passing by Ironside. My place is with you. General Vargen is more than capable of running things here."

Merssa nodded. Though one more warrior made little difference, a bit of hope returned. "We will be all the stronger with you among us."

Arkor gave a nod.

Merssa cleared her throat before addressing the room. "Trannum is aware of our presence, of that there is no doubt. Arkor was able to knock one of his finest warriors into the chasm. Whether the Death Lord survived, I am unsure, but the necromancer has surely taken notice. His spies and minions will be on alert, and entering Denvale will prove difficult. Does anyone have an issue with a mission of stealth?" Merssa looked at Landerik. In her younger days, she would rather have been captured than play the role of a thief. But the years had opened her mind to many things.

"No, my lady." Landerik's eyes were downcast, but his fidgeting revealed deep conflict, for Brondor prohibited such actions.

"Good." Merssa gave a nod. "We will pass through Denvale as quietly as possible and make for Mentrial Forest. We will then follow the Belsal River to Krimbror River, and then on to Kembald and Castle Lambrak. If scouting reports are still correct, Gulthar will be there. The information may be inaccurate, however, since the necromancer has made adjustments to prepare for our coming.

"As I mentioned earlier, we cannot lay siege to the castle." Merssa walked around the table. "So we shall infiltrate. Once inside, we'll make such a commotion that all eyes will turn our way. In this matter, I will count heavily on Wezlok."

The elf nodded.

"The enemy will be forced to deal with us," Merssa continued. "But it is important that we withstand the initial assault. I realize this sounds impossible, and it very well may be. But their first strike will only be to test our strength. We must succeed if we are to draw all surrounding evil to us, and in doing so, grant others access into Trannum's stronghold." Merssa gazed out the window. The open curtain fluttered with the sound of the rising wind, but the snow had stopped. "I only pray Trannum has not learned of their approach."

"I will do everything within my power to achieve success," Wezlok said.

"As will the rest of us," Arkor added. "It is a hopeless quest, but the bravery of Ironside did not diminish with Vikur's passing."

Merssa turned back to the table. "Then it's time to get to work."

They searched the fallen enemies, procuring garments to disguise themselves as Marc soldiers. The uniforms bore a terrible smell, having been worn by the undead, and were damaged and stained, but Merssa hoped the defects would go unnoticed in the night. At least the cloaks were thick and would provide warmth. Arkor then gave final instructions to General Vargen, and the company set out.

Dark clouds remained overhead, but it was not yet evening and Merssa led the way. They traveled light, carrying little more than their armor and weapons, and though the snowfall had ceased, the wind continued to howl across the road, cutting through Merssa's layers. They hugged the wall and followed the icy path on foot—even if any horses had survived the assault, it would have been impossible to ride into Denvale unnoticed.

After a mile, sheer rock replaced the chasm and cliff walls towered to either side. Untouched snow then covered the pass, and drifts of the powder climbed the northern wall to heights of ten feet in several places. But the trek was not difficult. As night arrived, Wezlok took the lead.

The wind calmed while the elf veered around the slicker parts of the road, and Merssa was unsure if it was her imagination, but it also seemed the air had warmed. Soon the snow was only an inch deep, and they increased their pace, making better progress than during the day. As the night grew late, two points of light appeared ahead and to the left, fifty feet above the pass. The Denvale watchtowers rose like black spires, and a solid gate barred the way between them.

Merssa placed her hand on Wezlok's shoulder, halting the elf. She saw nothing outside the dancing torchlight within the tower windows.

"How many guards?"

Wezlok peered at the distant structures. "Two each. Armed with crossbows. One bears a horn. The gate is closed."

"How do we to pass through undetected?" Cavalor asked Arkor.

"A breach beyond the far tower." The one-armed warrior stared ahead, as if lost in memory. "Vikur discovered the opening when we were kids, and we used it to sneak out when trouble found us. It's not obvious to the eye... I only hope it has gone unnoticed."

"That may not matter," Cavalor said. "We'll be as dark insects on a white blanket. They'll see us and sound the alarm."

"Can you hide our approach?" Merssa asked Wezlok.

The elf stared at Merssa for a couple of seconds. He then scanned their surroundings. "It will be an unwelcome return, but it should work."

Merssa gave a nod.

Wezlok whispered unintelligible words, wiggling his fingers at the peaks above, and a breeze descended, growing stronger with every second. The company looked around in alarm, as if Trannum had sent forth another storm to bury them, but Merssa knew it was Wezlok's doing and soon everyone was aware of his plan. The wind lifted loose snow from the cliffs and rushed it down and across the road, swirling and obscuring the pass.

"Hurry!" Wezlok darted into the torrent.

The company followed. Merssa remained as close to the mage as she could, and though she lost sight of the elf, the way was straight and no one strayed. The road broadened upon reaching the gate, and everyone came to a halt before the tall wooden doors. The bases of the towers were visible to either side, but blowing snow obscured everything above ten feet, including the lights within the turrets.

"This way," said Arkor, just above the wind, and he pressed farther.

Beyond the southern tower, a wall of stone stretched twenty yards to the cliff. Near the edge, where the wall met the mountain, the stone was pitted and riddled with cracks. Arkor made a quick search of a particular crevice, and through the snow Merssa saw him nod.

Had the breach escaped enemy eyes? Or did the evil forces not care enough to address the issue? Merssa moved in for a closer look. A few feet above the ground, deep within a wide groove and roughly three feet in height and two feet across, a hole penetrated the wall. Only when peering directly into the crack could one notice the hole passed all the way through, and Merssa understood how the breach might go unnoticed from this side. She nodded for Arkor to proceed.

Arkor used his good arm to pull himself into the opening. It was a tight squeeze, but after removing his weapon belt he pushed through. Merssa went next, followed by Cavalor, Borse, Landerik, and then Wezlok. Cavalor had difficulties as well, but he made it with some effort. As the mage pulled his last leg into the tunnel, the winds ceased and the snow drifted to the ground.

On the other side of the wall was an unattended corner of Denvale. Many large stones had accumulated from past rockslides, and ice packed the rubble together. After strapping his weapon belt in place, Arkor led the way over the pile and into the end of a long alley, where a mountain of frozen garbage was discarded. Merssa doubted any of Denvale's citizens had knowledge of the breach.

"Where to now?" Cavalor frowned at the snow-covered refuse.

"Lead the way," Merssa said to Arkor with a wave of her hand.

The company followed Arkor up the alley until it joined an empty street. It appeared the village had not experienced snowfall for some time, and what snow did exist was hard packed along the edges of buildings and alleyways, leaving the street clear. Still, the air was chilly.

Merssa poked her head out, but retracted it when a dozen guards rushed by in the direction of the pass. They were not zombies, ghouls, or dunarchins, but living men. Though Merssa despised the fact that living beings served the necromancer, she was glad the city was not infested with the undead.

"Do you think the wind caused an alarm?" asked Cavalor.

Merssa was unsure. She had hoped the city watch would assume Wezlok's wind was sent by their master. If they began a search now...

"Find the Wild Boar Tavern," Arkor said. "It's down the street on the left. I'll meet you in the alley next to it."

Before Merssa voiced her objection, the one-armed warrior sped off to join the guards. The platoon disappeared around a corner and all was quiet.

Merssa shook her head. But it was for the best. She needed to know if their presence was realized. With a deep breath, she led the way along the barren street.

The tavern was not difficult to find, as it was well lit and music sounded from within. Through frosty windows, Merssa spied figures drinking and laughing, as if life were normal. With a sneer, she stepped toward the alley next to the building.

"What're you doin'?" barked a Marc soldier, stepping from the shadows of the alleyway. "You know only those on duty are allowed on the streets after dark. Now git yer raggedy hides indoors! Startin' to look like the undead..." The man slunk back into the darkness.

"How does he know we're not on duty?" Cavalor stared at the alley.

"He bore an armband," said Wezlok. "We best step inside."

Merssa reluctantly opened the tavern door.

Marc soldiers filled the room, as well as hobgoblins and krukari, and a few larger krukari wore red surcoats bearing a bleeding eye upon the chest. Merssa recognized them as Zurkan, and she wondered what had brought them so far south.

A few open tables existed, and Merssa led her companions to one suitable to accommodate them. Several patrons looked puzzled by the company's attire, but no one seemed interested enough to comment. A disgusting man in a soiled apron then approached.

"Fresh from battle, eh?" The barman grinned, revealing deformed black teeth as he observed their uniforms. Seeing no answer was forthcoming, he cleared his throat. "Whatcha be havin'?"

"Five beers," said Merssa.

"I wasn't speakin' to you!" The man caught the company by surprise.

"Five beers." Cavalor emphasized the words, rising to his feet to glare at the servant.

The barman cowered. "To be sure. No need to be raisin' yer voice. We all have a job to do." He headed for the bar.

"This place is worse than Neja," Merssa muttered. Her head then snapped Borse's way, but her husband paid the comment no mind.

"Watch yourself," Wezlok said as Cavalor sat. "I find these people as revolting as you, though for other reasons. But an order exists." The mage nodded toward a group of krukari. "Zurkan are in charge. The Marcs clear at their approach. We must play our part if we are to remain unnoticed."

"What about you?" asked Landerik. "I don't see an elf in this establishment. Will they not take notice of that fact?"

"What they see is not necessarily what you see." Wezlok brought confusion to Landerik's face.

"Why would Zurkan be in charge here?" Merssa eyed the table of krukari. "Their master rules over Kalmaar."

The slob-servant placed the beers on the table. Without mention of a price, he walked away.

The drinks were disgusting—a watered-down brew served in soiled clay mugs—and the company sipped slowly. Before Merssa was forced to consume too much, Arkor entered. Merssa noticed he now wore an armband.

"I said the alley," Arkor whispered as he took a seat next to Merssa. Upon seeing her glare, he nodded in understanding. "They know the wind was not normal. They've quadrupled the guard at the pass and are watching for us."

"Then they do not realize we have already passed through," said Cavalor.

Arkor gave a nod. "But I think it best we leave soon. Someone spoke of a Lord coming."

"A Death Lord," Merssa murmured. She then looked around the tavern. Was it paranoia? Or was every patron staring? "Let's go."

They headed for the door. But as they walked by the table of Zurkan, one of the krukari stuck out his boot and caused Cavalor to stumble. The evil warrior rose, glaring at Merssa's son.

"How dare you kick me!" the Zurkan growled.

Cavalor composed himself and bowed, doing well to hide any anger. "I apologize for my clumsiness, sir."

"That won't do." The Zurkan held a malevolent grin. "There's a price that must be paid."

Landerik stepped forward, pulling his pouch. "Take it." He offered the small bag.

The krukari looked at Landerik and snarled. "Somethin' 'bout you has an odd smell." The Zurkan sniffed. "I don't like it."

"Be that as it may," Landerik used his condescending tone, "this should more than make up for everything." He bounced the pouch to make it jingle.

"I have no use for your coins!" The Zurkan slapped the pouch from Landerik's hand, spilling its contents. The tavern fell silent, with the exception of gold and silver coins rolling to places near and far, and all eyes were on the confrontation. "I want blood!"

"On my word," Wezlok said to Merssa and Borse, "make haste to the alley we first entered."

The krukari pulled his blade, his face aglow with excitement, but Landerik was quicker. The young paladin unsheathed his sword and plunged it into the Zurkan's chest before the krukari could take a swing, and the tavern erupted as weapons were drawn.

"Run!" Wezlok shouted.

Merssa and Borse ushered the company toward the door, and behind them was a brilliant flash. Merssa heard shouts of confusion as she stepped onto the street, but there came no immediate pursuit. She knew not what magic was at work, and there was no time for questions, so she ran as fast as she could.

More shouts sounded as guards appeared, but no one paid any heed to the company. Instead, soldiers were occupied with looking at each other or gazing at their reflections in windows. As Merssa neared the alley, horns blared and more guards rushed about, but still no one gave her or her companions a second look. Once they were from sight, she halted.

"Arkor," Wezlok said. "Can you get us out of this place?"

Arkor nodded. "I know the alleys well enough. There's no wall on the eastern side, so we should be able to slip out if we're not spotted."

"That is not likely to happen." Wezlok exuded arrogance. "Unless someone more powerful than myself is about."

"What have you done?" Cavalor asked.

A soldier rushing by slowed to glance at the company. He shook his head and continued on his way.

"We must move," Merssa said. "The rest can wait." They had no time for the wizard's cryptic explanation.

They scurried along the alleyways while trailing after Arkor. Every now and again they were forced onto the streets for short jaunts, and still no one took notice of them. Not until they exited the alleys a fourth time and a large Zurkan ran toward them. Arkor reached for his weapon, but Wezlok cautioned him to stay his hand.

"Have you seen them?" the Zurkan asked in hobgoblin.

Merssa understood the speech, and she made sure Cavalor was well versed in the language so he could communicate when necessary. But it was Wezlok that answered without hesitation.

"No. We have not seen the human scum!"

Merssa thought the choice of words rolled too easily off of the elf's tongue.

"Keep your eyes and nose open," the krukari said. "We'll never be able to spot them with all of us looking like Gurix. But I hear one smells like a pala—" The warrior sniffed. "Wait a minute." He sniffed again, leaning toward Merssa.

Merssa grabbed her mace.

"Here!" Wezlok called out in hobgoblin, pointing at the krukari. "Here!" the elf repeated in the common tongue. "We have one of them!"

The Zurkan backed away as all eyes on the street fell upon him. "No!" he said in horror, but his voice went unheard as Arkor joined Wezlok in shouting and pointing.

At that moment, Merssa noticed her reflection in a window. She looked like the Zurkan Landerik had slain in the tavern. She began shouting and pointing, as did the rest of the company.

"No!" The krukari turned to run. But before he made it ten paces, a hobgoblin, three krukari, and four humans butchered him in the street.

"Go," Wezlok hissed at Arkor.

Arkor led them back into the alleys, leaving the screams behind. Minutes later, they cleared the final buildings of Denvale and were off into the dark countryside. The snow was shallow, only an inch or two in its deepest patches, and they ran until the lights of the city were faint. There, they stopped, and everyone panted while looking to the west.

Wezlok narrowed his eyes. "They are not following."

"That is good news," Merssa said between breaths. "But we must move on until we are sheltered from the sky. Dawn is not far away."

CHAPTER 25

DARK DECISION

Merssa halted her company within a copse of evergreens, five miles east of Denvale. The snow was patchy, as most of it had dissolved into puddles of slush, but the trees were on a small rise, providing dry land and allowing for some rest. Wezlok was the first to fall asleep. The power the elf unleashed in Denvale had surely left him drained, and while the others were placing furs over the bed of pine needles, the mage curled into a ball, appearing nothing more than a harmless child.

Merssa and Arkor remained awake and alert. There came no signs of pursuit, but just before the dawn, the familiar sensation of dire cold swept by on a breeze from east to west. A Death Lord had flown by, concealed by the storm clouds lingering overhead. Merssa knew it would learn of their passing through Denvale, and there would be little rest from that point. The sky then brightened, illuminating the land through the gray clouds.

"Wake them," Merssa said.

Arkor carried out the order, and everyone was soon on their feet. While they readied to move on, Merssa addressed Wezlok.

"What do you see?"

"A thick haze conceals the mountains," the elf said, gazing to the west and north. "To the east, the fields stretch far, but nothing moves. There is no snow ahead."

Merssa nodded. She did not know what to make of the depleting snow. According to Selanna, it covered all of Marcove. But the thought of warmer weather was encouraging.

Trees became scarce, forcing them onto open fields while they headed southeast toward the Belsal River. Nothing stirred, save for a few birds here and there. The air grew hotter with every step, carrying with it the smell of summer, and when night descended, Merssa found it as warm as the day.

They shed their furs at last, stashing the bulky cloaks among a group of elms, and there they sat upon the ground to rest their weary legs. The break was brief, for traveling beneath the open sky made Merssa nervous, and after a couple of hours they moved on in the darkness.

Wezlok took the lead, and they walked a steady pace until dawn, continuing the downward trek into the valleys of Marcove. Boulders were gathered in several areas, some round, some flat, and others like pillars of granite, and it was within one such grouping that the company stopped for the day. The stones were tall, and a crawlspace existed to offer shelter from the sky.

It was nearing noon when the clouds became scattered and the sun shone upon the land. Merssa held her breath and squinted to see through the illusion, but the sunlight remained. She saw the temptation in her company's eyes; the desire to leap out and bask in the warm rays.

"Perhaps you should have a look around," she said to Wezlok.

The elf nodded and poked his head out to scan the sky. After a moment, he climbed onto a boulder.

"The sky is clear," he said. "The river is not far to the south. We can reach it—" Wezlok's attention snapped to the east. "They watch the river. At least a hundred soldiers."

"I should've known," Merssa muttered. "The river's no good." She bit her lip. Following the waterway would have made for an easier journey.

"Get down!" Arkor hissed at Wezlok.

From out of the west came rolling black clouds, traveling fast and without wind. Wezlok sprang from the rock and joined the others, and shortly afterward the sunlight faded as darkness encompassed the land. High above, a dragon of bone glided beneath the billowing mass, and the air cooled, causing Merssa to shiver. The dragon headed southeast, disappearing into the distance, and the clouds rolled with it. The scattered rays of the sun returned and the day grew hot.

"Do you think it spotted us?" asked Cavalor.

"Who knows?" Landerik furrowed his brow. "We'd have to count ourselves lucky for it to have missed us."

"Can you conceal us from above?" Cavalor looked at Wezlok.

Wezlok's brows drew together. "I have only just recovered from getting us out of Denvale. And now you wish for me to make us disappear altogether?"

"We'll just have to pray we have not been seen," Merssa said. "Now let's get some rest."

The day progressed without mishap, but any sleep gained was short-lived. Come dusk, the company headed due east, staying a good three miles north of the river. The sky remained cluttered and the growing moon provided ample light, and after a few hours, the terrain leveled. By morning the land began a gradual climb, slowing the pace, and trees grew more numerous. They had not yet reached Mentrial Forest, but the clusters of trees made locating a suitable campsite a simple task.

"Perhaps we should take to traveling by day again," said Cavalor while they pulled blankets from their packs. "With the return of the trees, we should be able to keep hidden. Besides, who knows what we're missing in the night? The enemy likely sees in the dark much better than we do."

Merssa nodded. "You're right. All the same, we'll rest a few hours."

Beneath the morning sun, Merssa leaned against a tree and gazed to the east. She had ordered Arkor to get some sleep, and she kept watch alone. There was a sudden movement behind her and she reached for her mace... It was Cavalor. Concern was etched on his youthful face. He worried for her, Merssa knew. But it was not his place.

"When is the last time you found rest?" her son asked.

"I shall find no rest." She sighed. "Even in sleep, I am troubled. I may as well remain awake and do the company some good."

Cavalor frowned. "You do good every day. So please —"

"As your mother, I thank you," Merssa said. Then her tone was cold and serious. "As your commander, I insist you return to your blanket. We can't have all of us weary with the coming days."

"Mother —"

"Rouse the others." She turned away. "It's time to move on."

The day passed, revealing no signs of the enemy. Though spirits lifted while the company marched through patches of sunlight, no one lost sight of where they were, and all eyes constantly darted about the trees and sky. Travel was easier, and they covered twice the distance than they had through the night, and when dusk arrived, they stopped beneath a canopy of leaves.

Merssa allowed Cavalor to guard with Arkor, much to her son's satisfaction, and she forced herself to lie down. Rest was difficult, but she was sure she slept for at least an hour. She was already awake when Cavalor's gauntlet touched her shoulder.

"It's time," he said.

Merssa rose, feeling just as weary as she had before they stopped, and Arkor and Cavalor took their places on their blankets. She guarded the rest of the night alone, and with the slightest hint of a brightening sky, she roused the company.

They marched on, the day much like the last. No one spoke a word that Merssa could hear, not even the usual encouragement from Borse. Lunch came and went and they kept moving without a break to eat. After another hour had passed, Merssa spoke quietly to Arkor.

"What can we expect within Mentrial?"

Arkor shrugged. "It housed thieves and hobgoblins in the past. The king allowed them to remain, so long as they left royal caravans undisturbed. Wolves have never been an issue, but cats large enough to pounce a horse roam the trees. Since the coming of the necromancer, there's no telling what awaits us."

Merssa nodded. It was useless information, really. She was not even sure why she asked. Perhaps she needed to hear someone's voice.

A few hours later, with the sun low in the west, the company halted atop a hill. Below, the Mentrial Forest stretched beyond sight to the north, south, and east. Merssa saw maples, oaks, and birches, but here on the western edge, pines outnumbered them all. She sighed and surveyed the sky. The clouds were brighter than when the day began, and there were no signs of Death Lords or bone dragons.

They descended the hill and entered the forest. A road through the woodland existed south of the Belsal River to offer a direct route, but Merssa wished to remain as far from it as possible. The river would have provided guidance through the forest as well, but with the water being patrolled, Merssa would have to find her own way. Why not? Nothing else had gone according to plan.

Their mail jingled and their boots crunched on the hard needles covering the forest floor, and the only other sound belonged to the birds fluttering about for a last bit of fun before bed. After two hundred yards, the shadows had grown too dark and they stopped to gain some rest.

Distant noises greeted Merssa's ears throughout the night. They were animal-like at first, but then came moans and shrieks to the south and east. Cavalor and Landerik pulled their blades at one point, but Merssa assured them no evil was near, and Borse concurred. This did little to ease Cavalor's mind, and he remained restless for the remainder of the night, even in his sleep.

An hour before dawn, an intense chill permeated the forest, and everyone's breath was thick as they woke from their slumber. Merssa's heart raced, and the dreadful hiss of an undead dragon filled the sky as the monster flew low and against the treetops. Branches rustled and pine needles showered the company, but then everything became still and the evil aura faded.

"Do you think he knows we're here?" Landerik asked.

Merssa nodded. "I felt him. And I'm sure he felt me as well."

They moved on. Wezlok led the way until the forest brightened, and then Merssa retook the lead. They crossed a few hunting trails, but Merssa ignored them and continued eastward, venturing deeper into the woodland. Though feelings of evil remained far off, she did not slow her pace, not even for food or drink. With the arrival of night, she stopped at last.

"Don't set up camp," Merssa said. "We can only spare an hour, so find what rest you may. If the Death Lord has sent forth its soldiers, they will not be stopping with the night."

After the hour was up, the company resumed the eastward trek beneath the dark trees. They marched into the following day, until half of it was spent and all were weary, and Merssa came to a halt. The hair on the back of her neck had risen and her scalp tingled. She looked at Borse with alarm.

Borse nodded. "I feel it too."

"I hear horses," said Wezlok. "They are distant, but headed this way."

"Ready yourselves." Merssa pulled her mace.

They moved at a quickened pace, veering to the north. The evil became stronger, and then came the sound of horses to Merssa's ears — several hooves pounding back the way they had come.

"Take positions!" She spun around.

Borse stood behind Merssa, while Cavalor and Landerik took her right and left flanks. Arkor was a few paces before her, locking his crossbow into place on his wooden arm and loading an arrow. Wezlok stepped beside Borse.

From beyond the trees came a group of dunarchins on horseback. The animals were undead, their eyes shining the same blue light as their riders, and upon spotting their prey, the evil warriors unsheathed their swords. One dunarchin blew into a horn that alerted all things for miles, but Arkor cut its tone short when his arrow pierced the undead warrior's skull between the eyes. The dunarchin fell from its horse and tumbled into a tree.

The enemy was then upon Arkor, and the one-armed warrior pulled his sword to parry a dunarchin's blade while dodging the stomping hooves of its steed. With a spin, he brought his weapon across the animal's rear leg, slicing through the limb and spilling beast and rider to the ground. Arkor plunged his sword into the back of the dunarchin's skull before it could rise, and its eyes went dark.

Merssa charged with her mace held high, and her golden aura surrounded her. The horses became spooked, and the riders did all they could to control the beasts, but to no avail. Merssa destroyed two undead firstborns attempting to dismount while the others dropped quickly from their saddles. The animals then bolted beyond the trees and disappeared.

Three dunarchins charged, but when they came into contact with Merssa's light, smoke arose from their decaying flesh and they hissed. Merssa struck down two and Arkor destroyed the third.

Merssa saw a pair of dunarchins at Landerik's feet and two more near Cavalor, and Cavalor sent another sprawling across the ground after severing its leg. Borse's hammer crashed onto the creature's head, causing its limbs to spasm wildly for a moment, and when he lifted the weapon, nothing remained of the skull but a pile of dust on the forest floor.

The dunarchins were defeated and all was quiet. But then a distant horn resonated to the north, followed by a horn to the west. Two more sounded, one to the east and one to the south, and the latter was much closer than those before it.

"This isn't good." Cavalor looked at the trees to the south. "This was only a scout party. They're closing in on us."

"Let's not tarry, then." Merssa put her mace on her belt. "We're easier to find if we stand still."

"But we grow weary with every step," said Landerik. "Borse looks to collapse at any moment. We should gather what strength remains and make a stand!"

Merssa looked at her husband. Borse was pale and leaned heavily on the haft of his hammer. As if sensing her pity, he swung the weapon over his shoulder and put forth his strongest face. But his eyes betrayed him.

"Let's continue." Borse gave a nod.

They headed northeast, trying to put some distance between them and whatever force lay to the south. There came nothing more throughout the day, and they traveled almost to the forest's northern edge before Merssa stopped at last. Dusk was upon them, and already the full moon peered onto the land, illuminating the forest through breaks in the trees. The essence of evil was still present, but it had grown distant, so she allowed time to dress any wounds received from the dunarchins and a chance to gain some rest. Worn and weary, the company found sleep.

Arkor and Merssa stood guard. After an hour, Merssa closed her eyes and concentrated. No evil had drawn any nearer.

"Wake Wezlok," she said to Arkor. "And get some rest. You'll need your strength in the days to come."

Arkor frowned. Wezlok had never been made to guard, and Arkor surely did not understand her order. But he complied without question.

Moments later, Wezlok approached with brows furrowed. He studied Merssa, as if attempting to read her face. His expression then softened, and he nodded, as if he understood. Merssa motioned for him to watch to the south, and he sat on the ground there and closed his eyes.

Merssa leaned against a tree to the north of her sleeping companions, her mind troubled and constantly drawn to Cavalor, as it had been every time she stood guard. Her son slept, appearing almost peaceful. But what would tomorrow bring? Her thoughts again drifted to his childhood, and again she hated herself for raising him to fight this war. He should have known a better life. He rarely played with other children while growing up; his days were filled with studies and combat training. Once, Cavalor painted a picture for Merssa, of her defeating a skeleton with a glowing blue eye. She should have recognized it then, but it was not until recently that she realized her obsession had become his own. She could not remember the last time she heard him laugh joyously about anything. Cavalor was a beautiful man, and he should be wooing women and singing and dancing. Well, not the singing part; he was terrible at that. Merssa enjoyed a small smirk, but it faded. This was the life she chose for Cavalor, and he would likely perish without ever reaching the objective his entire existence pointed toward. Merssa shook her head. Cavalor deserved a better life. He deserved a better mother. She should never have brought him here, and now there was no turning back. The undead hunted them like wild game and would overcome them before they ever saw the walls of Kembald. Even if they could evade the hunters, the forest was ending. Rough terrain existed between the woodland and the largest city of Marcove, and nothing would hide them from the eyes of a Death Lord.

An icy presence interrupted Merssa's thoughts. The Death Lord was not too near, but close enough to give her a chill. Back at the campsite, Wezlok was alert and Borse had awakened. Borse's gaze met hers, and he gave a knowing look; and once the chill faded, he nodded.

"Wezlok," Merssa said quietly. "I need your help."

Wezlok rose to his feet and approached, and Borse followed. Her husband placed a loving hand on her shoulder and looked at her with moist eyes.

"I love you," he said.

Merssa put a finger to Borse's lips. "Our love will endure all." She kissed him. "Take care of our son."

It was not yet light out, and Merssa held her mace overhead, its golden aura shining like a beacon. The moon illuminated the rolling hills north of the forest, and many stars dotted the dark blue above.

Her companions followed at a distance of thirty feet, matching her pace, and with a deep breath she ran, leaving Mentrial Forest behind.

Merssa headed north, and then northeast, and it was not long before the Death Lord took notice. Her breathing became visible as storm clouds consumed the sky from out of the west, but the undead king did not show itself. The clouds continued into the east, taking the chill with it, and the moon and stars returned. The hiss of the undead dragon then sounded in the distance, but Merssa knew it would return.

Morning arrived, and its cool, moist air rushed deep into Merssa's lungs while she raced up and down the rolling terrain until she could run no more. Winded, she panted while taking in her surroundings. Her companions remained behind her, and trees were scattered about undulating fields as far as she could see. Above, the fading stars sparsely decorated the brightening sky. The sun then peeked over the horizon, and Merssa drew in a long breath while a tear rolled down her cheek. With a sigh, she headed north.

Hours passed while Merssa continued running and walking as her energy allowed. The sun traveled high, bringing a moist heat that saturated her with perspiration, and as the bright orb began its descent into the west, the presence of evil returned. Moments later, distant horns sounded, first from the east, and then to the south, west, and north. Bracing herself, Merssa walked a steady pace to conserve strength.

The day waned, and Merssa wondered when the Death Lord would choose to strike. Her answer came with the return of the dark clouds out of the south, banishing the final traces of the sun's light. The air became deathly cold, tasting like an old crypt, and the scream of an undead dragon nearly caused Merssa to jump from her skin.

Though hidden from view, Merssa knew the Death Lord to be riding within the clouds. Was it circling? What was it waiting for? Next, ranks of soldiers approached from the east carrying banners Merssa had never seen — red flags bearing a black triangle with a blue oval breaching two of its sides. Whether undead or living, Merssa could not tell, but there were no dunarchins among the marching force, for their eyes were dark. Turning back, she saw more soldiers to the north, east, and south — four small armies, at least five hundred strong each, come to battle a few rebels! The Death Lord then revealed itself, landing its dragon at the bottom of the hill upon which Merssa stood, and she knew immediately that it was Cadorn.

Cadorn dismounted before unsheathing his sword and pulling the black mace from his belt. He then appeared almost as a dark statue while his shining blue eyes attempted to pierce Merssa's soul.

"Cadorn!" Merssa pointed her golden mace at the evil king.

The figure remained motionless a few seconds longer, and Merssa could now see the surrounding soldiers more clearly. There were Zurkan and Benasti warriors to the west and south, Marcs to the east, and zombies and ghouls glared with hatred from the north, where the Death Lord stood. The black helmet nodded once. He accepted her challenge.

The dark lord ascended slowly, and Merssa's heart pounded harder with every step he took. His soldiers spread around the hill, moving part way up the slope to get a better view, and Merssa's company remained several paces behind. Once Cadorn reached the top, the battle began.

Merssa waved her mace overhead, and the golden aura surrounded her. The Death Lord put forth his mace in response, speaking a strange word in his hollow voice, and the weapon took on a glow of its own. Unlike Merssa's holy light, the evil mace spewed a black, cloud-like vapor that exploded into a dark flash, and all living soldiers surrounding the hill screamed out in terrible agony. Cadorn paid them no heed; his eyes never strayed from his prey.

Merssa felt as though every bone in her body was being torn from their sockets. She fought to remain standing, and as the Death Lord advanced, it took all her energy to knock aside his evil blade and dodge the mace. The power of Cafior then surged through her soul, and her golden aura swelled, freeing her from the dark magic and granting her strength. Steam rose from the seams of Cadorn's armor where the holy light touched it, but if the Death Lord suffered any pain, it was not apparent.

Merssa fended off several more attacks before chancing one of her own. She brought her weapon in a wide arc that left a ray of gold in its wake, and her mace connected with Cadorn's as he raised it in defense. A brilliant flash of gold and black encompassed the hill as a loud *crack* echoed across the land, and the Death Lord stumbled back a step. The evil mace was sundered.

Merssa pressed, but Cadorn dodged her attack and spun, bringing his blade around with great speed. The edge sliced her left arm, cutting through steel and into her flesh, and searing pain became an icy chill from her shoulder to her fingertips. Merssa faltered, but she found her balance in time to duck her foe's next slash. She then brought her weapon up, striking the bottom of Cadorn's chin and knocking his helmet free.

The world slowed as the black helmet tumbled down the hill, and Merssa gazed upon her enemy. Cadorn's head was that of a skull, but over it was the spectral image of a dark blue face. From deep within the eye sockets shone points of blue light, and steam emitted from ghastly boils on the transparent skin. The undead king's ghostly lips moved.

"You shall pay for that!" he said in his hollow voice with a slight hiss, and he advanced.

Cadorn's sword weaved to the left and right as he launched a flurry of attacks, and Merssa did her best to fend off the blows while backing away from the towering Death Lord. Two of the strikes found their marks, issuing nasty wounds to Merssa's leg and stomach, and a chill penetrated deep inside as it crawled through her veins. She refused to yield and swung her mace, striking Cadorn with all the force she could muster. There was a loud *snap*, and the Death Lord's arm went limp.

The briefest moment of shock held Merssa, realizing his bones could be broken. But her thoughts returned to the battle, for she had overextended herself on the attack. She pulled back, but the Death

Lord's blade struck her golden mace. Her aura faded as the weapon fell to the ground, and the dark lord kicked it down the hillside.

A smile formed on Cadorn's blue lips. But his smile transformed into a scowl when he looked upon her company with a new light. None of them came to Merssa's aid. In fact, they had become transparent. Wezlok's power was strong, but it diminished as the distance between Merssa and the elf grew too large. The illusionary companions then faded altogether, leaving Merssa alone with the Death Lord atop the hill.

While Cadorn contemplated this new knowledge, Merssa searched for anything she could wield as a weapon. There was nothing. Cadorn hissed as he stepped forward, his eyes burning brighter, but Merssa refused to accept defeat. Reaching deep within her soul, her lips moved in a prayer to Cafior, begging for the strength to throw down her enemy; and Cadorn balked when the golden aura returned, more radiant than before and encompassing the entire hill. All evil soldiers, undead and living, were tortured as the holy light engulfed them, and they collapsed with shrieks of agony—even the skeletal dragon.

Steam billowed from Cadorn as his image appeared to be melting, and he roared with pain Merssa did not believe possible. She sprung, with Cafior's Might coursing through her body, and wrapped her gauntlets around the undead king's ghastly throat. Cadorn stumbled, falling onto his back, and Merssa did not feel the dark sword pierce her chest as she rode the Death Lord to the ground. She continued to chant in prayer, and Cadorn coughed a yellowish gas as his eyes grew brighter still. The blue lights then winked out and his ghostly shape vanished, leaving behind bones that crumbled within the black steel shell.

Merssa lay atop the armor, watching the skull break loose and roll several feet away. The dark clouds parted and the air warmed as the moon shone upon the hill, and her prayer came at last to an end. But the holy light persisted, and she still felt no pain. She had conquered the Death Lord, the captain of all Death Lords, perhaps allowing her companions and loved ones to venture a bit farther and reach Kembald.

Merssa rolled onto her back, gazing up with blurred vision, and the moon and stars melded together. Bright forms appeared, drifting toward her on wings, and as they came into focus Merssa saw they were angels, the very ones that once adorned the street outside the Grand Cathedral of Palidur. They had come to relieve her of all troubles from this world, and to take her to a place where evil could never touch her again; and she smiled as they took her hands. Her body slumped and the golden light faded, leaving behind an empty shell: Merssa Goldmace, High Paladin of Cafior.

CHAPTER 26

MUD LAKE

Having cleared the Fire Hills, Soren took the lead, and Rholmar was at his side. Pallit joined Lorylla to the rear, the ranger's skills not as critical for the way ahead, and between the four walked Rybeal and Nilborg, the elders of the group.

They left the white furs behind and headed east beneath a blue sky, passing over fields of dry grass ranging from several inches to a couple of feet in height. A few streams crossed their path, but the water was shallow and easily traversed, and the heat rose steadily and the air grew thicker, reinforcing that it was summer.

Before the day was spent, the southern peaks of Varlimor loomed ahead. The sun shone red in the west, and to the north, dark clouds hovered above snowy mountains. What held Soren's attention, however, was the pond of brownish-orange substance before the company, aptly named Mud Lake by Selanna.

The mountains presented an impenetrable barrier to the left, and to the right, the Twin Rivers carried water swiftly to the jungle of Tarn Arum, as well as to Dright Swamp. Selanna believed a mountain stream fed the bizarre pond, passing beneath its thick layer of mud, and this belief was reinforced by the clean water rushing from the lake's southern edge. The plan called for Soren's company to cross the Twin Rivers thirty miles south of the pond, where the currents calmed. But without horses, the journey would take three days at least, and they would arrive at the dark stronghold too late. Fortunately, a contingency plan existed, in case of the horses' demise. Unfortunately, that plan was to cross the lake on foot.

According to Selanna, the mud could support an armored warrior, provided the warrior did not linger in one place too long. Selanna claimed to have crossed safely more than once in such a manner. As Soren watched the muck bubble in several places, he did not look forward to attempting it, and his companions' expressions echoed these thoughts.

"Well," he murmured, "I'll go first."

After a quiet prayer to Soleran, Soren placed his boot on the mud, and warmth seeped through the sole. As his foot sat upon the spot for more than a few seconds, the boot sank, slightly at first, but then more rapidly as the sludge grabbed hold. Soren pulled back, but the lake was unwilling to give up its new treasure. He used more force, almost yanking his foot from the boot, and with a great sucking sound he claimed victory.

"Would you like me to go?" Rholmar asked.

Soren gave the Arronaus paladin a level gaze. "I was only testing it."

With a deep breath, Soren stepped onto the pond and took to a brisk walk. While he kept moving, the mud could not gain a decent hold—its only consolation was to coat his boots with its orange filth. Soon he was halfway across, twenty yards from the opposite shore, and he chanced a glance over his shoulder to see his companions following. The action caused him to stumble, and although he righted himself, the mud grabbed hold of both feet. He lifted his knees high for several steps, reclaiming his original gait, and the lake yielded.

The strange bubbling grew closer, and Soren quickened his pace as a sense of urgency overcame him. His eyes shifted back and forth and his hand moved to his sword, and with ten yards to go, he spied movement to his right. He turned, but there was only mud. His gaze then snapped forward when he detected the movement again, and this time he knew he had not imagined it. Something swam beneath the mud! The form appeared serpent-like and looked to be at least twenty feet long; and as it slithered to Soren's left, he pulled his blade and veered right.

"Something's afoot!" he called out, but the snake delved deeper into the muck, leaving no trace as to its whereabouts.

Only a few more steps, and Soren would be safe on the western shore. He thought of running, but then Rholmar shouted a warning.

"Soren! Behind you!"

Turning, Soren was face to face with a hideous serpent. Orange mud coated its scales, making it impossible to discern its true color, but its monstrous size was unmistakable. The creature rose over ten feet, though much of it was still immersed in the mud, and it dipped to look Soren in the eyes. Its body was at least two feet thick and its head the size of a large man's, but the most unnerving feature was the serpent's face. The snake-like eyes were golden, but its nose and lips appeared human-like. It smiled, revealing several pointed teeth, and a forked tongue fluttered from within. As mud dripped from its head, Soren noticed the scales ended about the edges of its face, where skin began.

"Ssso," the serpent hissed, the dark tongue lashing in and out, "ssstrange daysss have brought ssstrange morssselsss."

Soren held his blade ready, but he did not strike. Something about the serpent's face stayed his hand, and the longer he viewed it, the more familiar it became. It continued to speak, but its words sounded far off, as if in a dream.

"No matter," the snake said. "A meal isss a meal. Even ifff it isss coated with sssuch a hard ssshhhell."

Soren heard muffled cries. Were they calling to him? Rubbish. He was meeting with a good friend, seated in his favorite tavern within the walls of Palidur. Soren's friend smiled and toasted his good health, but outside the tavern there was a commotion. Rholmar was yelling in the street. Strange. Paladins did not run about Palidur, screaming. Such an outlandish thing to do. What was Rholmar yelling? It was Soren's name. But why was Rholmar waving his sword and charging the tavern window? Soren's good friend suddenly lunged to the side in serpent-like fashion, the man's body becoming elongated as he evaded Rholmar's attack.

Soren shook his head, and the tavern vanished. He was back in the wilds, south of the Fire Hills and waist deep in Mud Lake. Rholmar fought the enormous serpent, and the creature's face was unfamiliar, appearing more snake-like than it had only moments ago. But Soren's immediate concern was that the lake continued to pull him downward. Struggling only made him sink faster, and the further he sank, the hotter the mud became. He needed help.

Rholmar's feet moved constantly as he swung his blade, but the serpent glided through the mud as easily as if it were water and remained out of reach. Pallit then issued a wound to the serpent's flank. Without breaking eye contact with Rholmar, the monster brought its tail from below and slapped Pallit in the back, knocking the ranger facedown. The pond took hold, and Pallit fought to lift his head for a breath while his arms and legs sank. Rholmar then came to an abrupt halt, staring at the creature with his mouth agape.

"Mother?" Rholmar asked.

Soren saw only the horrific serpent.

An arrow pierced the scales, and the snake whirled around, seeking the source of its pain and freeing Rholmar from its gaze. Lorylla stood thirty yards away, and already another arrow launched from her bow. The monster evaded the missile and sped toward her, leaving Rholmar to extract his boots from the mud.

Lorylla slung her bow over her shoulder and pulled her sword. Her feet showed only traces of the mud, and she seemed unhindered as she moved about, as if on dry land. The creature lunged, and she stepped clear of its path and slashed her sword across its back, scoring a minor wound. Soren then realized the elf's plan: she only sought to distract the snake. While the serpent concentrated on Lorylla, Nilborg headed toward Soren, and Rybeal aimed for Pallit.

Pallit's arms were submerged to the elbows and his legs had disappeared. Rybeal came to a halt and chanted with palms up, struggling as if lifting a heavy object, and Pallit rose from the mud. The lake fought against the spell, but Rybeal's power proved too strong and it released its prize. The mud then bent its will upon Rybeal, pulling the mage down past his ankles.

Soren was now chest deep, and the mud burned like fire on his feet. Nilborg took hold of his right arm and pulled, but the pond did not yield. The priest only slowed Soren's descent while sinking himself. They needed more help.

Rholmar rushed to Lorylla's aid while she danced with the monstrous serpent. In its efforts, the creature failed to notice the Arronaus paladin's approach, and Rholmar dealt a mighty blow, cutting deep into its long body. The reptile screamed, sounding like a woman, and created a five-foot splash as it sank into the mud. Rholmar held up his arm to protect his face from the wave while searching the lake's surface. The snake had disappeared.

Pallit was on his feet, almost completely coated by the orange muck, and he ran to Soren while Lorylla rushed to Rybeal. Rybeal had been laboring to pull his boots free, and with the elf's assistance he broke loose. Nilborg continued to lift Soren's arm, but the priest was now buried to the knees.

"Help Nilborg," Rholmar said to Lorylla and Rybeal as he arrived, and while the two complied, he and Pallit moved to either side of Soren and grabbed hold beneath his shoulders.

The fire on Soren's feet faded as his companions pulled with all their might, freeing his chest. Rholmar and Pallit then freed their boots before returning to the arduous task. On the next try, they extracted half of Soren's body, but a sharp pain coursed through his leg, as if teeth had grabbed hold, and he cried out as he was jerked back down to his chest.

"It's biting my leg!"

Rholmar and Pallit strained to keep Soren from sinking farther, and Rybeal now assisted with magic from the shore. Soren rose slowly, but the teeth did not relent, and he cried out again.

Rholmar pulled his sword and turned the blade down. "Which leg?"

"Left!" Soren grimaced as the teeth bit deeper into his flesh.

Rholmar fell to his knees, thrusting his sword downward, and his arms submerged past the elbows as he drove the blade into the mud. Soren was released, and Pallit extracted him from the lake with the help of Rybeal's magic.

Floating inches above the mud, Soren was bootless, and his leg showed a mixture of blood and filth. Rybeal stood on the shore with hands outstretched, holding Soren in place and speaking to Lorylla, and the gray elf ran back onto the pond while Pallit freed Rholmar's arms and sword. Soren continued to hover as Lorylla led him from the lake by the hand, and Rybeal set him on the ground.

Pallit and Rholmar were close behind, and everyone was soon upon the bank. The orange mud coated most of everyone's bodies, except for Lorylla, and they panted while watching for pursuit, but the snake did not resurface. Without a word, Rholmar hoisted Soren over his shoulder, and they moved over the next hill until Mud Lake fell from sight. Soren was then placed on the grass.

Nilborg began an immediate inspection of Soren's wounds, and Soren could see where the teeth had torn open the flesh of his left leg. As well, his feet appeared to be charred. But he felt no pain, and his mind wandered. What was it that burned within the mud? And just how far below was the alleged water that fed the Twin Rivers? He then heard the voices of his companions, and though groggy, his focus returned to the tall grass where he lay.

"What in the Abyss was that thing?" Pallit's voice sounded muffled.

"Selanna gave no warning of such a monster." Rholmar's words were distorted as well, as if spoken from another room.

"Perhaps she did not know of it," Lorylla said. "Your movements surely gained the serpent's attention."

"And judging from Lorylla's light feet," added Rybeal, "it probably knew Selanna's passing to be nothing more than a breeze brushing over the surface."

"Let us hope there are no more surprises," Pallit said. "The war against Trannum must not fail because we're unable to show."

"We have a problem." Nilborg hovered over Soren. "His legs are paralyzed. The venom of the snake, no doubt."

"Can you cure it?" asked Rholmar.

"I will try."

The fog lifted from Soren's mind, and he found his voice. "Leave me. We're losing time. The war is of greater importance than my life."

"Hush." Nilborg placed his hand on Soren's forehead. The priest closed his eyes and whispered a prayer, and upon completion, he opened his eyes and released a deep sigh.

"What's wrong?" Rholmar asked.

"I'm not familiar with the poison that runs through his veins." Nilborg shook his head. "Without such knowledge, I have not the power to cure it."

"Leave me, old friend." Soren looked at Nilborg; the man he had known his whole life. They had presided as High Paladin and High Priest of Soleran in Palidur for so many years, and Nilborg had been there several years already when Soren was appointed. Though they were peers, Soren always considered Nilborg more of a father. "My arms are tingling—"

Soren's body convulsed.

Rholmar felt powerless, holding his breath while Soren shook for several seconds. The Soleran paladin then became still and his eyes glazed over. Rholmar could not believe his colleague's time had come. Soren had been one of the greatest representatives of Palidur for so many years... He deserved a better fate.

"Is he...?" asked Pallit.

"No," Nilborg replied. "The poison holds him."

Rholmar stooped to lift the ailing paladin, but Nilborg grabbed his arm.

"As much as it breaks my heart, he is correct," the priest said. "We must leave him."

"What are you saying?" Rholmar glared at Nilborg. Was it not the Soleran way to help the helpless? Rholmar refused to leave a friend to die in a strange land.

"He will only slow us," Nilborg said. "He knows this. And we must think of Vaeldor, and all the people that call it home."

Rholmar shook his head, looking in the lake's direction with ire in his heart. The priest was right.

"Take care, my friend." Nilborg closed Soren's eyes. "I will see you in the Blessed Realm before long."

Chapter 27

Maak Maak

It was dark. Greyor was not sure how far he had fallen, nor how much time had passed since he landed. All he knew was that his body ached.

His eyes adjusted and he looked around. Dust was heavy in the air, making it difficult to see very far, and a stream of small rocks drizzled from a shaft twelve feet overhead. His pack was missing, as was his hammer. Reaching to his waist, he pulled his knife.

"Millord?" Greyor used the common tongue, in case any of the others were present.

"I'm here," Millord grumbled to the left, speaking in the dwarfish language, and Greyor could just make out the shape of his friend rising from the floor. "Where are we?"

"Dunno." Greyor brushed the dust and stones from his mustache and the upper portion of his beard. "We're still in the mines. The lower levels, I'd guess. Is Clanghorr with you?"

"Trannum could not pry Clanghorr from my fist!"

There was moaning nearby. They were not alone.

"Shh!" Greyor hissed. He then spotted his torn pack, and from within he pulled a torch. Keeping watch on the darkness, he extracted the flint from his pocket and struck it several times until the oil ignited.

They stood in a small chamber. Tables of granite and thick wooden chairs lay broken and a large boulder covered most of a well. A couple trickles of blood ran down Millord's dust-covered face and his pack was missing, and several pale-skinned mine dwellers were present, having accompanied Greyor and Millord on their descent. Some humanoids remained motionless, while others rose slowly to their feet.

Millord lifted Clanghorr and gave a growl. "Arm yourself, Greyor!"

Greyor looked for his hammer, but he still could not locate it. He readied his knife.

The humanoids shaded their eyes, appearing frightened as they backed away. "Maak Maak!" one said, looking at the shaft overhead and then around the chamber. "Maak Maak!"

"Don't speak your curses at me!" Millord advanced. "I'll have your tongue!"

"Wait!" Greyor halted his companion. "I don't think he's cursing us. I don't think it's *us* he fears."

"Then I shall teach him to fear us!" Millord gained a few more steps before Greyor halted him again.

"No! That's not what I mean. I think they fear the creatures that dug these tunnels."

Ten mine dwellers now stood. Four were obviously dead, and the rest appeared too wounded to move without assistance. The one who spoke chanced a few steps forward and held up his hands, his eyes reflecting red in the light as he squinted.

"Maak Maak," he said again. Then, placing his thumbs beneath his fingers, he made hand puppets the way children do to create shadow monsters on the wall. He moved his thumbs, opening and closing the puppet mouths, and growled and hissed. The puppets then lashed out, striking unseen targets.

"Snakes?" Millord frowned.

The humanoid raised his hands as mighty claws and growled some more, bending over to swipe at stones on the floor. He became so engrossed in his role that spittle began spraying from his mouth. His hands returned to puppets, and he hissed in Millord's direction, sending forth the saliva that had accumulated.

"That's it!" Millord raised Clanghorr.

"No!" Greyor grabbed hold of his companion's arm before the weapon fell, and the mine dweller retreated to join his people, bringing an end to the performance.

Millord wiped the moisture from his face, glaring at the one responsible.

"Maak Maak," the pale-skinned humanoid repeated softly.

"Maak Maak," Greyor said to himself. Then a thought occurred to him. "Maak Maak?" He held up one finger. Then two. Then three. He continued until all of his fingers on one hand were raised.

The humanoid lit up with realization. "Maak Maak!" He held up two fingers.

Greyor nodded. "Maak Maak?" he asked again, holding his hands a couple feet apart.

"Maaaaak Maaaaak." The mine dweller strained to hold his hands as far apart as he could.

"What's this?" Millord's frown deepened. "You understand him?"

"I understand enough, I think." Greyor gave a small nod. "Maak Maak must be what they call the two lizards that dwell here. And from what I gather, they're much larger than the ones we've seen so far." Greyor looked around the chamber. There were three exits, two behind him and one beyond the mine dwellers. Pointing at the single exit, he asked, "Maak Maak?"

The humanoids backed away from the dark archway with eyes wide. After a moment, they turned back to Greyor, all of them frowning. The speaker's face then lit up again, and he pointed at one of the far exits.

"Maak Maak."

Greyor nodded and turned toward the arch. "Well, let's go find these things."

"What?" Millord's expression was one of shock.

"I don't know what happened to Selanna and the others," Greyor said, "but I'll wager some of them survived the fall as well, though we'll likely never see them again. And since we don't know where we are or how to get outta here, the least we can do is make sure these Maak Maaks don't get them before they find their way through."

Millord stood silent, absorbing the words. "What makes you think they'll get outta here?"

Greyor shrugged. "Eraim." He had seen enough to know a simple collapsing of the mines could not deter that elf from her mission.

Millord looked back at the pale-skinned creatures and pointed Clanghorr in their direction, causing them to cower. "What about these things?"

Greyor glanced back. "Let them be."

He moved toward the arch, but halted when he heard a grunt. A humanoid held Greyor's hammer, and the creature bowed and offered it. Greyor accepted the weapon and grinned.

"Let us find these beasts!" he said with a stronger spirit.

Millord scooped up his torn pack and nodded. "Let's go."

"Is anyone there?" whispered Eraim as loud as she dared.

The oil of her shattered lantern burned over a five-foot area, illuminating only a portion of the large chamber where she had been deposited, and the pungent odor of rotting flesh stung her nose. Nothing stirred, save for the trickle of stones pelting the floor from the gaping hole that had delivered her. Though she fell over forty yards, Eraim used her hands and feet to slow the descent and received only a few cuts and scrapes.

She searched for her companions, and dread coursed down her spine when she discovered dozens of mine dweller corpses in various states of decay. Portions of their anatomies were missing, having been bitten off by large teeth, and it appeared as though they had been there for a few days at least. It was as if she had fallen into a feeding room.

"Some light, please," Eraim whispered to Mithkahr, and the blade shed a soft glow.

Moving deeper into the room, she released a gasp upon finding Arrikan beside a large boulder. Blood seeped from the ranger's scalp, and many scratches were visible on her arms and face in the dim light. Eraim placed her hand before Arrikan's mouth, and she was relieved to find her companion still breathed.

"Thank Galenfial."

Eraim inspected the ranger's head wound. There was a gash, but it did not appear too serious and she fished healing herbs from her pack. They were the same herbs Eraim had placed within Candermane Tunnel for those marching to Darmhorng. While she treated Arrikan's cut, she wondered about Magneer and his companions. Were they able to follow her map and make it safely into Kalmaar? She shook these thoughts and concentrated on the matter at hand.

With the wound properly dressed, Eraim inspected the rest of Arrikan's body. Luckily, there were no broken bones, and the remaining injuries appeared light.

Arrikan awoke, looking around and furrowing her brow, as if she had fallen asleep within a comfy inn and awakened in a strange place. Her eyes opened wide and she sat up; and Eraim steadied her as she wobbled and almost fell sideways.

"Where are the others?" the ranger asked.

"I am not sure." Eraim spoke in a whisper, holding a finger to her lips to warn Arrikan against loud speech. "We have been separated, and we need to leave this room in haste."

Eraim helped Arrikan to her feet, and the ranger quickly realized the state of the chamber and wrinkled her nose.

"The sooner the better!" Arrikan whispered in disgust.

Pulling a torch from her pack, Eraim lit it upon the dying fire, and at that moment she noticed the last corner of her Lornibur map burning away. With a sigh, she allowed Mithkahr to dim and helped search for Arrikan's equipment.

The ranger's bow was sundered and her pack torn, its contents splayed about a twenty-foot area. They collected all but the food, as it was lying among the decaying bodies, and found Arrikan's blade intact, though the weapon belt was ripped and the sheath snapped in two. Eraim was then impressed to see the ranger fashion a belt from a scrap of leather, complete with a loop to hold her sword. After one last sweep of the room, they were satisfied none of their companions were present and they readied to depart.

There existed four large archways, one centered within each of the room's walls. Eraim had no bearing on which led south, and the identical openings provided no clues. She closed her eyes to concentrate and slowly exhaled. The mines remained stale and unrevealing.

"I guess one is as good as another for now." She sighed. "Let us get away before suppertime. Then I will regain my bearings."

Eraim chose the archway she believed led southward, though she could not be sure, and the familiar rail system returned. It was in worse shape than in the mines above, and from the deep gouges, Eraim guessed the claws that destroyed it to have been at least six feet across.

They uttered few words while they walked, for every noise traveled far along the many tunnels. Eraim made no sound at all, but Arrikan was a larger person, bore several wounds, and...she was not an elf. The ranger staggered now and again, as dizzy spells attempted to get the better of her, so Eraim allowed for several breaks. After each period of rest, Eraim was encouraged to see Arrikan grow stronger.

They pressed on for a few miles, pausing at every intersection for Eraim to make a mark upon the gray walls with a piece of colored rock—best not to travel in circles. Eraim then sensed that the day had grown late, and from the look of her weary companion, she knew Arrikan to be in dire need of sleep. They began searching for a place where a couple of fatigued warriors might defend themselves, but the chambers were too large or possessed too many points of access—or both. Just as the task seemed hopeless, they happened upon a small room appearing adequate.

The chamber looked to have been a lounge of some sort. Broken furniture of wood and stone littered the floor and smashed kegs were present, as well as many shattered mugs. A large, stone-framed sofa dominated one side, and Eraim could not help wondering if its cushions were missing, or if dwarves had no need for such things. Two tunnels entered the room, the one they had used and another upon the opposite wall, and Eraim and Arrikan huddled in a corner behind the sofa, where Eraim extinguished the torch and kept an alert ear.

Several hours passed before Eraim roused Arrikan. The ranger looked much better for the sleep, and the herbs had already closed her head wound. After sharing a small meal from Eraim's pack, they readied their weapons and Eraim lit another torch.

"I am not entirely comfortable with some of the decisions I made," Eraim said as they exited the room the way they had come. "We'll have to double back a bit."

Arrikan nodded, offering no opinion on the matter. Eraim always appreciated traveling with those wise enough to put complete trust in her. She wished more humans were like Arrikan.

They retraced their steps for nearly a mile, stopping by each of Eraim's original marks to add a second one. Eraim then located a tunnel that felt right, one they had not taken previously, and they turned onto the new route.

Over the next few hours, they encountered several large lizards. Eraim avoided them when possible, but the reptiles became too frequent, forcing her and Arrikan to slay a few. Eraim used her bow after passing the torch to Arrikan, and Arrikan's sword finished any that were not felled by a well-placed arrow or two.

"Have you noticed they've been getting larger?" asked Arrikan.

Eraim nodded. "I have. The last one was twenty feet long. I hope this trend does not continue."

They walked more cautiously, stopping to examine every sound they thought they heard. Then another problem befell them: Eraim's last torch was failing. She had packed only a few before leaving Sendorum, counting on her lantern to light most of the journey. Had that failed, the dwarves always carried more than enough torches for everyone, not to mention Selanna's magical light. Eraim was confident her vision could carry her safely through if need be, but she feared Arrikan would be helpless in the dark underground. As the flame fluttered and diminished, Eraim unsheathed Mithkahr.

"I need your light, my friend," she whispered, and the weapon shed its soft glow. The illumination revealed little beyond the immediate area, but it was better than nothing. "Stay close," she said to Arrikan, and they continued along the corridor.

The lizards proved more dangerous from that point. Even with Eraim's sight, it was difficult to spy the reptiles upon the cold stone. Most times she detected the scraping of their scales when they moved, providing her ample warning, but a few lizards remained still until she and Arrikan were within striking range. After the third such occurrence, Eraim slowed her pace.

A couple of days passed while they walked through the dark mines of Lornibur, resting as often as they could. The population of lizards dwindled, much to Eraim's relief, but she kept up her guard. She continued marking walls with the colored stone, and she never saw the symbols again, so she was confident they were getting somewhere. Eraim often wondered if others of the company had survived the fall, but there was no time to go looking for them, and neither she nor Arrikan brought the subject to light.

Just after midday of the third day, as far as Eraim could tell, they spotted a light in the distance, and from that direction came a slight breeze carrying a wet, stale odor. They proceeded along the tunnel, which was surprisingly clear of debris, and at the end was a large archway. Beyond, lights danced upon the walls, and Eraim knew that a pool of water existed therein.

The room was enormous. But unlike the rest of the mines, it was only half finished. The floor was expertly chiseled into large squares, but forty feet ahead rested an underground lake beneath a collection of dangling stalactites. Bizarre flames sprouted from the water here and there, fluttering in the breeze and reflecting dully off crystalline formations to illuminate much of the chamber. To the right, several more arches lined an inward-arcing wall, evenly spaced over a two-hundred-foot span. The wall displayed the same craftsmanship Lornibur had exhibited thus far, and the ceiling above the worked stone was high enough that Eraim could not discern it among the shadows. Other than the dancing flames, nothing stirred.

With a finger to her lips, Eraim motioned for Arrikan to follow and they entered. Eraim felt small within the vast chamber, and all noises were swept into the darkness above, where they bounced around for several seconds. No signs of the cart rails existed, making Eraim ponder what purpose the chamber served in days of old, and the air current was constant, surely entering through one of the other archways. With no genuine sense of where she and Arrikan were, Eraim hoped the draft would lead to an exit.

They made their way from arch to arch, hesitating before each while Eraim held out her hand in hopes of discovering the source of the breeze. The first five were dark and stale. Three-quarters of the way along the arcing wall, Eraim noticed they were drawing nearer to the fiery water and the feeling of dread returned. With a deep breath and a firm grasp on Mithkahr, she continued.

The next archway did not differ from the previous ones, and as Eraim took another step, she was startled by Arrikan's hand on her shoulder. With a glance, she saw the ranger's gaze fixed upon the water.

Ripples raced toward the shore now less than twenty feet away. Something had moved. Eraim handed her bow to Arrikan, an action seeming to shock the ranger almost as much as Eraim herself. It was the only bow she had ever known, having made it from an oak sapling two hundred years ago, and it would likely be the last. But she was unwilling to sheath Mithkahr, and she slid the quiver back as well.

Arrikan put the quiver over her shoulder and nocked an arrow. The ranger then trained the bow on the water while they crept toward the final two archways.

A splash sounded from a distant, dark corner of the lake. Eraim froze, as if standing still would erase the noise, but it was not so, and a monstrous, reptilian head emerged near the midpoint of the water. The head was set atop a serpentine neck, rising twenty feet from the pool's surface, and it possessed a maw large enough to swallow a horse. Deep-set eyes surveyed the chamber while its forked tongue tasted the air, making it appear snake-like, but then its mouth opened with a hiss, revealing many teeth and appearing more in likeness to a giant crocodile. It turned toward Eraim and Arrikan with a snap of its neck, taking notice of their presence, and it seemed to smile.

Arrikan pulled back the bowstring, but she balked when a second head rose to the left of the first. The first head turned and hissed, and the second one responded with a low growl. The creatures then began moving toward the shore. Their necks stretched longer as they approached, and it became obvious they belonged to the same body, as they were joined between two powerful shoulders from which enormous claws rose from the pool.

"Shoot!" Eraim shouted.

The arrow was released, but it bounced from the creature's scales.

The monster neared, and the right head lunged for Eraim. Eraim tumbled through the next archway, and the jaws stopped short with a loud gnashing of teeth. She rolled to her feet and returned to the room, just as the head drew back and the other attacked Arrikan. The ranger dodged to the left, but only evaded part of the blow; and although the teeth failed to reach her, the enormous snout knocked Arrikan into the wall.

The right head lunged again for Eraim, and she leaped to the side and slashed its lower jaw. Mithkahr bit through its scales and into its flesh, and the monster jerked back. The left head turned Eraim's way, as if it had tasted the cold steel as well, and rage was evident within its serpentine eyes. It readied to strike, but a booming cry filled the chamber, and both heads turned to the middle arches.

"Maak Maak!" Millord's words echoed as the dwarf charged into the room, waving Clanghorr overhead. To Millord's flank was Greyor, and at least two score of the mine dwellers followed in their wake. It was almost enough for Eraim to question if she was dreaming.

Even within the light of the lake fires, the mine dwellers did not balk, and the front ranks carried clubs and rail-spears while the ones to the rear lugged bulky sacks. The latter came to a halt, spreading out and pulling stones from their packages, and the others continued, screaming every bit in the fashion of the charging dwarves. The two-headed reptile appeared only slightly annoyed by the rocks, as most of the stones bounced from its hide and splashed into the water, and the left head moved to answer the threat while the wounded head returned its attention to Eraim.

Arrikan released another arrow, and the missile flew true, burying deep into the long neck of the right head. The reptile reared, drawing in a deep breath, and then lurched, belching a stream of scalding water. Eraim dodged beneath the chin of the beast, avoiding the attack, and thrust Mithkahr upward before the head could retract. Her sword bit deep, and the monster retreated with an angry roar.

Greyor was knee deep in the lake when he noticed scattered fires about its surface. But the water was surprisingly cool. Five paces ahead, Millord led the charge, and when one of Maak Maak's heads attacked, Greyor's companion made no attempt to evade it. Instead, Millord swung Clanghorr, and the weapon removed two of the monster's many teeth. The reptile scored a hit as well, but only managed to knock Millord into the water, as Greyor's hammer crashed into its jaw and deflected the attack.

The puppeteer and his friends had followed Greyor and Millord, and several mine dwellers joined while they traversed the maze of tunnels. They entered the melee, and most of them attacked with rail-spears or swung clubs while the rest threw stones from the shore. The reptilian head punched forward, releasing boiling water, and the stream washed over the stone throwers. Terrible cries were amplified by the shadowy ceiling, and seconds later the humanoids collapsed, appearing to have partially melted. The mine allies were then reduced to a dozen.

Millord emerged beneath Maak Maak's left head, less than twenty feet ahead of Greyor and waist deep in the lake, and he hacked into its massive scales. Clanghorr sliced deeper with every blow, and Millord was soon covered in the creature's greenish blood. The neck curled back as the monster retreated, and Greyor spotted the second head approaching fast. He yelled a warning, but Millord continued to press; and Greyor gaped in horror as his friend was scooped into the air. The jaws clamped shut, but Millord's torso protruded, and he continued swinging Clanghorr with his free hand.

"Millord!" Greyor's voice was lost to the roar of the beast and splashing water.

Maak Maak continued chomping its massive teeth, and Millord yielded at last to the considerable damage his body had sustained. With one last effort, he heaved the mighty axe toward the shore, and Maak Maak turned its head upward and swallowed. Millord was gone.

The other head spit its scalding jet at Greyor.

Eraim retrieved her bow and quiver from Arrikan, the ranger cringing in pain and unable to stand after the scalding water washed over her legs. Eraim then moved closer to the lake's edge, taking aim, and with the expertise of better than two centuries she let loose an arrow. The missile pierced the left eye of the head that had devoured Millord, just as the other head released its breath upon Greyor and his new friends. The stream ceased, and Eraim saw only four mine dwellers standing. Greyor was gone.

While the half-blinded head writhed, Eraim held the left head's undivided attention, and she felt her luck wane as the creature bolted forward — there existed no cover and she was too far from the arches for a retreat. But then the room erupted with bright light, and a pair of spheres exploded on the monstrous heads. The left head collapsed into the water while the other hissed angrily in the direction from where the fiery balls had come.

Standing in the first archway was Selanna, the vapor trails of the spell still rising before her outstretched hands, and Brem was close behind. With a gesture, Selanna shouted a command, and dirt poured from the ceiling as stalactites broke loose and descended onto the reptile. The creature retreated to the far end of the lake and quickly submerged, steam rising with a hiss from where it was last seen.

Selanna lowered her hands and the rumbling ceased. She looked at Eraim, releasing a smile and sigh of relief, and Eraim could not help but do the same.

The water calmed, save for the ripples of the monster's departure. Then came a splash near the shore. Greyor emerged with Clanghorr in hand, his face grim as he surveyed the lake. But the creature was gone.

CHAPTER 28

RETURN TO DARMHORNG

Nidor watched Sullis and Magneer ride into the night upon Umbarc, bound for Morimont. Soon they were nothing more than a passing shadow, and then they were gone.

Without a word, Vecnor stepped into the Morimont River. The water engulfed the large man's boot, and as he continued across it climbed no higher. Xorlunder walked behind the warrior, and Nidor went next with Melac. Gruelenor moved last. The current lapped against their boots in a vain attempt to impede them while they crossed its breadth, well over a hundred feet, and after reaching the opposite bank, they followed the river back east. They proceeded in silence for several miles, finally stopping outside a small grove off Lake Garaard.

"Morning is upon us." Vecnor scanned the brightening sky. "We best shelter for the day."

Within the trees, the company dropped their packs and sat on the cool ground, making themselves as comfortable as possible. The terrain was clearer with the daylight, but appeared no less dreary beneath the gray clouds. While chewing on a light breakfast, Xorlunder ventured a question.

"How are we to gain access into the dungeon?"

Though Nidor saw nothing moving and sensed no evil that was near, the uncanny feeling that someone was listening made him understand Xorlunder's desire to speak just above a whisper.

"A secret passage." Vecnor spoke in a normal tone. "One Eraim discovered many years ago. She does not believe it is known to the enemy."

Xorlunder nodded. After a brief silence, the elf posed another question.

"Where have you been all these years? Several times, Merssa sent messengers to seek for you before the war began."

"I'm here now." Vecnor offered no other explanation.

Xorlunder nodded again, though he appeared unsatisfied with the answer. Nidor could see the gray elf intended to press the issue, perhaps ask if it was Vecnor that met with the Death Lord that night in the mountains. But the large man seemed unwilling to explicate further, so Nidor changed the subject.

"How strong are the forces of Elloria?"

Vecnor shook his head. "There is no way to know. I pray it is enough to make a difference."

"All must not be well with the war," said Melac, "if we are to place hope with an unknown force. Do we at least know that Elloria lives?"

Vecnor gave the mage a grave stare. "Nothing is certain. And whatever her condition now, it may not be so when we arrive."

His words failed to instill confidence, and the grove fell silent, as if things might worsen with additional questions.

They tried to sleep, guarding in shifts while the day passed, but there was little success. With the waning of the light, they gathered their gear and continued across the dark land.

The near-full moon illuminated the way, shining through breaks in the clouds while the company followed the lake's edge. The terrain rose and fell sharply, and boulders of various sizes dotted the landscape, as well as smatterings of vegetation. Small groupings of trees persisted, but they became less frequent over time. Those that did exist were twisted in strange angles as they reached from the sloping lands to compete for nutrients. Farther south, the trees were almost nonexistent.

For three nights, they marched with no signs of the enemy—or anything else for that matter. On the fourth night since crossing the river, the sky grew dark and thunder shook the land. But even as rain soaked the company, they did not falter from the hard pace.

With the fifth day a few hours off, Vecnor stopped among a group of trees. Many large boulders existed within, and the warrior took a seat upon one, dropping his pack onto the muddy ground and drinking from his flask.

"Make yourselves comfortable." Vecnor wiped his mouth with his hand. "We'll be here a couple days...if luck finds us."

They settled in without question.

The trees, while tall and bearing many leaves, did little to keep the company dry, and comfort was a pleasure left unfound. They continued to watch in shifts, but nothing stirred in the dark, wet night.

Come morning the drizzle ceased, though rain clouds remained overhead, and it became obvious why Vecnor had chosen the spot. Not far to the east stood Darmhorng Castle, sitting atop a small hill and butted against the lake. South of the stronghold was the city of Burmagaard, surrounded by a wall of stone and covering a rolling area of greater than four miles from the north gate to the south gate. Dark figures moved along the walls, and above both the city and castle waved flags of various colors, but Nidor could not make them out. Xorlunder did not share in Nidor's limitations, and the elf related what he saw.

"There is the bleeding-eye standard of the Zurkan, and two others I do not recognize. One is of a spear with lightning striking the tip. The other is a black banner with a red triangle and blue oval."

"That one is the union of Trannum and the Zurkan." Vecnor showed no emotion.

"I assume the spear-flag has something to do with Gruzim," said Melac. "From what we know."

"What about the figures on the walls?" Nidor asked the gray elf.

"It is hard to say if they are among the living," Xorlunder replied. "But they do not move like zombies or ghouls, and they lack the eyes of the dunarchins."

"In the end, it matters little," Vecnor said. "They are the enemy."

A cool breeze penetrated the grove, and everyone's attention shifted to the sky. Nothing flew overhead. The air then warmed as the sun pierced the clouds, and the illumination made the thicket appear friendlier than it had through the night. The trees were tall and straight, unlike those seen over the past several days, and wild flowers grew in defiance of the surrounding evil. It was a breath of fresh air; a glimpse of a time before darkness tainted the land. But the vision lasted only a moment, and the sunlight vanished, returning the copse into gloom.

"The creatures upon the walls are among the living." Xorlunder grinned. "With the coming of the sun, they did not seek shelter."

Though no one seemed to share in Xorlunder's enthusiasm, Nidor looked forward to fighting an enemy that bled.

Conversations were minimal throughout the day, and all attention was constantly drawn to the castle. Being so close to the doors of evil placed Nidor's nerves on edge, but the time passed without mishap.

The night brought heavy rainfall with gusting winds, and flashes of lightning provided glimpses of Darmhorng and Burmagaard, making them appear more ominous. Nothing stirred, and the many windows of the towers and buildings remained pits of darkness—it seemed not even the undead wished to venture into the violent storm. The sky brightened with the morning, and the thunder and lightning ceased and the winds calmed, but rain continued to wash the land as the day came and went.

"How much longer do we remain here?" Melac asked while they consumed a cold, soggy supper. "With every day that passes, we risk being discovered."

"Not to mention we have just about depleted our rations," Gruelenor added.

They were the first words the krukari had spoken since before crossing the river, when he wished Magneer a safe journey. Nidor noticed Gruelenor's darkening mood after that night, and he had wanted to speak with his friend, but Gruelenor was still avoiding him and he left it alone.

"We don't dare enter too soon," Vecnor said, "lest the entire army of Burmagaard become aware of us. We must wait until the time is right."

"When will that be?" asked Xorlunder.

"We'll know." Vecnor turned his attention to Darmhorng.

The downpour continued, and the night added frozen winds. The company huddled close, shivering beneath soaked blankets, and raindrops turned to sleet.

"A Death Lord has arrived." Vecnor's breath was thick upon the air.

Another night passed, and with the sun's return, the rain subsided near midday. The sunshine persisted, bringing with it a taste of summer, but Nidor noticed its rays did not touch Darmhorng, which remained beneath unmoving storm clouds. As the sun faded into the west, the sky cleared, making for a warm, dry evening.

The company settled in for another night, only to be roused a few hours before dawn. Xorlunder had been on watch.

"*Mees!*" the elf hissed, and everyone was quick to rise. "A legion of undead! A hundred yards to the southeast."

Standing among the dark trees, nothing seemed amiss. But distant moans, hisses, and the odor that soon followed gave the creatures away. Vecnor hurried to the edge of the grove and gazed into the shadows, as if his human eyes could pierce the darkness.

"They aren't aiming for us." Vecnor's shoulders relaxed. "They're headed west."

"Morimont must be marching," said Melac.

Dread crept into Nidor as he thought of Magneer and Sullis. "Is there any way to send warning?"

"We must trust it to the gods now." Vecnor sighed. "But do not fear. The dwarves of Morimont are the greatest warriors of their race, in my opinion. And they will know resistance awaits them."

"Shh!" hissed Xorlunder. "They are almost upon us."

Darkness fell over the trees as clouds rolled overhead, and no one moved. They watched while greater than five thousand zombies, skeletons, ghouls, and dunarchins made their way west, all but the latter uneven and undisciplined. Nidor saw no commander to lead or drive them; they simply walked a brisk pace. The army passed by the copse with malice in their eyes, and if they smelled the presence of Nidor and his companions, it was not obvious.

"Gather your gear," Vecnor said after the undead were beyond sight, taking with them the patch of dark clouds. "We move now."

While they collected their things, Vecnor searched among the collection of boulders. He traced a large square with his finger in the wet dirt and then stood.

"The entrance was here the whole time?" Melac raised a brow. "The one Selanna used when visiting King Karrak?"

"It is most likely latched from beneath," said Xorlunder. "And it is too fine a seam for a blade to pry open. But, perhaps with the proper magic —"

Vecnor pounded his heavy boot onto the door, sundering it in a single attempt.

"It won't be much of a secret after today," he said in response to Xorlunder's questioning look.

The large man dropped through the opening, and the others descended the iron rungs after him.

Two feet of muddy water covered the floor of a long, dark tunnel. The way was narrow, restricting the company to proceed in single file, and the low ceiling was only inches above Nidor's head, giving the corridor a cramped feel. Vecnor was hunched over and practically walked sideways to fit within the confines.

Nidor spoke his silent request to Silcor, bringing his sword to life with the fire-like glow, and he sloshed behind Vecnor, trying his best to light the way ahead. Water dripped from the ceiling, sometimes in a steady trickle, and after a mile the corridor sloped gently upward, lifting them from the flood. Two hundred yards farther, the passageway ended.

Vecnor fiddled with a protrusion on the tunnel wall to the left until the back wall opened slightly. Through the gap rushed a deep chill, and Nidor's stomach soured—a Death Lord was near. Vecnor placed his gauntleted hand onto the secret door and gave a shove, creating a loud grating sound as he pushed the panel deeper into the wall to widen the entrance.

Without concern for the noise, Vecnor drew one of the large swords from his back and entered a storage chamber. He made his way around crates and barrels to the opposite side, where the room's only visible door existed, and tried the latch. It was locked. With a single kick, he launched the door from its hinges and into a dimly lit hallway.

"Sullis would have loved his approach," Gruelenor mumbled to Nidor.

From the apprehension in Gruelenor's eyes, Nidor was sure his companion shared his uneasiness with Vecnor's lack of stealth.

Vecnor strode down the passage and to an intersection bearing left and right. Before reaching the end, two guards appeared from the left branch and were startled by the company's presence. Without hesitation, Vecnor thrust his sword through one and pinned the other to the wall by the throat. He then snapped the soldier's neck before an alarm could be voiced and released the body to the floor.

"There are cells to the right," Vecnor said, as if the encounter with the guards had been a minor nuisance. "See if Elloria is there."

"What about you?" asked Nidor.

"There are more cells to the left," Vecnor replied, "or so I'm told. I'll find the keys. You find the prisoner."

Nidor stared after Vecnor as the warrior headed for an iron-bound door a short distance to the left. While the large man forced the door open and passed through, the words of Sullis returned, warning Nidor to remain cautious. But if Vecnor *was* a traitor, they would have failed long ago. Nidor shook his head.

"Let's go." He hurried along the passage to the right.

The corridor stretched fifty feet before ending, and to either side were five wooden doors, each reinforced with steel bands and possessing a small window of bars. By the light of his sword, Nidor peered through the openings to discover dirty cells, each holding a few occupants. The prisoners shielded their eyes and cowered. None of them were female.

"She is not here," Xorlunder whispered, the elf having looked himself.

Distant screams sounded from the direction Vecnor had gone.

"Ready yourselves!" Nidor rushed down the hall.

The iron door clung to a single hinge, and as Nidor neared, the screaming ceased. He listened. The dungeon was silent. But his skin began to crawl.

"Do you hear anything?" he asked Xorlunder.

"No. But it smells foul. And feels..."

Nidor nodded. "I feel it too."

He stepped past the ailing door and into a guardroom, expecting to find dead soldiers littering the floor. But there were none. It was dark, the only light provided by Nidor's sword, and a few chairs, a keg, and a table were present, as well as mugs and game cards. Everything was in disarray, and there was no sign of Vecnor.

Nidor again heard Sullis's voice, cautioning him to be wary of the man that appeared to them looking like a Death Lord. He suddenly wondered why they had sat idle within the trees while an army of undead marched off to confront the dwarves. At the time it made sense—they were too few to stand against such a force. But now Nidor was unsure. Could they have at least sent a warning? Surely, with Melac's magic, something could have been done. No. Vecnor wanted to avoid discovery. The large man had been cautious... Until they reached the dungeon.

"Blast!" Nidor was filled with the horror that he had made a grievous mistake. His company, put together to perform a specific task, was convinced to split up. Now they followed a stranger into the jaws of the enemy, while Sullis and Magneer likely rode into a trap. Sullis warned Nidor to stay alert, but he had sensed no evil in Vecnor, and now the war might be in jeopardy.

"Fear not, Paladin of Flame," Xorlunder whispered. "Vecnor is with us."

The elf's words did little to ease Nidor's anxiety, but there was no choice other than to carry on.

Across the room was an iron door, and to the right another sat ajar. Nidor crept toward the open door, halting when he spied movement within the darkness. Turning, he saw nothing but shadows.

"What was that?" Melac looked to the left.

"Wraiths!" said Gruelenor.

Nidor spotted a wraith near the ceiling, and its glowing eyes were flying straight for Gruelenor. Gruelenor staggered back as it reached for his throat with ghostly hands, but its attack fell short when Nidor's flaming sword sliced through its incorporeal body. The monster vanished in a hiss of black vapor.

Three more wraiths emerged from the shadows, and one assaulted Nidor. Nidor's eyes flared, chasing away all darkness and revealing the fiend to him; and the creature shrieked when an aura of deep orange arose. The fire-like glow engulfed Nidor but brought him no harm, and the pleasant warmth removed all pain and fatigue he might have harbored, replacing it with strength and energy. The wraith hissed as it sought escape, and Nidor's blade silenced it forever.

A wraith held Melac pinned to the floor, its dark claws penetrating through clothes and flesh and into the mage's chest. Melac was frozen in horror, and Gruelenor attempted to give aid without success—his sword passed harmlessly through the wraith's ghostly form. The glowing eyes then turned on Gruelenor, and he gave ground as the shadowy spirit lunged for him, avoiding its reach as best he could.

Xorlunder had also been driven to the floor, and the wraith plunged its claw into the elf's chest. The evil spirit's eyes grew bright with excitement, but a large blade sliced through its body and it vanished with a hiss. Standing above Xorlunder was Vecnor.

The wraith upon Gruelenor abandoned its attack and fled through a small shaft in the ceiling. The dungeon was silent.

"One got away," said Gruelenor, and he gazed at Nidor with concern.

"To warn its master, no doubt." Vecnor's brow furrowed while he eyed Nidor.

Nidor allowed the flames about his eyes and body to fade, leaving only his blade alight.

"We need to keep moving." Vecnor pulled Xorlunder up before tossing a ring of keys to Nidor.

The large man walked to the closed door and shouldered it. The portal did its best to turn away the assault, but it could not withstand the warrior's strength and he entered the passageway beyond.

Nidor glanced at his companions. Melac leaned on Gruelenor, and Xorlunder's grayish skin was a shade paler, appearing almost white. Nidor wished to heal them, but there did not appear to be time. With a deep breath, he followed Vecnor.

The corridor contained another ten cells, each with a door of bars and holding at least two occupants. The final cell on the right, however, held a single prisoner; a woman seated on the floor against the far wall. Though the other cells possessed cots, hers was bare of furnishings, save for the shackles and chains that afforded her little movement.

"Elloria?" Xorlunder stepped next to Nidor, his voice hoarse.

The woman raised her weary head to look at them. She was older, nearer to Sullis in age, with graying black hair and sad blue eyes. Upon seeing Xorlunder her expression changed, and an inner fire was kindled. From her, Nidor sensed spiritual strength.

"Xorlunder?" she said in a dry, raspy voice. "Can it be?"

"It is I, my lady." Xorlunder bowed.

Elloria released a hard sigh with a smile. "Thank Brondor!"

Nidor gazed at the keys in his hand, wondering why Vecnor bothered to retrieve them. The large warrior did not seem concerned with the well-being of doors. But then Nidor noticed a strange construction within Elloria's cell: rafters rigged from the door to the middle of the ceiling. He did not quite understand the set up, but he was sure a forced entry would crush the priestess beneath several feet of stone. He approached the door.

Chapter 29

Kembald

Cavalor awoke with a start. He thought he heard the distant scream of an undead dragon. It was nearing dawn, and all remained still, save for Borse and Wezlok whispering to the side of the campsite. Landerik and Arkor were sleeping. Merssa was nowhere to be seen.

Rubbing the sleep from his eyes, Cavalor did not think much of his mother's absence. Then he noticed his father's long face, and he knew something was amiss. As well, Wezlok avoided eye contact, appearing remorseful. It was an odd expression for the elf.

Cavalor went to his father, and a rush of emotion nearly overwhelmed him as he realized he would never see his mother again. He stared at Borse, hoping he was mistaken.

"She is the bravest soul I have ever known." Wezlok continued to avert his gaze. "I will wake the others."

Cavalor looked at his father. "Why?"

Borse placed his wrinkled hand on Cavalor's shoulder. "It was something she needed to do."

"We must go after her!" Cavalor said with urgency.

Borse sighed, as if struggling with the same notion himself. "There is still a goal to achieve. To go after her would undo the time she has afforded us." He scanned the branches overhead. "The evil has faded. They follow her now. Would you place her bravery in vain?"

Cavalor heard the others stir. Whispering followed, and then silence. Wezlok had informed Arkor and Landerik of the latest news.

"Let's move." Cavalor turned away as a tear rolled down his cheek.

He was angry with his mother for leaving. But also it saddened him that he would never again see her face or hear her commanding voice. Anger welled up inside as he gathered his gear, and his focus shifted to the enemy. He hoped minions of Trannum would surface soon.

They headed east, Arkor leading the way through the forest along its northern edge, and nothing hampered them while the day passed. An hour before dusk, a patch of dark clouds rolled out of the southeast, riding frozen winds and stealing the sun's light. The company sought cover, but the clouds rushed past, disappearing into the northwest, and the light returned.

They pressed on, and as the air cooled with the final traces of the sun, there came the screech of an undead dragon from far away. Moments later, a darkness flickered in the distant north. A brilliant flash of gold and black followed, accompanied by a faint crashing sound, as if something had snapped a tree in half.

Cavalor averted his gaze while his companions stared. A terrible pain seized his heart and he could not bear to look. His eyes were then drawn back, for it appeared the sun was setting a second time. But the light was northerly and golden in color. It grew bright, lasting almost a minute, and then it was gone. Next came a warm breeze out of the north, and it filled Cavalor with hope and washed away all fatigue. It looked as though the others shared in this relief, except for Wezlok. The elf had seemed tired throughout the day, and now he appeared exhausted.

The company eyed one another, none of them finding any words. Arkor issued a questioning glance toward Wezlok, and the mage nodded. Without a word, they resumed their trek.

They marched most of the night, stopping for a few hours of sleep come morning. Upon the evening of the following day, they reached the eastern edge of Mentrial Forest. Broken, desert-like terrain stretched as far as Cavalor could see, incapable of supporting most plant life. To the distant south, Moon Lake was nestled against the woodland at the bottom of a valley, and the Krimbror River cut a deep path on its way to the sea. Kembald and Castle Lambrak were a couple of hard days away.

"We should take advantage of the forest tonight," said Arkor. "We shall not find better cover once we exit."

The night passed, and with the dawn the sun shone brightly. There was still no sign of the enemy, and the company's luck continued throughout the day while they trekked across the desolate land. Cavalor could not help but feel his mother's ploy, whatever it was, had worked. But he turned his thoughts to Castle Lambrak.

Shadows stretched long with the setting of the sun until melding with the darkness. The aging moon then partially illuminated the way, and though Wezlok continued to show signs of fatigue, he gave no objections while they walked through most of the night. A few hours before dawn, at Arkor's insistence, they halted among large boulders to get some rest.

Cavalor was the sole guard through most of the day. Sleep was impossible, as sorrow, hatred, and confusion continued to plague his mind. When it came time to wake Landerik for the final shift, Cavalor declined to do so and remained on watch. His father had attempted to ease his heart earlier, while they ate a cold breakfast, but Cavalor refused to hear anymore words about bravery, or how Merssa had found her place within the Halls of Cafior. He wanted her back, and he was angry with her for leaving.

When evening arrived, Cavalor watched the sunset in silence. A warm breeze rushed over him, and he imagined his mother was there, but the daydream ended when a large creature flew overhead. Cavalor jumped, and the rattling of his armor stirred the others. It was only a bird.

He felt ashamed. Had it been the enemy, they could have killed his entire company while they slept. His mother's voice came to him.

"Keep your mind about you! You're no good if you're dead!"

"Yes, Mother," Cavalor said quietly before looking at his companions.

Arkor released a sigh while eying Cavalor. "Let's continue."

They gathered their gear and headed east.

The night passed, and the company continued into the following day. The sun traveled overhead and dropped into the west while they climbed stony hills, slid down rocky slopes, and depleted nearly all of their water supply within the blazing heat. As dusk neared, the dying light reflected off the gray buildings of Kembald.

The walled city sat atop a green hill at the bottom of the next valley, and within the shadows of the settlement, upon a neighboring hill to the east, was Castle Lambrak. Farther still, scattered trees filled the valley below the stronghold. The Krimbror River weaved its way around the southern side of the city before curling north and rounding the castle. From there, it raced off to the Endless Sea, a grayish-blue wall in the distant east.

"We've made good time," said Arkor. "We could reach Lambrak before the light fails. Perhaps we should wait for nightfall."

"Darkness provides little help when dealing with the undead," Wezlok said.

"What do you suggest?" The one-armed warrior raised a brow.

The mage shook his head. "Only that we remain aware of where we are."

They continued, moving more cautiously. The slope into the valley was mild in most places, but steeper in others, and loose rocks waited for the slightest misstep to try and send them tumbling. They remained well north of the city, finally stopping for rest below a large outcropping of rock.

Cavalor now held a better view of the hills beneath the waning light. The streets of Kembald were barren, and to the east a bridge led to Castle Lambrak, where towers stood tall above an iron gate.

"What do you know of the castle?" he asked Arkor.

"The only way in is the bridge," the one-armed warrior replied. "Long ago, the Marcs shaved the hillside about the castle to create sheer drops. Even if we scaled it, there's a fifteen-foot wall of smooth stone and towers every fifty yards."

"What of the gate?" Landerik posed.

"Two towers bar entry with an iron portcullis between them," Arkor answered. "And then there's a second portcullis beyond that."

The Brondor paladin frowned. "So how do we get in?"

"If Merssa had a plan, she said nothing to me." Arkor shrugged. "But I doubt she did. I'm sure she would have come up with something once we arrived." He looked at his Marc livery. "Perhaps our uniforms will help."

Cavalor considered their tattered clothing and shook his head. Even at night in Denvale, the outfits had turned heads.

"Then we best put out the moon and walk like zombies," Landerik waved a contemptuous hand, "lest we can make ourselves appear as dunarchins or ghouls." He gave the mage a sidelong glance, surprising Cavalor with his sudden acceptance of employing stealth.

"My powers will be necessary once we are inside," Wezlok said flatly. "I have not fully recovered, and if I use what strength I have to gain access, I will be of no more use than a *human* peasant."

Cavalor was not sure why Wezlok emphasized the word human, but he decided not to waste any thought on the matter. They needed to bend their minds on forming a plan. It was Borse that spoke next.

"Perhaps we can enter without expending *any* power. And if we're lucky, without a fight."

After the sun was set, they traversed the dark countryside. They arrived to where the Krimbror River flowed between the hills, and above the water was a bridge of land connecting the city to the castle. Fine stonework arched above the waterway to form a tunnel, most likely for support, and Cavalor wondered if the current had always traveled thusly, or if the tunnel had been bored and the river's natural course shifted at some point.

A narrow patch of grass led up to the street, just east of the city, and the company ascended with little effort before stepping onto the stone path. No lights issued from Kembald, and large wooden doors stood open, revealing lifeless, two-story buildings. The wide road stretched fifty yards to Castle Lambrak, where twin towers rose forty feet to either side of the entrance. The left tower windows revealed torchlight while the right tower's exhibited pits of darkness, and both portcullises were firmly in place. Three-foot walls lined the edges of the street, chipped and worn, and the flagstones were marred by time, but the construction appeared sound and the road sturdy.

The night was silent, and it seemed no one had taken notice of Cavalor and his companions. With deep breaths, they approached the gate, and every step weighed upon Cavalor's nerves. Soon they stood before the first portcullis. The iron bars were thick and spaced a foot apart, and a large chain rose from each gate and into the upper floor of the left tower, where the flickering light revealed the silhouettes of two figures. Though the southern tower remained dark, Cavalor felt eyes watching from within.

"Hail!" called Arkor.

"Who goes there?" a voice demanded from the illuminated tower.

"We have caught an elf wizard!"

Arkor jerked Wezlok to the front. No longer garbed in the ill-fitted Marc uniform, the elf appeared wounded and his hands were bound before him.

Murmuring issued from the lighted tower, and Wezlok tilted his head, as if to listen.

"They are confused," the mage said. "They have had no word of incoming prisoners." He sighed. "It is not going to wor—" He turned his attention to the dark tower. "Another voice. Sharp. It speaks of Merssa and the invaders, spotted three days ago. It mentions that an elf mage was with her."

A shrill voice pierced the night, issuing from the dark tower. "Let them in."

Cavalor could not begin to imagine what had spoken with such a voice. The winch began turning, as if the occupants of the lighted tower feared to delay, and the chain was pulled taut. The first portcullis then rose until it was just above the company's heads.

"Step forward," the voice from the lighted tower shouted.

The company passed beneath the gate, and the portcullis crashed down behind them, almost causing Cavalor to jump. Within seconds, several guards appeared beyond the second portcullis with torches. They looked to be among the living, and suspicious eyes scrutinized the company's bloodstained uniforms, paying special attention to the slashes and puncture holes in vital regions.

"I am Captain Crismar," said one guard at last. "Who are you?"

Cavalor's heart stopped. He was sure the captain had traced a symbol on his chest with the middle finger of his left hand. His mind raced back to when Nidor mentioned such a gesture, one shared by a secret force within Trannum's ranks. Zhokards, Cavalor believed the Dale called them. Though he had seen it only once, when the barbarian paladin gave a demonstration, he spent weeks afterward, watching for other rebels hiding in plain sight. As these thoughts occurred to him, he began to doubt he had truly seen it on this occasion. But when Arkor's mouth opened, Cavalor spoke.

"I am Cavalor." He repeated the gesture as best as he could recall. "We captured this elf in Mentrial Forest."

It seemed an eternity passed while the captain eyed Cavalor. Had he been mistaken? Did he trace the symbol wrong? Perhaps Crismar had not made the sign at all. Cavalor wished he had let Arkor speak. The one-armed warrior was much more experienced in the ways of Marcs, and he might have given a better response than blurting out his true name.

"Ah, Lieutenant Cavalor," the captain said. "I almost forgot you were coming." Crismar called up to the tower, "Open the gate!"

Chapter 30

Castle Lambrak

Cavalor and his companions followed the guards across the courtyard, and Captain Crismar passed the time speaking of news and events since the "invaders" were spotted. Most of it was meaningless to Cavalor. Once they neared the castle, and the last of the accompanying soldiers had left them, Crismar's face became somber and he took a quieter tone.

"You are obviously not zhokard." He came to a halt. "But your reply was close enough that you know something about us." He looked at the others, and the feeble bindings on Wezlok did not escape his notice. Crismar's attention returned to Cavalor. "Who are you?"

"We fight for the same cause as you," Cavalor replied. "At least, I was led to believe so by one who went by the name of Grimmen."

Crismar's face was unreadable, but Cavalor sensed turmoil in the man's eyes.

"I suppose I'll have to trust you for now," the captain said. "But it is not up to me. So watch your step. My kind have escaped detection for many years, and we will not risk discovery over a small band of mortals."

Cavalor glanced over his shoulder. His companions had questions, he knew, but they remained silent.

"Let's go inside," Crismar said. "There are safer places to talk." The captain shot a glance toward the dark tower above the gate.

They proceeded to the southern side of the castle and through a servants' entrance. A short corridor gave way to a large kitchen, where four women were cleaning up after a meal. Several plates bore a red substance, and Cavalor felt ill wondering what the main course had been — did Death Lords eat?

The servants smiled at Crismar. Crismar made a gesture Cavalor could not see, and the smiles were replaced by glares for the company. One servant moved to the opposite end of the chamber to peer through a large archway. She nodded, and a woman bearing unkind eyes opened a pantry door. Beyond were several sacks, casks, and jars, but the servant ignored them, reaching to the side and fiddling with something until the wall next to the pantry opened. Revealed was a staircase descending into darkness. Crismar motioned for Cavalor to enter.

Cavalor hesitated, wondering if it was a trap. But what choice did they have? He moved down the steps, and his companions followed.

The stairs led twenty feet to a dark, dank room. The walls, floor, and ceiling were of dirt and uneven, appearing to have been excavated in haste with less-than-adequate tools, and taking up most of the space was a table and eight chairs, barely visible within the glow of the kitchen. Upon the table rested a lantern and little else, and Wezlok dropped his bonds and ignited the wick with a touch of his finger. The light revealed a large map of eastern Vaeldor spiked to the far wall, and on it were several unfamiliar symbols. Unmistakable was a blue oval over a black triangle in Nomedd, marking the stronghold of Trannum.

The kitchen door closed, leaving them alone, and all eyes turned to Cavalor. Before any could voice a question, he shared the story of the encounter between Nidor and Grimmen, as told to his mother. The room stared in silence.

"Sullis spoke of this fire paladin." Landerik appeared as if he had eaten something foul. "This information might have proven useful earlier. We could have used the zhokards, as a distraction or —"

"It was my mother's decision." Cavalor did not care for the direction Landerik was headed. "She did not wish to place hope with an unknown force. Nor trust within creations of the enemy."

"And who could blame her for that?" Arkor seated himself at the table.

Everyone but Landerik followed Arkor's lead and took a seat. The Brondor paladin paced with a furrowed brow. Cavalor listened to the faint rustling and muffled voices from the kitchen for a while, but he doubted even Wezlok could discern the words. It seemed like an hour passed when the door opened and Crismar descended into the chamber.

"We do not have long." Crismar took a seat, and for a moment Cavalor noticed a blue shimmering within the captain's eyes. "The queen will hear of your arrival soon, if she hasn't already."

"The queen?" Arkor frowned.

"That's what *they* call her." Crismar sneered. "The Ice Witch is more to my liking. She is Mayry, wife of Gruzim, and she rules by the might of her son, Horx. He is her steel and muscle while her husband reigns over Kalmaar. She has strong hopes Horx will one day become a Death Lord, like his father."

"The same Mayry that was espoused to Duke Tarm?" asked Arkor.

Crismar nodded.

"She was a woman of great beauty," Arkor said. "How could she choose a life such as this? And wedded to a krukari?"

Crismar held a wry smile. "She has given herself to Trannum for power. The necromancer's magic keeps her to her liking. She is neither wholly living nor undead, much like myself. Only *she* needs daily elixirs to maintain her existence."

"Just as Malgabi." The wrinkles on Borse's face appeared deeper than in recent days.

"The same." Crismar gave a nod.

"Is there no Death Lord within the castle, then?" Landerik's frown showed disappointment.

Crismar shook his head. "They come and go. But one has not remained here for months. Not since learning of your plans to march."

"Then you know of us?" Cavalor asked.

"Of course," Crismar replied. "Besides what the Death Lords have told us, we received additional news from a scout of our own." He glanced Cavalor's way. "Grimmen was his name." He returned his attention to the company. "Unfortunately, Cadorn the Vile sent an army into Kalmaar nearly a month ago, and Grimmen was among them. Cadorn remained for a while afterward, but when no word came from Jurak in the mountain pass, he left for Denvale."

"Our friend, Arkor," Borse nodded toward the one-armed warrior, "knocked Jurak into the gorge outside Ironside Keep."

"Please, Borse." Arkor held up his hand. "I was not alone in that battle. And besides, the Death Lord may very well have survived the fall."

"We have had no word of the fate of Jurak." Crismar sat back. "Not even after Cadorn returned a few days later. All he would say was that your party had entered the realm, and he sent what remained of Kembald's soldiers to search for you in Mentrial Forest." His eyes narrowed. "He arrived recently to inform Mayry of your presence in the northwest, and he departed to deal with you personally. That you are here and he is not gives me hope he has been defeated." The captain looked from Arkor to Cavalor, as if awaiting confirmation.

No one spoke. Cavalor did not know what had become of Cadorn or his mother. Was it possible that she conquered the Death Lord? Might she come marching into the castle at any moment? Cavalor almost lost his breath at the notion, but also a chill ran down his spine at the thought of Cadorn finding his mother alone. He banished the image from his mind.

"Is Kembald empty, then?" Arkor asked.

"Hardly." Crismar shook his head. "A couple weeks ago, it seemed Nomedd emptied its lands of the undead. Thousands of them now inhabit the city, and all living beings were forced to leave. Most of them headed north, into Kalmaar."

It appeared to Cavalor that his mother's plan was working, though not as originally laid out. All attention was bent on Kalmaar and Marcove, and nothing was said of the companies passing south of the Fire Hills or through the mines. He accepted this as a good sign, and his father's expression revealed the priest to feel the same.

"Do you have news of events in Kalmaar?" Borse asked.

"Only that all forces are concentrated on Darmhorng," the captain replied.

"The North Army must be intact." Arkor almost smiled. He turned to Crismar. "How many within this castle are loyal to Mayry?"

"There's Horx," Crismar searched the ceiling, "as well as some dunarchins and Zurkan—Mayry has developed a taste for the krukari."

Cavalor had no wish to inquire as to what the captain meant by *taste*.

"Along with a handful of zhomians and the bandits from Mentrial," Crismar continued, "I'd say there are at least three score. But I'm only counting what's inside the castle. Within the courtyard and gatehouse are an additional fifty."

"What of your kind?" asked Landerik.

Crismar eyed the Brondor paladin. "I am not at liberty to share that information." He turned to those at the table. "I have said too much already. But I *will* admit that my folk are outnumbered, even if we were to add you to our ranks."

Cavalor frowned. "Will you not help us?"

"I do not yet know your plans," the captain replied, "nor what helping you would entail."

Cavalor looked at his father, unsure of how much to reveal. Borse then spoke.

"I am Borse, priest of Cafior and husband of Merssa Goldmace, a name I am sure you are familiar with. We are here to take control of the castle."

Crismar stared in disbelief. "Perhaps I wasn't clear. There is an army of undead within Kembald."

This news did nothing to interrupt the stone faces of Cavalor's companions. It seemed they were all committed to seeing the mission through.

The captain lit up with sudden realization. "There's more than you're willing to say. You do not fully trust me, nor I you." He shook his head. "But it is not my decision. I am only here to determine where your loyalties lie. Another will determine your fate."

A soft tapping fell on the door. Crismar's face darkened.

"Alas, time grows short and the sun rises soon." The captain stood. "I must now take you before the queen." He eyed Wezlok. "I don't know if she will buy your story of the captured elf. But you best refasten your bonds all the same, since that is the story you have given."

They followed Crismar up the stairs, where he scratched the secret door twice. Moments later, it opened and they stepped into the kitchen. Only three women were present.

After verifying the mage's bonds were in place, Crismar led the company from the chamber. They walked corridors lined with tapestries of wondrous designs and landscapes, as well as paintings of a lovely woman wearing a magnificent tiara, and more than a few human and krukari soldiers watched Cavalor and his companions with hateful eyes. Crismar turned down a wide hallway, and at the far end was a pair of hefty wooden doors and two large krukari. The guards wore the usual Zurkan garb, blood-red cloaks draped over black armor, and they scowled at Crismar and his guests as they opened the doors and stepped aside.

Beyond was a majestic chamber, where twelve massive pillars created a long aisle. The columns were carved into the likenesses of powerful men supporting the ceiling thirty feet overhead, and before each stood a Zurkan warrior. A violet carpet ran along the center of the aisle and to the far end, its only interruption a fountain in the middle of the room seeming out of place with the overall grandeur.

The fountain had surely been an impressive construction of a horsed soldier holding aloft a sword, but the soldier's head was missing, the blade sundered, and brownish liquid drizzled from the mount's broken jaw.

Across the room, a pair of wooden thrones were atop a dais, and the carpet ascended three arcing steps before surrounding the elaborate chairs. One throne was inlaid with gemstones of various colors, and upon it sat Queen Mayry, more beautiful than the portraits and appearing no older than her early twenties. The second chair was smaller, but equally magnificent, and seated was a large krukari in black armor reminiscent to that of a Death Lord's. At the company's arrival to the thrones, the krukari's lips curled into an evil grin.

Arkor slid behind Borse in an apparent attempt to remain hidden. Cavalor assumed Arkor had made the queen's acquaintance at least once in the distant past, and even if she did not remember the man, who could forget the wooden arm? Cavalor and his companions followed Crismar's lead as the captain bowed.

"Captain Crismar." Mayry's tone was drenched in arrogance. "I was beginning to think you were entertaining without me."

"Many apologies, my Queen." Crismar bowed lower. "I only wished for them to get a bite to eat, for they had been on the road for days."

"I see." Mayry gazed down her nose at the company. "And what gift have they brought to me?"

"They have —"

"I wish to hear from them!" The queen's sharp words caused the captain to flinch.

"A prisoner." Cavalor stepped forward. "From Mentrial Forest."

Mayry looked at Cavalor with a raised brow. Her cold eyes then returned to Crismar. "That will be all, Captain."

Crismar bowed and turned, shooting Cavalor a concerned glance. The captain's footfalls echoed as he strode from the chamber, and the shutting of the doors reverberated about the hall.

"What is your name, knave?" Mayry spat once the echoes had ceased. "And this time, you had best practice proper decorum."

"Cavalor, my Queen." He bowed his head.

She nodded in satisfaction, and her lip twitched with the slightest of smiles. "So you say you have a prisoner, Cavalor?" Mayry gave a sidelong glance at the krukari seated next to her. "Was there any word of a prisoner, Horx darling?"

"None." Horx stared at Cavalor.

Horx was the most hideous krukari Cavalor had ever seen. He often thought the one called Gruelenor appeared more hobgoblin-like than human, but Horx combined the worst traits of either race into a truly horrible visage.

"Cadorn sent us—" Cavalor said.

"*Lord* Cadorn!" Mayry rose from her seat with rage in her eyes. "How *dare* you speak his name so!"

"Many apologies, my Queen." Cavalor bowed again. "For my insolence I will surely suffer his wrath, as well I should."

Mayry's mouth hung open for a couple of seconds. But then her smirk returned, and she retook her seat. "Well, then." She chuckled. "You wish for your punishment to come directly from *him*? That is brave of you. And it shall be arranged!" Her last statement was venomous.

"Very good, my Queen." Cavalor bent his knee, bowing low enough to avoid eye contact.

"You may continue." Mayry waved her hand, as if she were growing bored.

"Lord Cadorn still hunts the paladin," Cavalor kept his knee bent, "but he ordered us to bring the elf for questioning."

"Is that so?" Mayry nodded to Horx.

The krukari raised his left fist, and the Zurkan drew their swords. Cavalor rose, his hand moving to the pommel of his blade, and he took a step back. His companions did the same, though none of them pulled their weapons.

"The way I understand it," the queen frowned, trying to appear perplexed, "there were to be *no* prisoners. They were to be slaughtered, from what Lord Cadorn told *me*." She smiled. "So please, Cavalor, slay this elf."

Cavalor looked at his companions. They had no answers. Unsheathing his weapon, his mind raced for something to say or do. He found nothing.

"Wait!" Mayry stood. "Face me."

Cavalor turned back, and her brows came together as she gazed upon him. Stepping from the dais, she moved uncomfortably close and lifted his chin with an icy finger.

"Durl?" She spoke just above a whisper.

Cavalor was confused. A chill exuded from her body, and her dark eyes pierced his soul. He retreated a step.

"Durl!" Mayry said again, stronger this time. "It *is* you. My darling Durl! After all these years, you've returned to me at last!"

Cavalor shook his head and looked at his father. The priest's eyes grew sad and became downcast.

"I always wondered where that *bastard* hid you!" Mayry smiled, turning Cavalor's face to meet hers. "He stole you from me. It's me, Durl. Your mother."

Cavalor's mouth opened, but nothing came out. A few years ago, his parents revealed he was not of their blood, after he had grown depressed at failing to achieve paladinhood. He accepted the news and their love, never desiring to know his birth parents. Now, faced with the pale woman before him, questions and emotions coursed through him. But still he could think of nothing to say. Could she be speaking the truth?

"It *is* you, Durl." Mayry brushed her frigid hand along his cheek. "A mother knows her son. I do not care for the name they have given you, but what's important is that you've returned. My firstborn, returned at last! I am so sorry for what you must have endured all these years. But now you're home. Now you can begin the life you were destined for. Have you seen Solinin, your brother?"

Cavalor gazed into Mayry's eyes; her dark, cold, bottomless eyes. She had no soul. Were it possible, she might have shed a tear. But there was sincerity in her voice. Cavalor then met Horx's gaze, and the krukari's grin was replaced by malice, not at all pleased with the thought of sharing the throne. Or, perhaps, he felt forgotten and insignificant in the presence of his human half-brother.

"My darling," Mayry said. "Look at me. Look at your mother."

Cavalor sensed the eyes of his companions upon his back. Deep inside, he twisted and churned as his heart was torn, wishing for the void left by his mother, Merssa, to be filled. In that moment, he realized the true wisdom of Cafior; why paladinhood was forever beyond reach. It had nothing to do with birth parents, nor the blood that coursed through Cavalor's veins. Cafior knew Cavalor's destiny; knew what was in his heart. And never could a paladin of His Order turn from honor and give in to such temptation. But Cavalor could not help himself.

"My mother's dead!" He thrust his sword into Mayry's chest, burying it to the hilt.

Mayry gasped and fell to her knees, and dark liquid issued from her gaping mouth.

"No!" Horx stood, unsheathing a curved blade with teeth along the edge. "Kill them all!"

The Zurkan advanced, and one of them stopped to blow into a horn. The alarm was sounded.

Cavalor pulled his sword from the queen's body, allowing her corpse to fall, and he drew his knife as Horx arrived. The Zurkan towered over Cavalor, and he brought down the curved blade with impressive strength, forcing Cavalor to his knee as he parried the attack.

"Now it's time to die, *brother*!" The krukari prince ran the teeth of the sword along Cavalor's blade, snapping it in two with a shower of sparks.

Cavalor dropped the remaining shard and rolled to the side, leaving Horx's next blow to strike the stone floor. The krukari then gazed upon the queen's body, and Cavalor raced onto the dais.

"I'll skin you!" Horx snarled. "You'll beg for death!"

"Come then!" Cavalor grinned, enraging Horx further. "Come if you dare!"

Cavalor said a quick prayer as Horx charged, but it was not to Cafior. "Mother. I need your guidance."

His spirit rose as all the training she had given him, the lectures and disciplines of combat, flooded his mind. He sidestepped the next powerful swing and brought the pommel of his dagger to the back of Horx's head, causing the warrior to stumble. Horx was beyond rage and unbalanced, and as Cavalor realized this, he heard his mother's words.

"Keep your mind about you. You're no good if you're dead! Fight with passion. Fight with your head. Never with your heart or anger. The heart does little to win in combat, and anger kills you quickest. The skills are there. Trust in your reflexes. Trust your instincts. Trust in Cafior! Fight!"

Horx charged with a two-handed swing, and Cavalor dodged at the last second. He then feigned a thrust, drawing Horx's next attack, and lunged as the curved blade struck the flagstones. Cavalor's knife plunged into Horx's chest, and though the krukari grimaced and staggered, he did not fall.

"Nobody does that to me!" Horx shoved Cavalor aside and pulled the small weapon from his body.

"Then do something about it!" Cavalor fueled the krukari's fire. "I'm unarmed. Surely you can best me now. Or can you?"

Horx looked as if he might explode, and he cast the knife across the room and charged. Cavalor dodged several attacks, but one grazed his forearm, scoring a minor wound, and another struck his side, where the teeth left a burning gash.

Cavalor maintained his wits, and he used the thrones as obstacles. His patience paid off when Horx lunged over the smaller seat, and

Cavalor seized the warrior's arm and delivered a sharp blow to the ribs with his gauntlet. He failed to free the weapon from Horx's iron grip, and he twisted the arm, spilling the krukari onto the floor.

Racing from the dais, Cavalor saw his companions were faring well. Arkor fought two Zurkan while three others were dead at his feet, Landerik had slain two and faced one, and Borse stood near Wezlok, pitted against another. Two Zurkan lay dead before Wezlok, though there was nothing obvious to show how the feat was accomplished, and a krukari ran for the doors with a wary eye upon the mage.

Cavalor scooped the sword of a fallen Zurkan, and Horx was right behind him. He dodged around a nearby pillar, leaving the krukari's blade to *clang* off the stone, and spun just as Horx rounded the column. Cavalor thrust his sword into the krukari's stomach — a wound fatal to most, it only staggered the evil prince.

Cavalor went on the offensive, and he drove Horx back. But the prince's strength was not spent, and Horx parried every blow as the wicked grin returned. The krukari then pushed forward with powerful swings, and as the teeth of the curved blade notched Cavalor's newly acquired sword, he twirled the weapon, causing Horx to stumble. Cavalor plunged the blade into the krukari's chest, and the prince coughed blood as he was driven to the floor.

The chamber fell silent as Horx's eyes glazed over. No Zurkan stood.

"Crismar must have come through." Arkor glanced around the room. Though a Zurkan had sounded an alarm, not even the guards outside the doors had come to the aid of their queen.

"Let us hope that is the case," said Landerik, cleaning his blade on the red cloak of a slain enemy.

"There is a commotion outside." Wezlok cocked his head to the side.

Everyone was quiet, and Cavalor noticed a faint horn blaring. One of the doors then swung open, and a woman from the kitchen entered.

"We have put our fate into your hands," the woman said, looking different than she had earlier. She was a cook, the one that had opened the secret door, and an air of authority surrounded her. She almost reminded Cavalor of his mother. "We have secured the castle, but are undermanned and in need of your assistance to hold it."

Battle lust filled Landerik's eyes. "To the entry hall!"

"Two of you shall report to the front hall." The woman spoke in a commanding tone. "And we need two in the northwest tower, preferably skilled with the crossbow." She turned to Wezlok. "*You* shall accompany me."

"And who are *you*?" Landerik's arrogance returned.

"I am Chandrella," she replied. "Commander of the zhokard." While she spoke, a few soldiers arrived. "These men will lead you to your posts."

Arkor followed his escort to the castle tower. He did not hesitate to volunteer for archer duty—even when Vikur ran Ironside Keep, it was Arkor that trained the bowmen. He was glad to have Cavalor with him. Being the only other warrior skilled in the use of the crossbow, there were no other options.

They climbed four stories and stepped onto a turret beneath the growing light—dawn was not far off. Six crossbows were present, and a pair of tower guards fired the weapons while a young boy kept them loaded. To the left of the turret, five additional archers occupied the southwest tower. Below, the courtyard teemed with Zurkan and humans, and several of them swung a thick log into the front doors of the stronghold.

Arkor slid the crossbow pieces into place on his wooden arm and began firing, dropping a target with each of his first four shots. Cavalor used a tower crossbow, proving his years of training had not gone to waste. Incoming arrows then raced above the courtyard from the northern tower of the gatehouse, most of them shattering upon the merlons, but a couple struck one of the zhokard crossbowmen.

The tower guard grimaced, pulled the arrows from his body, and continued to shoot while blood momentarily seeped from the puncture wounds.

Arkor trained his bow on the attacking tower, picking off three of the four bowmen with his next five shots. Lightning then launched from the dark tower of the gatehouse, striking the southwest tower. The archers there disappeared, but rose moments later and continued to defend the castle. Arkor was glad to have the zhokards on his side.

He and Cavalor turned their focus to the castle's main entrance, but they could not deter the ram wielders, as soldiers stood ready to replace any that fell. Spells of fire then washed over the entryway — likely the workings of Wezlok — and the enemy there was devastated.

With only a handful of survivors left, the attackers withdrew, fleeing beyond the gatehouse and onto the road.

The courtyard quieted. The first assault had been thwarted. But then came the blaring of horns, and a dark mass marched from Kembald. It was then that Arkor saw Cavalor stumble against the battlements.

"What's wrong?" Arkor steadied the young warrior, and as he did so, he noticed Cavalor's left side was soaked with blood.

"Horx got a good one in," Cavalor said through clenched teeth.

"Why did you not say anything?"

"There was no time." Cavalor tried to appear strong, but his face paled and his legs shook.

"Stay alert," Arkor said to the zhokards. "We shall return."

The guards looked at each other. But there was little they could do when Arkor led Cavalor to the stairs.

Descending grew more difficult with every step, and upon reaching the second floor, Cavalor leaned heavily against the wall as he panted and coughed. Arkor noticed a woman running along a nearby corridor.

"Wait!" He caught her attention. "Where are the others of my company? The ones who arrived this morning?"

"I... I'm not sure," the woman said. "Some may yet be in the front hall. Or the servants' quarters at the other end of the castle, perhaps."

Arkor used his good arm to steady Cavalor as the lad's eyes began to fade. "There's no time," he muttered. Then a thought occurred to him, prompted by something Crismar mentioned earlier. "Where are the queen's chambers?"

"Not far." The woman gazed at Cavalor with pity. "But why—"

"Just take us there!"

"Follow me." She hurried down the corridor.

Arkor lifted Cavalor and trailed after the woman. She turned right at the end of the passage, and the next hallway ended with a beautiful wooden door, ten feet in height and adorned with carvings of flowers and trees. Someone other than the original artist had made alterations, however, and added a few demonic creatures to spoil the scene.

The woman opened the door, revealing an extravagant bedroom. Mayry had spared no expense, providing herself a magnificent four-poster bed, as well as a wardrobe, wash table, and vanity, all constructed of solid oak. Upon the vanity were several vials and jars of various colors.

Arkor set Cavalor on the bed and went to the vanity. Unsure of which container he needed, he pulled his knife and placed a cut just above his wooden arm. He then picked jars at random, smearing their contents onto the fresh wound. The first few made it burn, but the fourth one eased the pain and sealed the cut.

He rushed to the bed with the jar, where Cavalor clung to consciousness and struggled to breathe. Cutting loose the breastplate, Arkor pulled the armor free and found the nasty gash Horx had inflicted. He rubbed the salve over the wound, but nothing happened and he feared it was too late. The cut then closed, and he sighed in relief. The injury was soon gone, and Cavalor's color returned.

"Poor, fragile mortals." The woman shook her head. "I am amazed Chandrella decided to help you, being there are so few of you and you are so easily broken."

A few unpleasant words raced through Arkor's mind. But he said nothing. He looked at Cavalor, and he was suddenly haunted by Mayry's revelation. Knowing of Cavalor's true lineage, he could see Solinin in the warrior's face. Arkor was not sure why he never noticed it before. How many times had he dined with Ballrik's friends in Duke Rholmar's castle without realizing the similarities?

Cavalor breathed in deep as his eyes opened. He looked at Arkor, appearing more himself.

"How are you?" Arkor asked.

"I feel fine." Cavalor sat up.

"Thank the gods." A weight lifted from Arkor's shoulders. "Let's find the others."

Cavalor nodded, and they exited the chamber.

"Thank you," Cavalor said after the woman disappeared down a neighboring corridor. "I had always heard what a great warrior Vikur was. But I have since learned of another noble warrior of Ironside, as well as a resourceful one."

"Thanks, kid." Arkor gave a wry smile. "But my resources are about to run dry." He paused to gaze out a window overlooking the road to Kembald. Thousands of soldiers now marched on the castle. It was hard to tell what they were, but with the sun shining, Arkor knew there to be no ghouls or wraiths among them. "I don't know what we're to do against that army."

Cavalor looked out the window, releasing a sigh as he shared Arkor's view. "Mother, give us strength."

After reaching the first floor, they received directions from a soldier and raced to the front hall. Two massive, solid-oak doors exhibited long cracks at the far end of the wide room, but a thick crossbar held them in place. Spiral steps led up on either side of the entryway to a balcony, where archers gazed through arrow slits.

Borse and the others were not present.

Arkor was about to ask for the whereabouts of his companions, but he was compelled to have a look and he climbed onto the platform. The balcony was thirty feet across and ten feet deep, and most of the floor was recessed, containing hundreds of murder holes that overlooked the entryway. Around the perimeter was a two-foot ledge that the archers stood upon, and a large cauldron sat cold to the side. Arkor stepped on the ledge and gazed through the arrow slits, spying a horde of skeletons and zombies within the courtyard, the latter appearing to be semi-fresh corpses of Marcs and Nomish. The undead stood facing the entry doors, and not one of them made the slightest movement.

Turning, Arkor grabbed an archer. "Where are they?"

"Umm..." The guard thought for a moment. "The throne room?"

Chapter 31

Under Siege

Cavalor walked beside the one-armed warrior. His side felt as if the dire wound had never existed, and he wondered what was in the salve Arkor had used. The more Cavalor thought about it, the more he concluded he did not want to know.

They found their companions in the throne room, but the room was not how they had left it. The hall was cleared of dead bodies, though blood stains proved the battle against Horx and the Zurkan had occurred, and Chandrella sat upon the larger chair. Cavalor thought the difference too great to ignore, as Mayry's beauty and arrogance were replaced by a woman of humble countenance, still wearing her kitchen garb. An aura of authority continued to surround Chandrella, and wisdom shone in her eyes, again reminding Cavalor of his mother. Standing before Chandrella was Captain Crismar, who flashed Cavalor a curious look before turning back to his commander.

"Where have you been?" Landerik asked Cavalor in a hushed tone. "Crismar sent for you some time ago. And where's your breastplate?"

Cavalor did not answer. The conversation at the throne held his attention.

"How strong are we?" Chandrella asked Crismar.

"There were no casualties."

Cavalor saw several zhokards fall, but keeping them down was another matter.

"We gained a dozen soldiers before we had to seal the doors," the captain added. "I'd say we have thirty men after we dispatched the zhomians."

Chandrella pursed her lips. "How are the defenses?"

"All entrances have been barricaded and the men deployed," Crismar replied. "But there's no telling how long we can hold once the attack begins."

"Why have they stopped?" Cavalor asked, gaining Chandrella's attention. "I mean, they must realize they outnumber us. Why do they wait?"

"They are to contain us for now," Crismar said. "They will await a Death Lord for further orders. And since Cadorn has not returned, I'm not sure who it will be."

"Gulthar, most likely," grumbled Chandrella. "And his evil scepter."

Cavalor detected a hint of apprehension with her last words.

"We've seen it," said Arkor. "He used it against us in Sardina."

"Then you are lucky to be alive." Crismar stared at the one-armed warrior. "Its dark power can rip the very life from anyone it touches. Including zhokards."

"So we just sit and wait?" Landerik's condescending attitude returned. "Wait for the Death Lord to come mount an attack?"

"Would you charge into an army with thirty men?" Chandrella raised a brow. "We have not survived for years among Trannum's minions by being hasty and foolish. We shall await the Death Lord and choose our reaction accordingly."

Landerik was not satisfied with the response. "But what awaits us outside cannot kill *you*. Why not deplete the enemy's numbers before the undead king arrives?"

Chandrella stared at the paladin. "I am amazed you made it this far."

"What can we do to help?" Borse spoke in a respectful tone.

"We shall decide where you will best serve our purposes." Chandrella turned to Borse. "Until that time, Crismar will take you to the kitchen to get something to eat. It is breakfast time for your kind, is it not?"

"And I thought humans were insufferable," Wezlok mumbled to Cavalor.

Cavalor and his companions were left alone in the kitchen with a meal of bread and cheese, as well as a couple pitchers of beer — the only liquid, it seemed, there was to drink. Landerik barely touched the food, still visibly upset.

"This is not why we have come!" The Brondor paladin tossed a piece of bread onto his plate.

"Isn't it?" Borse raised his brows. "We have gained the attention of an entire army, and soon a Death Lord. Was that not our purpose? To draw the enemy's forces our way? It would appear we have done well, under the circumstances."

"Circumstances you created, let us not forget." Cavalor glared at Landerik.

Landerik gave Cavalor a sidelong glance before addressing Borse. "But are we to just sit here? Sit, eat, drink, and await Gulthar to kill us? Is there not more we can do? I, for one, refuse to go down without a fight. And, by Brondor's Might, I will slay enough of them to open the doors to His Palace!"

"Don't be in a hurry to die yet," Arkor said. "We have only accomplished our immediate objective. Now we must hold the castle for as long as possible. Others are depending on it."

"How are we to do that when we are under the command of that *zhokard*?" Landerik stood. "For all we know, she'll have us loading crossbows for her feeble archers!"

"That will not be the case," said Crismar from the entrance.

Cavalor wondered how much the captain had overheard.

Crismar filled a mug and took a sip. "Chandrella has been apprised of the skills you exhibited. And though she places no trust in mortals, she cannot deny your talents are needed." He took a deeper drink before wiping his mouth with his sleeve. "I have put my faith in you, although you still have not divulged your plans to me. I only hope whatever you have in store works, and soon."

Silence followed.

Cavalor was uneasy. The captain was awaiting some grand plan to develop—a plan that had nearly run its course already. Guilt gnawed at Cavalor's stomach, and he could not justify allowing the ruse to go on any longer.

"We have no intentions of surviving this siege."

Crismar stared at Cavalor with his mouth open. His brow then furrowed.

"We are but a small part of a larger mission, I assure you," Cavalor added. "But being here now, and still alive... That is our part."

Silence returned while Crismar absorbed this knowledge. Then he spoke.

"So it is martyrdom, is it? There is no army coming?"

Cavalor shook his head. "We are all that's left of our force, once forty thousand strong. We suffered greatly on the mountain pass."

Anger replaced Crismar's shock. "I do not think I would have pressed Chandrella to aid you had I known this."

Borse gave a sympathetic smile. "That is why we could not tell you. Though I regret having withheld such information, there is a larger matter at hand, and all who live in this world depend on its outcome."

"I understand." Crismar's face was grave—most likely at the thought of explaining this to his commander. "Were our roles reversed, perhaps I would have done the same. But now I must take my leave. I shall return in an hour. So relax, if you can."

Several hours passed, and the company grew anxious. Borse buried his nose in a cookbook to keep busy while Wezlok sat in meditation, and Landerik sharpened his sword, as well as a blade provided for Cavalor by a soldier. A servant discovered Cavalor's breastplate and brought it to the kitchen, and Cavalor spent his time repairing the straps with Arkor's help. At long last, Crismar appeared in the entryway, and the captain's face was unchanged.

"There's still no sign of the Death Lord," Crismar said. "We don't know what to make of it. I can only assume the parts of your plan you have chosen not to share have given the necromancer trouble. Perhaps the battle to the north goes well."

"That would be good news," Arkor mumbled.

"How much longer are we to remain in this kitchen?" Landerik stared along the edge of his blade, giving the sword a thorough inspection.

"Actually," Crismar said, "I have come to collect you. You are to report to the front hall."

Landerik's grin stretched to one side of his face, and he sheathed his weapon.

Crismar led them to the castle's main entrance, where the large doors were now reinforced. Tabletops had been spiked across the fissures left by the battering ram, and a pair of beams were added for extra bracing, their opposite ends set within freshly dug holes in the stone floor. Cavalor, Arkor, and Landerik joined half a dozen soldiers just beyond the beams, and Borse and Wezlok ascended the spiral steps, joining a single archer above the entryway.

Upon the balcony, Cavalor saw his father peering through an arrow slit. Borse... The greatest Cafior priest one could hope to find—Cavalor's biased opinion aside. Cavalor had not been able to say goodbye to his mother; he would not allow that to happen with his father. He climbed the stairs.

A cauldron of boiling oil was suspended over a fire to the right, and through metal rings on one side of the pot ran a thick iron bar. Next to Wezlok on a ledge surrounding hundreds of murder holes was Cavalor's father, leaning on his oversized hammer as if it were a staff. Wezlok held a bow, and a quiver of arrows was at his feet. The elf frowned at Cavalor.

"It has been greater than a century since I last used a weapon such as this." Wezlok shrugged. "Because I am an elf, I *must* be skilled in archery." He sighed. "I suppose I can still find the mark if necessary."

Cavalor received a smile from his father, one aged and weary. The old priest always seemed to know what Cavalor was thinking.

"What an eerie sight." Wezlok gazed through an arrow slit.

Cavalor glanced through the openings to spy the undead. They filled the courtyard and spilled onto the bridge, covering most of the distance between the castle and Kembald. The abominations remained perfectly still.

"They seldom move unless instructed to," said Crismar. The captain stood behind Cavalor. "That is why we must defeat the Death Lord. Without him, they are less organized and more easily destroyed. Even dunarchins cannot control them for too long."

"You're joining us?" asked Cavalor.

"It was my request." Crismar sighed. "I'm the one who convinced Chandrella to risk everything. If things go awry, I should be at the brunt of it. And now, I think you and I should take our places below with the others."

Cavalor shared one last look with his father. The priest gave a nod, and Cavalor returned the gesture before descending.

The day seemed an eternity, and hours passed with no movement outside the stronghold. But as dark clouds rolled in with the coming of dusk, it was obvious Trannum had not forgotten about the siege. The wind grew stronger with the dying light, howling fiercely through the gaping mouths of the gargoyles high atop the castle walls. Moments later, Wezlok reported snowfall, and a chill penetrated the front hall. Though the zhokards appeared undaunted, Cavalor shivered.

"Fetch some furs for our guests," Crismar ordered a guardsman. It was the only time his breath was visible within the icy hall.

"Thank you, Captain." Cavalor looked at the other zhokards. None of them seemed to breathe. Perhaps they only required air when they spoke. As torches were lit, Cavalor could not help wondering if zhokards needed light to see.

Outside, the snow had grown thicker, and Wezlok reported the courtyard to be hidden from view. The night dragged on, and the slightest noises received immediate attention, but there were no attempts to breach the castle. When morning arrived at last, the winds calmed and the courtyard was revealed.

"They have not moved." Wezlok's voice held a trace of curiosity. "They are buried to their knees."

Snow continued to fall throughout the day, and fatigue crept into the castle sentinels. Cavalor's eyelids grew heavy, and it surprised him to learn that zhokards needed rest as well. Crismar separated soldiers into shifts, and everyone gained a few hours of sleep within nearby quarters.

Another night passed, and still the undead did not move. The snow ceased by noon of the following day, and though the latest report claimed the awaiting army to be half buried, Cavalor knew the besiegers to hold no discomfort.

The castle was now a block of ice, and Arkor took charge of lighting fires in all nearby fireplaces, so their company might find warmth when necessary. As the day passed and night returned, horns sounded from the towers, and everyone reported to their posts.

"The undead are trampling the snow," Wezlok said, still keeping watch.

"He has arrived!" Crismar rushed up to the balcony.

An intense chill penetrated the castle and frost crept along the walls. There was no mistaking the Death Lord's presence.

"Here they come!" Wezlok shouted.

Though Cavalor could not see the courtyard, flaming arrows were visible through the breaches in the large doors, raining from the towers. But the zombies were likely frozen, and the attack would have little effect.

"A battering ram," Wezlok said.

The oaken doors shuddered as the ram struck, but the beams held. They shook again a couple of seconds later, and a steady rhythm began.

Cavalor saw Crismar and the zhokard archer step to either side of the cauldron.

"Get on the ledge," Crismar said to Borse.

As Cavalor's father stepped up next to Wezlok, Crismar and the archer lifted the metal bar. The giant pot tilted, showering boiling oil through the murder holes and onto the area outside the entryway, and steam rose through the fissures in the doors.

"You have cleared the area," Wezlok said. "But others are taking their places."

The mage fitted an arrow to his bow and took aim at the floor; and the tip of the missile flared, as if on its own. The elf let loose, and a *whoosh* sounded as the oil caught fire. The flames grew bright, and though the pounding of the ram did not cease, the effort was lacking in strength.

"They continue to replace the fallen." Wezlok seemed amused. "But they burn up before they can bring any damage."

"The fire will not last," Crismar said.

Wezlok nocked a second arrow and chanted. Taking aim at the floor again, he fired through a murder hole and an explosion ensued.

"Let us see how they fare without their ram," the elf said.

Flames continued to dance within the cracks of the entryway, and Cavalor worried that the wood might catch fire. His concerns grew when the doors heaved, as if being struck. How had it been accomplished without the battering ram?

"Lightning from the gate tower!" shouted Wezlok.

The doors rattled two more times, and the crossbar cracked and the beams shifted. Borse rushed down the spiral steps, moving more swiftly than Cavalor thought possible, and made his way just beyond the beams before facing the doors.

"Fall back!" he yelled.

"Back off!" Cavalor ushered the zhokards away to give his father space. He did not know what the priest was planning, but he knew better than to ignore the command.

With a crash, lightning splintered the doors and the beams were sundered. Undead issued through the breach with a frozen wind at their backs, and Borse swung his hammer overhead and onto the floor. The impact rang like thunder, and the stone before him cracked and shook, collapsing skeletons and hindering the advance of the zombies. A fissure then opened within the courtyard, swallowing undead by the hundreds before closing again. It was the most breathtaking sight Cavalor had ever beheld, and he stared in amazement while the display lasted. The shaking ended and the castle guards advanced, dispatching all undead remaining in the hall.

The enemy withdrew beyond the gatehouse, ending the assault and leaving the courtyard barren. Whether the retreat was due to the divine power Borse exhibited or some unheard command, Cavalor was unsure. The intense cold faded, but the chill winds continued to sweep along the chamber through the open doorway.

"The wave has ended," Crismar said. "And now it will get worse. They'll send more worthy foes. Perhaps the Death Lord himself."

Cavalor watched his father climb wearily up the spiral steps and back onto the landing. After all these years, there was still more to the priest than he knew. Maybe more than he would ever know.

Several hours passed, and nothing entered the courtyard. Zhokards attempted to nail planks over what remained of the burned and broken doors, but they grew frustrated when the wood splintered further and abandoned the task. A gentle snow drifted to the ground, quickly becoming a raging storm, and sheets of ice blew across the windows and into the front hall. The storm prevailed throughout the night, but came to an abrupt end with the dawn.

Surprisingly, only an additional foot of snow had fallen, and it was the only element of the dark courtyard Cavalor could make out. But then shadowy figures slunk atop the white ground, staggering to the left and right, and more shapes flew from the gate towers.

"Wraiths!" called the archer from the platform.

"Ghouls!" shouted another soldier, peering through the broken doors. "Hundreds of them!"

"This is it," Arkor said to Cavalor.

Cavalor gripped his weapon. He thought of his childhood; a childhood devoid of fun and games. But he did not care. He thought about the words of Mayry, and he scowled at the memory. Evil, it seemed, had brought him into this world, and now he would make his final stand against it. He had known nothing else his whole life, but that fact did not bring him grief or regret. The love of his family and devotion to his deity were all that mattered. In the end, he had lived so that others *could* live, and he was content with that knowledge. His mother was gone, but Merssa had been the best mother he could ever have hoped for.

Cavalor raised his sword. "For Mother. For Father. For Cafior."

"For Vikur, Ballrik, and all of Vaeldor," said Arkor.

"For Brondor." Landerik joined them. "May we carve down our enemies one hundredfold before the end!" Unlike Arkor, the paladin's eyes gleamed with excitement.

The three faced the entrance, awaiting the undead. Around them, eight zhokards stood ready, though puzzled by their comments. The wind rushed through the broken doorway, dancing with torches as frost drifted the length of the hall, and Cavalor's heart pounded harder and harder. But then something unexpected happened.

The wind ceased, and almost at once the clouds dissolved and the early sun touched the castle. It was as if summer had won the battle against the unnatural winter. Ghouls packed the courtyard and wraiths filled the sky, and beyond the gate marched ranks of dunarchins across the bridge. The ghouls hissed at the sun as their skin bubbled beneath its bright rays, and most of the wraiths dissipated into flashes of sickly black vapor. The dunarchins were undaunted, and they continued their steady pace.

Several wraiths found shelter, darting back into the gatehouse or into the castle, whichever was closer, and a dozen entered the hall through arrow slits, windows, and the open doorway. Their ghostly forms smoked and their eyes were dim, and they attacked anyone within reach, yearning for living souls to mend their ghastly existences. But the zhokards lacked the life force the dark spirits craved, and the soldiers fought without fear, destroying most of them.

A wraith reached for Landerik, and the paladin spun out of the way, bringing his sword about and ending its existence. Two others attacked Arkor, and the one-armed warrior struck down one while the other locked its claws around his throat. Cavalor smote the creature before it could bring any harm.

Ghouls then poured through the doors. Smoke rose from their melting skin, making their appearance more hideous than usual, and as they passed beyond the landing Wezlok released spheres of flame. The fire finished what the sun had started, incinerating more than a dozen.

Cavalor led the soldiers with Arkor and Landerik at his sides, and they destroyed another score of ghouls with little resistance. Cavalor received a few burning scratches in return, but there was no time for concern, and he continued hacking into the enemy. Borse and Crismar descended from the balcony and felled several ghouls as well, but dozens more drove all defenders back from the entrance.

Wezlok remained atop the landing with the sole archer, and while the zhokard fired arrows, the elf unleashed magic without mercy. Some ghouls attempted to scale the stairs to confront the two, but they met terrible ends when Wezlok assaulted the stairwells with lightning.

The air then grew deathly cold and the sun ceased to shine; and the ghouls became excited, attacking with greater ferocity. Moments later, a zhokard fighting next to Cavalor collapsed when a bolt of darkness struck him. Ghouls dragged the corpse away, and others filled the void to seek meals of their own.

Standing in the entryway was a Death Lord, tall and foreboding. In one hand was a curved sword, and in the other was the scepter that revealed him to be Gulthar. Ghouls danced from the undead king's path as he strode into the castle, and his glowing eyes turned to the landing above. Wezlok backed as far from the ledge as possible, and from the scepter issued the evil pulse, striking the archer. The zhokard went limp and fell into the hungry mob, and several ghouls scrambled up the spiral steps. Gulthar then returned his attention to the castle defenders, and he snuffed the life from two more zhokards.

"He must be destroyed!" Landerik hacked more forcefully, destroying a ghoul with each of his next few swings.

The glowing eyes fell on the paladin, and it seemed to Cavalor that Gulthar stood taller. The ghouls then opened a path between the two, showing no interest in Landerik, and the paladin charged.

Cavalor battled toward his father, splitting his attention between the ghouls and the Death Lord. Landerik flailed his sword with great speed, but Gulthar knocked the blows aside. The evil lord countered with the curved blade, striking Landerik's side, and Landerik remained strong, driving the Death Lord back with a solid hit to the leg.

Cavalor received another burning wound when a crawling ghoul bit his leg. He destroyed the creature, as well as two others, and he was very near to his father now. Landerik, meanwhile, still battled the Death Lord.

Gulthar's eyes flared, and the undead king attacked with sword and scepter, but Landerik parried one attack after the other. The paladin countered with a thrust, and his blade pierced the breastplate, sinking into the heart of his opponent. Unfortunately, Gulthar's heart had long been silenced, and while the sword was held by the black armor, the Death Lord struck Landerik's helmet with the scepter. The paladin reeled, and the curved blade slashed his neck.

"No!" Cavalor gasped as Landerik's body was lost to the sea of undead. He then decapitated a ghoul and reached his father's side at last.

Gulthar's eyes turned on Cavalor, and his mind raced as the dark rod was pointed his way. But the evil magic did not issue. Crismar had battled through the ghouls, arriving seconds too late to assist Landerik, and his sword knocked the scepter from the Death Lord's hand. Gulthar cut the captain down within seconds and fed his body to the ghouls, and the last sight Cavalor held of Crismar was the beating black heart raised in triumph.

"Dunarchins have entered through the kitchen!" a voice shouted. "They are coming!"

Cavalor continued to battle, and he could not keep his mind from wandering. To his left, Arkor fought valiantly, while his father labored to his right. And somewhere above the entryway, among a score of ghouls, Wezlok had his hands full—if the mage still lived. The undead had them pinched between dunarchins and ghouls, and the Death Lord was depleting their numbers quickly. Cavalor's mother would have been proud then, as his thoughts moved to Selanna and Soren, and he hoped he had bought them enough time to complete their missions.

CHAPTER 32

MARFESNA

Eraim was relieved that the two-headed monster did not reappear from the lake. The strange fires on the water continued to sprout here and there, but other than Greyor sloshing from the large pool, the chamber was still.

Eraim turned to Selanna. "What took you so long?"

Selanna gave an annoying glance at Brem. "The half-*human* thought he knew the way. If not for the marks you left, we would likely be back in the Fire Hills!"

Brem checked on Arrikan's wounds. The ranger's leather pants were soaked, and after the priest unlaced the sides, Eraim saw the woman's legs were badly blistered. She was about to reach for her herbs when Brem pulled a jar from his pack. He used his fingers to extract a thick salve, and Arrikan winced while he spread over the burns.

"I'm sorry," Brem said. "It's the only way to apply it."

Arrikan nodded with a grimace, but her expression eased as the blisters faded. The salve was certainly a faster option than Eraim's herbs.

While the marteese helped Arrikan strap her armor back together, Eraim noticed Greyor standing near the water with his helmet removed and head bowed. She had witnessed Millord's fate, and she was unsure of what to say. The four surviving mine dwellers remained several paces behind the dwarf, bowing their heads as he did. Greyor then replaced his helmet and turned to the company, his expression grim.

After seeing Eraim's injuries were minor, Brem approached Greyor. The dwarf's exposed skin exhibited scratches, bruises, and fresh burns, but Greyor held up a large hand, denying any treatment.

"I must suffer the pain to honor Millord."

Eraim would never understand dwarves.

"Do you know where we are?" Selanna asked Eraim.

Eraim shook her head. "I never studied this part of the mines, and the map is lost. But I have strong hopes this last archway will reveal something."

"What is with the mine creatures?" Selanna looked over her shoulder at the pale-skinned humanoids dragging their dead from the lake.

"I am not sure." Eraim shrugged. "They came with the dwarves."

Selanna gave a small sigh. "There is no telling how much time we have lost in this maze. I regret we cannot give Millord a proper service, but we must be going."

Selanna spoke to the mine dwellers, attempting to find the correct path. She used her hands, speaking loudly and slowly, but the humanoids understood nothing. Greyor provided no help, claiming he held only a small comprehension of their squeaks, chirps, and grunts.

"They've probably never seen the outside," Greyor said. "I doubt they'd know the way."

The dwarf ordered the mine dwellers to return home, pointing and grunting at the arch that delivered them. But they appeared determined to follow their leader wherever he went. Greyor urged them with a bit more force behind his voice, and though he seemed confident they understood, they furrowed their brows and appeared confused. He threw his hands up in frustration, and he was further annoyed when they mimicked him.

"Time is short," Selanna said with waning patience. "Either bring them with you or stay here."

Greyor snorted in Selanna's direction, and he waved for the humanoids to follow. Lifting their weapons, two rail-spears and a couple of table legs, the mine dwellers seemed to smirk as they fell in line.

Eraim led the way through the final archway and along several corridors. She paused at every intersection to sense for the right path, and continued using her colored rock to make sure the twisting hallways did not lead them in circles. The lizards plagued the tunnels again, but Selanna's light revealed them with plenty of warning, and Eraim's bow and Clanghorr's edge did the rest. With each reptile Greyor hewed, the mine dwellers cheered, receiving sharp hisses from Selanna to keep quiet.

After two days, the lizard population dwindled until there were none. Near the end of the third day, Eraim discovered stairs climbing over fifty feet and through the ceiling. She ascended with renewed hope, only to find yet another maze of tunnels.

Part way through the fourth day, the mines grew bitterly cold. The humanoids appeared unused to the sensation and looked nervous at seeing their own breath, but they continued to follow, clutching their weapons tighter while their eyes darted left and right.

A mile passed, and Eraim detected a breeze from a tunnel on the left. The air was frigid and lacked the stale scent of the mines, and as they followed it, the chill became almost unbearable. The mine dwellers shook and their teeth rattled, and Greyor did all he could to quiet them, but there was no suppressing their shivers. Eraim did not blame them, as the biting cold had worked its way to her bones.

"It does not feel like a Death Lord," she said to Selanna.

"No." Selanna pursed her lips. "But evil is ahead."

"Most of us don't speak elf!" Greyor made it seem as though Millord was there. "Is there something we should know?"

"*Nish!*" Selanna hushed him in dwarfish. She then spoke in common. "We know nothing for sure, so let us not announce our coming."

They walked another hundred yards and the tunnel ended, and at its termination was a large hole in the floor that shed a gray light. Eraim held up her hand to halt the others, and she crept forward to have a closer look. After a moment of thought, she motioned for Selanna to follow.

Through the hole, Eraim saw an enormous cavern, dully illuminated by an unseen source. The floor was well over a hundred feet below and covered in snow, and beneath the hole was a pile of boulders that rose to within fifty feet—most likely useless rubble discarded by dwarves of Lornibur. Poking her head further, Eraim discovered the source of the glow. A large opening led to the outside, and though dull and gray, the light stung Eraim's eyes. Many stalactites and stalagmites existed, and a pond of ice was near the middle of the cavern, feeding a frozen stream that passed through the cave opening.

An icy wind slapped Eraim's face, and she spotted movement beyond the pond. Facing the cavern exit and almost transparent was a throne-like chair made of ice, and a large figure sat like an ominous sculpture, also made of ice. It was bestial, with sharp features and crystal-like skin covering its translucent body, and cold blue eyes were set deep beneath a jutting brow and above its pointed nose. Eight-fingered hands rested on the arms of the throne, and the statue's ears and fingers were like icicles. The figure shifted its head, and Eraim realized it was alive. She withdrew from the hole and turned to Selanna.

"You best have a look," Eraim whispered. "A creature of ice, sitting on a throne of ice at the far end."

Selanna kneeled to take a peek. After the briefest moment, she pulled back, and her face was pale. "That is how he does it!"

"Does what?" Eraim furrowed her brow.

"That *creature of ice,* as you put it." Selanna looked at Eraim. "It is called Marfesna. And it is not of this world. It is a demon from the coldest regions of Hell, and Trannum uses it to create the eternal winter."

"How are we to get past it?" Eraim feared the answer.

Selanna shook her head. "There is no easy way. I doubt even *you* could sneak by unnoticed. We must fight."

"Will that not alert Trannum to our presence?" Brem asked, having joined them.

"It most certainly will." Selanna sighed. "But what choice have we? We cannot seek another route. We might not find our way out again until the war is over."

Eraim looked at the hole and then back to Selanna, her shoulders slumping. "Is there a curse upon my head?"

"Ready Mithkahr, my friend," Selanna said. "I will inform the others."

Eraim squatted near the hole and took in a slow breath before releasing it. She was not sure if the plan she and Selanna had come up with would work, but she could think of no other alternatives.

Selanna and Brem appeared calm, and Arrikan stood with a sympathetic hand on Greyor's shoulder. Greyor's face was unchanged since the serpent battle, although his eyes were a bit red — the loss of Millord was surely on his mind. Though the mine dwellers understood nothing of what was said when the plan was revealed to the company, they were ready.

The humanoids had adjusted well to being in the light, and the more Eraim viewed their faces, the less savage they appeared. They were not goblin-like at all, and she was sure they could pass through just about any town unnoticed — that is, if they wore normal clothing, their skin was not grayish, and their eyes were not sunken so deeply beneath their brows.

Selanna cleared her throat, shaking Eraim from her thoughts and reminding her it was time to begin.

Eraim pulled the coil of rope from her pack while eyeing the descent. She then grabbed her tools, and after a nod from Selanna, she spiked the rope to the hard, icy floor. With each fall of the hammer, the spike drove deeper into the stone, but no noise was emitted. Selanna's magic did not allow it. Once the rope was secure, Eraim nodded.

"Remember," Selanna whispered. "Wait for the second explosion."

Selanna stepped over the hole and dropped into the chamber. Eraim watched her companion freefall most of the distance, but as Selanna neared the pile of boulders, her descent slowed until she hovered just above the rocks.

Marfesna's head rotated to face Selanna. The demon remained seated, showing no emotion—not even when Selanna launched a ball of flame from her hands. The spell streaked toward its target, but Marfesna vacated the throne before it struck, and an explosion of searing flames destroyed the large chair.

Selanna dropped onto the rock pile in a seated position. She then spun and slid down the snow to the backside of the mound. Marfesna released a hollow roar, sounding more like a wailing, and hundreds of icicles fell from the ceiling just below Eraim's feet. Selanna held her hands overhead, summoning a barrier of green light, and she was unscathed as the shards shattered upon contact.

The shower subsided, and Selanna rushed around the rocks. Marfesna stood atop the frozen lake, and with a word, Selanna launched another ball of fire as the demon spit a globe of ice. The spells collided halfway between the two, resulting in a second explosion.

With an eye on her companion, Eraim dropped the rope and slid down as quickly as she dared. Selanna continued to hold the demon's attention while racing for the cavern exit, but when Marfesna lifted its hands, the snow rose to Selanna's waist. Selanna uttered a word of magic and leaped onto the snow, standing atop it as firmly as if it were stone.

Eraim reached the mound of rocks and moved aside as Arrikan arrived. Greyor touched down next, but the dwarf's weight caused a boulder to break loose and tumble to the cavern floor. Eraim froze as Brem set foot on the rock pile, her eyes moving to the demon.

Marfesna spun, and upon spotting the new intruders he began to pant. The air within the chamber swirled, becoming a wintry torrent and obscuring vision beyond a few feet. Eraim slid down the back side of the boulders, and Arrikan and Brem followed. Greyor disappeared down the front. Of the mine dwellers, two made it safely onto the rocks, but the other two were blown from the rope and vanished into the snowstorm, their screams swallowed by the rushing wind.

Eraim rounded the hill of rocks, feeling relieved as the storm weakened enough to allow for a better view. She was sure it was Selanna's doing, for she could just make out her companion chanting and waving her arms. Eraim then noticed Greyor, only ten yards from the lake, and Marfesna stood before him.

The demon lashed out with its long, pointed fingers, piercing Greyor's shoulder with one of its icicle-claws. Greyor's arm went limp, but he remained strong and brought Clanghorr around with his right hand. There was the sound of breaking glass as the blade severed three of the eight fingers on the demon's left claw.

Marfesna leaped over thirty feet back and onto the lake, releasing a high-pitched wail that rattled the ceiling and dropped a second volley of icicles. Though the smaller shards were caught up in the wind and blown away, the larger ones pelted the floor with deadly force. Eraim dodged a couple of icy spears, and she saw Brem push Arrikan from the path of another. The marteese collapsed with a cry of pain after the missile left a gash on his leg. The two mine dwellers avoided the icicles by pure luck as they hurried to join their leader, and Greyor focused on his opponent while a few missiles landed around him.

Eraim let loose an arrow to aid her stout companion, but the wind was too strong, and she missed her target by a wide berth. Her bow was useless under the current conditions. She slung it over her shoulder and pulled Mithkahr.

With his left arm dangling, Greyor pushed through the snow and to the edge of the pond; and the demon studied the dwarf while blue blood dripped from its hand. A ball of fire then struck the lake and the ice exploded.

Marfesna leaped away again, this time landing within a couple feet of Selanna. It swung its claw, and Selanna jumped headfirst into the snow, evading the attack.

Greyor stole the demon's attention with a battle roar. The runes upon Clanghorr were burning with a white light, and the dwarf charged faster than Eraim would have thought possible. He was undeterred, even as the snow climbed above his waist, and to either side the humanoids waved their weapons and grunted. The demon sprang at the three, piercing one of the mine dwellers with all eight fingers of its good hand. The icicle-claws bore through, and not even a yelp escaped the mine dweller's lips as it was instantly killed. Greyor swung his axe, shaving part of the demon's right leg, and the second mine dweller struck the monster with its club, but its weapon shattered.

The humanoid remained impaled on Marfesna's claw, and the demon held the corpse between Greyor and itself like a grisly shield. Eraim felt pity for the mine dweller that had followed Greyor beyond the borders of its home, giving its life for him. She thought she spied the same pity in Greyor's eyes as the dwarf swung Clanghorr, slicing through the mine dweller's body and into the demon's arm. Again, Marfesna wailed and leaped away.

The demon now descended toward Eraim. She calculated the trajectory of the creature's path and maneuvered about the snow; and as it touched down, she plunged Mithkahr into its chest. A stream of fire sprouted from Selanna's hands and washed over the monster, and Eraim tumbled away. She caught a taste of the heat as she rolled across the snow, and Marfesna's scream rose beyond hearing until the creature exploded in a shower of ice crystals. Eraim buried her face as hundreds of razor-like shards pelted her back, reminding her of the shattering orb within the cabin of Sistama.

The wind stopped, and all was quiet. Eraim raised her head. Greyor was splayed protectively over the last surviving mine dweller, and Selanna stood behind her magical shield, unharmed. Nearby,

Brem lay on the snow, looking around while Arrikan moved toward him.

A single ray of sunlight entered the cavern, and a hot breeze followed.

Chapter 33

Velgaad

After seeing that Selanna was safe, Eraim checked on the others. Brem had just finished applying his healing salve to his leg, and he was using pieces of wood to form a splint. Eraim thought it odd, since the ointment had worked so quickly on Arrikan. Arrikan appeared to have escaped harm, and after she pulled Brem to his feet, they joined Eraim.

Greyor winced while he held his limp arm. Clanghorr's runes no longer glowed, and every few seconds he shooed away the mine dweller, who looked eager to inspect the wound left by the demon.

"My arm is frozen!" Greyor said when Eraim neared. "The numbness is creeping into my shoulder."

Eraim wondered if Greyor knew the difference between numbness and debilitating pain. Either way, her herbs could not treat such an injury.

"Let me see if I can help," said Brem.

The marteese held Greyor's hand and recited a prayer to Frayorna. Greyor cried out, and a blue liquid oozed from the hole left by the demon's claw. Brem then applied the salve, which eased the dwarf's suffering. Greyor nodded in thanks, and Brem dropped the empty container onto the snow.

That was that. There would be no more aid coming from the marteese.

They made their way to Selanna, who stood near the cavern's exit. Eraim stepped outside, squinting as the sun reflected off white hills rolling for miles to the south, east, and west. Upon spotting what had to be the Trethel River away to the southeast, she knew where they were.

"We are closer than we would have been, had we taken the original path," Eraim said to Selanna. "This is good news. Perhaps we have not lost much time at all."

"Winter is ended." Selanna gazed at the sky. "A bit quicker than I would have hoped. We best leave this place far behind before Trannum's minions come to investigate."

Eraim saw Greyor speaking to the mine dweller. The dwarf pointed to the cavern exit, but the humanoid shook his head—he would never walk beneath the sun. Greyor put his arm around the humanoid's shoulder, offering what looked like food from his pack. The mine dweller accepted the gift and headed back to the rock pile, where the rope still dangled. Eraim hated to leave the rope behind, but she would need the humanoid's assistance to detach it, and she did not possess the time or energy to try and explain the necessary steps.

"How is your leg?" Selanna asked Brem.

The marteese looked at his handiwork. "It will be fine soon. I dared not use all the salve it would have required, not if I wished to help Greyor."

That explained the splint. Eraim nodded. Brem was not so bad...for a marteese.

Arrikan and Greyor took the lead, and they left the cavern behind. The day wore on and the sun prevailed, burning away all straggling clouds until there were none, and pools of slush riddled the hills as the midsummer's heat thawed the land. An hour before dusk, they halted within a small grove. The trees were spread thin, leaving very little cover from above, but many boulders existed to keep them off the saturated grass.

Sitting on the large rocks, they enjoyed the sunshine while nibbling on what rations remained. Brem's leg and Greyor's arm were well on their way to recovery, and after the meal the marteese discarded his splint. Brem then mixed healing herbs from his pack with water from the melting snow, and he said a prayer over the pasty concoction before treating the minor injuries Eraim and Arrikan received from the demon's explosive demise.

As the sun set, the company settled in for some rest. They did not build a fire, but the night was warm and refreshing all the same.

Selanna drew in a deep breath. "It is not home. But if I close my eyes, Salenti surrounds me."

Eraim closed her eyes, allowing her mind to take her to Dominelli. She sat beneath her favorite tree, and Lilli was resting at her side. She only wished the forest did not smell like a wet mountain.

Eraim awoke to Arrikan's touch. The ranger had been on guard with Brem, and she reported seeing nothing beyond a starry sky. Brem stirred Greyor, and he and Eraim took their places to watch the remainder of the night.

All was well for the first hour. But then the screech of an undead dragon broke the silence. The company needed no prodding as they grabbed their weapons and rose, and Greyor climbed a boulder to search the sky. The dwarf sniffed the air and turned north, where the screech sounded again.

"No doubt something's learned of our work," he said.

Eraim spotted a dark form flying beneath a patch of black clouds. "It comes this way!" As she finished her warning, the aura of a Death Lord crept into her bones.

"Seek shelter!" said Selanna.

Eraim readied her bow and kneeled in the mud behind a boulder. Next to her was Greyor, holding Clanghorr and whispering a prayer to Meldar. Selanna, Arrikan, and Brem put their backs to trees. The rolling clouds consumed the moon and stars, and moments later, the dark presence passed overhead, carrying the odor of a grave on an icy wind. The undead dragon flew by in haste, and mounted upon it was the Death Lord. Eraim held her breath as the dragon continued south, but then it turned back in a wide arc.

"Prepare yourselves!" Selanna stepped out into the open.

The skeletal beast flew over again, this time just above the treetops, and Eraim saw the Death Lord clearly. Upon the dragon rode a stout figure, similar to Greyor in stature, and she knew right away it was Velgaad, dwarf king of Lornibur in its final years. There were several legends describing the evil dwarf and his voracious appetite for wealth and power, and they all shared the same bitter end: Lornibur, birthplace of the dwarfish race, was lost, and the one responsible for its demise had disappeared. Eraim noticed the ire in Greyor's eyes—he obviously knew the legends as well.

Greyor scrambled onto the boulder as the Death Lord approached a third time. "Velgaad! Come fight me, you dog!"

The dragon's neck twisted toward Greyor, and it belched its nauseating gas of death. But Selanna summoned a wind gust, dispersing the cloud even as it spewed from the skull of the beast.

The undead mount continued south before making another wide turn to approach from the southwest. Eraim stepped next to Selanna, releasing a couple arrows that pierced Velgaad's chest, but the Death Lord did not veer from his path.

Velgaad lifted a flail and began spinning a pair of spiked iron balls. Thunder shook the ground, and a flash of lightning struck the weapon, causing it to pulsate with white light. Moments later, it discharged, casting lightning at Eraim and Selanna.

Eraim dodged behind a large pine while Selanna jumped away. The bolt splintered the tree's trunk, and Eraim scurried from its path to avoid being crushed. She then regained her feet as the Death Lord flew overhead, and she stared in shock when she saw Clanghorr sailing end over end into the dark sky.

Greyor gaped in disbelief, as if he had not thrown his weapon. But his aim was true, and Clanghorr shattered the dragon's neck. The head descended into the hills, landing somewhere to the west, and the body crashed north of the trees. Eraim pulled Mithkahr and charged, the blade shedding its red glow as it sensed the evil presence, and Greyor followed with his hammer in hand.

Upon reaching the top of the hill, Eraim found Velgaad unhindered by the crash and already twirling his flail. Fear gripped her stomach as the spiked balls came her way, and she brought up Mithkahr to parry the blow. The chains entangled her blade, and the undead king wrenched it from her grasp and sent it flying into a bush.

The flail circled again, and Eraim rolled away, evading the attack. Greyor then arrived with a roar, and Velgaad's attention shifted to the dwarf. Eraim crawled to where Mithkahr had disappeared, keeping her eye on the battle.

"Die traitorous scum!" shouted Greyor in the dwarfish tongue as he brought his hammer about.

Velgaad dodged the blow, and the flail crashed into Greyor's side, knocking him prone.

Selanna's light appeared as she reached the top of the hill with Arrikan and Brem. Arrikan charged and swung her blade, but the weapon bounced off the black armor. The dark dwarf turned on the ranger, and he forced her back until she stumbled and fell. He twirled the flail and brought it down again, but one of Selanna's balls of green light struck him on the chest. The spell had no apparent effect, other than to allow Arrikan time to escape.

Eraim reclaimed Mithkahr and rejoined the battle. With Velgaad's focus on Selanna and Brem, she arrived unnoticed and pierced the Death Lord's back. The undead king spun, and his evil eyes were bright with rage. He drove Eraim several paces with powerful swings, leaving no room to counter, and Eraim employed all her skills to keep her weapon from becoming entangled while she awaited help.

"Clanghorr!"

Greyor must have discovered his axe. Help was on the way!

One of the spiked balls struck Eraim's left arm, knocking her to the ground. Velgaad then turned, and Eraim saw Greyor emerge from the crash site of the undead dragon with Clanghorr held high. The runes on the ancient weapon were aglow with the white-hot light, and Eraim was sure Velgaad's eyes paled.

Velgaad raised the flail in defense as Greyor attacked, and the axe cleaved the chains and continued through the Death Lord's neck. The helmet tumbled across the ground as Velgaad's knees buckled; and as the dark dwarf fell, the clouds vanished, and the chill faded in favor of the warm summer night.

"Is everyone all right?" asked Selanna.

Eraim rose, holding her left arm close to her body. It was broken for sure, and the pain radiated across her ribs. The runes upon Clanghorr then lost their glow and Greyor dropped to his knee, as if the injury the Death Lord inflicted had suddenly returned.

Brem rushed to Greyor and inspected the dwarf's side.

"You fought well for one with such an injury," the marteese said.

Perhaps Greyor had suffered broken bones as well.

"Clanghorr defeated the evil traitor," Greyor said through clenched teeth.

"I was hoping to save what spiritual power I possess for Trannum's stronghold." Brem sighed. "Hold still."

He placed his hands over Greyor's ribs. Reciting a prayer, a green light encompassed the dwarf's side, and Greyor appeared much better for it. Brem examined Eraim next.

"I am afraid I cannot fight this way," Eraim said. "The herbs I have are strong, but they cannot mend a broken bone."

"I'll do what I can." Brem repeated the procedure he performed on Greyor. Upon completion, his face paled and he frowned. "I wish I could do more."

Eraim moved her arm in a circle. The bone was whole, but there was still considerable pain. At least her ribs felt better. She nodded to Brem in thanks.

Selanna stood apart, gazing south at the declining hills, and Eraim joined her. The snow was almost gone, and the wet ground reflected dark beneath the pale moonlight. Though the night was warm, a creeping, cold presence wafted up from below.

"We must go," Selanna said. "Before anything else comes."

Selanna's magical light faded, but before the illumination had diminished, Eraim noticed her companion's troubled expression.

Greyor and Arrikan resumed the lead, and the company continued south on the downward trek. The way was not difficult, but much of the land was flooded, and at times they slid along patches of mud.

Eraim walked behind Selanna beneath the brightening sky, her mind unsettled. Selanna was the most powerful mage Eraim knew, outside of Elgarroth of course, but she could not stop thinking about her friend's lack of effect on Velgaad.

"What happened back there?" she asked quietly. "Your magic…?"

"Trannum has afforded his generals some protections." Selanna's expression was grim. "I was useless against Velgaad. I will have to try another approach with other Death Lords."

"This will not do." Dread crept over Eraim. "It took all of us to combat one! Without your magic —"

"Perhaps the other missions have drawn away the rest of them." Selanna's tone was hopeful, but her eyes betrayed her.

The hills became tame, and old trails made travel easier. But the company proceeded with caution, and no shadow or movement escaped scrutiny. Once the sun appeared on the eastern horizon, its rays were immediately felt, and any snow having survived the night soon found its end. Though Eraim had never been to Nomedd, she understood the realm to suffer brutal summers, and it was not long before she began to perspire.

The sun beat down as lunchtime came and went without a break. Just after midday, the heat made breathing a chore. Eraim could not remember a time when she had experienced such temperatures, and she was grateful when the heat declined with the approaching evening.

They walked until the sun was low in the west, and Greyor came to a halt. Below, where the hills ended and just east of the Trethel River, stood a small castle, dark and foreboding. No light from the dying sun reflected from its surface, and there existed no windows that Eraim could see.

The company stepped from the path and hid among rocks and scattered trees. Eraim scanned the barren land, but not even a bird revealed itself. Her mind was then given to concern, as a horrible thought occurred.

"What if Nilborg and Rholmar have arrived already?" She looked at Selanna. "I would hate to think we failed them."

Selanna shook her head. "There is no way to know. We will have to leave it to hope that they have not. In the meantime, we will keep watch for them."

CHAPTER 34

DRIGHT SWAMP

Rholmar led the way with a heavy heart. Lorylla, Nilborg, Rybeal, and Pallit followed in single file. Every now and again Rholmar glanced over his shoulder, but he was sure Soren's body was beyond even the gray elf's sight. Nilborg was struck hardest by the fall of the High Paladin of Soleran. The priest had known Soren for more years than Rholmar cared to count, and Nilborg was the last to leave the paladin's side.

Deep down, Rholmar knew they were doing the right thing. Without horses, it would take twice as long to reach Trannum's stronghold, and they could not afford to slow their pace further by carrying the body. What weighed heaviest on Rholmar was leaving Soren alive for scavengers to toy with. Just as the others of the company, he could not put the paladin to death, not even after Nilborg assured him Soren was beyond sight and feeling. Rholmar tried to take solace in the fact that Soren would soon succumb to the poison, if he had not already.

They headed south, following the eastern fork of the Twin Rivers. Had they been there under better circumstances, Rholmar might have marveled at how clean the water ran outside of Mud Lake, but he walked, almost as if in a trance.

Night fell, and with it came thousands of insects that preyed on their flesh. The company moved their campsite from the water's edge, but the critters found them all the same—even the many bats darting about could not cut into the number of bugs the wild country harbored. The moon was full and the evening warm, but they received little sleep. Besides the insects, Rholmar was sure the memory of Soren and the lake creature haunted everyone's minds.

Morning brought with it a much hotter day than the previous one. The air was thick, and Rholmar's clothes were tight against his skin with perspiration, though it was not obvious beneath his armor. The only consolation was that the daytime pests were not so numerous.

Returning to the river's side, they resumed the southward trek. The land rolled before them as they veered ever closer to the Varlimor Mountain's southern peaks, but the hills were gentle and presented no hindrance. The river fell below, having cut a trench into the terrain, and its current became rapid and drowned out most noises. After half the day had passed, the water slowed and Lorylla brought everyone to a halt.

"Horses!" The elf looked over her shoulder.

Rholmar detected only the rushing water at first, but then the unmistakable sound of distant hooves reached his ears.

"Who could have followed us into this land?" Pallit searched the terrain behind them.

"I don't know." Rholmar shook his head. "Let's put some distance between us and the river. See if we can lose them in the hills."

They moved fifty yards from the gorge, but still Lorylla detected horses headed toward them. The animals were not in sight, but a whinny gave them away just beyond the last hill. A moment later, four horses came into view.

"Only two bear riders," Lorylla said. Then she gasped. "Soren!"

"It can't be." Pallit squinted to get a better look.

All Rholmar could tell was that one rider was taller than the other. As the animals rode down the hill, he and Pallit drew their blades.

"We cannot be too careful," Pallit said. "Trannum is cunning."

"Hold your swords." Nilborg's expression brightened. "I sense no evil. In fact, it's quite the opposite. It *must* be Soren."

The riders neared, and Rholmar saw them clearly at last. The taller one certainly appeared to be Soren, and the other was an elf garbed in a green cloak. To Rholmar's further amazement, the horses were the very steeds they had set free in the Fire Hills.

Lorylla said something in elfish Rholmar did not comprehend, but the final word he recognized to be *Elgarroth*, and she ran to meet the new arrivals. Indeed, it was the legendary wizard riding with the Soleran paladin. Soren's face was grim, and he was wearing fresh leggings and boots.

"I believe you will be needing these fine animals," Elgarroth said in the common speech as they dismounted. "They were the only survivors, I fear."

"Even one horse would have been grand." Lorylla looked at the Soleran paladin. "But the return of Soren..."

Nilborg raised his hands to the heavens. "Praise be to Soleran!" And he embraced the paladin.

"I'm sorry we left you." Rholmar placed a guilty hand on Soren's shoulder.

"You did what you had to do." Soren nodded. "And it was the right decision at the time. But now things are changed. I am healthy and we have horses. Trannum's luck has taken an ill turn at last."

"But how...?" Nilborg looked from the elf wizard to Soren.

"I awoke to find Elgarroth kneeling over me," Soren said. "And in my mouth was a strange leaf. Whatever it was, it conquered the venom and restored my life."

"We owe you many thanks, Master Elgarroth." Nilborg bowed before the wizard.

"He had not reached Death's Door just yet," Elgarroth said. "All I provided was a simple herb to counter the poison."

"Simple?" Nilborg raised an eyebrow. "Somehow I doubt that."

"In any case," Elgarroth's expression became serious, "there is no time for celebration. You must not delay."

"What news have you of the other missions?" asked Rybeal.

Elgarroth shook his head. "Not much that is good. But you must remain concerned for *your* part."

"With the return of these noble beasts," Lorylla patted the horse that had borne her from Sendorum, "we shall make good time!"

"Will you be accompanying us, then?" Rholmar asked Elgarroth.

"Alas," the wizard spread his hands, "I must be off. There are matters more pressing than yours at the moment."

"*More* pressing?" Rholmar raised a brow. "That does not bode well."

"But where are you off to?" Pallit inquired.

"The northwest," Elgarroth replied.

Disappointment was obvious on Pallit's face. The ranger had surely hoped for more information—perhaps word on those traversing the mines of Lornibur. Nilborg pressed further.

"Master Elgarroth. Can you tell us how Merssa has fared? Since last night, I have had an ill feeling."

Elgarroth stared at the priest without speaking. The wizard then shook his head slowly, and Nilborg's eyes sank. Rholmar's heart stopped.

"Do not trouble yourselves with her fate," Elgarroth said. "There is too much at stake, and time is of the essence."

Nilborg nodded, and Elgarroth began walking up the hill, leaning on his staff with every other step. The company watched until the elf made it to the top, where he turned back.

"The hardest road is yet ahead," the wizard called out. "Keep your wits about you!"

Elgarroth stepped over the ridge and was gone.

"Pallit. You'll ride with Nilborg." Soren resumed his authority. "Lorylla and Rybeal will share a horse as well."

They mounted and continued south with Rholmar and Soren in the lead, each on his own horse. Though all expressions were improved with the return of Soren, the company remained silent for a while. Rholmar's mind wandered to the *other* matters that led Elgarroth away, and his concern for Merssa grew.

"Are you all right?"

Pallit stirred Rholmar from his thoughts. Rholmar shook his head clear and looked back to respond, but then he noticed the ranger had addressed Nilborg.

"Quite so." Nilborg cleared his throat. "I was just thinking about the path ahead."

Rholmar was sure the priest's thoughts had been in line with his own.

They rode out the remainder of the day and camped only a few hours that night. Under the warm, starry sky, they continued along the river as it veered eastward and became level with the land; and come morning, scattered trees and fields of tall grass replaced the hills.

The next day grew hotter still, and the distant, snow-covered mountains to the north looked inviting—even with dark clouds hovering above them. A pride of lions lounged across the river, too lazy to hunt the gazelles to the east; the large cats panted, lacking even the energy to show interest in Rholmar's companions beyond the occasional glance.

That evening, they shed all remaining cloaks and excess clothing, and Nilborg and Lorylla removed their armor and strapped it to their horses. Still, the persistent heat made rest difficult and the night stretched long.

Upon the following day, the river became stagnant and the air hazy, and tall reeds plagued the water's edge while lilies dotted its green surface. Hordes of insects feasted on the company, and their chorus played just as loud as the previous night's. They had reached Dright Swamp.

As the sun faded, they set up camp under a willow upon a small hillock. Dark circles were evident beneath all but Lorylla's eyes, but the humid night did not allow for solid rest. If Rholmar even came close to slumber, insects intervened, buzzing near his ears or pricking his skin with long needles. After a couple of hours, all attempts to sleep were abandoned, and they took to checking their gear by the light of the moon.

"According to Selanna, the marsh crawls with the undead." Soren's voice cut through the drone of the swamp.

"Guardians of the rear entrance." Rholmar gazed into the dark east. He did not fear the undead. But after the close call at Mud Lake, he wondered what else had escaped Selanna's notice during her travels.

"There's no telling how far west they roam, so be on your guard." Soren turned to Lorylla. "Do you have the map?"

"Right here." The tall elf pulled a leather tube from her pack. "We could leave now if you like."

"Though your eyes see much in the night," Soren said, "the rest of us would be at a great disadvantage. We shall await first light."

Soren breathed easier with the arrival of morning. Lorylla's offer to lead them in the darkness had been tempting, for the night was long and uncomfortable, but he needed to place common sense above impatience.

They rode beneath the brightening sky, and by noon, the surrounding land gave way to the river and its water branched in every direction. Most streams were shallow and easily crossed, and as the company came upon a second large willow, Soren brought them to a halt. They had reached the next checkpoint on Selanna's map.

"Lorylla," Soren said.

The elf rode forward, and Rybeal dismounted to leave her alone atop the horse. While the wizard joined Soren in the saddle, Lorylla pulled the leather tube from her pack and produced the map. She took the lead, and Soren rode to her left.

From what Soren could see, the detailed drawing showed a couple of routes deemed safest, as well as areas to avoid at all costs.

It seemed easy enough to follow, and he wondered how long Selanna had spent within the marsh to sketch it so well.

Trees were gathered in large patches, standing tall and covered by algae, and vines draped across the ground, playing with the horses' hooves. Nearer to the many rivers and ponds, cattails grew to extraordinary heights, and occasionally the company had to venture through fields of them. Pallit and Rholmar dismounted in these areas to hack a path with their blades, all the while prodding ahead to avoid sudden drop offs in the water.

For three days, they weaved through Dright Swamp with no sightings of the undead. The nights were dark and sticky, and insects swarmed in larger masses than before; and while some dealt painful bites, most were only annoying and loud. On the fourth day, the sun disappeared behind low, dark clouds and the air cooled. A light drizzle descended with the night and they donned their cloaks; and Nilborg and Lorylla put on their armor as well.

The rain ended before morning, leaving a thin layer of frost and a chilly start to the day. The swamp was gray and grew colder still, becoming winter-like near midday, and the insects abandoned the company for warmer regions of the marsh. As dusk fell, Soren halted.

"Perhaps we should continue," said Rholmar. "We must surely be nearing the end of the bog, and all's been too quiet. I fear staying in one place for too long."

"The night grows too dark." Soren looked around. "But we'll move a bit farther." He understood the Arronaus paladin's concern, for he sensed a distant evil drawing nearer as well—the hairs on his arms were standing.

"We should light torches." Pallit reached into his pack.

"There's likely nothing in this marsh relying on sight," said Rybeal. "The undead will follow our scent and come onto us in the night. We may as well be able to see *them*."

"Light them." Soren gave a nod.

The mage used his magic to bring flame to three torches provided by Pallit. Pallit then carried one, Rholmar another, and Rybeal the third.

They continued, and Lorylla rode closer to Rholmar's torch to better see the map. But after a mile, they stopped. Fifty yards ahead, a line of snow stretched beyond sight to the north and south. Soren dreaded the thought of entering another region plagued by winter, but there was no choice, and he urged his horse forward.

They crossed the border, and the horses grew hesitant. It was as if they recalled the trek through the Fire Hills, and Soren detected a slight shudder from his mount. After a bit more coaxing, the animals returned to a steady pace.

The snow was not deep, but frigid gusts swept over the company, seeking routes beneath Soren's cloak and cutting to the bone. They had not ridden far when everyone began to shiver.

"We must stop," said Pallit through chattering teeth. "We'll freeze to death without a fire."

"I wish we hadn't left the furs behind." Nilborg glanced back, as if he could see the heavy cloaks lying on the grass hundreds of miles away.

Soren agreed with the sentiment. The swamp must not have been frozen when Selanna last passed through; she would have mentioned that. There was no choice but to light a fire and warm themselves.

Everyone dismounted, and Rholmar and Pallit fed ice-covered vines and branches into a small fire fueled by Rybeal's magic. Soon, they huddled around a decent flame.

The night was quiet, revealing nothing outside the crackling fire wavering in the wind. But then the air calmed, and Soren thought he detected groaning. He stood and readied his weapon, and the others did the same. The wind returned and the moaning faded, but Lorylla voiced an alarm.

"They are nearly upon us!"

"I feel them," said Rholmar.

Soren sensed the approaching evil as well. Even the horses stirred.

"They're all around us." Nilborg's head spun left and right.

"Backs to the fire," said Soren.

From every direction, zombies staggered into the firelight. They appeared Nomish, and how long they had been dead, Soren was unsure, for the winter had preserved their cold, blue bodies. Hatred burned in their eyes, and they hissed and moaned louder, causing the horses to bolt. The animals trampled several zombies as they disappeared into the night.

Soren charged, and Rholmar was next to him. Together they defeated ten zombies with little effort, and to Soren's flank he heard Nilborg damning the abominations. Soren glanced to see the priest standing over two zombie corpses with his morningstar held high. Pallit and Lorylla had destroyed six more on the opposite side of the fire, and Rybeal surveyed the undead with his hands raised.

Nilborg moved to Soren's side. "Is the entire population of Nomedd within the swamp?"

Indeed, the zombies were endless.

Soren and Rholmar continued their onslaught, but the sheer numbers forced them back. Immense heat then arose as a mass of flame billowed outward to the north. The fire washed over the zombies, destroying more than a score, and another mass streamed over the undead to the south. Once the fires dissipated, smaller spheres flew about, incinerating zombies one at a time. Rybeal possessed powerful magic, indeed!

Well over a hundred undead littered the ground, and the bodies were piling up. Not far away, the horses cried in the darkness, no doubt having become a meal for the horde.

"Rybeal!" Soren called out. "We need a path!"

The billowing flame returned, reaching to the east and stretching twice as long as the previous clouds. A wide berth resulted, lacking snow and filled with glowing ashes and burning bodies, and at its termination were more zombies.

"Fly!" Soren rushed down the alley.

Zombies hissed to either side, hesitant to enter, and for a moment, Soren enjoyed the heat against his body. Rholmar ran beside Soren and the company followed, carrying only their weapons and leaving all else behind. The zombies grew bolder nearer to the end of the path, and Soren and Rholmar carved down any daring to impede their progress.

Rybeal cast his fire again, extending the alley, and still there was no end to the undead. The wizard repeated the spell twice more before finding a break in the horde at last, and they fled into the night as fast as their legs could carry them.

Frozen air pierced Soren's lungs, and he stumbled in the darkness, slipping on patches of ice and tripping over debris. But everyone was safe, and they helped one another until the sounds of the zombies were long faded. Soren then stopped, and his breath was heavy upon the air as he leaned against a tree and panted. The others were just as fatigued, except for Lorylla—the tall elf continued to amaze Soren, appearing ready to continue all the way to Trannum's stronghold.

"Rybeal." Soren turned to the wizard. "Some light, if you would."

Rybeal cast a spell to illuminate the area. Snow weighed down the trees and plant life, and it appeared as though the company had just crossed a frozen pond.

"They're far behind now," Nilborg said between breaths.

"But they won't rest." Pallit blew into his hands. "They'll pursue, have no doubt."

"At any rate," Soren said, "we must move on before the cold gets the better of us."

Lorylla shook her head, looking at the map. "I am no longer sure of our location."

"Our destination lies east," said Rholmar. "I suggest we continue that way."

Lorylla looked doubtful, but she did not argue. Soren nodded in agreement.

The chill was unbearable while they walked through the night. Before long, Soren's hands and feet were numb, as well as his face, and the march became laborious. The sky brightened with the dawn, but the sun failed to penetrate the dark clouds. Instead, a light snow greeted the company.

They continued for most of the day, halting only when Nilborg collapsed. Soren quickly helped the priest into a seated position.

"We're going to perish here!" Pallit said through chattering teeth.

Soren looked at Rybeal. The wizard was as pale as the others, though Soren doubted it was completely due to the chill or lack of sleep. After the power Rybeal exhibited against the zombies, it surprised Soren the mage could walk. With reluctance, he issued his next command.

"We must have a fire."

Rybeal nodded and closed his eyes. He released a slow breath, reciting a chant, and a flame appeared atop the snow, much smaller than the last one. Pallit and Rholmar fed it with nearby sticks, and it was not long before the wood ignited. Rybeal sat heavily onto the ground with his head bowed.

The company gathered close, but the fire provided little warmth. Pallit was right. They were going to perish in the swamp. Their path was secret, and Soren still believed the necromancer had no knowledge of their approach. And yet, with no horses, no warm gear—no gear at all—and zombies in pursuit, they were going to fail. Soren had not felt such defeat since the fall of Palidur. He bowed his head and prayed to Soleran.

The snowfall ceased. Then a warm breeze brushed over the swamp, growing warmer with every second.

"What's happening?" Pallit voiced Soren's question aloud.

"Trannum must have suffered a blow!" Rholmar had a gleam in his eye. "Merssa's doing, no doubt!"

Soren nodded in agreement, his hope returning.

The gust continued, becoming hot and thawing Soren's limbs. The clouds then parted, and the sun was revealed in the west. Its light was nearly lost through the haze, but its warmth was unmistakable.

"Let's get moving while we can." Soren rose to his feet. "The cold may yet return."

They marched another mile through melting snow while the sun dipped lower and the clouds all but disappeared. Every now and again, they stopped for Lorylla to assess their position, but none of the landmarks on the map matched their surroundings. As darkness settled, they halted.

Soren gazed at the moonlit swamp. Streams and ponds nourished sagging trees, and snow was but a bad memory. He sensed no immediate danger and allowed himself to relax.

"We can only rest a short while." He sighed. "Let's not forget our pursuers."

Fatigue was heavy upon Soren, and he could only imagine how Nilborg and Rybeal felt. But neither posed an objection.

Though the night was hot, they lit a small fire. Lorylla studied the map while everyone nibbled on what little food they carried in their pouches, and after an hour the elf gasped.

"I think I found us!" She shook her head. "It is not good."

"What is it?" Rholmar looked over her shoulder.

"If I am correct," Lorylla said, "we have drifted to the south. Selanna marked this area as dangerous."

"Quicksand?" asked Pallit. "More zombies?"

"No." The elf furrowed her brow. "She drew an undead dragon."

"Well, she drew the torso of a dragon," Rholmar pointed out.

"Could be one of the Death Lord's beasts," said Soren. "In any case, we need to get moving." He looked at Lorylla. "What do you suggest?"

"It depends on whether we are north or south of the creature." The elf pursed her lips. "Your guess is as good as mine. I wish I had had more time in Sendorum to go over this with Selanna." She shook her head again.

"Let's go east," Rholmar said. "We've lost the horses again, so a direct route would be best. Others are waiting for us."

"Besides," added Pallit, "if it is a Death Lord's mount, it may no longer be there. Selanna drew that map years ago."

"I agree." Soren gave a nod. "We'll chance a direct route."

They headed east, passing through several groupings of trees. The waning moon did little to light the way and they possessed no more torches, so Soren entrusted Lorylla to lead them through the darker regions—he dared not ask Rybeal to expend any more power. The swamp was soon flooded in most places, and at least one of them needed the assistance of a steady arm on occasion. Sometimes deeper bodies of water impeded progress altogether, and they were forced north or south a few hundred yards before turning back to the east. After a couple hours, the ground became solid and the trees more numerous. Just as Soren began to feel grateful, Lorylla halted.

"What was that?" The elf stared at a large grove to the left.

"There's evil there," Nilborg said.

Soren sensed it, too, and Rholmar nodded in agreement. They readied their weapons.

Within the trees appeared two points of blue light, ten feet above the ground. Next came a horrific screech, and from the shadows the head of a skeletal dragon emerged. The monster hissed and its eyes grew bright, and from its gaping maw issued its yellowish gas, appearing brown in the moonlight. Pallit attempted to push Rybeal from its path while the company scattered, but both the ranger and the wizard disappeared within the cloud.

Soren and Rholmar charged the fell creature, and its breath ended as it turned on Rholmar with gnashing teeth. Soren then understood Selanna's drawing, for the monster lacked hindquarters—perhaps an incomplete skeleton discarded into the swamp. Rholmar tumbled across the ground, evading the creature's attack, and Soren struck the dragon's skull. His blade rang off the thick bone, leaving a mere crack.

The dragon swung its head like a club, launching Soren into a nearby tree. The world was then spinning and all sound muffled, and Soren saw two skeletal dragons towering overhead. He rolled aside as both mouths lunged, and the twin heads bit into trees at the same time. Soren then spotted Lorylla and Rholmar, or rather two of each, and they struck the beasts with their blades. The undead creatures turned and hissed.

Soren climbed to his feet, dizziness threatening to overwhelm him. To the right, two Nilborgs stood over four bodies, and he staggered toward the priests, knowing he could not continue without the aid of his longtime companion. He found a pair of Pallits and Rybeals writhing on the ground, their skin turning yellow and beginning to shrivel.

"Save Pallit." The Rybeals wheezed, leaning on their staves and struggling to their feet.

Soren faced the melee while the Nilborgs prayed over the Pallits, and thirty yards away the dragons turned, as if sensing the divine power. Soren shook his head, determined that no harm would come to his friend, but his vision remained impaired. Hopefully the Loryllas and Rholmars could keep the monsters contained.

The muffled prayer continued, and the radiance of Soleran's healing touch was a blessed sensation on Soren's back. The double visions drew together, and he looked to see Nilborg's hands on Pallit's chest; and even as Rybeal's skin flaked, Pallit's color returned. But then Nilborg swayed. Soren righted the high priest with his free arm, nearly falling for his efforts.

"It's taking a lot out of me." Nilborg panted, sounding as if he were far away, and Pallit immediately faltered.

Nilborg's expression became determined as he repeated the prayer more forcefully, and Soren turned to keep guard, welcoming the aura's return. It was still hard to focus, but he saw Lorylla and Rholmar hounding the skeletal beast, now twenty yards away. The dragon knocked Rholmar to the ground with its claw, and its eyes burned brighter as it hissed at Lorylla.

"No!" Soren charged.

Lightning raced across the swamp, halting Soren after only a few steps. His head cleared, and he saw Rybeal. The wizard's wrinkled skin hung loose, his hair had fallen out, and he appeared much older than only moments ago, but lightning issued from his outstretched hands, enveloping the dragon's body. Lorylla and Rholmar fled while the monster screeched and thrashed about, and as the dragon collapsed into a pile of bones, the lightning ceased and Rybeal fell.

Nilborg rushed to the wizard. But it was too late.

Rholmar pulled a healthy Pallit to his feet, and they joined Lorylla next to Soren. They then bowed their heads while Nilborg recited a prayer. Upon completion, Nilborg placed a small symbol of Soleran onto the chest of the withered, lifeless body, and he remained on a knee, staring with unbelieving eyes.

Even as the poison was draining the life from Rybeal, the wizard found the strength to pour every ounce of his power into one last spell. If not for Rybeal, none of them would have survived the swamp. Because of him, they had a chance to complete their quest and free the world from the necromancer's clutches.

"We must go." Soren put his hand on Nilborg's shoulder.

CHAPTER 35

BATTLES IN THE NORTH

After unlocking Elloria's cell, Nidor opened the door with a wary eye on the rafters. But the key seemed to have rendered the strange contraption inert, and the trap did not spring—if it was a trap. Xorlunder joined Nidor as he entered and unlocked Elloria's shackles, his nerves still on edge. The rafters remained intact. Nidor breathed a sigh of relief and tossed the keys to Gruelenor, who immediately began opening the other cells.

"Just when I had lost all hope." Elloria placed a tender hand on Xorlunder's cheek as the gray elf helped her to her feet. "How are you, my friend?"

"I have seen better days," Xorlunder replied. "The wraiths have put a drain on me."

"The wraiths often visit us for the same purpose." Elloria shuddered. "The enemy desires to keep us alive, for reasons I do not know, but they can't afford for us to regain our strength. So the wraiths keep us weak." Her face twisted. "Gruzim is as cruel as his master! Every week his Zurkan take one of my men… I don't dare imagine what for. Nor do I think about what's in store for me."

"You may put those feelings to rest," Nidor said, receiving a curious look from Elloria. How was it that almost no one had ever met a Dale? "But a wraith has gone to warn its master of our presence," he added. "We must be moving."

"Alas," Elloria's face saddened, "that is not the way of Brondor. The God of Battle does not permit acts of stealth. I sense you are a paladin, dark one, and you surely understand that."

"If it's battle you wish," Vecnor stooped to enter the cell, "then that is what you shall have. We are not here to steal you away, Priestess, and there has been no secrecy in our approach once we arrived. Two armies will soon converge on Burmagaard, and they need your faithful following to defeat the enemy!"

Nidor suddenly realized Vecnor's reason for entering the way he did, without a care for alerting the castle's sentries. It was necessary, so Elloria could emerge from the dungeon without shaming herself before her deity—or perhaps it was just Vecnor's way. Did Vecnor worship Brondor?

Elloria looked at Vecnor, held in awe for a moment. "I do not know how many of my folk remain." She shook her head. "It has been longer than I can recall since my imprisonment. Any soldiers not captured may have indeed sought refuge to await my return. But whether they have escaped enemy eyes, I cannot say."

"Rise, Priestess!" Vecnor's tone caused her to flinch. "It is time for battle! Time to put the enemy down and reclaim what was taken!"

Elloria's face took on a more youthful appearance, and she somehow stood taller. "Yes." Her voice grew in strength. "Yes! The time *has* come." Elloria looked at the score of men gathered within the corridor; her loyal soldiers from the neighboring cells. They were pale, but their faces rekindled with her words. "We will take back what is ours! Or we will die in combat!"

"Brondor!" the men cheered, raising a fist, and no one seemed concerned with the sound echoing to unknown ears.

"Who are you, stranger?" Elloria looked at Vecnor.

"He is Vecnor!" Xorlunder said. "The ageless warrior, come to us in our time of need."

"Vecnor?" Elloria furrowed her brow. But then a smile crossed her face. "It *is* you! I met you once, when I was but a child. My, how you have not changed. But it must be you. I can feel it."

"I remember," Vecnor said softly, bringing confusion to Nidor. How was that possible? "But first, some of my companions are in need of aid. Can you help them?"

"Already I feel my power growing." Color returned to Elloria's face as she spoke. "I have no herbs, but I'll do what I can."

Nidor, not wanting to stand in the way of Elloria's triumph, handed her what remained of Eraim's herbs. The priestess looked at them, and she smiled at Nidor and gave a nod.

She first tended to Xorlunder, preparing the herbs much in the same fashion Sullis had, and chanted a prayer while doing so. Xorlunder looked relieved once she was finished, and she eased Melac's suffering next. Her men then kneeled before her in turn with heads bowed, and she cured their ails, as well as her own.

While Elloria worked, Gruelenor arrived with the prisoners from the first set of cells—Nidor had not realized Gruelenor had left, and he was glad to see his companion's safe return. Knowing the priestess would possess no more herbs for the newcomers, Nidor entered the corridor and called upon Silcor's Healing Flame. They gaped, appearing hesitant to receive his touch, but after the initial shock and pain, they expressed gratitude while continuing to gaze in awe.

The task took some time, and no soldiers of Darmhorng arrived to intervene. When done, Elloria looked to have been drained of spiritual power, but her flesh remained strong. She turned to Vecnor and grinned.

"Now all I need is a sword...or two."

Vecnor led the way to the guardroom and through the open iron door, where Nidor was sure he had gone to procure the keys. Stone steps ascended to a smashed-in door and another guardroom, this one possessing a dozen dead soldiers. The bodies revealed many wounds, and each had been decapitated.

"Do not forget the evil effects of the Death Lord's presence," Vecnor said. "The living will need to be put down twice."

There were enough weapons to arm Elloria and most of her men. She did not bother with armor, but several of her following donned the bloodstained chain shirts. They then ventured up a second stairway that ended at a small landing, where a heavy door with a shuttered window barred the way. Vecnor lowered his shoulder and busted the door from its hinges.

The chamber beyond teemed with soldiers holding loaded crossbows, and they appeared confused when Vecnor entered, appearing as a Death Lord in his black armor. They realized their error too late, and he slew half of them with his massive swords before the other half discharged their weapons. Two missiles bounced off Vecnor's dark plates while another pierced his right side, but he showed no pain, and the remaining bolts caromed off the walls. The guards were then overwhelmed when the company stormed into the room. As the corpses stirred, they were slaughtered again.

The rest of Elloria's men outfitted themselves, and the priestess lifted a second sword. She swung it through the air, showing no signs of having spent years within the dank prison of Darmhorng. Turning to Vecnor, she raised a blade.

"Let our enemies litter the ground beneath our feet! And may Brondor give us the strength to claim victory! Or the courage to carry on until the last of us has perished in combat!"

"Brondor!" her men resounded, as did Vecnor.

Nidor looked at Gruelenor, and Gruelenor nodded. The day had arrived. They set out several weeks ago, and had reached their destination at last, though by a different road than was laid before them. The time had come to see if they could occupy the forces of Trannum in the north, so that others might enter the necromancer's stronghold and destroy evil at its core. Nidor only hoped the other companies had accomplished their goals, lest the ensuing battle be in vain.

Vecnor led the way along the castle's various halls and chambers, seemingly familiar with the layout. They slew the enemy wherever they found them, consisting of living guards at first, but they soon encountered dunarchins and ghouls. The battles were more difficult then, and some of Elloria's men fell. Moments later, those soldiers were put down again, as zombies.

They were surely nearing the main halls when the castle grew colder. A Death Lord was near. Nidor recalled the feeling other Death Lords had placed on his soul, one of immense fear, but this was different. He was not sure if it was the presence of Elloria, or perhaps Vecnor, but the sensation was not so dire as in the past.

"Is it Gruzim?" asked Melac.

Vecnor shook his head. "They all feel the same. But I do not believe it is he that dwells here at the moment."

Elloria gazed at her remaining soldiers, twenty-four in all. She then turned to Vecnor. "I must make my return known. Without more warriors, we'll not survive long enough to see your armies arrive."

Vecnor nodded, his attention veering from the wide staircase ascending to the upper levels. "Take your men and make for the city. Xorlunder and our mage will assist you. May Brondor guide your swords."

"You shall not accompany us?" Elloria's brows drew together.

Vecnor looked up the stairs again. "The rest of us have matters elsewhere."

Nidor and Gruelenor shared a nervous glance. They were going after the Death Lord.

Elloria nodded and smiled, and after slapping blades with Vecnor, she dashed down the corridor with Xorlunder at her side. Melac hesitated a moment, giving Nidor a questioning look. Nidor gave a nod, and the mage joined the soldiers in pursuit of the priestess.

Vecnor climbed the staircase, his strides falling upon every other step, and Nidor and Gruelenor hastened to keep up. Shouts and the clash of steel became clear below, as Elloria surely found resistance in the entry hall, but the sounds soon faded into the distance.

While the first floor of the stronghold maintained the appearance of a normal castle, the second story was marred and scorched, and the odor of decay hung like a cloud. Statues lay smashed and tapestries were shredded, and bloody garments and discarded bones of past meals were strewn across the floors. Ghouls, dunarchins, and a few wraiths stood in opposition, but Vecnor cleaved through the enemy while Nidor and Gruelenor destroyed all foes attempting to sneak up from the rear.

They entered the throne room at last, a vast chamber with a high ceiling supported by four rows of pillars. The inner columns looked to have once resembled figures, most likely past monarchs, and the north and south walls exhibited portraits resembling women, possibly queens. Presently, the sculptures showed excessive chipping, and the paintings were decorated with blood and other colorful fluids. At the far end, a grand throne of dark wood was situated upon a dais, but the seat was unoccupied. The east wall opened onto a large balcony, where the king may have sat with his court and addressed crowds, but now it was home to the undead dragon that roosted there. Many Zurkan warriors occupied the room, and also present was the source of the chilling fear—a Death Lord, standing just inside the opening on the eastern wall.

The undead king unsheathed a sword and pulled an axe from his belt. It was Anduiff, ancient Lord of Benasti centuries before Gruzim's rule, but of the same bloodline. Weapons ready, the Zurkan advanced.

Vecnor twirled his blades, carving down all who opposed him. The Soldiers of Blood attacked with axes, swords, and spears, but no weapon found its mark against the mighty warrior. Nidor and Gruelenor fought to either side, taking on those attempting to flank the large man, and destroyed any Zurkan converting to zombies. Many curses flew Gruelenor's way in the hobgoblin tongue, but Gruelenor did his talking with his sword. Flames engulfed Nidor's blade, and he felt invincible while he hewed a dozen of the Benasti soldiers. He was sure he received a few wounds, but the injuries were insignificant and failed to hinder him.

Before long, dozens of Zurkan littered the floor, and still the Death Lord watched. As Vecnor defeated the final Soldier of Blood, his gaze met the glowing eyes of the enemy.

"Anduiff!" Vecnor exhibited no fear.

There came a screech from the distant sky, and the Death Lord glanced over his shoulder. The dragon on the balcony gave a return screech before turning its attention to the undead king.

"Another time," Anduiff said in a deep, hollow voice. The Death Lord sheathed his sword and jumped onto the beast, and with a jarring shriek, the dragon took to the sky.

Nidor and Gruelenor joined Vecnor as he rushed to the balcony. The morning sun peeked over the horizon, and within the walls of the city below, a battle was taking place. To the east another battle was at hand, a mile from Burmagaard, and above the melee, black clouds produced lightning every few seconds. Anduiff flew to the west beneath another gathering of clouds, and he and his beast grew smaller as they sped into the distance, taking the dark canopy with them.

"He does not aid the battle for the city?" asked Nidor. "Or join the battle to the east?"

"No." Vecnor furrowed his brow. "He flies to the dwarves." His gaze fell onto the city. "To Burmagaard!"

They ran back through the hall.

Chapter 36

Burmagaard

Nothing opposed them as Nidor and Gruelenor followed Vecnor from the castle. Once outside, Nidor detected the clash of steel in the distance, and a trail of bodies, both friends and foes, lined the short road to Burmagaard. The city gates were open, and the gate towers appeared dark and unmanned.

Just beyond the large wooden doors, a group of men fought desperately against krukari and hobgoblins. Vecnor's approach sent many of the soldiers scattering in fear, but they realized he was no Death Lord when he, Nidor, and Gruelenor dispatched the enemy. The bodies fell and did not rise again—the Death Lords were too far away.

Vecnor addressed the men. "Where's Elloria?"

"To the south, I believe," one man replied. "But who are you?"

"I am her faithful servant." Vecnor bowed his head.

Looks of relief and excitement lit up their faces, and the men eagerly joined forces.

Vecnor led the way south along the streets, the large man again seemingly familiar with his surroundings. The city appeared to be free of the undead, and only bandits, traitor-Kalmirans, and Benasti warriors opposed them. After a couple of hours had passed, they found the priestess.

Elloria was full of life, and she grinned at Vecnor's approach. Xorlunder and Melac were with her, as well as eight of her fellow dungeon mates and no less than five hundred new recruits. Nidor was amazed at how many of her followers had been hiding within the city, but he believed some of the men were soldiers that had recently sided with the enemy, judging by the dirt smeared over the red portions of their garments.

"The enemy's numbers are failing!" Elloria said. "I have two full squads clearing the streets to the east and west. We will win Burmagaard before the day is out!"

Moments later, the air grew deathly cold, as if in response to Elloria's proclamation. Anduiff had returned. The Death Lord flew just above the buildings, and many soldiers cowered at the sight. Fallen warriors rose, former allies and foes alike, and the battle began anew.

The undead attacked all living souls, including a group of hobgoblins and traitor-Kalmirans that had emerged from alleyways to the north. The traitor-Kalmirans were quick to turn on the zombies, but the hobgoblins laughed, welcoming death and their ultimate rebirth. Elloria cursed Anduiff while the dragon circled, but the dark king paid her no heed. The Death Lord and his mount then sped off to the southeast, toward the battle outside the city.

Nidor wondered if the return of Anduiff meant the dwarves would not be coming, and he was filled with dread for Magneer and Sullis. His attention then returned to the matter at hand, for zombies closed in around them.

Nidor advanced upon the corpses with his sword still ablaze, and his foes were reduced to cinders with every strike. Gruelenor fought at his side, and they battled through more than fifty zombies before Nidor realized they were separated from their allies. The path they had cleared was gone, filled in by twice as many undead as before, and they were attacked from all sides.

Back to back, Nidor and Gruelenor kept the enemy at bay. But as the battle wore upon Nidor, his arms lowered and he knew he and his companion would soon be overwhelmed. Nidor's inner flame grew, rising up his spine until his head felt as if it might explode. The pressure released when streams of fire shot from his eyes, and the flames passed from zombie to zombie. Within seconds, all that remained were their ashes floating to the cobblestones. Over a hundred undead had been destroyed, and the streets were empty. Vecnor and Elloria were gone, as was Elloria's army.

"You're always full of surprises." Gruelenor held a look of astonishment while catching his breath.

Nidor did not know how it happened. "I am as surprised as you. I am but a tool of Silcor, and through me He makes His Will known."

"You must teach me to thank Him when this is over," Gruelenor said.

Nidor grinned. "Done!"

The sound of battle came from several directions. Nidor and Gruelenor returned to where they had last seen Vecnor, but found only corpses and destroyed zombies.

"Judging by the bodies," Gruelenor scanned the street, "they split into three groups. The larger groups headed east and west. Another took that alley." He pointed at a dark path between a pair of two-story buildings.

Times like these made Nidor grateful his friends were skilled trackers.

"Look!"

Gruelenor pointed at a group of zombies approaching from the north. The undead were turning to move away at a quickened pace while eyeing Nidor. It was odd, but they seemed fearful. Nidor led the charge, and he and Gruelenor slew the abominations before they could escape.

"Let us follow the path with the most slain enemies," Nidor said to Gruelenor. "Surely that will lead to Vecnor."

Gruelenor nodded, and they sped off to the east.

An hour passed, and they found no further signs of Vecnor or Elloria—only undead that needed to be destroyed. Nidor felt they would never see friendly faces again as the battle for the city claimed the day and shadows grew heavy; and with the disappearance of the sunlight, ghouls and wraiths abandoned their hiding places to enter the fray. Nidor's eyes lit up, revealing to him every dark corner along the streets, and any wraiths attempting to ambush them met a swift end.

Within a market square, fifteen soldiers battled more than a score of ghouls, and the guards were backed against a wall.

Gruelenor scowled. "Humans in Benasti garb!"

"But they fight the enemy," Nidor said.

"Help us!" one man shouted.

"I have half a mind to stick them like the pigs they are!" Gruelenor spat as Nidor led the way toward the melee. "But it isn't worth the effort to have to kill them twice."

Nidor's core temperature rose, and flashes of fire intervened every time a ghoul attempted to touch him. He fought with reckless abandon, and he and Gruelenor defeated half of the ghouls. The soldiers finished the rest.

Nidor addressed the men while they gaped at him in awe. "We will fight with you this night. But you will answer for your crimes against Vaeldor when all is done."

The thirteen survivors nodded with shameful looks.

"We seek a large man in black armor," Nidor said. "He is no friend of the undead, and he accompanies the priestess, Elloria."

"I've heard rumor of Elloria's return," one soldier said. "But I have not seen her or the man you speak of."

Nidor looked at Gruelenor.

Gruelenor sighed. "I think we should double back. I don't believe there's any chance Vecnor has been this way."

Nidor shared that belief, and he nodded.

The men followed as Nidor and Gruelenor returned the way they had come. They traversed the streets for an hour, battling through packs of ghouls and zombies that cost them four lives while a wraith claimed another. Still, they saw no allies, and Nidor wondered again if they would ever find their companions among the expanse of buildings.

"Did you see that?" Gruelenor said. "It looked like fire."

Nidor followed his companion's gaze, and a flash of light illuminated the distant sky. "Melac?"

"It must be."

They hurried north with the traitor-Kalmirans close behind. More ambushes greeted them, as ghouls continued to jump from dark places, and after the fourth such attack, Nidor noticed the soldiers were lagging. He looked at Gruelenor, and his companion's eyes reflected the same fatigue the men displayed.

The sounds of battle remained distant, and there was no hope of finding Vecnor any time soon. Nidor scanned nearby buildings until spotting a dark structure with a battered door, and he led the way inside. It was a store, stocked with travel gear, and its wares were in shambles. But it was otherwise empty.

Gruelenor barked orders, placing the eight surviving soldiers in positions to keep watch through the doorway and a couple of broken windows. The men appeared fearful of the krukari and obeyed without question.

"We will not tarry long," Nidor said. "Find what rest you can. But no one sleeps."

Half an hour passed, and no undead attempted to gain access to the store. But screams and groans haunted the night, keeping Gruelenor's nerves on edge.

Though the Dale's eyes ceased to burn after entering the building, the paladin's blade remained wreathed in flame until he finally sheathed it. Gruelenor did not know what to think of the fire that had issued from Nidor's eyes to destroy the undead, and a touch of fear filled his heart—what if those flames were ever meant for him? He shook the thought, glad to have Nidor on his side.

Gruelenor was grateful when Nidor called upon his fiery hand to mend all wounds received throughout the day, and the traitor-Kalmirans watched in awe before turning their attention back to the street. Nidor used his healing on the soldiers as well, amazing the men further, and once finished, the fire receded and the store was dark. The Dale appeared as the tall, muscular paladin Gruelenor had always known.

While Nidor had been tending to the others, Gruelenor located a small keg of beer and refreshed himself. At Nidor's urging, he allowed the traitor-Kalmirans to partake as well. Once everyone was settled back into position, Gruelenor took a seat on the floor next to Nidor, and they sat for several minutes without speaking. Gruelenor then interrupted the distant clamor of combat.

"Have you stopped to wonder? What if the war is already over? What if we've lost and just don't know it? Trannum's forces could be marching on us right now. By morning we could be surrounded by Death Lords." It was a thought that haunted Gruelenor throughout the day, but he never mentioned it while Nidor led the way along the city streets, appearing as a man on fire—flames producing no smoke, but shedding a large amount of heat.

"I cannot accept that to be true." Nidor shook his head. "Not while Silcor gives me strength." He gazed at the Kalmirans scattered around the room. "Have you ever wondered what drives men such as these to fight for the necromancer? I pity them." He looked Gruelenor in the eyes. "Everyone has their reasons; the experiences that lead them down the roads they choose." Nidor returned his gaze to the soldiers. "They seldom have control over what travels that road with them or against them, and often face dilemmas when splits occur. Sometimes they have time to choose their paths carefully, and other times they make life-changing decisions without clearly knowing the consequences those decisions will bring. I believe these men would go back and change their paths, given the opportunity. They are good men at heart."

Gruelenor sighed, an uneasiness coming over him. He looked at his companion, a shadow within the darkness, and dreaded what he was about to say. But he did not want to die before sharing the truth.

"I made a promise to Xorlunder, to reveal who I truly am to my friends." He spoke just above a whisper. "Though I have never shared my past in all the years you've known me, I wish to speak of it now." Gruelenor paused, searching for the courage to continue. "I am the eldest son of Gruzim."

The statement did not escape other ears within the building, and all attention moved briefly to Gruelenor. Gruelenor's stomach churned as he worried what Nidor would say next.

"I believe I already knew that," the Dale said after a moment. "At least, part of it."

"That elf!" Gruelenor grew angry with Xorlunder. Perhaps his teachers of old were correct in their lessons to distrust gray elves.

"It was not by Xorlunder's lips," Nidor said, "but your own. Back in Nira, when we first encountered Gruzim. I heard you two talking, though I did not understand the words. Then there were the wolves, first in Vermallon and then Benasti. They viewed you differently than the rest of us. And the tone in which the Zurkan warriors spoke to you in the throne room earlier today."

"Oh." Gruelenor felt ashamed. Had Nidor known all along? Why did the paladin say nothing?

"Do not concern yourself with such things," Nidor said. "I know what is in your heart, and I always have. Such a lineage does not trouble me, nor make you evil. It is your actions that make you who you are. You have chosen wisely the roads you have taken. You are one of the strongest men I have ever met."

Gruelenor rarely accepted compliments. People had complimented him his whole life for different reasons. He was strong. He was skilled. He was scary. Only those wishing to stay on his good side offered compliments, or those desiring to use him. Then he met Ballrik. Ballrik had been genuine, more so than Magneer or Solinin. Magneer was a decent man and a good friend, but he always considered Gruelenor last in times of import, and Solinin never fully trusted Gruelenor. But Nidor... Nidor had never given a reason for Gruelenor not to trust him. Nidor was the truest friend Gruelenor could ever hope to find.

"I'm glad you're here with me," Gruelenor said. "If I am to die this night or tomorrow, I am grateful to have had a friend such as you."

Nidor stood and drew his sword, and it flared bright with flame. "Then let us return to the fray...my brother."

Gruelenor rose and unsheathed his blade. "For Silcor!"

For the first time in his life, Gruelenor spoke a deity's name with true feeling behind the words. A strong heat emanated from the paladin's body, but it was a divine heat, and Gruelenor's spirit soared higher for being within its warmth.

With renewed energy, they lit torches from the store's wares and exited the building. Four ghouls and a couple of wraiths waited outside in ambush, and though the fiends were destroyed, three more lives were lost.

The distant flashes they had been following were absent, but Gruelenor and Nidor continued northward. Before long, they came upon a street littered with corpses and surrounded by scorched buildings. Their companions had been there, Gruelenor was sure, but they were gone.

"Let's continue north," Nidor said.

With no better options, Gruelenor nodded.

They pushed farther until reaching the north gate, and dread entered Gruelenor's heart. A mass of ghouls poured through the large doors, followed by ranks of dunarchins, and though he saw no skeletal dragon overhead, the presence of a Death Lord was unmistakable.

"South!" Nidor called out. "Quickly!"

They retreated, running for at least a mile before slowing. The streets remained dark and there was no sign of pursuit. A group of soldiers then rushed toward them.

"Brondor!" they cried with their swords held high.

"Halt!" Nidor stood tall with his weapon blazing.

"They're among the living!" the lead soldier said, and the platoon came to a stop. But their weapons remained ready and their eyes suspicious.

"We are of Vecnor's company," Nidor said.

"And you march with a krukari and traitors to Kalmaar!" The man glared at Gruelenor and the others.

"There is no time for petty squabbles!" Nidor's tone caused the soldiers to take a step back. "An army of undead has arrived through the north gate. Do you not *feel* the Death Lord?"

"Yes, I have felt it," the man said. "And I apologize for my harsh words. But we have lost many men this night, and slain both friend and foe, in one form or another. I am Captain Fremar."

"I am Nidor, Paladin of Silcor." He bowed. "Have you seen Vecnor or Elloria?"

"Away to the southeast," Fremar replied. "We were deployed to keep watch on this area."

"I suggest you fall back," Gruelenor said. "You do not have enough to oppose what is coming. The entire city may not be enough."

The man glared at Gruelenor. "Our orders come from the priestess."

"Dying here only serves the enemy," Nidor said. "You will rise again under a new leader. Does your priestess wish for that?"

While the paladin spoke, Gruelenor glanced over his shoulder to see if the undead were in sight. The streets remained dark.

Fremar looked at his men. Fear was in their eyes. "Fall back! All except the scouts!"

Nidor's sigh of relief did not escape Gruelenor's notice.

Captain Fremar led them southeast, but after a mile he froze. A high-pitched horn reverberated across the city.

"That was the south gate." Fremar turned to Nidor. "The enemy is there as well. Priestess Elloria will be moving to combat them. She is not aware of the army to the north. She'll be surrounded!"

"Make haste then!" Nidor's eyes flared, causing Fremar to stumble back a pace. "We must get to her before it is too late."

Fremar bit his lip, his brow furrowed. He then nodded, and they continued south.

Soon, a battle came into view. Vecnor fought with one of his large swords, and nearby were Elloria, Xorlunder, and Melac. Elloria's force was over eight hundred strong, and they were locked in combat with a host of dunarchins. The forces appeared to be matched, but living soldiers would join the enemy after they fell, and the priestess would be outnumbered.

Gruelenor and Nidor raced to Vecnor's side as the giant warrior grabbed a dunarchin by the throat and swung the creature like a club. After striking three undead firstborns, he cast the body into its own ranks.

"Vecnor!" Nidor called above the din.

"Glad to see you two alive!" Vecnor grinned as he severed a dunarchin's leg.

Nidor battered the shield of a dunarchin. "We are being flanked!"

Vecnor's smile faded, and he surged forward with a sense of urgency. Reaching back, he pulled his other sword and hewed the enemy twice as fast.

Back down the street, the ghouls had arrived.

"They're here!" Gruelenor yelled.

He charged to meet them, and Nidor joined him, as did their team of Kalmiran-traitors and Fremar's platoon. The ghouls licked their bloodstained teeth as they approached, and beyond them marched undead firstborns in perfect ranks. The dunarchins' eyes animated the dark street, and a few of them toyed with crackling energy about their fingertips.

Gruelenor's mind went back to the question he posed in the store. Had the war already been lost?

There was a roar to the northwest, and Gruelenor saw Sullis, sitting atop Umbarc and hacking into the dunarchins' flank. Behind the Brondor paladin was the host of Morimont.

The dwarves had arrived!

Chapter 37

Dark Army Approaches

Gulthar stood in the front hall of Castle Lambrak. At the Death Lord's feet, the corpses of Landerik and Crismar did not stir, and in his hand was the black scepter, having been returned by a faithful ghoul. Cavalor saw the blue eyes turn his way again, and he feared the worst when the evil king raised the dark rod. But a screech pierced the stronghold, and Gulthar's attention turned to the courtyard. The skeletal dragon issued a second screech, and the Death Lord departed, bearing a slight limp.

Leaderless, the ghouls attacked in a frenzy, hesitating only when an explosion resonated from the balcony. The undead that had ascended there rained onto the hall in pieces, and Wezlok stood alone, bleeding from several wounds.

Anger was plain on the elf's face, and he clapped his hands with a thunderous boom. Dozens of ghouls were smashed together, as if caught between invisible walls, and the display of crushed bodies and black blood nearly turned Cavalor's stomach. The corpses fell to the floor, and any ghouls lucky to have evaded the attack scrambled out the door, racing after their master. But the evil aura faded as the dark clouds rolled across the sky, and the ghouls writhed beneath the sun with terrible shrieks. Their skin smoked and blistered, and they crumpled within the courtyard and ceased to move.

The ghouls were destroyed, but the zhokards had their hands full with dunarchins at the opposite end of the hall. Chandrella stood at the forefront, smiting the enemy with a mace, but the undead firstborns outnumbered her and her soldiers. The lightning from the dunarchin mages seemed only a nuisance to the zhokards and failed to keep them down, but any time one was felled by the blade, their black heart was removed, making death permanent.

Cavalor and Arkor joined the melee, with Borse close behind, but they were not enough to slow the enemy's advance. Spells of fire then arrived from the balcony, taking out the undead mages first, and the dunarchins' numbers failed at last.

The castle became still. But it was not over—not while Gulthar existed. The sound of distant horns then reached Cavalor's ears.

"What's happening?" Chandrella asked Cavalor.

"I do not know," he said. "More dunarchins? Zurkan?"

"An army approaches!" Wezlok was gazing through the arrow slits. "They are almost to Kembald, and the Death Lord rushes to join them."

Cavalor's heart sank. But it was all part of the plan. To have drawn yet another army was another success. He doubted even his mother had hoped to make it this far.

"It's the Dales!" shouted Wezlok. "An army of barbarians!"

"The Dales?" Cavalor could not believe his ears. He bolted from the castle.

Holindale had not answered the call to arms. But there they were, unexpected and unlooked for outside the western gates of Kembald. Arkor and the zhokards joined Cavalor in the abandoned courtyard, gazing at the distant army beneath banners of green that Cavalor knew to bear images of fire. The dark-skinned warriors looked to be at least ten thousand strong, and their horns continued to cry out with hope renewed.

A mass of dunarchins raced from the city to meet the Dales, and Gulthar circled the battlefield, a foreboding shadow beneath black clouds. The dragon swooped, releasing its deadly breath, and the dark king cut into the barbarians' ranks with the evil scepter.

"This is not good." Arkor looked at Cavalor. "Every Dale he kills will rise against us. He's raising another army!"

"Have your men fetch bows!" Cavalor said to Chandrella.

The commander of the zhokards frowned at Cavalor, but the zhokard soldiers responded, rushing into the castle and returning shortly with crossbows. A zhokard child handed a loaded crossbow to Cavalor, and he patted the lad on the head. But then he realized the kid might very well be older than himself—it depended on how long ago the black heart started to beat.

"The battle's too far away," Chandrella said. "No bow can reach that distance."

"Have you any strength left?" Cavalor asked Wezlok.

Wezlok was pale, and bleeding wounds bordered by darkening skin covered his body. He inhaled a shaky breath and gave a nod.

"You'll not drop him with arrows," Chandrella said. "Regardless of what magic your elf conjures."

"I agree." Cavalor turned to Wezlok. "I only intend to gain his attention."

Arkor stood next to Cavalor, the one-armed warrior's crossbow-arm ready. Cavalor looked at the zhokard archers. They were ready as well.

"Aim for the Death Lord." Cavalor raised his crossbow. "Wezlok, if you please."

Cavalor held a steady gaze with his left eye shut. In the distance was the small figure of the skeletal dragon, and barely discernable was the Death Lord atop its back. Were it not for the dark flashes of the scepter, Cavalor might not have been able to see the evil king at all. But then the view changed. It was as if he stood just outside the battlefield, within a hundred yards of the Death Lord, and the image of the undead king became clearer. Cavalor assumed the other bowmen shared his view, and he gave the order.

"Fire!"

The missiles sped across the sky, and Cavalor was amazed as his vision flew with them over the road, above the city, and across the battlefield. Wezlok's magic carried the arrows far, but only four of the zhokards found their marks. Cavalor's own arrow struck beneath the helmet, near the Death Lord's neck, and a smaller bolt, one he knew to belong to Arkor, pierced the eye slot.

Cavalor's vision returned to the courtyard, and he saw Wezlok's shoulders slump. Returning his focus to the Death Lord, he spied the undead dragon speeding toward the castle. The plan had worked! The crossbows were reloaded, and as Gulthar neared, Cavalor gave the order again.

"Fire!"

They released another volley, this time without the elf's assistance. Only three arrows found the target, and again Arkor's proved most precise, piercing the center of the breastplate. Cavalor and Arkor then pulled their swords.

Dark clouds blocked the sun, and the aura of fear returned as the Death Lord pointed his scepter. A black dart issued, striking Chandrella, and the commander collapsed. The zhokards cried in outrage, cursing Gulthar as his one eye gleamed with delight—the other had been extinguished by Arkor's arrow.

The undead dragon descended, releasing its sickly breath, and a pair of zhokards shoved Cavalor and Arkor from its path. They were spared while the soldiers took the full blast, but when the withering vapors dispersed, the zhokards were unharmed.

Making a wide circle, the dragon hissed as it returned from the direction of Kembald. It swooped low, following the road between the city and castle, and that is when Cavalor saw his father.

Borse stood near the gate towers, where the portcullises were raised. He shouted as he struck the northern tower with his hammer, and the structure trembled. He then hurried to the southern tower and did the same. The undead dragon rose above the towers before swooping down with a gaping maw, but as it came to within a few yards of the retreating priest, the towers collapsed. The monster disappeared beneath a cloud of dust, and its screech sounded again and again until all was silent.

Everyone stood, watching and waiting. Cavalor knew Gulthar had survived, for the dark clouds and the chill remained. As the dust settled, the bones of the dragon could be seen protruding from the mound of rubble in various places, but the monster did not move. A few rocks then rolled down the pile as Gulthar emerged.

The Death Lord's armor showed several dents, and he continued to walk with a slight limp—the blow received from Landerik. He stepped from the debris, and his eye flared as he pulled his sword. The scepter was missing.

Arkor was first to challenge the undead king, and the two exchanged attacks. Though damaged, Gulthar's skills were remarkable, and he drove Arkor back several paces.

Cavalor was not sure why he hesitated. Perhaps it was the aura of evil that froze his legs. But then visions of Landerik and Crismar plagued his mind, and he moved to join the battle. He arrived at Arkor's side, and it was Gulthar's turn to take a defensive position, as Cavalor and Arkor operated in perfect sync—it was as if they had fought together for years. A pair of zhokards joined the melee, but their skills paled in comparison and they were struck down several times. They always returned to the fray, however, as their black hearts pumped life into their bodies.

Gulthar continued to fend off all attackers while issuing savage strikes, and his armor seemed impenetrable. But then Borse's voice rose above the clash of steel, chanting in prayer, and steam oozed from the seams of the Death Lord's armor. Gulthar became desperate, launching a flurry of attacks, and Arkor fell when the dark blade sliced into his thigh. The glowing eye then turned on Cavalor.

Cavalor's heart raced. His father's chant brought the Death Lord obvious pain, but the evil king was unstoppable, and the wicked sword fell again and again. Cavalor stumbled over loose debris while retreating a step, and Gulthar lunged. But the Death Lord was caught off guard when Arkor's wooden arm crashed into its steel boot. The arm shattered, and Gulthar was left unbalanced.

Cavalor brought his sword across, putting into the swing all the strength he possessed. The blade sliced through the Death Lord's neck, decapitating the evil king, and the helmet bounced several feet away. The aura of dread faded as Gulthar collapsed, and the clouds dispersed, allowing the sun access to the courtyard.

Cavalor's focus returned to the Dales. To either side of him stood the zhokards, fifteen in all after the last survivors arrived from the far corners of the castle. He looked to his father, who kneeled over Arkor, and Borse nodded. Arkor would be alright.

"To battle!" Cavalor said, and he sped off down the stone road with the zhokards in his wake.

Chapter 38

The Swarm

Selanna was restless. At the base of the hills stood Trannum's castle, darker than the aging night. She saw nothing entering or exiting, but she knew the necromancer was there. She could feel him. A shiver overcame her as she recalled the horrors she witnessed therein, and the constant screams haunted her still. She doubted she could ever tell the full tale, even to Eraim.

Selanna's thoughts shifted to the questions plaguing her mind. How had Merssa fared? Did Sullis reach the dwarves? Would Soren arrive soon, if at all? And after surviving the trials of Lornibur and Maak Maak, did she and her company have the strength to combat the necromancer? Surely Trannum realized his enemy was near—the fact that Velgaad did not return could not have escaped his notice. The element of surprise was certainly lost.

"They will come." Eraim's voice stole Selanna's attention. "Soren will make it."

Selanna sensed doubt within the wry smile her companion offered. "That is not all that troubles me."

"My thoughts mirror your own, I believe." Eraim glanced at the stronghold. "What is he doing in there? How much longer should we allow him to prepare for us?"

"Do not kid yourself," Selanna said. "He is ready."

Selanna gazed at the dark realm. No animals roamed the wide fields, large or small. The only sign of life was the horde of insects buzzing about. The critters were annoying, flying near to everyone's faces and always ready to avoid a swatting hand. A few found themselves tangled within Eraim's hair, and Selanna absently ran her fingers through her own, making sure it did not house any captives of its own. Already her legs and arms were covered with bites, and the urge to scratch was becoming unbearable.

As the night progressed, a breeze rose out of the south, carrying the odor of rotting corpses. It reminded Selanna of Sistama and she wrinkled her nose, although the foul reek of that swamp could never be equaled. She decided it best to distract herself, and she shifted her attention to her companions.

Eraim was nearby, fighting a losing battle as she tried to clean her equipment. Brem sat on a patch of moist grass in meditation, appearing more worn than Selanna would have thought. Normally she would tease that his human half led to his weaknesses, but she was in no mood to joke. In his condition, she wondered what assistance Brem could provide from this point on.

Arrikan and Greyor sat apart from the priest, speaking quietly to one another. Selanna heard their whispered words as they conversed in dwarfish about Millord. Though Greyor hid it well, he was upset about the loss of his friend—Selanna could not bear the thought of losing Eraim. Arrikan insisted they would not have made it safely from Lornibur without the late dwarf's battle skills, bringing a grin to Greyor. Greyor then spoke of better days with Millord, spanning more than a hundred years of sampling taverns and hunting goblins. The conversation carried on for some time, but then Arrikan gasped after swatting her neck and inspecting her hand.

"Selanna!" The ranger spoke louder than Selanna was comfortable with. "The bugs! Have you looked at them?"

The growing number of insects was annoying, but that was the extent of Selanna's thoughts on the subject. With the stockpile of corpses Trannum kept within the castle, not to mention the zombies that wandered Dright Swamp, she expected the buggers. She hoped that by ignoring them, she would be able to avoid scratching.

Arrikan ran to Selanna, holding out her hand. The crushed insect on her palm continued to move, even with half its blackened guts on display. It was undead!

Selanna checked her arms. Every swollen bump contained a black spot within its center. She scrutinized the swarm that had settled over them, as did her companions, finding mosquitoes, horseflies, gnats, and several species she did not recognize buzzing about, and all were darker than usual. Centipedes, spiders, and beetles of many sorts crawled upon the ground as well. They were missing wings, legs, antennae, or even half of their bodies. Still, they feasted on the company.

"We have to go!" Selanna said aloud. "They are from *him*. He knows we are here!"

"What vile poison have they been infecting us with?" Eraim slapped wildly at her body to remove the creatures.

Selanna looked at the silent castle, and she could almost hear Trannum laughing. He was toying with them.

"Shouldn't we wait for Soren?" asked Arrikan. "We'll arrive too soon."

"We have no choice," Selanna said while they gathered their gear. "We must go!"

They descended the hillside, leaving behind any insects lacking the ability to fly or failing to stow away in their equipment. The bites now itched more than ever. Some even burned.

"Brem." Selanna came to a halt. "Is there anything you can do?"

The marteese pursed his lips. "Maybe for some of us. But I doubt I have the strength —"

"Whatever you can manage, you must," Selanna said. "And hurry!"

Brem looked around until spotting a maple tree. Hastening to it, the priest put his hand on its bark and closed his eyes. His mouth moved in a whisper Selanna could not hear, and his eyes opened.

"Please, as much as you can spare," he said softly, and he pulled his knife.

Brem placed a small cut on the bark, and from it issued sap that he gathered into a vial. After the flow ceased, he waved his hand over the cut and the bark was unmarred. Brem thanked the tree and turned, looking as though he had not slept in a month. He handed the vial to Selanna.

"Use as much as you need and no more," he said in a hoarse voice.

Selanna's eyes returned to the stronghold. "Perhaps I should expend some power of my own."

She had resisted the temptation to do so, fearing the use of magical energy might gain Trannum's attention. But that was pointless now. Upon completion of a short incantation, a breeze swept over them, and though it did not seem overwhelming in strength, it bore away all insects of the flying variety. Selanna then gave the vial to Eraim.

Eraim applied the sap to her many bites, one fingertip at a time. Once finished, she handed it to Arrikan. The ranger held up the container—it was half empty. With a sigh, she passed it to Selanna without using a drop.

"Your skills are more important than my own," Arrikan said.

Selanna did not argue. There was no time for good manners, and the ranger was right. They could little afford for Selanna to be distracted by the itching and burning that grew more severe with every passing moment. She applied the sap, feeling the cool healing powers of Frayorna, and the irritation subsided. The vial then contained perhaps enough for one other person.

Arrikan and Greyor looked at the bottle and then at each other.

"You have been most skilled in your arts," Greyor said. "You use it."

"Nonsense." Arrikan put her hand on the dwarf's shoulder. "This is a battle for Clanghorr! And only *you* can wield such a weapon."

Greyor took in a deep breath and nodded, accepting the vial.

"I'll do what I can," Arrikan said to Selanna while scratching her arm.

"I'm sorry." Brem scratched itches of his own.

"You have done more than enough." Selanna issued as appreciative a smile as she could muster. "I only wish there was something more I could do."

Once Greyor finished treating his skin, they headed downhill beneath the brightening sky; the dawn of another day. The castle loomed closer with every step, and it would not be long before they stood before its doors.

CHAPTER 39

NECROMANCER'S CALL

With the arrival of the dwarves to Burmagaard, the undead were overwhelmed and slaughtered without mercy. Nidor noticed Anduiff had arrived to watch the battle from above, but the evil king never assisted his troops. Upon the enemy's imminent defeat, the Death Lord returned to the east.

As the final dunarchin fell, the sky brightened with the beginning of a new day. Cheers resounded throughout the streets, and Nidor spotted Sullis. The Brondor paladin saw Nidor as well, and they worked their way through the crowd to clasp arms.

"It is great to see you!" Nidor said with genuine feeling. He knew his eyes no longer burned, for his vision was not tinted orange, but his sword was still alight. "I had almost lost hope."

"The road was not an easy one." Sullis grinned. "But we carved a path that shall never be forgotten! How I love the way these dwarves work!"

The company was reunited, and upon finding Nidor and Gruelenor, Magneer embraced his friends.

"I began to doubt I'd ever see you two again," the ranger said with watery eyes.

Nidor smiled. "Silcor smiles on us."

Gruelenor nodded.

"It is not over!" Vecnor's voice captured everyone's attention. "Feel good about this battle. But the war continues!"

"Where are the folk of Rornibur?" asked an approaching dwarf. Age lined his face and he bore a mighty war hammer, and upon his brow a jeweled-encrusted crown sparkled in the growing light. Behind him, the dwarves' faces were grim, unmoved by the victory. "I was informed that they march with the North Army."

Vecnor bowed low, and all non-dwarves followed his lead.

"King Kolermane, Lord of Varlimor." Vecnor rose. "Your kin lie to the east with what remains of the North Army. Beside them stand citizens from nearly every realm of Vaeldor, human and elf, and they have been locked in combat for more than two days. How they've fared thus far, I do not know. The Death Lord, Gruzim, leads the enemy there, and Anduiff races to join the battle."

"Then let us waste no more time with words!" The king faced his army, greater than five thousand strong. "To battle!"

Though likely worn from days of marching already, the dwarves raised their weapons and cheered a single grunt. They then headed toward the east gate, and Kolermane turned back to Vecnor.

"You fight with the strength of many dwarves," the king said. "It would honor me to have you and yours at my side."

"The honor is ours." Vecnor sheathed his swords on his back and nodded at Elloria.

The priestess gazed upon the Kalmirans, Marcs, and Nirans gathered before her, greater than two thousand warriors in all. "We march!"

"Brondor!" shouted half of the soldiers.

Nidor looked at Gruelenor, who returned a confident nod. They then turned to Magneer, who bore a wry smile.

"Guess there's no finding a tavern first," the ranger mumbled.

Nidor grinned, and it surprised him to see the slightest of smirks cross Gruelenor's lips.

The dwarves carried a steady pace across the plains of Kalmaar. There were no songs or chants, and not one of them exhibited a hint of fear. They were armed with axes, hammers, swords, and spears, and within the rear ranks were five large ballistae, each requiring four dwarves to carry. Twenty dwarves marched beside the giant crossbows in pairs to transport ten missiles — wooden shafts several feet in length and tipped by steel bands rather than points.

Kolermane led the way, with Vecnor and Elloria to his right. Nidor walked with Sullis, Gruelenor, Magneer, and Xorlunder behind the king, and farther back, among Elloria's forces, Melac sat atop Umbarc. The mage had expended much of his power to take the city, and he rode the enormous horse, hoping to regain his strength for the fight ahead.

Nidor squinted as the sun shone in his eyes, but a dark fog defied the light above the battlefield only a mile away. Commoners emerged from farmhouses to cheer as the army passed, and more than a hundred grabbed pitchforks, scythes, spades, and the like and ran to join them.

The battle came into view, and though the cloud hid much from Nidor, he spied nearly every type of undead: zombies and skeletons were unorganized and hunted all living beings; ghouls savagely attacked, some of them leaping onto their victims; dunarchins battled with discipline and skill; and wraiths circled overhead, diving in and out of the skirmish to wreak what havoc they may. The undead consisted of almost every race Nidor knew, as well as a few he had never seen, and Zurkan fought alongside the terrible wolves of Benasti.

A large village stood in the middle of the melee, with more than half of its buildings razed to the ground. One of the traitor-Kalmirans Nidor rescued in Burmagaard mentioned that Gruzim chose the town because of its population, and that the Death Lord ordered every citizen to be slain to increase the size of his force. The wide streets and fields were littered with mutilated corpses of both friend and foe; and though allies having received the Blessing of the Dead were spared from a false afterlife, those recruited along the journey knew no such protection, and they rose to fight for the enemy upon their deaths.

Most of the North Army was hidden from view, and the soldiers Nidor could see were divided. A group of Nejans were backed against a large building, possibly an inn, and surrounded by ghouls; a squadron of Philanders bore into a host of zombies while their flank was being devastated by Benasti wolves, and the Zurkan were close behind; a score of gray elves stood upon rooftops, raining arrows onto the enemy while fighting off wraiths. All appeared desperate, but as the forces from Burmagaard entered the haze, they fought with strength renewed.

The cloud was darker than it seemed from the outside, and the foul reek of evil and death assaulted Nidor's lungs. Some of the surrounding soldiers coughed and gagged, and Nidor resisted the urge to hold a cloth over his mouth. Though unseen, the presence of the Death Lords was unmistakable, and the aura sent the farmers screaming back to their homes.

Anduiff descended from his hiding place within the fog, halting the advance of the dwarves and Elloria's soldiers. The undead dragon released its poisonous breath onto the Morimont warriors, and a score of the mountain folk collapsed, their bodies aged and shriveled.

The ballistae bearers readied the enormous weapons as the dragon circled back. Each crossbow required three dwarves to balance the front ends onto long, y-shaped poles while another pair cranked the winches. Once the thick cords were locked into place, they loaded the blunted missiles. A dwarf commander barked orders throughout the process in their own tongue, and he continued to do so as the bottom ends of the giant bows were rotated to take aim. The commander then shouted a short, loud order, and they released the cords. Steel-capped logs soared into the sky, and although two missed the mark, the others flew true. One cracked the dragon's hind leg, and another shattered its ribs. The final projectile smashed into the creature's jaw, destroying its skull, and the dragon crashed away to the south in an explosion of dirt and bones.

Nidor could see why Sullis held such high regard for the way the Morimont folk operated!

The army of humans and dwarves roared as they charged into the village, and Vecnor advanced upon a mix of zombies and ghouls with both swords, dropping all undead within reach. The dwarves veered to the right of the large warrior's path, and Elloria and her guard fought to the left; and while Xorlunder worked his way toward the gray elves, Sullis and Melac were separated and disappeared.

Nidor remained near Vecnor, with Gruelenor by his side and Magneer nearby. Nidor's vision was tinted orange as his eyes flared, doubling his sight within the cloud, and his flaming blade required a single hit to drop his enemies. The protective flashes of fire returned, keeping his body pure, and any undead daring to touch him were severely wounded or destroyed.

Several cells of the North Army were then reunited. A group of Mocs freed the Nejans from the ghouls that surrounded them, and Vircans intercepted the Zurkan before the Benasti warriors reached the Philanders. Beyond a pile of rubble, Salenti elves fired arrows at an army of ghouls and used magic against wraiths, and surrounding the elves were a couple hundred Sendors that fought back advancing zombies and skeletons.

But the necromancer was not finished, and from the south wailed an eerie horn. No less than four thousand dunarchins then arrived with Anduiff at the lead, the Death Lord having recovered from the crash. The undead king pointed his sword, and the evil warriors drove a wedge between the Morimont soldiers and all others.

"We're cut off!" called Magneer.

The dwarves had disappeared, and Elloria and her men were gone, having rushed into the mass of zombies attacking the Sendors. The nearest soldiers of the North Army were no less than thirty yards away, and ghouls filled the gap between them. There was nothing to do but fight, and Nidor charged the advancing dunarchins.

The undead firstborns hesitated, appearing fearful of Nidor, and he reduced a dozen of the evil warriors to ashes. An enemy sword slashed his left arm, as the protective fire failed to deflect the blade, and though Nidor felt no pain, he altered his tactics to afford himself some protection.

Vecnor was nearby, equaling Nidor's number of slain dunarchins, and Magneer and Gruelenor protected their flanks, slaying ghouls. Nidor's friends fought admirably, but they lacked the strength of Vecnor and the Flames of Silcor, and they grew weary as the battle raged on. Nidor was amazed at how well four warriors fared in the face of impossible odds, but their luck could not last.

Help arrived when Elloria returned with five hundred soldiers, and Sullis was with her. The priestess wielded swords in either hand with great proficiency, and Sullis fought with the skill of many years. Behind them trailed onetime companions of Burmagaard—fresh zombies from the battle.

"This day will never end!" Sullis struck down a ghoul. "We must defeat the Death Lords if we are to achieve victory!"

"Anduiff is to the south!" Magneer called out. "I've not seen Gruzim!"

"I'm going after Anduiff!" Sullis said. "But I'll need a path!"

Elloria issued orders, and she and half her men bore into the dunarchins. Sullis joined them, disappearing into the mass, and the undead firstborns filled in behind.

Nidor sensed an ill wind to the southeast. Turning, he spotted a dark warrior bearing a long, wicked spear, and from its tip crackled flashes of lightning. It was the same Death Lord he had seen in Nira. Gruzim sat atop a skeletal dragon as it alit just outside the battlefield.

"There he is!" Nidor pointed his sword. "Gruzim is there!"

Sullis fought alongside Elloria and her soldiers. The warriors were well trained, and Elloria was exquisite in the way she handled two blades, never favoring one over the other. Sullis wished he had time to admire her technique longer, but he spied Anduiff, slaying dwarves with sword and axe and sending their newly animated bodies to do his bidding.

Ire filled Sullis's heart, a fire he summoned from deep within to abolish all fear. He remembered all too well that night in the cave, when he first experienced the aura of a Death Lord, and he swore he would never be affected so again. His cowardice had insulted Brondor, and now his chance of redemption was at hand. The glowing eyes of the undead king found him, and without a command, the dunarchins cleared a path.

Sullis advanced, and he and Anduiff were quickly locked in combat. Having trained since he could walk, Sullis put on an exhibition to drive the Death Lord several paces. He scored a hit on the dark warrior's leg, but it was minor at best, and Anduiff answered with a flurry of slashes. Giving ground, Sullis fended off the evil lord until the axe shattered his blade. He danced back, seeking another weapon, but there were none within reach. He was defenseless.

Kolermane's hammer crashed into Anduiff's shoulder, stealing the undead king's attention and surely crushing the bone. The sword fell from the Death Lord's grasp, and Anduiff countered, slicing into Kolermane's breastplate with the dark axe. The Morimont king collapsed.

Sullis cursed under his breath. He did not welcome assistance in this matter. This was single combat with a worthy adversary, and he would rather die fighting than win with the help of another! He slammed into Anduiff, shouldering the frozen armor and seizing the handle of the axe, but the chill the dark king exuded penetrated deep into Sullis's soul and his strength failed him. Anduiff lifted Sullis and cast him aside; and the wind was knocked from his body when landed on the unforgiving ground. He struggled to rise, but Anduiff brought down the axe, and the evil weapon sliced through steel, flesh, muscle, and bone, severing Sullis's left arm.

Through watery eyes, Sullis saw Elloria join the fray, her swords striking the black plates multiple times but failing to penetrate. The Death Lord turned on her, and she danced back several paces, avoiding the bloody axe. Anduiff pressed, and Elloria stumbled into a dunarchin and nearly fell.

"Finish her!" Anduiff commanded, and four dunarchins forced the priestess to abandon her battle with the undead king.

Sullis prepared for the worst as the blue eyes returned to him, but Anduiff lowered the axe and looked into the sky, unmoving for several seconds. The Death Lord then scanned the battlefield until his gaze met another Death Lord's, fifty yards away. It had to be Gruzim. The two seemed to exchange words, but Sullis heard nothing. Gruzim's attention appeared bent on Vecnor as the large man hacked through the undead, and when Gruzim turned back to Anduiff, he shook his head. Anduiff's eyes grew brighter, and again Gruzim refused.

Anduiff reached up his arm, and a skeletal dragon swooped from the clouds, grabbing hold with a bony claw and lifting the Death Lord from the battlefield. The dark king swung atop the creature and rode to the south, disappearing in great haste.

Vecnor witnessed the exchange of the Death Lords, and he could guess what had transpired. Years ago in Neja, Gruzim had wished to challenge Vecnor, and as the glowing eyes fell upon him now, he knew Gruzim still harbored that hunger.

Gruzim strode forward, and all in the Death Lord's path met their ends on the tip of the deadly spear, regardless of allegiance — lightning enveloped the bodies, causing them to convulse for several moments even after the weapon was pulled free. The enemy then cleared the way. Whether by fear or silent command, Vecnor did not know.

From Vecnor's armor protruded the broken shaft of an arrow that had pierced him during the exodus of Darmhorng Dungeon, and he had received wounds to his arm, leg, and chest since. But he pushed away all pain, as he had done for days now, and readied his swords.

Gruzim made the first move, slashing with the long spear. It was a feeble attack, meant to draw Vecnor closer, but he refused to take the bait and they circled.

"You cannot win," said Gruzim.

Though deeper and hollow, Vecnor recognized the krukari's voice. "Your days are numbered! Look around you. Your war is lost."

Even as they exchanged words, the alliance of humans, elves, and dwarves was proving too much for the undead army.

"You know nothing!" Gruzim lunged, this time with lethal force.

Vecnor knocked the spear aside and countered with both swords, but Gruzim was equal to the challenge, fending him off with the haft of the long weapon. The Death Lord slashed with the sharpened edge of the spear and Vecnor parried. He did not anticipate lightning racing up his blade, and as his left arm convulsed, he dropped the sword.

Gruzim's eyes pulsated with delight, and he brought up the butt of his spear, driving Vecnor back with a blow to the breastplate. The Death Lord pressed, swinging the spear-blade, and Vecnor danced from its path, not wanting to lose his other sword. Gruzim then halted when an arrow pierced his helmet. The missile drove deep, its point puncturing one side and passing through the other. Vecnor turned to see a familiar gray elf standing tall and proud.

Xorlunder held his bow, and at the elf's feet were two dunarchins, a ghoul, and three Zurkan, all with smoking wounds. With great agility, Xorlunder drew his sword and decapitated a ghoul approaching him from behind. He then sheathed the weapon and fit another arrow to the bowstring.

"Be gone!" Vecnor shouted, but it was too late.

From Gruzim's spear came the crackle of energy, and it released a bolt of lightning. Xorlunder's body lit up as he was struck, and he flew several yards away, disappearing into the scrum. Gruzim turned back to Vecnor with the arrow protruding from either side of the helmet.

Vecnor twirled his sword from side to side, and Gruzim fended off the blows and countered, attempting to sweep Vecnor's feet from beneath him. Vecnor leaped over the spear and came down with the pommel of his sword, denting the black helmet. Gruzim staggered a couple paces and Vecnor pressed, flailing his weapon and keeping the Death Lord on the defense. He then spun, catching Gruzim with a low swing and cutting deep into the evil warrior's left thigh. His sword became lodged within the cold steel, and it was ripped from his grasp when Gruzim gave him a shove.

The Death Lord moved with a limp, and he jerked the blade free and cast it aside. Vecnor lifted a sword from the battlefield as the spear lowered, and lightning discharged, driving him to one knee. Gruzim maintained a steady stream while he approached, and Vecnor could do nothing to prevent it.

"Now you die slow!" Gruzim said. "Now you can gaze upon your master as life is wrenched from your body. And I'll have your corpse as my personal servant for all eternity!"

The lightning ceased when a sword hewed the spear in two. Standing in blood-soaked armor was Gruelenor, panting with fatigue.

"You fool!" Gruzim struck Gruelenor with his gauntlet, knocking the krukari to the ground. Gruzim's eyes were almost white with rage. "You mean nothing to these vermin! You're an abomination!"

Gruelenor rose, fresh blood issuing from his mouth, and glared at the Death Lord. "Go to Hell where you belong!" He spit at Gruzim's feet.

Gruzim drew his sword, preparing to finish the one Vecnor knew to be the Death Lord's eldest son, and Gruelenor stood his ground, seeming to welcome his fate.

Vecnor roared and charged, every muscle twitching from the lightning, and he and Gruzim squared off again. Sword against sword, the weapons clashed, and they both inflicted wounds upon the other, but only Vecnor suffered any ill effects. His body ached as the foray into Darmhorng, the contest for Burmagaard, the current battle, and the agony the lightning imposed took their toll. Gruzim surely limped due to structural damage, and likely felt no pain.

With a deep breath, Vecnor executed his next move. With a feigned attack, much like Gruzim attempted at the beginning of the fight, he lured the Death Lord forward. He slapped the dark sword aside and slashed Gruzim across the chest, and the sword emitted sparks as it snapped in two. The force pushed Gruzim back several paces, and Vecnor followed with a punch to the helmet and drove the Death Lord a few more. Scooping Gruzim's broken spear from the ground, Vecnor swung its sharpened edge, and the blade passed through the black armor with ease. Vecnor struck again and again, severing the Death Lord's left arm and then the right. With a final blow, he cleaved the helmet from atop Gruzim's shoulders.

Gruzim's body fell, and the evil aura dissipated. The sun broke through the dark fog and the remaining ghouls and wraiths scattered, but they found no shelter before the rays of light devoured their forms. Leaderless, the zombies and skeletons were overwhelmed, and arrows pursued the fleeing dunarchins.

As the last of the clouds dissolved, the battle was over, and humans, elves, and dwarves cheered as one into the blue sky.

Vecnor's knees buckled, and he collapsed.

Chapter 40

Battle Rages On!

Cavalor led the way along the streets of Kembald, with the zhokards close behind. The city was silent, and buildings stood cold to either side; and if any undead lurked within, they did not make their presence known. As they neared the western edge, a few hisses sounded from alleys and other dark places. But still nothing emerged beneath the sun, and Cavalor did not deter from his path.

The western gates were wide open, revealing the battle beyond. The Dales wore furs and mismatched armor of chain and rings, and they wielded axes, hammers, swords, spears, maces, and mauls. One thing common to every barbarian was their orange-and-red hair, colored to show their dedication to the fire deity. They outnumbered the evil forces, and in the absence of Gulthar's aura, their dead remained dead and the enemy received no reinforcements. The Dales hewed zombies with little effort, and they might have overwhelmed the dunarchins as well, were it not for the spell casters—eight robed dunarchins released lightning from atop the city wall, killing dozens of barbarians at a time.

"To the walls!" Cavalor led the way to the north gate tower.

They raced up two flights of stairs that emptied onto the battlements. The dunarchin mages remained focused on the battle below, and as Cavalor struck the nearest one, the zhokards continued toward the remaining seven. The creatures' glowing eyes turned on the zhokards and they unleashed their magic; and while bolts of energy threw several zhokards from the wall, the mages were quickly defeated.

Cavalor watched the fallen zhokards regain their feet to return to the battlements, and he shook his head and grinned. "I'm glad to have you on my side!"

A nearby zhokard looked at Cavalor, the soldier's face grim. "We're not on your side. We only share your goal for the moment."

Returning to the street, they charged through the gates and into the rear ranks of the evil forces. The zhokards showed no mercy, and they put on a display; and though Cavalor lacked the ability to return from the dead, he rose above them in skill, slaying greater than a score of dunarchins. Before long, the zhokards were recognized for what they were, and a few of them failed to rise after their hearts were removed.

"Watch the left flank!"

A zhokard issued the warning, and Cavalor saw an army approaching from the south. Zombies and skeletons made up the front ranks, and behind them marched another legion of dunarchins. Soon, he and the dozen remaining zhokards would be pinned between two armies.

His mind raced, but then he heard the voice of his father, loud and commanding above the roar. He did not understand the words, but a resounding clap of thunder told him Borse's hammer had struck the ground. A tremor resulted, and the land beneath the approaching army shook as it opened up. After swallowing nearly a third of the undead, the fissure closed. The hammer pounded again and again, devastating the reinforcements before they ever reached the battlefield.

"You didn't think I'd remain behind, did you?"

Arkor was next to Cavalor; and though he lacked his wooden arm, he hewed three zombies and a couple of dunarchins. Together, Cavalor and Arkor destroyed undead beyond count.

The battle ended, and Cavalor, Arkor, Borse, and the remaining zhokards met the Dales on the field. The barbarians balked, realizing the warriors before them to be among the living, and they held their weapons ready. A large Dale clad only in the skin of a leopard and decorated in war paint then barked orders in his tribal language, and hundreds of Dales gave chase to the dunarchins fleeing to the south.

"Sorry we are late." The large Dale spoke slowly, using the common tongue.

Arkor grinned. "I'd say you arrived just in time."

"We didn't think you were coming at all," Cavalor added.

"At first," the man frowned, searching for the words, "maybe not. Nidor sends word. Tells us of the importance of this war. But fighting against non-living creatures..." He shook his head. "That is bad luck. No one of my people wished to do such things."

"What changed your mind?" asked Arkor.

"Small elf-man," the Dale replied. "He visits us and shows us what will happen if we do not fight against non-living. In the end, bad luck for the living is better than no luck for the dead. So we gathered our army, and he led us here."

"Elgarroth?" Arkor furrowed his brow.

"Yes!" The Dale raised a finger. "That was his name."

"Where is he now?" asked Cavalor. "Is he with you?"

"No." The man shook his head. "Elf-man headed south after we pass through mountains."

Cavalor nodded. It would have been nice if Elgarroth had accompanied the Dales. Perhaps the wizard could have told them if their seeming victory was in vain.

His attention turned skyward when black clouds rolled out of the north. The mass of darkness moved overhead, blocking the westerly sun, and beneath it rode a Death Lord holding an axe. Cavalor knew it to be Anduiff, and an eerie chill captured the battlefield as the fallen Dales stirred.

"He must be stopped!" Cavalor felt powerless. The skeletal beast was moving faster than anything Cavalor had ever seen, and all around him, zombies were rising.

A ball of flame streaked across the sky, its speed unmatched even by the dragon. It struck the mount upon the skull, shattering it, and the monster fell away to the south, taking its rider with it. The clouds dissipated and the sun's light returned.

Standing at the city gate was Wezlok with an outstretched hand. Though Cavalor believed the mage to have been drained of strength, the elf found the power to unleash the attack. It must have been truly taxing, for Wezlok collapsed.

The castle defenders joined the Dales as they battled corpses of their onetime allies, friends, and family members. Cavalor was sure this weighed upon the barbarians' hearts, but still they cried out in victory once the fighting was done.

Cavalor saw his father tending to Wezlok, and he turned his gaze to the south, wondering what Anduiff's arrival meant. Had Trannum called for his generals to return? Or perhaps the North Army had failed and the undead king was on his way to inform his master.

A hand touched Cavalor's shoulder, stirring him from his thoughts. It was Arkor.

"We have done all that we can," the one-armed warrior said. "Now it's up to others to finish it."

CHAPTER 41

DARK ONE'S THRONE

After exiting the foothills, Eraim led the way across a wide field of dead weeds toward Trannum's stronghold, her heart beating faster than she could ever recall. Following were Selanna and Greyor, and Arrikan and Brem trudged along as best they could, fighting the urge to scratch the bites that now oozed pus and blood. As they drew nearer to the dark structure, the unmistakable aura of a Death Lord brought Eraim to a stop.

"I guess it would've been too much to have hoped for no Death Lords," Greyor mumbled.

"I would have been shocked if at least one was not present," Selanna said.

"Who do you suppose it is?" Arrikan rubbed her sores.

"I do not know." Selanna frowned. "Cadorn, I would think. Trannum would want one of his stronger generals nearby, and Radaam is often at Ironside Keep."

The castle lacked normal defenses—there was no moat, no towers, and no surrounding wall. The only entrance Eraim noticed was a single wooden door, twenty feet in height and ten feet wide, and carved upon it was the familiar black triangle and blue oval.

"Is there no other way in?" Eraim asked Selanna. The last thing she wished to do was walk through the front entrance and announce their arrival. She doubted the necromancer was in the mood to entertain.

Selanna stared at the door with a grim expression. "One other way."

They followed Selanna to the west side, between the stronghold and the Trethel River. On the third level, a large opening existed in the castle wall.

"That is where the dragons are created," Selanna said.

"How do we get up *there*?" Greyor frowned. "I'd rather just smash down the door!"

"I will take care of it." Eraim reached for her rope. But then she remembered it was still dangling within the chamber of the ice demon—that is, if the mine dweller had not taken it home as a new toy.

"Do not worry." Selanna sighed. "It is my turn. Everyone hold hands."

They did as instructed, forming a circle, and Selanna closed her eyes. Eraim then felt weightless as they rose from the ground. Greyor gasped, and Brem and Arrikan winced as the dwarf squeezed their hands. Greyor shut his eyes and prayed while they floated over thirty feet upward, and once they reached the oval opening, they drifted into the castle. They were set gently onto the stone floor of a large chamber, and Greyor opened one eye. He stomped his boot to test the flagstones and released a long breath.

The aging sun illuminated the room, but it brought no warmth into the frozen stronghold. The light revealed bones of immense sizes, separated into piles, and tables existed along the edges, holding various tools and jars of strange liquids. Without a word, Selanna walked to the only set of doors the chamber possessed.

After pausing to listen, Selanna opened the doors. Beyond, a dark corridor stretched left and right. She looked both ways before heading left, and her small light materialized and rose above her head.

Eraim and the others followed in single file. The hallway was cold and stale, and the very air soured Eraim's stomach and made every breath laborious. Other than the heavy footfalls of Greyor, the castle was silent as a tomb—the dwarf's armor rattled with each step, echoing about the high ceiling.

"Whoa!" Greyor said, halting Eraim and Selanna near the corridor's end.

Eraim looked to see that Brem and Arrikan had turned blue, and both of them shivered. The venom of the undead bugs was not finished with them.

"I am sorry," Selanna said. "There is nothing I can do."

"C-c-c-continue." Arrikan nodded. "D-don't worry ab-b-bout us."

Selanna released a sympathetic sigh and proceeded.

The passage ended at a flight of stairs descending to the second level, and the company crept downward and into a chamber filled with large vats. Though the containers were empty, Selanna shuddered, most likely remembering things she would rather forget.

Five dunarchins entered through a door, brandishing swords, and Eraim and Greyor charged to meet them. Eraim darted about, evading attacks and carving down one with Mithkahr while Greyor sliced two others in half. Eraim then ducked an attack before cleaving another dunarchin, and she and Greyor converged upon the final one, slaying it without delay.

"I think it best you two take the lead." Selanna nodded toward the door the dunarchins had used.

Eraim and Greyor passed through the door and into a hallway. Doors lined the walls of its fifty-foot length before it turned left.

"These are laboratories," Selanna said. "Keep moving around the bend."

They traveled the corridor with weapons ready, and Eraim listened as best she could while passing each door. Outside of Greyor's movements, there were no other sounds. At one point she motioned for Greyor to remain still, thinking she had heard something, but all remained silent.

Around the corner, the hallway contained several doors to the left side. Selanna held up three fingers, and Eraim walked to the third door and placed her ear to the wood. Silence.

Eraim pulled the door open, and a rush of icy air greeted her. A single torch partially illuminated a large chamber devoid of furnishings, and upon the walls were splayed strange runes. At the far end to the right was a wide, curving staircase descending into an area of flickering light, and to the left of the steps, a solid wood railing overlooked the lower level. From the shadows below, Eraim detected faint whispers.

She motioned for everyone to stay put and crept in without a sound. Fear gripped Eraim's stomach, becoming almost painful, and she thought she might vomit. Choking down the compulsion, she crouched low and continued. By the time she reached the railing, she was practically crawling.

Eraim took in a few deep breaths before rising tall enough to see the area below. It was a throne room, dimly lit by a couple of torches. Upon a seat of bones was a skeletal figure robed in black, and from beneath the hood shone one blue eye. Trannum. The necromancer sat, facing the left side of the room, and he was not alone. Slightly behind the morbid chair within the shadows, a set of glowing eyes revealed a Death Lord Eraim knew to be Radaam, and in the center of the chamber stood a score of dunarchins. The undead soldiers were different, for their eyes were dark, and they did not move. Did dunarchins sleep?

The whispering chant continued, though no one moved, and try as she might, Eraim could not make out the words. She was startled when Trannum's head turned, rotating toward the stairs. It tilted back to gaze upward, and she fell behind the railing, hoping she had not been spotted.

"So you've arrived at last," came a scratchy voice; a voice Eraim had heard many years ago within the Stone Eagle Mountains. "You may use the stairs. Come. Now!"

Trannum's tone rose in both strength and pitch with the final word, making Eraim's head spin. She lost all sense of up and down until something tugged at her arm, and her eyes fluttered, as if she awoke from a trance. Selanna held Eraim's right arm, and she realized she had been walking toward the stairwell.

"Where are you going?" Selanna whispered, pulling Eraim down and behind the railing.

"Thank you." Eraim released a controlled breath. "I guess I could not resist his command."

Selanna frowned. "What command?"

The pain returned to Eraim's stomach, and she placed her back against the railing. "He's down there."

Selanna stood, with no attempt to conceal herself. Eraim reached out, thinking the necromancer had cast a spell on her companion, but Selanna brushed away her hand and turned to the throne with angry eyes.

"Ahh! Selanna." Trannum cackled aloud. "You've returned. Your appearance was much more appealing the last time you passed through these halls."

Selanna gasped.

Did Trannum know all along that Selanna had been infiltrating his stronghold for years? Had Selanna been but a pawn in Trannum's plans? It seemed to Eraim that her companion was suddenly short of breath.

Eraim put her hand on Selanna's arm. "Do not listen!"

Selanna stepped back and took in a deep breath. She appeared even angrier now, and she stepped forward again.

"Today you shall meet your end!" she said, and though Eraim knew anger flowed through her companion's veins, she noticed Selanna's legs were shaking. "Your reign is crumbling as we speak."

Trannum cackled again. "Fools! Do you think I care for your armies to the north? Even with your petty victories, your dead litter the land! There will always be soldiers waiting to rebuild my forces."

"You cannot raise the dead once you are destroyed!" Selanna said through clenched teeth.

There came a crash from below, and Eraim heard a familiar voice.

"By Soleran's Might!" shouted Soren. "Your tyranny has reached its end!"

Eraim rose to see the dunarchins' eyes were kindled. The undead firstborns drew their weapons and advanced, and Soren charged into the room, followed by Rholmar and Pallit.

"To battle!" Selanna said, and Greyor ran toward the stairs.

Eraim swallowed her fear and rushed past the dwarf, descending to the throne room in seconds. To her left, her companions from the swamp battled the dunarchins, and to the right were Trannum and Radaam. The necromancer and Death Lord watched in silence, perhaps enjoying the show in some twisted way.

Remnants of Dright Swamp covered Soren and company, as well as blood and signs of various wounds, but they fought with passion. Soren stood over the corpses of three dunarchins, and to his left, Rholmar had felled three others. Pallit destroyed a dunarchin, but he received a crippling gash to his right leg and he fell. Lorylla jumped before the ranger, defeating two dunarchins with speed and grace. Nilborg entered next, calling upon Soleran, and a dark blue glow surrounded the priest, similar to the one Merssa produced many times, although of a different color. The undead firstborns seemed fearful of Nilborg, and he slew two with his morningstar.

Eraim advanced on the dunarchins. She would need all the help she could get if she was to combat Trannum *and* one of his greatest Death Lords. She attacked the undead from behind, but Greyor did not join her.

Soren dropped another dunarchin before he noticed a small elf swinging a red-tinted blade into the rear of the enemy. It was Eraim. When Soren and his companions arrived, they saw no sign that the company from the mines had made it, and now his heart rose at the thought that Selanna was nearby.

"Prepare to taste Clanghorr's edge!" a deep voice boomed.

It was a blessed phrase, although uttered by one Soren did not expect. Greyor held the ancient weapon given to Millord before the march began, and Soren was sure he understood why. Greyor voiced his challenge to the Death Lord Soren recognized as Radaam, and the two stood before a hooded skeleton seated on a throne of bones. Though Soren had never met the necromancer, he knew it to be Trannum.

Radaam held a pair of black swords. The larger blade possessed many teeth along one edge and the hilt bore strange hooks, and the smaller weapon left a trail of greenish-black liquid while the Death Lord dragged its tip across the stone floor. Radaam's eyes grew bright as hollow whispers issued from beneath the dark helmet, somehow audible above the tumult, and the dwarf's body jerked about, as if in horrible pain. Greyor fell to his knees with a scream, and Radaam advanced.

Soren cut down the final dunarchin in his path and charged. He lunged with his sword before the Death Lord could strike the dwarf, and Radaam retreated a step and knocked his weapon aside. The dark warrior countered with the larger blade, an attack easily defended, and attempted to lock Soren's sword within the hooks. But Soren was no fool, and he twirled his blade, freeing the evil weapon from the Death Lord's grasp. It landed with a loud *clang* several feet away.

Radaam swung his empty gauntlet, as if backhanding an invisible insect, and Soren flew across the room and into the wall. Radaam then waved the gauntlet back, and Soren was pulled forward. He could not stop himself, not even when he spied the Death Lord's dripping sword held out to meet him, and the weapon was buried to the hilt. Soren gasped as a fog encompassed his mind, and everything began moving slowly, as if in a dream. Radaam kicked Soren from the blade, and he crashed to the floor. But he felt no pain.

"No!" gasped Selanna, almost in unison with Rholmar's voice below.

The melee versus the dunarchins had been going well enough, so Selanna focused on the throne, waiting to see what devilry Trannum unleashed so she might counter it. The necromancer, however, was unmoving. Selanna had tried to prevent Radaam's attack on Soren, but it had happened so fast that she was too late. And now the Soleran paladin lay crumpled on the floor.

Rholmar obviously shared Selanna's view, and the Arronaus paladin finished the dunarchin before him and charged Radaam. Greyor stood before the Death Lord, having overcome the evil magic, and he held Clanghorr ready as Rholmar arrived.

Rholmar attacked, drawing a parry from Radaam, and Greyor sliced through the dark steel and across the Death Lord's stomach. No blood issued, but Radaam retreated to take a defensive stance.

Trannum rose from the chair, lifting a long staff composed of bones and topped by a small, demonic skull. He rapped it on the floor, causing a clap of thunder that resounded throughout the castle, and dozens of hands punched through the flagstones. The grisly appendages were covered by decaying flesh and oozing sores, and they reached for the feet of the living. Trannum then waved his bony hand, and a shimmering portal opened to his left, allowing another score of dunarchins into the chamber.

Selanna launched tiny green spheres from each of her fingertips, and the globes sped around the room, striking the hands and causing them to shake and withdraw. The spell placed only a dent in the number that existed, however, and the hands hindered all but Nilborg—upon touching the priest's aura, they sank into the stone, smoking and quivering. Selanna cast her spell again and again, buying her companions the time they needed to defeat the original dunarchins. But more hands rose, and the evil reinforcements began the melee anew.

Lorylla remained near Pallit, dancing about with finesse, but the hands hampered her movement as three dunarchins arrived. Favoring his leg, Pallit destroyed one of the undead soldiers before slicing the appendage clutching Lorylla's left boot, and she fended off the other two while Pallit struck the other hand to free her. In his efforts, Pallit paid a terrible price when a dunarchin scored a gash across his stomach, and Selanna knew the wound to be deep. Lorylla stepped to Pallit's front to ward off the enemy, but more hands clutched at her and caused her to stumble. Selanna released additional green spheres, clearing the area around the gray elf, and Lorylla slew the dunarchin that had struck Pallit before squaring off with the other.

Eraim moved about, hacking the hands that reached for her feet. She then leaped onto the stairs as five dunarchins arrived, and spun, hewing the head from one—it was then that Selanna realized the steps were free of the morbid hands. The dunarchins pressed Eraim up to the balcony, and she dropped two more before receiving a terrible wound to her leg. Selanna released a wave of fire over Eraim's final attackers, and their burning corpses tumbled down the staircase.

Arrikan arrived to Eraim's side. The ranger still shivered, and discharge from the bug bites ran black and red on her bluish skin.

"I can no longer fight," Eraim said through clenched teeth as Arrikan helped her to the railing. "They need me down there."

Arrikan looked into the room, and Selanna knew the ranger spotted her husband, kneeling behind Lorylla and clutching his blood-soaked abdomen. With a deep breath, Arrikan drew her blade and descended the stairs.

"Arrikan!" Eraim shouted.

The ranger did not stop.

Selanna launched another score of green spheres to assist her companions, even if only for a moment. The dunarchins' numbers were then reduced to less than half, but the hands continued to hamper the living. Selanna wished to do more, but she needed to focus on the throne.

Radaam remained out of Clanghorr's reach, and Greyor and Rholmar were powerless to advance as sickly appendages held their feet and a pair of dunarchins opposed them. Greyor severed the limbs of his attacker, reducing the undead firstborn to a pile of body parts, and Rholmar freed one of his legs and maneuvered as best he could. The paladin then destroyed his foe, but not before suffering wounds to his shoulder and ribs.

Selanna sent more spheres to release Rholmar and Greyor from the grasping hands, but they still failed to reach the Death Lord as another group of dunarchins issued from the portal. Selanna then gaped in disbelief when Radaam passed through the gateway and it vanished. How was that possible? She knew Radaam had taken a couple of wounds, but was he capable of abandoning his master? Did he fear for his un-life the way mortals feared their own mortality?

Trannum was seemingly too occupied to notice Radaam's departure, and he lowered the staff at Greyor. The dwarf raised Clanghorr in defense as a black beam issued from the demonic skull, and the runes on the weapon glowed, orange at first, but becoming white. The dark beam disappeared in a flash of bright light, and Greyor was unharmed—there was more to that ancient axe than Selanna knew.

She cast another spell, placing more power into it than she had the green spheres, and from her palm launched a ball of fire that struck the staff of bone. The weapon shattered into thousands of pieces, and Trannum's eye turned her way.

"You wish to test me?"

Trannum's voice shouted in Selanna's head, and from his bony finger came a dart of pure black. The missile hit the railing before her and exploded, launching her across the upper chamber.

Eraim could not sit and hide. This battle was too important. And if they did not win... She dared not finish the thought. Mithkahr might be unable to help her at the moment, but she had her bow and seven arrows.

While Selanna focused on the throne, Eraim maneuvered until she could spy the room below. Arrikan fought desperately, but four dunarchins separated her from Pallit. Lorylla was before Pallit, and the gray elf danced about with incredible agility, severing the head of one attacker with a white-hot blade. But then a decayed hand anchored Lorylla to the floor.

Eraim took aim and fired, piercing the eye of a dunarchin and collapsing it. After doing the same to a second dunarchin, Lorylla and Arrikan slew the final one, and the rangers were reunited.

A flash emanated from the throne, and the ghastly hands shriveled and retreated into the flagstones. Eraim turned to see Greyor holding Clanghorr forward, and the runes upon the blade were glowing white. Had the axe banished the hands? Next, the bone-staff exploded, and Trannum launched a dark bolt toward the balcony. Eraim ducked, but the attack had not been meant for her. It destroyed the railing to her left, where Selanna stood. Eraim worried about her friend's sudden absence, but her companions needed her help and she returned her attention to the room.

Nilborg had joined Rholmar and Greyor, and the three battled dunarchins fifteen feet from the throne. But where was Radaam? At least a dozen fresh dunarchins were present, but the Death Lord was gone. Eraim fired a couple of arrows, dropping two of the enemy, but then the necromancer's head turned her way and she froze.

Selanna returned to what remained of the railing. Her robes were tattered and scorched, but her face showed more determination than fear. Eraim's confidence grew, and she fired another arrow while Selanna released a ball of flame. The fire sped from the balcony and toward the necromancer, but Trannum waved his bony hand and the missile swerved into Nilborg's chest. The priest flew into the wall, and the blue aura faded as his body slumped. Eraim and Selanna gasped in unison.

Greyor broke free of the dunarchins and rushed Trannum with a roar. The necromancer's eye turned on the dwarf, and a loud *crack* sounded as a portion of the ceiling descended from high above. Selanna waved her hands to the side, and the chunk of stone veered with her motion, but she could not stop it from striking Greyor. He was driven to the floor; and though the blow would have certainly killed most any man, he sat up, shaking his head.

Eraim shot down two more dunarchins, reducing their number to ten. She then sighed in frustration. Her quiver was empty. Now she *was* useless. She gazed at Trannum, filled with desperation, and a voice sounded in her mind. It was not the necromancer's this time, but her own, recalling words she had spoken to Selanna and Elgarroth many years ago in Tikken City.

My fear is that there may be six.

It was a thought that had occurred to Eraim while pondering the first verse from the Prophecy of Trannum: *Power of five, united by one.* Though the Council of Wizards believed there to be five orbs, Eraim was not so sure.

What if the one *is not part of the* five?

The phrase echoed in her mind.

What if the one *is not part of the* five?

Trannum's attention returned to Selanna, and as the bony hands rose, Eraim narrowed her eyes. Her vision passed into the skull, and she spotted it. An orb. It was smaller than those she had seen in the past, but she was sure of it. No one had given Trannum's eye a second thought, since all the necromancer's minions possessed the same glowing eyes. But an orb generated *this* light.

Eraim turned to announce her discovery to Selanna, but her companion was countering a black dart with a green barrier that cracked and vanished. Then another thought occurred.

What if he hears me?

Reflexively, Eraim reached into her quiver and withdrew an arrow—there was still one left! With a prayer on her lips, she took careful aim and released the bowstring. Time slowed while the missile crossed the room, and as it neared its destination, Trannum's head turned Eraim's way. She held her breath, for the target had shifted, but the arrow veered as well, and it pierced the eye socket.

There was a small explosion as the necromancer's skull shattered, and the black robes collapsed into a heap. The surviving dunarchins looked to escape, but Rholmar and Lorylla fought with renewed strength, and Greyor regained his feet and joined them. The undead firstborns were destroyed and the aura of evil faded. But the chill remained.

Anxiety entered Eraim's chest, and she found it hard to breathe. Was she dreaming? She gazed into the room below, and her ears seemed to work exceptionally well.

Arrikan still shivered, and she looked hideous with the oozing sores. But she smiled as she cradled Pallit's ashen face on her lap, and he smiled in return.

"I'm... I..." Pallit stammered.

"Hush, my darling." Arrikan brushed his hair aside. "No more words."

"Just...three." Pallit's voice was weak. "I love you."

Eraim's eyes welled up and her vision blurred, but in her mind was Pallit in better days, untouched by the filth of Trannum's stronghold and Dright Swamp. He was returning Lilli to her in Eastgate; leading her to the rorbak; marrying Arrikan; watching the birth of Magneer. Eraim wiped her tears and watched as Arrikan kissed her husband. Lorylla stood behind the rangers, the tall elf's face filled with pain and sorrow.

"He's alive!" Rholmar said, kneeling over Soren.

"So is Nilborg."

Greyor was next to the priest, and blood soaked the left side of the dwarf's head. He tapped Nilborg's cheeks, and the priest awoke with a start. After a quick survey of the room, Nilborg clutched his chest where the fire had struck him, and a dark blue aura briefly encompassed his hand.

"There are many that need your help," Greyor said. "That is, if you're able."

Greyor helped Nilborg to his feet, and the priest drew in a deep breath as he closed his eyes. He opened them again and scanned the room while exhaling, and his gaze fell on Pallit. Nilborg shook his head with a sigh. He turned to Soren, and again he shook his head.

"But he's alive." Rholmar held a cloth over Soren's wound as slow, raspy breaths moved in and out of the catatonic warrior.

"He's beyond help." Nilborg walked on shaky legs to the paladins. He looked at Soren, his longtime friend and companion. "The venom that burns within his veins... It is an elixir of Trannum's creation. The same used to create dunarchins, I believe. Soren *is* firstborn, of that I am sure, for I delivered him." Nilborg's look was grim. "I doubt even Elgarroth can save him this time. You know what we must do."

Eraim's vision blurred with tears again, and Rholmar bowed his head.

"Not here." Rholmar lifted Soren.

"Remove him from this place," Nilborg said, "and I will join you shortly."

While Rholmar carried the fallen paladin from the room, Nilborg climbed to the balcony and looked at Eraim.

"Please, help Brem—"

"Shh." Nilborg placed a tender hand on Eraim's shoulder. "Soleran will tend to all."

He recited a prayer, and a coolness ran through Eraim's veins. It was a pleasant cold, not at all like the chill the castle exuded, and her leg was mended. She rose to thank Nilborg, but he was already headed toward Brem.

Selanna sat with the marteese along the far wall. The horrible fluids seeping from Brem's sores covered much of his blue skin, making him appear ghoulish. Nilborg placed his hands on Brem's head and said another prayer, and Brem's complexion lightened and his shaking ceased, but the dark spots did not fade.

"I'm afraid that is the best I can do." Nilborg helped the marteese to his feet.

Brem nodded. "It is more than enough."

After Nilborg tended to Selanna's injuries, they all joined Rholmar and Soren outside the stronghold. Arrikan revealed surprising strength, and she bore Pallit's body from the fortress after politely refusing Greyor's help. Nilborg then cared for Arrikan as he had Brem; and just as with the marteese, her spots remained.

It was dusk, and still nothing moved or showed any signs of life upon the barren land. The company headed east beneath the moonlight until reaching a peaceful field of wildflowers, far from the castle, and there they stopped.

Though the night was warm, Greyor lit a fire, and Eraim wondered if sitting in the shadows would have been a better choice. Selanna, Eraim's lifelong friend, was an absolute mess, reminding Eraim of the days in Sistama—although Selanna did not have quite as much blood on her then as she did now. Eraim gazed at the others. Their disheveled and haggard appearances showed the hell they had endured, whether by swamp or by mines, and then within the stronghold of Trannum. They had just defeated the greatest evil since Uustaag the Dark, but one could not tell by their grim faces. There was no joy. Had it been the same for the heroes that conquered Uustaag several centuries ago? Soren, Pallit, Rybeal, and Millord had lost their lives along the way, as well as Vikur, Poluran, and Dellen, and she had yet to learn of how many others. Eraim was sure there were others.

Trannum was destroyed. So why did Eraim feel like crying?

Come morning, Rholmar and Greyor gathered wood and placed it into a pyre. They set Soren atop the bed, and everyone bowed their head while Nilborg said a prayer. As Soren's breathing ceased, they ignited the wood before the evil elixir could run its course.

Arrikan declined to have Pallit join Soren, wishing to bury her husband closer to home. She did, however, allow Rholmar to bear the body at the paladin's insistence, and Nilborg recited a prayer to preserve Pallit's corpse for the journey. They then readied to move on.

"What now?" Greyor looked at the brightening sky. Though it was only midmorning, sweat beaded on the dwarf's face.

"We head north," replied Selanna. "There are many who will be pleased to hear it is over."

Chapter 42

Aftermath

The war was over. Good triumphed over Evil. After Eraim's arrow shattered the orb within Trannum's skull, the surviving undead across the land sought escape. Hunting parties slaughtered the abominations wherever they were found, giving rebirth to the Death Hunters, but many dunarchins disappeared without a trace. Marcs, Kalmirans, Nirans, and Sards surfaced from places of hiding, but Nomedd remained barren, and was regarded as a haunted, uninhabitable place, much like Helmland.

Feasts and parties lasted for months after the war until winter arrived, and then smaller, more private parties continued indoors. As for the heroes, each followed their own path...

The North Army remained in Burmagaard for two weeks before learning of Trannum's demise. Word came from Marcove and rapidly spread throughout Kalmaar. No people erupted more joyously than the Kalmirans, and the anniversary was celebrated for years to come.

For the first time in the history of Kalmaar, a queen took the throne, for the Kalmirans revered Elloria, the savior of the realm. Two weeks later, Elloria married a man who had gained her highest respect on the battlefield, and though Sullis was king, he did not interfere with her rule. The Brondor paladin never returned to his temple in Harbnum after losing his sword arm, and his days of fighting were over. But he was content to be a teacher for young knights of Brondor, for Elloria assured him one could earn their way into the Halls of Battle without dying in combat.

Elloria reinstated the Tournaments of Brondor in honor of King Karrak, and during the feasts that followed the annual event, tankards were raised in the good king's name. A host of dwarves from Morimont always attended to pay their respects.

After Gruzim's fall, Gruelenor helped Vecnor from the battlefield and took him to Elloria for healing. Later that night, neither the legendary warrior nor his massive steed could be found.

A statue was built in Vecnor's likeness within the courtyard of Darmhorng, and knights would bow their heads before it as they arrived and departed from the castle.

Xorlunder was proclaimed a hero of greatest honor, though he never rose again after the vicious attack of Gruzim. The gray elf defeated more foes than most, but his last act cost him his life.

His kin returned him to Orlenfel and buried him among the forest's past lords. Every year after, the gray elves could be heard singing Xorlunder's praise on the anniversary of the Battle of the Dead Fields, as it was later known, for no life, plant or otherwise, was ever seen upon the site again, and the village was never rebuilt.

Melac remained in Kalmaar, too ashamed to return to Tikken City and the Council of Wizards, for his part in the final battle was small. He had ridden Umbarc into combat, and the horse fought valiantly, stomping the undead with its massive hooves. But Melac was too weak from the foray into Burmagaard, and he failed to remain mounted. He fell from the saddle and was knocked unconscious early on, and there he lay until hours after the fighting had ceased.

Elloria proclaimed Melac a hero, citing his bravery within the castle and city, and named him Castle Wizard. There, Melac advised Elloria and Sullis and resumed his studies of magic.

With the release of his last spell, Wezlok made sure Anduiff never reached Nomedd in time to aid Trannum. A later search revealed nothing of the Death Lord's whereabouts—only the dragon's bones were found.

Wezlok was taken into Castle Lambrak, and Borse cared for him while he remained in a coma-like state. The wizard eventually awoke to learn the war was over, and once he had received sufficient rest, he slipped from the castle while the others celebrated.

Wezlok did not stop for sleep or food, not even when he passed by Ironside Keep, and he avoided questions and praise upon crossing Palidur Bridge. He returned to Maple Lore Forest and was not seen again for several years.

After a couple of weeks of celebration at Castle Lambrak, Brem began his homeward journey. He had enjoyed the many parties in Marcove, and while passing through Kalmaar, he received more of the same. Upon entering Sendorum, his spotted skin drew stares from those unaware of where he had been and what he had seen. But he cared not. He longed for home.

Brem returned to Neja to lead a life in the same fashion Olinin had, before Trannum killed the marteese wizard in the Silent Marsh years ago. Brem worked with half-breeds, teaching them to cope with other races and preaching the ways of Frayorna; and just as Olinin, he became respected in the region.

Nidor, Gruelenor, and Magneer enjoyed many parties in Darmhorng while their wounds mended. But then Arrikan arrived, bearing Pallit's body, and Magneer's spirit sank.

The three accompanied Magneer's mother to the Coranthiar Mountains in northern Harbnum, where Arrikan and Pallit had shared their first adventure, and Borse was with them, for the priest had known the fallen ranger longer than anyone. Borse gave Pallit a proper Cafior funeral among the tall peaks, and no mountain creature disturbed the ceremony, nor the grave, for years to come.

After witnessing his mother's sorrow, Magneer's thoughts moved to Kalette, and he eagerly wished to return home. So with a heavy heart, he said goodbye, and he departed with Nidor and Gruelenor.

Upon reaching Philen, Magneer met his son Desser. Lorin and Della, widows to Ballrik and Solinin, had also given birth to sons, Romik and Daymyn. Magneer loved his family and spent as much time with them as possible, and he made sure Della and Daymyn were taken care of as well. He found little time for himself, and rarely saw mountains for several years, but he became content once again with hunting in Dakreal Forest.

Honoring his promise to Ballrik, Gruelenor looked after Lorin and raised Romik as his own. After a couple of years, Lorin grew fond of Gruelenor, seeing beyond the krukari face, and the two were married. Lorin bore another son, and though Baylun took after Gruelenor in appearance—much to Gruelenor's disappointment—Lorin showed the child every bit as much love as she did Romik.

Try as they might, Gruelenor and Magneer could not convince Nidor to stay. Nidor swelled with pride when learning of his kin's contributions to the war, and he wished to return home. But he promised to visit often, as Silcor allowed.

Nidor arrived at Holindale, and he was hailed a hero. Many ears were eager to hear of his journeys, but whenever Nidor told his stories, he neglected to mention the divine fires granted to him, for Silcor's Gifts did not exist to gain favor. As well, he always painted others as the true heroes, for without them all would have been lost.

Though Nidor enjoyed seeing familiar faces, something was amiss; and after six months, he realized life in the desert could never be the same. So he left Holindale to spread the Word of Silcor, returning once a year, and the road became his home.

Every summer, Nidor made his way into Marcove, for a few thousand Dales chose to remain where they had accomplished their greatest deed. Though the Marcs had never seen the dark-skinned barbarians before the war, the Dales were honored as heroes and led prosperous lives as both teachers and students. They always greeted Nidor with smiles and hugs, and he brought to the Mar-Dales news of their families, as well as delicious fruits that their new homeland could not yield.

After a few days in Marcove, Nidor would journey to Burmagaard and Darmhorng Castle. While there, he saw many Kalmirans carrying two holy symbols: that of Brondor and Silcor. Those that witnessed Nidor's display could not deny Silcor's hand in the war, and Nidor was recognized and welcomed. Queen Elloria was always pleased to see Nidor, and she canceled most of the week's engagements to honor his presence. But Nidor spent most of his time with King Sullis, walking the grounds and sharing philosophies, and he was often surprised by the old paladin's new outlook on life.

True to his promise, Nidor found his way into Philen at least once a year, and he never stayed for less than a month. He still provided no answers when Gruelenor and Magneer asked about the flames that sprouted from his body during the war, nor could he activate some of the powers on his own, and the questions eventually ceased.

Nidor never forgot Gruelenor's request to show Silcor proper thanks, and the two fashioned a small shrine in Gruelenor's house for such a purpose. Gruelenor asked many questions about Silcor's Ways, and Nidor was pleased to find that his friend continued to worship, even after Nidor departed.

In Marcove, Cavalor, Borse, and Arkor remained within Castle Lambrak after the battle outside of Kembald, awaiting a sign that the war was over while the Dales cleared the walled city of all remaining undead. Over a week had passed, and though there were plenty of opportunities to boast of victories and mourn lost companions, they spoke few words and kept watch. News came at last when the zhokards returned from their patrol of the southern border, and with them were the companies that faced Trannum at the dark stronghold. Hearts then burst as emotions flooded, and several tears were shed.

Cavalor was speechless, feeling true victory had been achieved. But he was also grieved to hear of Soren's downfall at the hands of Radaam, and his father was equally filled with sorrow at the sight of Pallit. The most disheartening tale, however, came when Cavalor spoke of Merssa's sacrifice—though he did not know firsthand that she was dead, Borse reinforced this belief without words. The news devastated Rholmar, and Selanna and Eraim were moved to tears. Nilborg, who prayed he had misinterpreted Elgarroth's meaning among the wild lands south of the Fire Hills, suspected it all along, but that knowledge did little to ease his grief after receiving confirmation.

"But let us not toil on such things right now," Cavalor said. "My mother's quest has been fulfilled, and her soul is at peace. Word must reach the rest of Vaeldor, and many toasts must be made and deeds be praised! That is the way she would have wanted it."

Celebrations ensued within Castle Lambrak and Kembald, lasting a month, but Arrikan, Greyor, and Lorylla departed after only a night's stay. Arrikan needed to take Pallit to the Coranthiar Mountains, and Greyor longed to return to Morimont, where he had not been in several years. And though Arrikan assured Lorylla Pallit's death was not her fault, the gray elf harbored guilt and promised to attend the funeral. The three journeyed on horseback into Kalmaar with Borse in company.

Upon reaching Burmagaard, Lorylla's kin were gone, having departed days earlier with their fallen general. From the lips of humans, elves, and dwarves, Lorylla learned of how valiant Xorlunder had been in taking Burmagaard, and again in the Battle of the Dead Fields; and they spoke of how the mighty elf warrior dropped many dunarchin mages and assisted in the destruction of Gruzim. But no matter how much pride Lorylla felt for her father's deeds, she desired his company more.

She was then filled with regret, for she had to break her promise to Arrikan, and Lorylla departed for Orlenfel at once to attend what would be a month-long funeral.

Greyor joined his folk within Burmagaard and received many grunting cheers. But before he and Arrikan parted, he gave her a powerful embrace, both in strength and emotion. Greyor then returned to Morimont, where he was regarded as a hero above all others, and a holiday was declared in his name by King Kolermane — the king survived the vicious blow dealt by Anduiff, as Elloria healed the wound just in time.

Greyor's thoughts remained upon Lornibur, and though he kept the mines a secret, he began formulating a scheme to rid the ancient dwarf home of the large reptiles and Maak Maak — if the creature still lived. Of the mine dwellers, Greyor was not sure what to do, and they were his chief reason for keeping the information from his kin. The dwarves would surely storm the tunnels and kill all things present, as Millord had desired to do. So Greyor continued to plan for the day when he could return.

Arrikan and Borse journeyed north without partaking of any feasts in Darmhorng, and Magneer, Gruelenor, and Nidor joined them. A few days after Pallit's funeral, Borse departed for Marcove, and Magneer and his friends left for Philen, leaving Arrikan alone.

Arrikan returned to the life she knew before meeting her husband, living off the land and assisting hikers and hunters to earn enough for supplies, and she renewed her friendship with the Andrians. She appeared aged and weathered, and the dark spots on her skin never faded, but her body remained strong, and she became a well-known hunter once again in northern Harbnum. She received visits often from friends and enjoyed reliving stories of the past, but never was the war discussed in her presence.

Lorylla arrived a month after Pallit's funeral, apologizing for her absence. Arrikan laughed, much to the elf's surprise, and insisted Lorylla was quite forgiven. The two became dear friends afterwards, and Lorylla returned when she could.

At least once a year, Arrikan and Lorylla hunted in Vermallon Forest among the hills and enjoyed good times. But Lorylla knew it would not last, for though she was much older than Arrikan, the ranger's days were advancing more rapidly. Lorylla was present when Arrikan was buried next to Pallit, and also in attendance were Magneer and Kalette, Gruelenor and Lorin, Della, all of their children, Borse, Selanna, Eraim, and Greyor.

Arkor never replaced his wooden arm. He did not tell anyone, but when he sundered it across Gulthar's leg, a chill crept into his shoulder that would not fade. He was sure Borse suspected something to be amiss, but Arkor preferred to keep the wound as a reminder of all that had happened, and he avoided the priest's probing questions.

Arkor enjoyed the festivities at Castle Lambrak before returning to Ironside Keep, where he planned to govern the mountain pass. He kept strong ties with Cavalor for the rest of his days, and their friendship grew to rival that of Arkor's bond with Rholmar. Arkor loved Rholmar and owed him much, but with both of their increased duties and responsibilities, he rarely saw the Arronaus paladin, and their relationship was largely reduced to one of letters.

In the years to come, Romik, the son of Arkor's late nephew, Ballrik, was often brought to visit by Gruelenor. Arkor showered the lad with gifts, and once Romik reached eight years in age, Lorin allowed the child to remain throughout the winter months at Arkor's request. He taught to Romik the everyday duties of maintaining the stronghold, much in the fashion Vikur would have.

"One day this will all be yours," Arkor would say, to which Romik always smiled.

Arkor could usually be found within the tavern of the keep, telling stories as Vikur had, but he never sat in the large chair Vikur had used. Instead, the sword of the Ironside legacy was placed upon it, returned to Arkor by Gruelenor, and there it would remain until Romik came to stay for good.

Rholmar journeyed with Nilborg to the ruins of Palidur once the celebrations in Lambrak had ended. The desolate city was as a graveyard, and there seemed no hope of ever restoring its glory.

Nilborg wept.

Upon returning to Philen, Rholmar gathered all the gold he possessed; and with leave of the king, he left the title of duke behind and returned to the Holy City with his wife, Princess Ladonia, and his son, Montac. He found Nilborg within the Soleran Sector, sitting on a pile of rubble and holding a tarnished blue star. It was a relic of Nilborg's that had been lost. Nilborg was pleased with Rholmar's return, though the priest's weathered face failed to show it.

Rholmar vowed to see the city rebuilt, and though his fortune would fall far short of such a task, it was a start. Before they began, the first order of business was to erect a grand monument of Merssa in the heart of the Cafior Sector. There, she would go into history as one of the greatest paladins ever to live, included with the likes of Vennimor, founder of Palidur. Also built was a statue of Soren within the Soleran Sector, and Hubrid in the Arronaus Sector, for the paladin's sacrifice during the fall of Palidur. Thousands of people flocked to assist in whatever way they could, but as the first year of construction came to an end, gold and materials ran low, and the city was only just begun.

It was at that time that Greyor passed through on his way to Rornibur, where he was to speak of Millord's part in the necromancer's destruction. Greyor met with Rholmar and Nilborg and learned of their limited resources, and upon his return to Morimont, he presented the story to King Kolermane. The king sent a thousand dwarves to assist in the matter, bearing a few hundred wagons of stones and seeking little reward; and though it took several more years to complete, New Palidur became a bastion for Good once again.

The Holy City resembled Palidur of old, but it was a warmer place, equipped with taverns and inns to welcome travelers with open arms. As well, every meeting of the new High Order included a representative of the outlanders, to present viewpoints of those outside the city's walls.

With no home to return to, Cavalor remained in Marcove; and with the realm in need of a king, he was uncontested in claiming the throne at Castle Lambrak. The Marcs welcomed Cavalor, overjoyed to be free from the rule of Mayry and the Zurkan.

As his first decree, Cavalor proclaimed the major deity of worship to be Cafior. There were no objections, for in all places where Borse's hammer shook the ground, lush vegetation spread. These areas were tilled and gardens planted, and crops grew to rival those of Sardina. Cavalor also employed royal marshals to roam the kingdom, and the days of bandits running rampant were left in the past.

With the deaths of Chandrella and Crismar, the zhokards lacked direction. They remained at Castle Lambrak and pledged their allegiance to Cavalor, the bravest mortal they had ever encountered. Cavalor accepted the zhokards without question, and afterwards he could be seen with his "ageless" guard while traveling the realm.

Borse was named High Priest by his son, and true to his nature, he traveled often, spreading the Word of Cafior from Kembald to Denvale. He held outdoor masses across the land and planted seeds when he was done.

"And with prayer and unyielding faith," Borse always said, "you will be rewarded."

As promised, all communities carrying out his teachings were blessed with rich soil upon the holy ground they helped to create, and Marcove was forever changed.

Early in his travels, Borse discovered the hill where Merssa and Cadorn fought their final battle. Merssa had not been found earlier, for the corpses encircling the hill warded off travelers, but Borse sensed remnants of her aura persisting.

Merssa's lifeless body lay next to a black armor shell containing nothing more than a decapitated skeleton, and Borse knew it to have once been the dreaded Cadorn. Time had been kind and Merssa was intact—no scavengers had desecrated her remains. Though she looked as if she had just passed, Borse realized she had been dead for weeks, and he thanked Cafior for preserving her for so long. A tear rolled down his cheek, but then a warm breeze touched his face, and Merssa's scent surrounded him. He smiled, and the desire to lie down and join her was overwhelming. But then her voice came to him.

"I will wait for you forever, my love. Take care of our son. He needs you now. I will always be with you."

Borse could no longer hold back the heavy flow of tears, and he refused to leave her side. Placing his fingers into the soil, he said a prayer.

Three days later, Cavalor arrived with his entourage. He knew not why he was drawn to the hill, but he swore the land had whispered to him and led him there. With the assistance of the zhokards, the site was cleared, and they buried Merssa on the very spot where she had been discovered. About the grave was constructed a shrine to Cafior and a statue in Merssa's likeness, and at the base of the statue was written:

HERE LIES MERSSA GOLDMACE. LOVING WIFE AND MOTHER. DESTROYER OF EVIL. PRAY TO HER AND RECEIVE HER PROTECTION AND CAFIOR'S BLESSING.

Ever after, upon the anniversary of Merssa's battle against the Death Lord, people swore they saw a golden light shining from the hill just after sunset.

Cavalor and Borse returned to the site when they could, and never did they miss Merssa's birthday. For the occasion, Cavalor left his bodyguards behind, and he and his father would spend the entire day with her. While the visit lasted, a sweet, warm breeze persisted, and lying upon the soft grass and closing their eyes, Merssa was with them. They shared conversations about good things and laughed often, and she always expressed how proud she was of her boys and how much she loved them both. At sunset, Merssa would leave them, blowing a kiss and saying, "Take care, my special men. Cafior be in your hearts."

Eraim and Selanna walked to the rear while Rholmar led the survivors of Trannum's stronghold across Nomedd, neither of them having the energy for jokes or teasing. They traveled for days with barely a word spoken, not even to each other. On the fifth night, while Eraim guarded, Selanna approached her.

"How did you know?"

Eraim shrugged. "Did you not see the orb pulsing in his skull?"

"I did not." Selanna pursed her lips. "But it would seem you were correct in your assumption. There *were* six orbs." Her brow then furrowed. "But still I am puzzled..."

"What?"

"Oh, nothing." Selanna shook her head. "Do not trouble yourself. The deed is done."

As they passed into Marcove, a group of mounted soldiers greeted them. The riders graciously allowed the weary company to ride to Castle Lambrak, and there they met all that remained of the South Army. News was then exchanged, good and bad, and the first of several parties ensued.

Once the celebrations ended, Selanna and Eraim left for Kalmaar. They were happy to find many smiling faces there—particularly those of their kin—as well as more parties and feasts. They were also delighted to learn of Vecnor's involvement, though sorry they had missed him. Eraim was especially disappointed, but pleased to know Vecnor still lived.

After a few days in Burmagaard, Eraim made a suggestion to Selanna.

"We should visit Master Elgarroth."

Selanna was taken aback. It was the first time Eraim had ever uttered such a phrase.

"I had planned to..." Selanna said. "But I did not wish to trouble you."

"But I wish to go."

"Very well." Selanna chuckled.

They departed before the festivities of Kalmaar came close to a conclusion.

Several days later, they arrived at the small house within Vermallon. Elgarroth did not seem surprised by their visit, and he embraced them each in turn. The three chatted throughout the day while the wizard's servant chopped wood, watered plants, and went in and out of the cabin. At one point, Eraim noticed a brief glance aimed their way, but as usual there came no word from the obedient elf.

As night fell and stars dotted the sky, the servant brought long pipes from the house, and Eraim, Selanna, and Elgarroth blew smoke rings. Fireflies danced about, zipping through the expanding circles as if to entertain, and for a while the war seemed years ago and far away.

"There are things that do not sit well with me." Selanna returned all thoughts to most recent days.

"I feel the same," said Eraim.

Elgarroth lifted his brow. "What troubles you?"

Selanna looked at Eraim, so Eraim spoke.

"Just before I destroyed the orb, a voice spoke inside my head. At first I believed it to be my own, but as I look back now, I am not so sure. There was a lot of confusion, and I was in a great deal of pain at the time, but I believe it to have been a voice different from my own. It was elfish, of that I am sure, but it seemed to be that of a male's. Perhaps...a wizard's?" Eraim eyed Elgarroth.

"That *is* intriguing." He puffed on his pipe.

"Then there is the arrow," Eraim added. "I have never lost count of those I have fired, but I had one more in my quiver than I should have. Beyond that, I purchase my stock from the greatest fletcher in Salenti. Though well crafted, they are otherwise unremarkable, but I swear that last arrow was darker in color, and it changed direction in mid-flight. And how did a simple arrow shatter the orb? Many other weapons had failed to achieve such a task. Even Mithkahr needed help from Selanna."

The wizard shrugged. "Perhaps the final orb was not so remarkable."

Eraim frowned. She had hoped for a better answer.

They were interrupted when the servant added more wood to the fire. He then returned to the house, and Selanna spoke.

"I have two concerns. The first is Radaam. Why did he abandon his master? And where has he gotten off to? Or Anduiff for that matter?"

"Indeed, those are interesting questions," Elgarroth said. "You will let me know what you find?"

Selanna gave a wry smile. "Second is the prophecy. The last verse, to be exact."

"What do you mean?" Elgarroth looked at Selanna.

Eraim recited the verse.

"Seek to end at dark throne,
Might and strength of Evil Bone.
Power shatters, dust does fall.
Eyes open in shadowy hall."

"The last line," Selanna said. "Whose eyes does it refer to?"

Elgarroth puffed several times on his pipe, gazing into the fire as if in deep thought. The tobacco within the bowl burned orange and smoke obscured his face. "Do not trouble yourselves with such matters," he said at last. "It is enough that the lands have been returned to their rightful owners. Enjoy life now, even if only for a while."

Selanna was not comfortable with his response.

The servant appeared, and he handed them each a glass of wine.

"What do you know of Vecnor's whereabouts?" Eraim changed the subject.

"Why do you ask?" Elgarroth took a sip.

"I have heard tales of his great achievements in the war," Eraim replied. "I would like to thank him."

"Why do you think *I* know of his whereabouts?"

Eraim shrugged. "Years ago, he mentioned a wizard had convinced him to journey into Sistama. From the way he spoke, I assumed he meant you."

"Interesting." Elgarroth said nothing more.

Again, Eraim heard chopping. The servant had returned to his duties.

"Well," Selanna rose, "we should be off." She drained her glass. "It feels like ages since I last saw the trees of Salenti. I fear I shall not recognize them."

Eraim was unimpressed with the answers they received, but she stood and they thanked the wizard for his hospitality. Before departing, she approached the servant.

"Many thanks, sir," she said. "You are quite a *strong* lad."

The servant nodded, still not uttering a word.

Eraim returned to the fire and gathered her gear.

"Master Elgarroth." She gained the wizard's attention. "If you see Vecnor, have him drop by and see me. I miss him." With her last words, she gazed at the servant.

"I am sure he misses you as well." Elgarroth smiled.

After saying goodbye, Eraim and Selanna headed northwest, leaving the wizard to puff on his pipe.

"Do you suspect she knows?" asked Vecnor.

Elgarroth glanced at the tall warrior holding an axe at the edge of the firelight. "She *is* a clever one." He turned back in the direction where the two had departed. "They are both quite clever."

This Concludes

MIGHT

AND

STRENGTH

OF

EVIL BONE

The story continues with

EYES OPEN

IN

SHADOWY HALL

Coming in 2023

Acknowledgements

My wife has provided incredible support, and I wholeheartedly thank her for making this chapter of my life possible. I am also very appreciative of my son and his contributions. I would like to add my continuing thanks to Mary Nichols and Peggy Kattelus for their encouragement and advice while balancing their own writing careers. A special thanks to my dad, who nurtured my love for medieval fantasy. Finally, I would like to thank my family members and friends for the hours of reading they provided to help my stories come to life.

About the Author

Ronald G. Bellar was born in Ohio and raised in Michigan, one of the middle children in a family of ten. He has an associate's degree in electrical engineering and a bachelor's in automated manufacturing, but his love for numbers led him to a life in taxes and bookkeeping. His passion for medieval fantasy began at age 11, when he was introduced to *Dungeons & Dragons*, and it was cemented after reading *The Lord of the Rings* by J.R.R. Tolkien. He began writing when he was 15, but did not take it seriously until he was encouraged to do so later in life. After coaching football for 31 years, he retired his whistle to pursue his writing career, but his love for sports endures. He currently lives in Michigan with his wife and son.

Ronald G. Bellar has also written Book 1 of the Fate of Vaeldor Trilogy, *Alas! The One that Evil Brings*, and coming in 2023 is Book 3, *Eyes Open in Shadowy Hall*. Beyond that, the adventures in Vaeldor will continue…

Visit Ronald G. Bellar's Facebook page at:
https://www.facebook.com/vaeldorhouse

Glossary of Names

Andria (an-DREE-uh): Barbarian realm north of Harbnum.

Andrian (an-DREE-uhn): Barbarian native to Andria.

Anduiff (AN-doo-if): Death Lord. First Lord of Benasti Forest.

Arkor (AR-kor): Younger brother to Vikur. Uncle to Ballrik. The one-armed warrior.

Arman (AR-muhn): Forest in northern Tenvale. Mysterious woodland known to possess magical properties.

Arrikan (AIR-ick-in): Mountain ranger, originally of the Coranthiar Mountains. Married to Pallit. Mother of Magneer. Assisted Merssa in the hunt for Trannum's orb in Andria.

Arronaus (AIR-uhn-us): Deity of the sky.

Ballrik (BAHL-rick): Son of Vikur and nephew to Arkor.

Batorn (buh-TORN): Gulf north of Kalmaar. Also a breed of horse from the region of the gulf, known for their beauty and great endurance.

Belsal (BELL-sahl): River in Marcove from the Varlimor Mountains and through Mentrial Forest.

Benasti (be-NAS-tee): Forest in northern Kalmaar. Largely inhabited by evil tribes of hobgoblins and krukari.

Berynyc (BAIR-in-ick): Castle for the baron of northern Kalmaar, just off the coast of the Batorn Gulf.

Boddrom (BOD-drum): Swamp in Tenvale.

Bormungdaher (BOR-muhng-DAR): Ancient dwarf king of Varlimor. Commissioned the construction of Palidur Bridge.

Borse (BORS): Priest of Cafior. Married to Merssa. Father of Cavalor.

Braak (BRAHK): Command word in hobgoblin language, used to send Benasti wolves to their pen.

Brakkeet (brah-KEET): Expletive in the dwarfish language.

Brazan (BRAY-zin): Journey taken by princes of Benasti Forest to become an adult.

Brem (BREM): A marteese. Priest of Frayorna from Neja. Assisted Poluran in hunting for Trannum's orb in Garthglen Swamp.

Brondor (BRAHN-dor): Deity of battle.

Burmagaard (BER-muh-gard): Capital city of Kalmaar.

Cadorn (kuh-DORN): Death Lord. Ancient ruler of Kalmaar. Led the attack against Palidur.

Cafdella (caf-DEL-uh): Village in Neja where Merssa met her husband, Borse.

Cafior (CAF-ee-or): Deity of the land.

Candermane (CAN-der-mayn): Waterfall in northern Varlimor Mountains. Also the name given to the secret tunnel passing beneath the falls.

Cavalor (CAV-uh-lor): Adopted son of Merssa and Borse. Given to Merssa by Selanna when he was a baby.

Chandrella (SHAN-drell-uh): Commander of the zhokard in Castle Lambrak.

Charal (CHAR-uhl): Lake near the border of Selt and Nira, fed by the Echo Valley Rapids.

Charndova (sharn-DOH-vuh): City in Sardina on the western edge of Varlimor Pass.

Clanghorr (KLANG-or): Ancient dwarfish battleaxe.

Coranthiar (kor-ANN-thee-er): Mountains across northeastern Vaeldor.

Dakreal (DAYK-ree-uhl): Forest in Philen. Home to Dakreal elves.

Dandi (DAN-dee): Salenti horse belonging to Selanna.

Darmhorng (DARM-horng): Castle for the King of Kalmaar, located outside Burmagaard.

Daymyn (DAY-min): Son of Solinin and Della.

Delarrin (duh-LAIR-uhn): Young farmer-turned-soldier in Steadshire.

Della (DELL-uh): Youngest daughter of Dezlo in Steadshire.

Demoligius (dem-uh-LI-gee-us): Evil deity of fire.

Death Hunter: Hunters of the undead.

Denvale (DEN-vayl): City in Marcove on the eastern edge of Varlimor Pass.

Desser (DES-sir): Son of Magneer and Kalette.

Dezlo (DEZ-low): Aged farmer in Steadshire. Father of Lorin, Kalette, and Della.

Dimarr (di-MAR): Former barbarian chief in Andria. Possessed one of Trannum's orbs.

Dominelli (DAHM-in-EL-ee): Largest village of elves in Salenti Forest.

Dright (DRITE): Swamp between Nomedd and the wilds north of the Tarn Arum Jungle.

Dunarchin (DOON-er-kin): Undead created from a firstborn. Elite warrior, able to walk beneath the sun.

Dunuthar (DUHN-uh-thar): Death Lord. Former king of Selt.

Durl (DURL): First son of Tarm and Mayry. Given away as a baby to Selanna by Tarm.

Elgarroth Sandanari (EL-guh-roth SAN-di-NAR-ee): Mysterious elfish wizard of Vermallon Forest. Mentor to Selanna.

Elloria (el-LOR-ee-uh): Brondor priestess in Kalmaar. Former Death Hunter. Assisted Vikur in hunting for Trannum's orb in the Serpent's Range.

Eraim (ee-RAYM): Salenti elf. Master of many talents and friend to Selanna. Wielder of Mithkahr.

Fendora (fen-DOR-uh): Kingdom in southwestern Vaeldor.

Frayorna (fray-OR-nuh): Deity of the forest. Mother of Nature.

Fremar (FREE-mar): Captain in Elloria's army.

Galenfial (guh-LEN-fee-uhl): Deity of the elves.

Garaard (guh-RARD): Lake in Kalmaar, north of Burmagaard.

Garthglen (GARTH-GLEN): Swampland in southern Moclen, where one of Trannum's orbs was hidden.

Gramborn (GRAM-born): Commander of Merssa's forces in Steadshire.

Grellmor (GREL-mor): Ancestor of Vikur and Arkor. Commissioned the construction of Ironside Keep in the Varlimor Pass.

Greyor (GRAY-or): Dwarf from Morimont in the Varlimor Mountains.

Grimmen (GRIM-min): Zhokard soldier working as a River Guard in Merssa's compound.

Gruelenor (GREW-len-or): Krukari warrior.

Gruzim (groo- ZEEM): Lord of Benasti Forest. Betrayed Merssa and her companions by assisting Malgabi in returning the orb from Garthglen Swamp to Trannum.

Gulthar (GOOL-thar): Death Lord. Former king of Marcove.

Gurix (GER-icks): Zurkan warrior in Denvale.

Harbnum (HARB-nuhm): Kingdom north of Sendorum. Protector of one of only two bridges crossing the Shield River.

Helmland (HELM-land): Wasteland north of the Stone Eagle Mountains, where the Ancient Enemy of the North resided.

High Riser (HI RYE-zer): Mountains in northern Philen. Home to the High Riser dwarves.

Holindale (HOE-lin-dayl): Barbarian territory south of Tenvale. Home to the dark-skins.

Horx (HORKS): Krukari prince. Son to Gruzim and Mayry.

Hubrid (HYOO-brid): Former High Paladin of Arronaus in Palidur. Died protecting the retreat of the city's last survivors before it fell.

Ironside (EYE-ern-side): Keep on Varlimor Pass. Surname to Vikur and Arkor.

Kalette (KAY-let): Middle daughter of Dezlo in Steadshire.

Kalmaar (KAL-mar): Kingdom in eastern Vaeldor. Conquered by Tarm in the name of Trannum. Once known for its strong military and dedication to the worship of Brondor.

Kalmiran (kal-MAIR-in): Citizen of Kalmaar.

Kembald (KEM-bahld): Capital city of Marcove.

Karrak (KAIR-ick): King of Kalmaar before Tarm took the throne. Died in battle in Darmhorng Dungeon after he was freed by Selanna.

King Arman (AR-muhn): The largest lake in Vaeldor. Located north of Arman Forest.

Kolermane (KOHL-er-mayn): King of the dwarves in the Varlimor Mountains.

Korban (KOR-bin): Bridge spanning the Squire River. Built by dwarves of Rornibur and named after their king of old. Made of rorbak.

Korgun (KOR-gun): Krukari warrior in Benasti Forest. Brother to Gruelenor.

Krelnamir (KREL-nuh-meer): Former Paladin of Cafior from Palidur that resided in Ironside Keep before the stronghold's fall to Trannum. Died in defense of the keep.

Krimbror (KRIM-bror): River extending from Moon Lake to the Endless Sea in Marcove.

Krukari (kroo-KAR-ee): One possessing both human and hobgoblin blood. Outcasts.

Ladal (lay-DAHL): Mountains separating the Desert of Fire from Tenvale.

Ladonia (luh-DOHN-yah): Princess of Philen. Married to Duke Rholmar. Mother of Montac. Assisted Selanna and Eraim in hunting for Trannum's orb in Tenvale.

Lambrak (LAM-brack): Castle for the king of Marcove. Located next to Kembald.

Landerik (lan-DEAR-ick): Paladin of Brondor from Harbnum. Follower of Sullis.

Larkorn (LAR-korn): Large city on the eastern border of Virch.

Lilli (LIL-lee): Salenti horse belonging to Eraim.

Lorian (LOR-ee-uhn): An elf from Maple Lore Forest.

Lorin (LOR-in): Eldest daughter of Dezlo in Steadshire.

Lornibur (LOR-ni-ber): Ancient home to the dwarves. Original birthplace of the dwarfish race.

Lorylla (LOR-i-luh): Gray elf of Orlenfel. Daughter of Xorlunder.

Magneer (MAG-neer): Mountain ranger. Son of Pallit and Arrikan.

Malgabi (MAL-guh-bee): The voice of Trannum. Also called the Marc.

Maple Lore: Forest along the Shield River. Home to the Lorian elves, a territorial race known to hold disdain for all other races.

Marcove (MAR-kohv): Kingdom south of Kalmaar. Conquered by Trannum.

Marc (MARK): Citizen of Marcove.

Marfesna (mar-FEZ-nuh): Ice demon.

Marteese (mar-TEES): One possessing both human and elf blood.

Mayry (MAY-ree): Queen of Kalmaar. Married to Tarm. Mother of Durl, Solinin, and Horx.

Mees (MEES): Elfish word for alarm.

Melac (MEL-ack): Wizard from Tenvale. Assisted Vikur in hunting for Trannum's orb in the Serpent's Range.

Melballa (mel-BAHL-uh): Mule owned by Poluran.

Meldar (MEL-dar): Deity of the dwarves.

Mentrial (MEN-tree-ahl): Forest in Marcove. Houses many bandits.

Merssa Goldmace (MER-suh): Paladin of Cafior. Ex-Palidurian. Married to Borse. Mother of Cavalor. Previously one of the High Paladins of Palidur.

Millord (MILL-ord): Stone Eagle dwarf from Rornibur. Cousin to Poluran.

Mithkahr (MITH-kar): Ancient elfish blade possessed by Eraim.

Moc (MAHK): Citizen of Moclen.

Moclen (MAHK-lin): Kingdom west of King Arman Lake. Home to Tikken City and the Council of Wizards.

Montac (MAHN-tack): Son of Rholmar and Ladonia.

Morimont (MOR-i-mahnt): Largest city of dwarves in the Varlimor Mountains and home to the dwarf king.

Neja (NAY-shjuh): Kingdom south of the Stone Eagle Mountains. The Bandit Kingdom.

Nejan (NAY-shjuhn): Citizen of Neja.

Nidor (NYE-dor): Paladin of Silcor from Holindale. One of the dark-skinned barbarians.

Nilborg (NIL-borg): Priest of Soleran. Ex-Palidurian. Assisted Selanna and Eraim in hunting for Trannum's orb in Tenvale. Previously one of the High Priests of Palidur.

Nira (NYE-ruh): Kingdom north of Kalmaar and south of Selt. The portion of the realm south of the Great East River was conquered by Trannum.

Niran (NAIR-in): Citizen of Nira.

Nomedd (NOH-med): Barbarian territory devastated by Trannum.

Nomish (NOH-meesh): Citizen of Nomedd.

Olinin (OH-li-nin): Marteese wizard from Neja. Killed by Trannum while investigating the Silent Marsh.

Orlenfel (OR-len-fell): Forest in northeastern Kalmaar. Home to the gray elves.

Palidur (PAL-i-der): Former Holy City. Located in Sardina. Conquered by a Death Lord and an army of the undead for Trannum.

Palidurian (PAL-i-DOO-ree-uhn): Citizen of Palidur.

Pallit (PAL-lit): Mountain ranger. Married to Arrikan. Father of Magneer. Assisted Merssa in finding the rorbak in the Stone Eagle Mountains and in hunting for Trannum's orb in Andria.

Peltagarr (PELL-tuh-gar): Large city in northern Kalmaar off the coast of the Batorn Gulf.

Philen (FYE-len): Kingdom in southwestern Vaeldor.

Poluran (POH-ler-uhn): Stone Eagle dwarf from Rornibur. Friend of Vikur. Led the hunt for Trannum's orb in Garthglen Swamp.

Prince Arman (AR-muhn): River connecting the King Arman Lake to the Queen Arman Lake. Border between Moclen and Tenvale.

Radaam (ruh-DAHM): Death Lord. Former king of Kalmaar. Led the attack against Ironside Keep.

Ragab (RAH-guhb): Demon.

Rasnar : (RAZ-nar): Baron of northern Kalmaar.

Rholmar (ROHL-mar): Paladin of Arronaus. Duke of West Palidur in Philen. Married to Ladonia. Father of Montac. Assisted Selanna and Eraim in hunting for Trannum's orb in Tenvale.

Rivercross (RIV-er-cross): Large city in Virch near the Korban Bridge. Famous for its markets.

Romik (ROH-mick): Son of Ballrik and Lorin.

Rorbak (ROR-back): Rare white stone native to the Stone Eagle Mountains. Used in the construction of Korban Bridge and Trannum's cabin in the Silent Marsh.

Rornibur (ROR-ni-ber): The largest city of dwarves in the Stone Eagle Mountains.

Rybeal (RYE-beel): Wizard from Philen. Assisted Poluran in hunting for Trannum's orb in Garthglen Swamp.

Salenti (suh-LEN-tee): Forest west of Moclen. Home to Salenti elves. Also a breed of horse that grows shorter and possesses long life and heightened intelligence.

Sardina (sar-DEE-nuh): Kingdom east of King Arman Lake. Conquered by the undead for Trannum.

Seac (SAY-ahk): The Seer. Member of the Council of Wizards of Tikken City.

Selanna (suh-LAHN-nuh): Salenti elf wizard. Friend to Eraim. Pupil to Elgarroth.

Selt (SELT): Kingdom north of Nira. Known for its dedication to the worship of Demoligius.

Seltan (SEL-tuhn): Citizen of Selt.

Sendor (SEN-dor): Citizen of Sendorum.

Sendorum (sen-DOR-uhm): Kingdom north of Sardina. Location of Merssa's compound.

Shield River: River separating the evil realm of Beit from the rest of Vaeldor.

Silcor (SIL-kor): Deity of fire.

Sistama (SIS-tuh-muh): Elfish name for the Silent Marsh.

Soleran (SOH-ler-uhn): Deity of mercy and light. Defender of the Defenseless.

Solett (soh-LET): Former wizard from Tenvale. Possessed one of Trannum's orbs.

Solinin (SOH-li-nin): Son of Tarm and Mayry.

Soren (SOR-in): Paladin of Soleran. Ex-Palidurian. Previously one of the High Paladins of Palidur.

Steadshire (STED-shire): Large village in Nira. Occupied by allied forces to train soldiers and supply troops guarding the Great East River to the south.

Stone Eagle: Mountains north of Neja. Home to Stone Eagle dwarves.

Sullis (SULL-is): Paladin of Brondor from Harbnum. Teacher of Brondor's ways.

Tarm (TARM): King of Kalmaar and Marcove. Rules at Trannum's behest. Married to Mayry. Father of Durl and Solinin.

Tenvale (TEN-vayl): Realm south of Arman Forest. Kingdom of Wizards, known for its strange laws.

Tikken City (TEE-kin): Free city located in Moclen. Governed by the Council of Wizards.

Trannum (TRAN-nuhm): Ancient necromancer, corrupted after researching Uustaag the Dark.

Trenny (TREN-ee): Little girl in Steadshire.

Trethel (TRETH-uhl): River in Nomedd.

Tribenor (TRY-ben-or): Capital city of Sendorum.

Umbarc (UHM-bark): Andrian horse belonging to Vecnor.

Urell Coast (YOO-rell): Kingdom on the western shore of Vaeldor.

Uustaag (OO-stahg): Warlord of Helmland of old. Ancient Enemy of the North.

Vaeldor (VAY-uhl-dor): The continent of all known kingdoms.

Vargen (VAR-gen): General of the South Army.

Varlimor (VAR-li-mor): Mountains separating Kalmaar from Sardina. Home to Ironside Keep and Varlimor dwarves.

Vecnor (VECK-ner): Mysterious human warrior. Also known as Black Rogue and Black Death.

Velgaad (VEL-gahd): Dwarfish Death Lord. Former king of Lornibur.

Vennimor (VEN-i-mor): Paladin of Soleran. Founder of Palidur.

Vermallon (VER-muh-lahn): Forest separating Harbnum from Nira. Largest forest of Vaeldor and home to Vermallon elves.

Vikur (VIE-koor): Lord of Ironside Keep. Brother to Arkor. Father of Ballrik. Led the hunt for Trannum's orb in the Serpent's Range.

Vircan (VERK-uhn): Citizen of Virch.

Virch (VERCH): Kingdom north of King Arman Lake. Known for its strong military. Protector of one of only two bridges crossing the Shield River.

Wezlok (WEZ-lahk): Lorian elf wizard from Maple Lore Forest. Assisted Merssa in the hunt for Trannum's orb in Andria.

Wornduir (WORN-dye-er): Barbarian village in Andria.

Xorlunder (ZOR-luhn-der): Gray elf of Orlenfel. Captain of the Orlenfel military. Assisted Vikur in the hunt for Trannum's orb in the Serpent's Range. Assisted Selanna and Eraim in passing unseen through Kalmaar.

Zhokard (ZOH-kard): Black warrior in the Andrian tongue. Creations of Trannum possessing black hearts. Neither living nor undead. Enemy to the zhomians and Trannum.

Zhomian (ZOH-mee-uhns): Black heart in the Andrian tongue. Creation of Trannum possessing black hearts. Neither living nor undead.

Zurkan (ZER-kin): Soldiers of Blood. Elite krukari warriors of Benasti Forest.